EUNICE FLEET

Jasmine Donahaye is a specialist in the Jewish literature and culture of Wales, and has published and lectured on Lily Tobias in the UK and the USA. She is a graduate of the University of California at Berkeley and holds a PhD from the University of Wales, Swansea. She lives near Aberystwyth.

EUNICE FLEET

by

LILY TOBIAS

With an introduction
by
Jasmine Donahaye

ICS

Published by Honno
'Ailsa Craig', Heol y Cawl, Dinas Powys
South Glamorgan, Wales, CF6 4AH

First published in England by Hutchinson & Co. in 1933
This edition © Honno Ltd 2004

© *Lily Tobias 1933*
© *Introduction Jasmine Donahaye 2004*

British Library Cataloguing in Publication Data

ISBN 1 870206 65 7

Published with the financial support of the Arts Council of Wales

Cover image of Lily Tobias courtesy of Annabella Shepherd

Cover design by Chris Lee

Typeset and printed in Wales by Gwasg Dinefwr, Llandybïe

To
My Brothers

Contents

Introduction

JASMINE DONAHAYE

IN THE 1930s, Lily Tobias' fiction was very well received, and enjoyed positive reviews by Frank Swinnerton, Louis Golding and Paul Goodman, among others. Nevertheless, notwithstanding the attention paid to her work by Mimi Josephson in *Wales* in 1958, and by Vera Coleman in the *Blackwell Companion to Jewish Culture* in 1989, being out of print has meant, effectively, that her work has been out of sight.[1] With this republication of her second novel by Honno Press, Tobias' work can begin to take its proper place in the traditions of Welsh writing in English and British Jewish literature, to both of which it contributes and belongs.

Lily Tobias was born in Swansea in 1887, and grew up in Ystalyfera, a tin-plating town in the Swansea valley, where her father, a Jewish immigrant from Poland, had opened a decorator's shop. The language of her community was primarily Welsh, but that of her home was Yiddish. Tobias' family was isolated from the Jewish community, but at the turn of the century her father's house was the meeting place for a local *minyan*, a group of Jewish men who came together to pray, some of them evidently walking many miles to join with other similarly isolated Jews in the Swansea valley. The working class and immigrant background of many of the Jews living in isolation in the Valleys was the source of some tension with the sizeable, more established and middle-class Jewish community in Swansea and Cardiff, a tension to which the early and unpopular Zionist beliefs of Tobias' father also contributed. The subtleties of these class conflicts among Jews, and between Jews and the non-Jewish community around them, are acutely observed in Tobias' stories and her first novel, *My Mother's House*, which was published in 1931.

Tobias' mother was traditional and religiously observant, and mistrustful of non-Jewish culture – according to a family anecdote, Tobias and her sister Kate had to resort to reading secular literature in the toilet in order to escape her disapproving eye. Despite the constraints imposed on her by her family, and the benefit of only a limited education, Tobias also came under the influence of the Jewish literary and debating societies that enjoyed a vigorous life in the Valleys in the early Edwardian period, and it was at a conference of these societies in London that she met her future husband, Philip Vallentine Tobias. Tobias had written short pieces for a local paper, and she went on to publish four novels, a collection of short stories, and numerous articles, as well as co-authoring the first dramatisation of George Eliot's novel *Daniel Deronda*, which was performed in London in 1927 and 1929.

The Jewish debating societies, which no doubt fostered Tobias' literary development, were themselves in part a response to the ethos of cultural improvement and political engagement in the society of which the Jewish community was a part –Ystalyfera, for example, where Tobias grew up, was home to the influential socialist paper, *Llais Llafur*, with which she was associated, and which was a focus for literary and political activity. In the 1920s, Tobias and her husband lived in Cardiff, in the garden suburb of Rhiwbina, a tenants' cooperative founded in 1912 as a mixed working class and lower-middle class community. At this time Tobias was heavily involved in the Zionist movement, co-founding the Cardiff and Swansea branches of the Daughters of Zion, a precursor to the Women's International Zionist Organisation, and serving as President of the Cardiff branch. It was during this period, too, that her stories comparing Welsh and Jewish political aspirations began to appear in the *Zionist Review* and the *Socialist Review*, and these were published as *The Nationalists and Other Goluth Studies* in 1921.

Rhiwbina was a vibrant intellectual enclave in the twenties and, as described by Iorwerth Peate in *Rhwng Dau Fyd*, was home to an impressive array of leading Welsh intellectuals and writers. Leo Abse remembers the ambience of Tobias' home in Rhiwbina as "a combination of pacifism, ILP socialism and the William Morris ethos", and this pacifism and socialism also informs her Zionism, her sympathy with the early Welsh nationalist movement, and the fight for women's rights, all of which are the subject matter of her work.[2] Her pacifism, of which *Eunice Fleet* is an expression, was perhaps crystallised by the experiences of her brothers during the First World War, for they were among the 16,500 men, a significant number of whom were Welsh, who, between January 1916 and the end of the war in 1918, stood before military tribunals as conscientious objectors. Their principled stand and the scorn heaped upon them by patriots is movingly depicted by Tobias in *Eunice Fleet*, a portrayal that is informed by her own experiences helping her brothers and other conscientious objectors in the war.

Like the possibly autobiographical figure of Laura Fennick in *Eunice Fleet*, Tobias' war-time contribution to pacifist and socialist activities in Swansea and Cardiff was considerable: she helped shield conscientious objectors, documented army abuses, promoted the No-Conscription Fellowship, an organisation formed by prominent socialists to oppose the war, and supported the Independent Labour Party. The

ILP had been created in 1893 by Keir Hardie, the socialist M.P. for Merthyr Tydfil, and in 1900 it joined with other left-wing groups to form the Labour Representation Council, precursor to the Labour Party. The ILP was active in south Wales, particularly in Merthyr and in the Swansea valley, and Tobias was for a time apparently secretary to its Swansea branch. The Labour M.P. Fenner Brockway described her to Leo Abse as a "young, battling, aggressive socialist pacifist" during the war and praised what he remembered as her "daring challenges to authorities".[3]

Brockway and other ILP members such as Keir Hardie, Ramsey MacDonald and Philip Snowden were all supporters of conscientious objection both on socialist and, in the case of Keir Hardie and Philip Snowden, on religious grounds. Many of these public figures suffered not only political and social censure but also verbal and physical abuse for their opposition to the war, and this idealistic and energetic political milieu in Swansea and Cardiff, of which Tobias was a part, informs her fictional depiction of historical events in *Eunice Fleet*.

The novel follows the emotional and psychological development of the self-interested title character, Eunice, who marries Vincent, a teacher in Cardiff. His socialist and pacifist convictions only truly register with her when conscription is introduced, he is called up, and objects on conscientious grounds. The novel's opening and closing sections take place in London in 1931, but the central section is a prolonged flashback to pre-war and wartime Cardiff, in which Eunice's narrow, selfish reactions to her husband's political commitments lead to disaster, a disaster whose consequences she is still dealing with in 1931.

The tragedy of Vincent and the narrative of Eunice's psychological development make compelling reading. Eunice is neither heroine nor anti-heroine – her amorality as a young woman is not ameliorated by mitigating circumstances, and although her later suffering makes her a more sympathetic character to the reader, her despair and contrition do not redeem her. The emotional renaissance she undergoes when she meets George Furnall in 1931, and her growing hope that she might make good her misdeeds in the past by supporting his political career, are particularly poignant, as is her disillusionment and second descent into despair towards the end of the novel.

The comfort that Eunice takes in the assertion by her Zionist friend that one must believe "in something – something big – not just in a man" is as much the political message of the book as is the pacifist polemic voiced by Vincent, and Tobias thus subverts the romance genre to which, in style, the novel in part belongs. However, the writing of *Eunice Fleet* is also overtly polemical in places, and Vincent's dialogue in particular shares a rhetorical style with much left-wing fiction of the period, fiction in which polemic takes precedence over characterisation, such as occurs in Lewis Jones' *Cwmardy*. Some of this polemic is historical material that Tobias seeks to convey through the medium of the Tribunal speeches, but even outside the courtroom Vincent never fully shrugs off this role. However, although his character is somewhat flattened by the primacy of his idealism and his politicised speech, the distress that he experiences as he suffers doubt in prison is as compellingly written as that of Eunice.

In addition to its literary interests, the historical context and content of the novel, particularly its wartime setting, also makes fascinating reading. *Eunice Fleet* contains an array of the historical figures whom Tobias knew or with whom she came into contact, and includes cameos of the South Wales Miner's Federation leader James Winstone; Winstone's opponent C. B. Stanton; the pro-war Prime

Minister Lloyd George; Ramsey MacDonald, and Helena
Swanwick, a representative of the Union of Democratic
Control. Many of these political figures make an appearance in Tobias' depiction of the confrontation at Cory Hall,
which took place in November 1916 in Cardiff. The so-
called Battle for Cory Hall in many ways typified the
violent confrontations between patriots and pacifists that
occurred in major towns throughout Wales and England,
but it was also characterised by elements specific to the
cultural context in which it occurred, such as the influence
of the Welsh pacifist tradition, which informed socialist and
non-socialist objections to the war, the tensions between
Stanton and Winstone, both of whom were ILP members,
and the union response to the threat of industrial compulsion. On the 11th of November, Ramsey MacDonald
and Helena Swanwick were to speak at a peace meeting in
Cory Hall, a meeting that was opposed by patriotic groups.
On having failed to ban the event, these groups organised a
counter-demonstration and violently broke up the meeting.
Unlike Fenner Brockway, who was physically attacked after
a similar event in Manchester, MacDonald escaped without
harm. It is this escape that Tobias fictionally enlarges, and
she describes MacDonald in adulatory language that re-
iterates his famous charisma. However the patriotic *Western
Mail* accused him of having slunk away.[4]

   Tobias portrays the events at Cory Hall as a pacifist versus
patriot confrontation from which the pacifists emerged
with the moral high ground, and this view is shared by the
ILP newspaper, the *Labour Leader,* which covered the event
the following week under the headline 'Mob Rule in Cardiff'. Politically the events were more complex, however:
the confrontation was provoked by Charles Butt Stanton
who, after Keir Hardie's death the previous year, had competed with James Winstone to be Labour candidate in the

Merthyr by-election. Winstone, a somewhat ambivalent anti-conscriptionist, had won the official candidacy, but was defeated by the inflammatory patriot Stanton, who ran as an unofficial ILP candidate. Tobias has simplified what she would have known was a complex political situation, but even though the depiction of the confrontation at Cory Hall is in this respect somewhat depoliticised, it reflects the popular perception of the encounter as a pacifist/patriot conflict, and Tobias' rendition of Stanton as "The Bloated Patriot" mirrors the reaction of many to his extreme anti-pacifist rhetoric.

The apparent simplification by Tobias of these events reflects a tendency throughout the novel to delocalise and depoliticise the setting, a reduction in cultural specificity that is in marked contrast to the overtly Welsh and Jewish concerns of most of her stories and her other three novels. In her first and third novel in particular she responds consciously to the tradition of Anglo-Jewish literature, particularly to the nineteenth century novels of Grace Aguilar and Amy Levy, but does so through the medium of her Welsh Jewish cultural consciousness and experience. In these novels and many of her stories she compares and draws parallels between questions of Welsh and Jewish ethnic identity, assimilation, culture loss and national aspirations. This central engagement with Welshness and Jewishness in her work is absent from *Eunice Fleet*, however, for here the primary engagement is with pacifism, and Welsh and Jewish issues are played down or coded, perhaps in an effort to universalise the novel's political message. Although the events at Cory Hall identify Taviton as Cardiff, and although several incidental Welsh towns are named, and a Jewish woman who has moved from Taviton to London remembers Eunice as "zat lonely gayl from zee old countree where we used to live", there is no overt indication that the

wartime section of the novel takes place in Wales and there
is no engagement with the specifically Welsh pacifist
tradition by which Tobias herself was in part politicised.

This is in contrast to her first novel, in which the character
Meurig Lloyd indicates his support of conscientious objectors
by observing: "Our nation it is that has most reason to
know the folly of opposing force to force. And shame it is
to every Welshman to join in the persecution of conscience".[5]
However, in the trial scene in *Eunice Fleet* in which a young
man pleads exemption on religious grounds, Tobias chooses
not to situate either him or his beliefs in any identifiable
cultural context other than a universal Christianity. This is
not for lack of familiarity with the particular political and
religious arguments being made in Wales against military
service at the time, for Tobias was not only intimately
involved in the movement but also almost certainly knew
– or knew of – many of the Welsh conscientious objectors
who went to prison, including such figures as the Welsh
language poet Gwenallt. Vincent himself may be modelled
on the high-profile case of Morgan Jones, a pacifist who,
because of his political views, lost his job as a teacher and
was imprisoned as a conscientious objector.[6] This possibly
coded reference is part of the heavily coded Welsh location
of the wartime section of the narrative.

Like the reduction of the Welsh context, in *Eunice Fleet*
Tobias' engagement with Jewish culture and politics is also
reduced: the portrayal of a Jewish conscientious objector,
his self-defence as an Englishman, and the small but highly
significant role played by the Zionist conviction of a friend
of Eunice constitute the only overt engagement with Jewish
issues. The sentiments of this Jewish conscientious objector,
who argues that his pacifism arises out of Jewish tradition,
echoes very closely sentiments expressed by Tobias' brothers.
But while some Jews, particularly those who were socialists,

were opposed to the war and to conscription, military service was seen by many members of the established, middle class Anglo-Jewish population as a means towards greater social acceptance for Jews in general, while the Anglo-Jewish poet Isaac Rosenberg enlisted out of a hope that this would help his impoverished family. Among more recently arrived immigrant Jews the response was more complex, particularly as many were not yet British citizens.[7]

The old charge of split loyalties, which in the war could now be laid against Jews who were unwilling to serve, is amply illustrated in the trial scene of the Jewish conscientious objector in *Eunice Fleet*, and the antisemitic implications in this trial scene, and indeed the antisemitism encountered by Tobias' brothers, which they report in a letter written from Kinmel Park where they were imprisoned, suggests one reason why Tobias should reduce overtly Jewish concerns in this novel: it appears very likely that this apparent anglicisation arose out of a desire not to provide ammunition to patriotic anti-Jewish opinion. Indeed, as one character remarks: "People talk as if a Christian C.O. was an unnatural coward or traitor, but a Jewish one a *natural* kind." It seems equally likely that Tobias also reduced overt Welsh markers in order not to provide such ammunition to patriotic anti-Welsh opinion.

Aside from her evident desire that the idealism and courage of conscientious objectors be recognised, and that the abuses they suffered both at the hands of the Tribunals and in prison not be repeated, the argument in the novel is against war in general, and Tobias perhaps also delocalised the setting and reduced these culturally specific markers in order to make her overriding pacifist message more palatable to an English audience. On the other hand it is possible that, having experienced the pressures exercised by a canonical tradition that disregarded "regional" fiction, Tobias sacrificed Welsh and Jewish cultural specificity for literary reasons, but as her later work returns to this cultural specificity, this seems less likely.

The depiction by Tobias of the abuses by the Tribunals and the torture of conscientious objectors in prison is historically accurate, and indeed some of the language used in the Tribunal scenes is very close to accounts that appear in the period in the *Labour Leader*. Her effective illustration of the hypocrisy of the Tribunals, which allowed those with class and political privilege to buy exemption for doing work of so-called "national importance", and of their refusal to honour the right to exemption on the grounds of conscience, reflects historical events. The subtle distinctions between the positions taken by conscientious objectors is conveyed through the stand made by Vincent: he does not request exemption from active duty only, which he is granted and refuses, but claims total exemption. It is because he refuses to accept any work that relates to the war that he suffers prison and torture, and is threatened ultimately with death by firing squad for refusing to comply with a military order. Conscientious objectors were illegally but routinely shipped to the front and ordered to comply under this threat, although these death sentences were commuted at the last moment to years of hard labour.

The central concern with the suffering of pacifists rather than the suffering of soldiers at the front distinguishes *Eunice Fleet* from much of the post-1918 writing on the First World War. The publication of popular work dealing with the suffering of soldiers during the war had reached a huge volume by 1933, when *Eunice Fleet* was published, and was typified by the successful West End play *Journey's End*, which Eunice attends in London in 1931. Much of the popular work published in this period was conservative in nature and sought to re-establish social stability in the chaos of post-war change.[8] But *Eunice Fleet* is, in contrast, a radical work, not only because it constructs the highly unpopular conscientious objector as a courageous and tragic hero, but also because as a pacifist polemic it argues for radical political change.

The novel was published at a time when the threat of a second war was looming, but it also constitutes an outraged response to the betrayals of MacDonald's government in 1931, when such stringency measures as the Means Test were introduced. Whereas during the war MacDonald had been a much-hated pacifist, in government, in Tobias' view, he betrayed not only socialist principles, but also the memory of conscientious objectors and ex-servicemen alike. Although her portrait of him at the end of the novel is moderate in its criticism, in an unpublished play that she based on the novel, entitled 'Where have I Seen You Before?', he is depicted as an outright traitor. It is in the context of these betrayals and the threat of another war that the *Socialist Review* welcomed *Eunice Fleet* as a topical and brave book that "has for its theme the tragedy, the humiliation, the abuse and misconception which all of us have got to face if we refuse to fight in another capitalist war".[9]

Eunice Fleet and Tobias' other four books went out of print and were quickly forgotten, like so many authors whose political commitments and whose particularity condemned them to obscurity. Several of these political women writers have been reconsidered in the collection *Rediscovering Forgotten Radicals*, and they form a group of writers among whom Tobias clearly belongs. The editors' assessment of the style and focus of this kind of work in the 1930s could as easily apply to her work as well:

Although [these authors] wrote during that troubled

period . . . called . . . 'modernist,' their concern was
not to find new ways to express new forms of
consciousness but rather to expose the resilience of
old forms of consciousness that prevailed then and
that still prevail today.[10]

The old form of consciousness that Tobias seeks to expose in *Eunice Fleet* is what Vincent calls the "wrong political
conception" and the "wrong human outlook, morally and
spiritually" which leads again and again to war. In 1933
Tobias used the First World War to argue against the
madness of a second war, and the pacifist message of her
novel is as topical now as it was then.

Sadly, Tobias' idealism suffered later in her life, and
disillusionment set in. In 1946, shortly before her sixtieth
birthday, when she was frail, lonely and ill, she wrote to
her nephew, Leo Abse: "Pacifism and appeasement are a
dead failure! – a belated discovery, you'll think. But one
clings to the illusions of a lifetime, somehow".[11] No doubt
the murder of her husband, family conflict, and events in
Europe and in British Mandate Palestine, where she had
gone to live in 1936, all contributed to her disillusionment.
With the exception of the war years, which she spent in
South Africa, Tobias lived in her father's villa in Haifa until
her death in 1984 at the age of 97. Her fifth book, *The
Samaritan: An Anglo-Palestinian Novel*, which is a sequel to
My Mother's House, was almost finished when her husband
was murdered in Haifa. She dedicated *The Samaritan* to him
in 1939 and published no further fiction.

One wonders what Tobias might have contributed from
her position in Israel, had she not been so traumatised by
these events, for in 1920, in an emphatic rebuttal to a mili-
tarist article published in the *Zionist Review*, she had written
passionately, and prophetically:

The authentic voice of Israel pleads for 'Peace – Peace – Peace.' It is not for us to hush a single note of that compelling cry. For, unless we fulfil its message on the soil of Palestine, we shall be false alike to the most vital teaching of our past, and to the greatest present need of racked mankind.[12]

SOME PUBLISHED WORK BY LILY TOBIAS

The Nationalists and Other Goluth Studies (London: C.W. Daniel, 1921).

My Mother's House (London: George Allen & Unwin, 1931).

Eunice Fleet (London: Hutchinson & Co., 1933).

Tube (London: Hutchinson & Co., 1935).

The Samaritan: an Anglo-Palestinian Novel (London: Robert Hale, 1939).

"Daniel Deronda, a play", *Jewish Quarterly* 23.3 (1975): 8-12.

NOTES

1. See Vera Coleman, "Lily Tobias", *The Blackwell Companion to Jewish Culture from the Eighteenth Century to the Present*, ed. Glenda Abramson (Oxford: Blackwell Reference, 1989), pp. 759-760, and Mimi Josephson, "Dual Loyalties", *Wales* (December 1958): 16-20. See also Henry E. Samuel, "Mrs Lily Tobias: A Welsh Emissary in Israel", *CAJEX* 8.2 (1958): 50-52.
2. Leo Abse, letter to the author, 22 December 2000.
3. Leo Abse.
4. For an analysis of the events at Cory Hall, see Brock Millman, "The Battle for Cory Hall, November 1916: Patriots Meet Dissenters in Wartime Cardiff", *Canadian Journal of History*, 35.1(April 2000): 58-83.
5. *My Mother's House*, p. 514.
6. See K.O. Morgan, "Peace movements in Wales 1899-1945", *Welsh History Review* 10.3 (June 1981): 398-430.

7. See Mark Levene, "Going Against the Grain: Two Jewish Memoirs of War and Anti-War (1914-1918), *Jewish Culture and History* 2.2 (Winter 1999): 66-95.

8. For discussion of this popular work, see Rosa Maria Bracco, *Merchants of Hope: British Middlebrow Writers of the First World War, 1919-39* (Oxford: Berg Press, 1993).

9. *Socialist Review* (Spring 1933).

10. Angela Ingram and Daphne Patai, eds. *Rediscovering Forgotten Radicals: British Women Writers 1889-1939* (Chapel Hill: University of North Carolina Press 1993) p. 6.

11. Leo Abse Archive, National Library of Wales.

12. "Zionism and Militarism: some other considerations", *Zionist Review* 4.5 (September 1920): 90.

Part One

PRESENT

Her Sister's Keeper

"WHAT! Going *out*?"

"Of course. Don't be horrid, Eunice. I told you before we left the shop – you know I hurried—"

Water splashed. The taps were still turned on, the pipes babbled, and the enamel soapdish fell off its ledge and clattered. Conversation through the bathroom door was difficult.

"Oh, I know you hurried." The figure in the dim corridor moved nearer, her long shadow bending as she stooped towards the lock. Such light as spread from a low-powered bulb showed a bone-clear face, the chin jutting to a fine point below compressed lips. As they parted, her voice came louder, not raised, but deepened. "You rushed me into forgetting the ledger-notes, and then when I went back for them you didn't wait—"

"I jumped on the first bus – thought you'd guess—"

"Well, I don't remember your saying you meant to go out – why, you were going to help me with these papers tonight—"

"Sorry, old thing. But I can't miss a dinner and show for the sake of those blithering accounts. Why don't you let Hava finish them? She's got a quicker eye for figures than you have!"

Dorry prolonged her laughter with such a shrewish tinkle that Eunice recognised the pun. She took no notice of it. Dorry must be feeling reckless as well as gay if her brain sprang to this mischievous humour. Her own mood was waspish – and aware of it, she made an effort at restraint.

"It isn't Hava's job. She's doing her share of the stock-taking. Everyone's got to – time's short." She paused. "Who's taking you out, anyway?"

There was no reply from the bathroom. Only more furious splashings, then the gurgle of the plug, the sucking outrush of water. Dorry, standing on the rubber mat with a towel in her hands, listened a moment in her turn, and heard the bang of a door.

"Eunice *is* mad. She'd be madder if she knew it was Blake—"

She chuckled, and stretched the towel, drawing the ends up and down in see-saw motion across her back. The pink, steaming flesh glowed ruddier in the friction. She dabbed at the round abdomen and rounder flanks of her sturdy, small frame, sprayed herself with talcum from the per-forated top of a bottle, pushed wet toes into blue silk mules, flung a terry-robe over her shoulders, and, clutching the ends, unlocked the door and slithered through the corridor into a bedroom. The air of the crammed little chamber was warm from a sizzling gas-fire. The girl let her robe drop on the Indian rug that reached from wall to wall, and began spasmodically to pull out drawers, the contents springing a medley of patterns on bed, chairs, and floor. Selecting a few things, she piled them beside the fire, and stood straddling a moment in the heat. Then with hasty jerks she began to dress.

First she drew on a pair of stockings, shielding the web-fine silk from her pointed nails. The nails, however, were more precious than the stockings. Their red-stained glint warmed the refraction of shell-cold eyes, bent critically on fingers smoothing pretty legs. These legs, too, could pass their owner's inspection – they were short, of course, since they belonged to a short body, but they were well shaped and, thank Heaven, not *fat*. The word shuddered visibly on her lips. She stood before the wardrobe mirror, and pride fled from her as she surveyed the rest of her nude young person. How awful – the heavy little globes of her breasts, the looming globe of her stomach! She slapped and pinched her haunches. The full firm curves might have enchanted Rubens, but her gaze was disconsolate. She tumbled the pile of garments and picked up a rubber corset, still in its tissue packing. Her hands, unrolling it, trembled with a pleased and furtive haste. Its brand-new smell enhanced her sense of guilt. What would Hava – what would Eunice say? – As she struggled to mould her flesh into this flexible yet inexorable prison, there came a knock at the door and Eunice called:

"I'm coming in, Dorry."

Useless to protest! The lock didn't work, and, anyway, Eunice walked in without waiting for an answer. She stared.

"You might have asked permission," she said. Her voice was not hard, and Dorry was too relieved to point out that the remark belonged in the first place to herself. She began her usual rattle of excuse and justification.

"Oh, Euny dear, you don't really mind, do you? I just *had* to try these darling things at once. I *did* mention taking a pair home, but I wasn't sure whether you heard and I didn't bother to repeat. Hava won't mind, I know – it won't affect the stock or the new display next week. And I'm simply frightful, just look – in spite of all the exercises and dry biscuits and knocking off potatoes and chocs. I bet this'll make far more difference – but how do you get into the damn thing? Do help me, there's a gem, I don't care how tight you squeeze."

"It's not a matter of squeezing, but adjustment—" Eunice used her long fingers deftly. "But these things aren't good for you, silly kid. Naturally it doesn't say so in the brochure

– but they're beastly unwholesome. You'll sweat horribly and probably get pneumonia."

She looked down with an ironic smile from what seemed a great height. Actually Eunice Fleet was not over-tall, but she appeared so beside the little figure of the younger girl. The half-sisters were totally unlike. They were daughters of the same father, and in stature and colouring Dorry resembled him, while Eunice perpetuated his first wife, her own slim, dark-haired mother: "Too thin" had been the verdict of the earlier generation on Beatrice Granger and her child, endorsed by Tom Granger himself. His second wife had not been thin, but neither had she been as fat or short as her offspring. Her prettiness, rather than her grace, had descended to Dorry. The stocky build, the flaxen curls, the rosy bulge of cheek and chin, were so much Tom's, that they could foil his elder daughter's hate of that lovely stepmother.

Beside, was there not something pathetic and childish in the naked creature looking up at Eunice – something that belonged only to herself? At seventeen Dorry Granger showed a sophistication of body and mind that offended Eunice Fleet, as old again in years, in suffering, and in temper. But mixed with this sophistication, this modern and native assurance, was a streak of naïveté, that may have been simplicity of age or of brain: whatever the source, its existence was undeniable, and as sure its power of reaching the heart. Eyes looked up to eyes; and shell-grey doves deflected the spring of coiled brown snakes.

"I knew you'd be sweet about it, Euny. You do like me to look nice and make a hit, don't you? It's good for trade, too. My – what a difference!" She strutted delightedly before the mirrors. "No chest – no hips – or hardly any – hooray! My frock's going to look twice as smart – my dear, it's a great ad. for Madame Eve's! Who said I'd be no good as a mannequin? Tell you what – I'll put in extra work with the rubbers, and you can talk to Hava about doubling my salary. Hadn't you better send the special brochures out at once? This new rubber's the find of the season. It knocks spots off the old – *literally* – see?" She pushed her fingers into the little round holes which patterned the corset, winked wickedly, and burst again into her tinkle of laughter. "Safe enough to sweat in these, you bet! Wait till the fat little Duchess sees me. She'll be on 'em like a bird – *in* 'em, rather. And what about Lady Bee, and Greta Sheldon, and the Crit girls – they're half-dead getting their weight down. Why, the guineas will pour in like – oh, what's that? – not the taxi? – My God, and I haven't done my face! Be a sport, Euny – call down the tube and tell the man to wait while I make the sparks fly."

She was, however, still "doing her face" when Eunice came back into the room. The rapidly changing texture of hair, skin, lips and brows had the effect of eliminating the "something childish." In no more than the rubber sheath, stockings, and cami-knickers like twin handkerchiefs, she was adult, cocksure, complete. The frizz of hair was sleeked to the skull, the forehead blazoned its arches; lid and nostril rose from purple shadows, the mouth marched with scarlet flags. Jezebel could have proclaimed no less when she looked from her window, thought Eunice. The image shocked her to revulsion.

"I hope you're not going to be late, kid. It's bad enough leaving me here to work on my own – but I don't mind that so much. It's your knocking yourself to rags and scamping your morning. You've done it too often lately. Any of the others would have had the sack long ago—"

Answer broke in quick and muffled. Dorry was working her way into her frock.

"I'm not afraid of getting the sack, old thing. Much more afraid of *looking* like one!"

"You're witty tonight. For whose benefit are you practising on me?"

"Blast! Now I've torn it!"

The flimsy georgette was intact, however. Dorry's head emerged immaculate from the opening, and she surveyed herself in a prudent whirl of satisfaction.

"There! What do you think of it? Glad I took your tip and had royal blue instead of sky. Don't I look marvellous? Fit for the Savoy?"

"Who's taking you there?"

"One of my pals, of course. Tell me how I look."

"Lovely – a picture – but—"

"But not as flat as *you*, all the same – I know—" She kept swinging on her soles before the mirror, discontent creeping into her gaze as she smoothed her hips. "Even in your old stays and that overall, you've got more style – your figure's just right. It isn't fair. You don't take any pains – you don't *do* anything – and yet you're just perfect—"

"Thanks – for very little—"

"Oh, of course, you were born tall, and that makes all the difference – no, it doesn't – not *all*—"

"If you're feeling so frank, Dorry, why can't you tell me who—"

"Go on. Be a cockroach." She snatched up a black velvet cloak glittering with sequins. "You don't know all my pals and you don't care for any you know – that's why they've stopped calling here and I've got to meet them elsewhere. Even Rita – I'm joining Rita tonight, if you want to know."

"But *she* isn't taking you to dinner. Who is?"

"I must be off – that taxi's ticking up—"

"Who's paying?"

"Well, of all— S'long, quizzy!" She opened the door and drew the air audibly through her nostrils. "Oh, what a scrumptious smell! Bet I shan't get anything as good as that chop Ginger's cooking for you. She just knows *how* since Hava showed her. Enjoy your dinner, darling, and don't grouse – you've preached enough and got it off your chest – bye-bye!"

"Come back straight from the theatre. If it *is* a theatre."

"Of course. We're going to see – oh, I forget the name of the piece, but Gladys Cooper's in it."

"I'll be waiting for you – got enough work till midnight. I'll have something hot ready."

"No – no – I'd tons rather you went to bed – shan't want anything. We're going on somewhere for supper – the Asulikit, I expect – there's a new cabaret on. Don't fuss, Euny – I'll be all right, I tell you—"

"Yes, but you won't tell me who it is you'll be all right *with*. Why this long spree on a week-night, anyway?"

"Well, Blake's going to Spain tomorrow for a month – oh, *blast*!"

"So it's Blake Pellew. I thought as much. And you wouldn't tell me because you know I hate your going about with him."

"Of course. And I might have known you'd worm it out of me. But look here, Eunice. There's no sense in your objections. He's quite O.K."

"He's not. He's a rotter."

"How do you know? It's only surmise!" – her shrewd glance stopped reply – "He gives me a good time, anyway, and I can jolly well take care of myself. Don't worry, old thing. And go to bed when you've done those beastly accounts. We needn't *both* be late in the morning. Bye-bye."

She was through the corridor and had banged the outer door of the flat. Eunice remained standing against the bedroom jamb. A slight poison reeked in the air, stimulating and sickening her. The brown snakes had uncoiled, had shot their charge, to find it darting off an unharmed spine.

She breathed back her own resentment in disgust. Always the same! The little puss either disarmed you with her look of innocence, or thwarted you with her mock and flair. Mostly one felt old and wise with the weight of experience; then suddenly, helpless, beside the cunning boldness of the child. Who could tell whether the fault was not in one's self – the nemesis of impotence, and not the warp of – what did she call it? – surmise? – *unjust* surmise?

She took the notion with her to her room, she washed and changed with it, and finally digested it with her dinner. The chop was delicious, as Dorry had foretold. Eunice sighed as she removed the crisp fringe of fat. How Dorry loved such morsels, yielding to desire in spite of vows of abstinence! Her slimming craze at least need never cause alarm. Easy for her to desist from potatoes, which she did not like, but not from savoury meats and rich sweet creams, like the pink-iced mould melting its favours before a languid, solitary spoon. That was Dorry – a greedy child. How did one treat greedy children? The woman who had been a wife but not a mother, leaned back in her chair and brooded. She was tired – tired – she had fought so long with her sense of failure, and won rest by acknowledgment. After all the misery and revolt, the rape of dominance and pride, she had snatched at the laurel of repentance and claimed her ease with it. Was it decreed that she should suffer a fresh incompetence – an incompetence of sisterhood? Be thou thy sister's keeper, their dying father had enjoined. She had not slipped into the yoke as lightly as she had bent to that of marriage. She hadn't wanted it, she had tried her hardest to avoid it. But that creature, the child's mother, so shamelessly abandoning her natural responsibility, had forced it upon her. The old man's wish had reason in it. There had been sweetness, too, in reconciliation, after the hostile years. And now – her promise bound her to an importunate ghost.

Well, she had done her best. She had brought Dorry to live with her in the flat, she had provided her with a job in the firm, and she had tried to adapt her own dry routine to the springing sap of youth. More than that, she had tried to love the child. With all those bitter memories behind, it was not an easy task. Yet it might have been easier had Dorry felt affection. What she showed was spasmodic cordiality, varied with bursts of envy and spleen. Frank the little puss could be – if crude unrestraint was a virtue. Eunice laughed drily to herself, without resentment. Yes – she had done her best. Had she? Did that mean this futile guardianship, which let Dorry spend her evenings – almost her nights – with a man who was a rake, perhaps a rogue?

She touched the bell, and a slight woman, neat in apron but with wisps of sandy hair straying to her eyes, entered timidly.

"You can clear, Mrs. Johns. I'm staying in to work, but I shan't want you for anything more tonight."

"Very well, mum."

II.

The Model

ONCE or twice, while Mrs. Johns moved about her duties, Eunice heard a sniff. But it made no more than a momentary impression. The lugubrious Mrs. Johns seldom cried, either visibly or audibly, in her employer's presence, though she always looked as if she had just been crying or was just about to cry. "Misery-face," Dorry dubbed her, alternatively with the nickname "Ginger." It was difficult, or at least imprudent, to show annoyance with one who did her work so well: and when she was less preoccupied, Eunice could be touched as much as vexed by the woman's wretchedness. A drunken husband, who beat and abused her, three troublesome children, a landlady for whom she scrubbed, washed, and cooked at unseasonable hours, in order to retain possession of a damp slum cellar – these were, perhaps, commonplaces of existence among the poor. But Mrs. Johns had been the daughter of a grocer in a village not remote from Taviton. As a girl of sixteen, she had "gone wrong" about a year too soon, unjustified by the licence of war. Her lover disappeared, and soon afterwards she fled or was ejected from her home. An aunt in Taviton, a dock labourer's wife, took her in, and kept the baby while she went out to work. But the aunt died, and nobody else would have her with her infant. Early in the war the defaulting lover was killed, and a soldier-mate who had been her aunt's lodger came to visit her and condole. He was a rough man twice her age, but seemed kind to her then and fond of the baby. They were married, and a month later the child died. "So I needn't a' married him, after all," was Mrs. Johns' mournful plaint. The husband went through the war without a scratch, but came home to drink, abuse her, and live on her earnings. She had five more children, two still-born. When her father died, leaving his house and business to a cousin, she was granted a sum of ten pounds as a final gift from "the estate." The money was spent when they drifted to London in search of work, which Johns never found or found only to lose. The melancholy drudge, who had "charred" for the Jays in Taviton, somehow chanced on Madame Eve.

That she had not always been melancholy and a drudge came gradually to Mrs. Fleet's knowledge, but most surprisingly as a result of the visit of a friend of Dorry's. A lanky, fringed girl – one of those modern chits Dorry picked up so enthusiastically. Eunice was far from enthusiastic about her. She disapproved the untidy dress, the nonchalant stare, the timbreless staccato speech. Odd, Eunice thought her, and even a little mad, when she said abruptly, watching Mrs. Johns depart with the tea tray – "I say – she's rather a beauty. I'll get my pad and pencil – would you mind awfully if I went into the kitchen? She needn't stop work – I'll do her in a jiffy—"

But Eunice had forgotten the incident when Dorry came in, a few weeks later, giggling over the cover of a fashion journal.

"Look what Rita's done of Ginger! Sketched her in the kitchen when she came to tea – I was in my room getting ready to go out, and didn't know she'd done it. Rita's got some funny ideas! Says Ginger's lines are perfect under her Noah's ark rags. In this gorgeous frock she looks a beauty – it's Ginger all right, just as she'd be if she were done up

– hair waved and eyebrows plucked, skin white and smooth – like her neck really is, Rita says, and I'm to look and see— Here, Gin – Mrs. Johns, what d'you think of your picture? Don't believe it, I suppose?"

Since Eunice didn't, she expected Mrs. Johns would not. But to her surprise, Mrs. Johns merely smiled a bashful, credulous smile at the smart fashion plate.

"It's a bit like me, miss, though I never did take a good photo. And I never had a grand gown like that – no back on it, neither! But my party dress was pretty when I was a gell, and everybody said I looked nice—" She blushed in retrospective modesty.

"That must have been a long time ago," said crude Dorry. She had torn off the colourful cover and pinned it on the kitchen wall, and was staring from it to the woman's worn, dingy face, with the screwed hair straying over red-rimmed eyes. Eunice stared, too: she saw at least that the curve of the cheek was good, the ears small, and the mouth shapely, despite dry, bluish lips with toothless gaps between.

"I'm just gone thirty-four," said Mrs. Johns, her un-youthful shoulders sunk as she rubbed some spoons. "But it *do* seem long ago – what with work and troubles – and the children, bless 'em—"

Her horny hands continued rubbing, but her eyes were moist and her dolorous voice trembling. Dorry cast a glance of horror at Eunice. It said plainly – "Misery-face is whining – she's going to cry – I'm off—" She fled, but Eunice, though frowning, stayed to ask—

"Hasn't your husband found a job yet, Mrs. Johns?"

"No, nor never will, mum." A dull resentment hardened the meek voice.

"Why on earth don't you leave him?"

"It's the children, mum – though he turns 'em against me, worse luck! The gells, poor dots, they don't know any better – he gets 'em sweets and plays with 'em – he's more time than what I have – so they're fond of him and listen to him when he tells 'em to do spiteful things. They coaxes me for money to give him, and if I don't give it, they goes on something shameful, using language what he teaches 'em. But my baby – oh, he's a little love, mum – and he clings most to me. The gells, they favour their father, but the boys be the image of me – it's as if they only belong rightly to me."

"I thought you had just the one boy."

The woman's face flushed and paled peculiarly. Her words trailed, plaintive, inconsequent.

"It's like as if the others – oh, I hardly know how to explain it – but this little 'un, he's the same colour and ways as my first—" She paused and seemed to struggle to recover herself. "You see, mum – he's so delicate – and where could I leave him when I goes out to work, and the gells in school? Not that their father minds any of 'em much. He's more often at the pub."

III

Invitation to Cabaret

IT WAS quiet in the flat. Seneschal Mansions edged a green space that split the mainway traffic of Maida Vale. Sounds were diverted and dulled before they reached the fourth floor, with its windows above the square. The faint noise of running water, chink of crockery, and slippered footfall, ceased with the click of the outer door. Mrs. Fleet had noticed them as little as the sniffs and sighs from the same unaggressive source. Unless encouraged to talk, Mrs. Johns kept her woes to herself. She knew as she let herself out that her mistress was absorbed in her own.

Sitting at her desk, with her office papers spread, Eunice lit a cigarette and brooded. She was obsessed by Dorry's painted face, her young strictured roundness, flanked by the dark elegant form of Blake Pellew. She saw his preying gaze, their contacts – and shivered with disgust and appre-hension. A bad man, Blake, if ever she had met one. Yet to use such a term in these post-war days was to invite a child's ridicule. It was not that for herself, she examined moral codes, or judged with rigidity. But Dorry – Dorry must be safe – must be protected from adventures.

Cigarette in mouth, she bent her eyes on the papers before her. Dorry and the uneasiness she caused must give way to consideration of business accounts. Tomorrow audi-tors would begin their annual exploration into Madame Eve's affairs. There was no need for anxiety here: on the contrary, an exceptionally good balance-sheet was due. The little shop near Oxford Circus was prosperous, the partnership proved a success. She and Hava Casson made an excellent combination. Hava's knowledge of the trade, experience in buying, sense of management, had developed under her mother's wing: Eunice brought complementary qualities of salesmanship and judgement that surprised herself more than her friend. Their equality had been established on a legal basis a year before Dorry arrived: and now there was a likelihood that "Madame Eve" might come to mean the younger partner alone. Hava had new plans for herself, it seemed. The prospect of sole ownership made mixed appeal to Eunice. Responsibility was not difficult to face: but she was too fond of Hava, or perhaps too used to her, to relish the idea of her disappearance from their common life. On the other hand, the chances for Dorry would improve. Yes, she must think of Dorry's future more than of her own – her own, that mattered, after all, so little. . . . Dorry must be cared for, must be made secure. She braced herself sharply, stubbed her cigarette in the tray, and began to total a column of figures.

But she could not concentrate. The imp of anxiety returned, danced in her brain, bedusted it. She had narrowed her eyes for a third attempt on the same column, when the telephone bell rang.

"That you, Bob?" Her root of a smile, that did not bloom in her eyes, pushed up slightly the corners of her mouth. "Yes, I'm home for the evening. No, I'm sorry. It's impossible. Alone? Yes, but – oh no, sorry, you can't. No, really! I can't have you here. *Work*, boy. Stock-taking accounts. Must be ready for the morning. Oh, about four hours, I should think. What? Nonsense. Yes, but—" She listened with humorous patience to the urgent voice, sweeping away her negatives. Why couldn't the good fellow leave her in peace?

Suddenly her vague gaze grew alert. A thought sprang into it. She broke upon the ramble of pleading with a decisive note.

"All right, Bob. I'll come. Oh, but wait – listen. Not to a show – not even a picture – positively no time. I must get in two solid hours at least. But if you can make it late? – good – then what about the Asulikit? Extension night, isn't it? New cabaret, eh? Very well – eleven. Not a moment before. Don't care if they do. No – simply can't be done. 'Bye."

She set the receiver on its prong abruptly, unconscious of curtness in act or voice. Her mind flowed warmly over her newborn plan. Dear old Bob. Butted in at the right moment this time. To sit in a corner and watch young Dorry – to join her somehow and contrive a homecoming together – what a halt to worry and the chance of mischief, at least for a month to come. Who knew what might happen on this night otherwise? It was strange, she realised with surprise, how she had been weighed down with a certainty of something happening tonight. The weight was lifting, but not the feeling of fate. Unused to forebodings, she was half ashamed of it. Anyway, she ought to be cheerful now – whatever was in the air, she'd got it in hand – in a firm, masterful business hand. She sat down briskly to her task, working for two hours without moving from the desk; shaping notes and figures into form, calculating, checking, summarising, not a shadow from her private mind clouding Madame Eve's sphere.

When the doorbell rang she was ready, though her clock had not yet chimed eleven. Bob stood like a schoolboy before her, guiltily expecting rebuke. But she smiled in greeting, and accepted his violets with a gracious air, pinning them promptly into her mole-skin cape. He wanted to linger – it wasn't so often they were alone in the flat together – but she hauled him out of the comfortable chair he plumped into, and made him pick up hat and gloves again.

"Just as you like," he said amiably. "Didn't know you'd want to clear at once – thought you'd blow me up for coming too soon. By gum, girlie, you look ripping!"

How Dorry would laugh to hear Eunice called "girlie." Eunice herself might laugh at any man but Bob, indulging in such patronising tenderness to her. But Bob was – Bob; a large, bluff, boyish male, whose friendly privilege held neither ridicule nor reason. Too deep for laughter had been her surprise at finding that, to him, *she* was an object of protective care, and Dorry – of uncomfortable fear. She could not bother, however, to probe and understand it.

"*Ripping*!" he repeated, standing with his big head askew.

And now she laughed a little, for sheer pity of his artless praise. Dorry's burst of petulance came back to her – you don't take any pains – you don't *do* anything – and yet you're just perfect – she had not given much thought to her appearance tonight, at any rate. Absently she had groomed her sleek brown locks, absently donned the wine-coloured velvet gown which swathed her slenderness. There was no colour in the long-boned cheeks, or animation in the deep-lidded eyes. A sinuous listlessness moved her limbs, and wound about her the cape which Dorry so often tried on in furious envy – because "it makes me look like a walking barrel"; whereas on Eunice – she had no words for the apprehension that on Eunice it wreathed itself like a veil of mist on a birch.

"Thanks, Bob," she answered him lightly. "And now let's hurry. After all, I might as well not miss too much of the show."

"Righto," he said. And took her down to a taxi without more ado.

IV.

Where Have I Seen You Before?

THE band was playing with the lights on, and most of the tables were occupied. She walked between them in slow grace, meeting glances with eyes like shields upon which they beat in vain. Her sight was long and quick. She knew at once that Blake and Dorry were not there, and she sat back in the corner that Bob found for her, prepared to wait. He fussed with wine and waiters, ordered and arranged, and imparted information which she acknowledged without note.

"See that little crowd on the left? In that alcove. Some of the Prince's friends there. Shouldn't be surprised if he walks in. . . . Too early yet. The fun won't begin till twelve. Jolly good idea of yours, Eunice, to pick on this place. Best programme in town. . . . That Spanish dancer's hot stuff. But d'ye know her partner's English? Fact. His name's nothing to go by – names never are. If you ask me, I don't think *she's* seen Madrid. Not in her baby-skin!"

She smiled, not at Bob and his big-dog air, but at the thought of Blake – going to Spain for a month. If only they'd walk in now and have their last fling before her. But still no sign. Couples were coming in faster and thicker. Soon the little hall of mirrors and tables would be jammed with standing as well as sitting figures. But from her vantage-point beside a pillar she could see from end to end.

"Hallo! That's Allanson with a party – over there. Wonder

I didn't spot him before – must have passed 'em coming in. That's his wife with him – in black – the girl in pink's his secretary. Don't know the fellow with her. Perhaps Allanson's new private man – he's just appointed another. Saw him last week about the Government's latest stunt. Did you read my little piece?"

She nodded vaguely. Just as vaguely her glance drifted over the Minister and his lady, the girl-secretary and her companion. The latter sat with his back to her, but as he moved she caught his profile, and her gaze stood still. There was something familiar about that nose and chin – still more about the gesture with which he lit a cigarette. He turned round fully and stared at her. It was so deliberate, so direct, a movement, that she knew instantly it was not made for the first time. He had seen her come in, he had watched her to her seat, he had kept twisting round to stare at her. The fact did not touch her in the least. She was used to men's glances. She had felt herself a magnet for their eyes, even when beautiful women companioned them – beautiful as she could not even seem to be. But this man – where had she seen him before? The question troubled her in some strange, hidden way. It distracted her attention from her quest. As the minutes swallowed the hour, she scanned newcomers with less and less impatience, until at last they ceased to matter. To watch the turn of one man's head grew more compelling. She did not care whether he looked at her or not. She wanted very much to look at him.

The band played on, in livelier syncopation. Dancers ebbed and flowed across the narrow floor. Twice Bob and Eunice swayed past the Minister's table, empty of its four occupants. At the third passage Bob's wish to greet them was appeased.

"Ally's sitting this out – I thought he'd get puffed pretty soon! Now we'll stop and introduce—"

"Not this time," murmured Eunice, and lay dreaming so content in his arms that he would not have paused for a hundred "Ally's." Yet he was delighted when, a little later, she broke the rhythm of the dance and stood still to say: "Perhaps we'd better meet your friends, though, now?" She had seen the younger couple returning to their seats.

"Righto. I say – the Allansons are going off. Seen me coming, you bet!" He grinned as the stout man of the party, standing over his dull-eyed wife while she collected wrap and bag, turned on being hailed and stared suspiciously.

"How are you, Sir John? Glad to see you looking in the pink."

"Um – er – ah, you're young what's-his-name – the press fellow who came along from the *Sunday Mail*—?"

"That's me, sir. Hope you liked the write-up."

"First rate," broke in the other man, in quick friendly tones. "You remember, Sir John, we agreed on that? – Winfield, I believe? – Lady Allanson – and Miss Grunbaum. My name's Furnall." He was glancing the whole time at Eunice, and she at him. She saw him still while her eyes moved to acknowledge introduction in her turn. Bob talked gaily, Miss Grunbaum made light retorts, Lady Allanson stood primly mute, and her husband tried to look gallant and genial while bowing himself free.

". . . Sorry, no time to improve charming acquaintance – must get off to prepare for early journey – can't sit up all night like you young folks – another opportunity, perhaps – good night, good night . . ."

"Won't you and Mrs. Fleet join us?" said Furnall.

"Yes, do," said Miss Grunbaum.

Eunice smiled pleasantly at the dark, curly girl with the dark, curly voice. It had an intonation that reminded her of Hava. But in appearance she resembled Hava's daughter, who was not as large or as handsome as her mother. In each girl the small, delicate bones and mobile flesh gave the same impression of warmth and intelligent restraint. Meeting Jess Grunbaum's eyes, Eunice felt an agreeable, almost an exciting, sensation of thaw. Whence the excitement? Those two bright pupils, gold in onyx, could scarcely be the fires at which her frozen soul might melt. Speech ran fluidly between them, an easy stream, easier in flux than that which trickled through the dance. There the current changed to rhythmic motion, with some strange accompaniment in blood, a deeper, faster harmony than words, mere pebbles now breaking the flow.

Furnall's voice was soft enough in her ears as they danced. But he said nothing that caught her mind until they paused, clapping their hands like the rest to make the band resume.

"Your name seems familiar to me, Mrs. Fleet," he said, "I mean—"

She watched him, intent, expectant. Was he going to add: "*You* seem familiar to me?" But he hesitated, and so long was the moment that she could not endure it.

"I know," she said, "it struck me, too—" The music went on, but she sat down as if unaware – they had stopped at their table – and instantly he sat down beside her. "I noticed you, looking round from your chair. I said to myself: 'Where have I seen you before?' Perhaps – perhaps you were saying the same thing?"

He smiled as if he found her gravity amusing.

"You said it to *me*, not to yourself! I wish I'd known. I thought you were just asking what I meant by it! What *I* said to myself when you passed me, coming in, was: 'George – you've never seen a beautiful woman before – you are seeing one now.' So George kept turning round and staring. Must I apologise?"

She turned down her lip, disappointed. A little puzzled air dashed his smile, but he chattered on.

"I wonder who it is that I remind you of? Lots of fellows look like me – I'm a hopelessly ordinary type. But if we'd met before, do you think I could forget?"

She said, indifferently:

"Then what did you mean about the name being familiar?"

"Oh, the name? Yes – it's queer. I don't know anyone called Fleet. But I've an idea I must have known – once. I don't forget names. Possibly I've met one of your family? – Perhaps" – he hesitated – "your husband?"

"My husband died. During the war."

Though she spoke quietly, almost coldly, her look embarrassed him, and he nodded several times in haste.

"Ah – you mean – service?"

"Service?" She did not repeat the word audibly, but weighed it, turning it round as if it were a toy in her hands. Service? Was it – wasn't it? It had seemed like that to Vin, but not to the majority of his world. How the present world judged, she couldn't decide. Meditating an answer, she found herself staring at the way in which Furnall manipulated his cigarette. She had noticed at once that he was left-handed. His gloved right was obviously artificial. The missing limb must mean that he belonged to that old majority. It made her answer harder. As she stared, the deft, unwonted gesture assumed a repetitive aspect, in her mental rather than in her physical sight. Suddenly memory unbarred a door. It revealed a scene, so clear, so startling, that she exclaimed aloud.

"Hallo, Eunice!" Bob, who had brought Miss Grunbaum back and was chatting animatedly with her, looked round in consternation. Her glance had jumped to him with her cry. Did she think he was "getting off" with the little dark girl? It was business, really. A journalist had to seize the chance of friendliness with a political secretary. She might give him useful tips, especially just now. Of course Jess

Grunbaum was a shrewd little nut, not to be cracked too soon by the soundest wisdom teeth. But she was jolly easy to talk to, and approved a fellow's funny bits. Eunice never seemed to listen much, anyway . . .

"Sorry," she said, with her absent air. "I just – remembered something—"

She accepted a cigarette from Furnall and drew at his flame, her eyes downcast. He was studying her intently, fascinated by the sudden flicker of life beneath her skin. So cool-cream the brow, the cupping lids, the long slope of cheek – was it his wavering match or some inner flame that ran a ripple through them? He had called her beautiful without insincerity, though her features were not cut to classic mould. If that flicker beneath leaped to radiance, there might be beauty of a rich, compelling kind. Meanwhile she moved superbly. One rarely saw such a spontaneous sweep of limb, such poise with flexibility. Had she really uttered that involuntary cry?

"Won't you tell me?" he asked, "what it was that you remembered?"

"Where you met my husband," she said. "And – where I have seen you before."

"Where – we—" he stammered.

"I grant you don't forget names," she continued calmly. "But you forgot me. I don't blame you. It was a long time ago. Years and years. And it wasn't much of a meeting." She blew out a long, straight puff of smoke. "I took you to see Vincent Fleet in a military detention cell."

The lights dimmed suddenly, as if sucked into one great beam that rode on a space of floor. In its shafts pranced a pair of magnificent creatures. Their dark manes, short, free, gleaming, swung on their necks as they leaped and whirled together. A gay shawl on one, a spangled cloak on the other, fell without sapping the brilliance of the strong, springing limbs. Their copper skins emerged from satin bands, swathed none too widely over breast and flank. With skill and energy rather than poetry of motion, they tore swift patterns from the hot, beamlit air, and in time with the crash of brassy instruments, wrenched at the senses of their audience. A clamant din of applause broke out. The dancers flourished their limbs in pyrotechnic flashes, the beam following their separate evolutions up the room. Wheeling back, they chased each other past the tables, mingling their breaths with the nearest onlookers. Here and there they halted, the female bridling at some man, the male snatching at wrists or heels to drag her off. She stood a second before Furnall, her arms making circles at his neck. Eunice was clapping as wildly as the rest, releasing into her hands the excitement in her veins. She saw the dancer's face like a magnified doll's, with poppet eyes leering and a rim of pink round her ears, where more art than sun had surfaced milky nature. Her fingers slackened, she kept her palms apart, and stared as Furnall grinned and gestured in return. The male dragged off his partner, still rolling her eyes, and Furnall thumped the table vigorously. But his thoughts were with Eunice and her revelation more than with the dancers' antics. For to him, also, a door had opened on the scene she evoked. Difference, if any, lay in the angle of vision. The door was the same – a rusty iron affair, creaking as the corporal pushed it. He could hear the beery gruffness of the soldier's voice: "Private Fleet, 'ere's yer wife 'n fren' to see yer. T'in't visitin' day, and can't let 'em stay long. So git it over – spry." There on the bench against the whitewashed wall, murky under a tiny grating light, was the man he had travelled over a hundred miles to see. What a leap of joy in the loosened body – could these agile dancers match it? The gripping hands, the eager voice, its pride and pleading, his own response, the grudging silence

of the sulky girl, stiffened against the door— Was it possible? That lanky creature, rude, stubborn, awkward – this
supple, gracious woman? A great rush of interest swelled
the current of casual admiration, bearing him on a broad,
warm tide.

"I remember it well – Taviton Barracks, of course! I
ought to apologise, all the same. And yet – something must
have told me. I couldn't stare at a *name*, you know, especially before I'd heard it! You've changed, though." His
voice could not drop lower, but it deepened, thickened. "By
jove, you're wonderful – to have mastered all your trouble,
and come out on top!"

"Have I? How can you know?"

"I can – guess. I heard what happened to Fleet. I never
knew what became of you. But – well – it's enough to look
at you."

They were almost whispering, in a sudden intimacy
charming to both. The semi-dark, their nearness, his head
inclined to hers, the loud clapping around them like a
shield of noise – everything projected them into a world of
their own. The bowing couple, a few feet away, might have
been as many miles distant. She moved a shoulder.

"You must have had a poor opinion of me."

"Not so bad as you had of me. Didn't you think me a
poisonous reptile? I believe you almost told me so—"

She laughed softly and sighed.

"I daresay. And now I've changed, as you say. But too
late."

"No, no – not too late – to help – to save others – from
another catastrophe—"

She was silent. The didactic note in his voice woke singular
echoes. She remembered its cogency in Vincent's ears – its
futility in her own. But now her sense seemed suddenly
attuned, acquiescent, not stilled, but ready – even for hope.

The cabaret had ended. Light diffused, music blared and whined, couples danced or sat on eating, drinking, talking louder and faster. While Eunice swung with Bob, she waited for the moment when Furnall would take her, his numb hand behind in magical hold. She knew he waited for it, too. Their glances raced together, and won to fulfilment in the surmise of both – the transcending harmony of their steps in a last tango.

"Absolutely your dance," said Furnall, letting her go with reluctance. "It's rounded off a perfect evening. I hope you've enjoyed it – the evening, I mean – half as much as I have."

"Oh, I have – as much, I should think!" Eunice smiled buoyantly. It was true. She had forgotten her lassitude, her gloomy fears. She had almost, though not quite, forgotten Dorry. She watched the streaming exit of couples as she had watched their incoming, but with anxiety submerged. She was resigned to the fact that Blake and Dorry had not come here: he – or she – had changed the venue. They had gone to a similar place, Heaven knew which, but it seemed absurd now to connect the jaunt with injury. Why shouldn't the child, too, enjoy these public hours? Nothing worse could happen than had happened already, all of it a past in process of fading out. The present was beginning in this dawn of tomorrow, when the association with Blake Pellew must inevitably end.

"I'm glad I turned out tonight," she said to Miss Grunbaum in the cloakroom. "*Last* night, rather – it's nearly two, isn't it? I didn't think I could manage it, I've so much work on hand. Business, you know, can't be neglected like politics."

"Oh, not much neglect – don't you believe it. We've done quite a bit here tonight. It's true the Guvnor's off to Monte for a week with his family – he's fixing them up there for three months, lucky nibs! But I've got to prepare no end of stuff for the campaign when he gets back."

"But the weekend's your own – doing anything Satur-day?"

She observed with amusement the lift of the thick black brows. Miss Grunbaum was powdering her face, rather clumsily and inefficiently, without looking into the minor that fronted her.

"Believe I've promised to do a show with your friend. Hope you don't mind."

Eunice laughed outright. She almost loved this girl with her lack of ceremony, combined with admirable mental control.

"Not in the least. I was going to ask you both to my flat. Come round, anyway, for tea – or a cocktail."

"Delighted. Furny coming, too?"

Eunice looked down her long, fine nose. The blunt inquiry hustled her half-born intentions.

"Quite likely – if he knows you are."

"Oh, he's tired of the sight of me, I assure you. The old man set me on to him hard this week with some Geneva stuff. Not that he doesn't know more than I can tell him. Being behind the scenes is rather limiting sometimes."

"Less inspiring, perhaps," said Eunice, she hardly knew why. Miss Grunbaum threw her a quick, droll glance, pursed her lips, and closed her bag with a snap. They moved to the door together, and Eunice added:

"Mr. Furnall's keen on League of Nations work, I sup-pose?"

"Oh, very. Disarmament's his special stunt. That's why he's going to be so useful to the old man. But I say – you're not really interested in my shop, are you?"

"No, I like you for yourself alone."

They paused a moment to smile in unison.

"It won't hurt you to throw a few crumbs to Bob," said Eunice confidentially. "He's very decent."

"So are you," said Miss Grunbaum, and looking both shrewd and generous, went on in her quick, decisive tones: "Furny's a coming man, you know. He's in the line of progress. And as soon as there's a by-election—" She arched her brows significantly.

"I'm not surprised. I mean – well, I'm not much of a politician, of course – but – oh, do you know, Miss Grunbaum – we found we'd met before – years and years ago – I know all about his views – and it's so interesting, this unexpected meeting here again tonight—" To her astonishment, she heard herself garrulous. A wild urge to talk about him to someone sympathetic yet unintrusive possessed her. But Miss Grunbaum merely nodded in her friendly way, checked, perhaps, in response by a number of women who passed between them. They drifted into the vestibule and found the men waiting.

In happy continuity the party began to walk, ignoring the taxis that lurched furtively by. The small March hours were dry and frostily clear. Naked with space and quietude between intermittent lights curved the new-breasted heights of Regent Street. Eunice offered her bare head proudly to them, craning her neck to match their smooth, firm lines; she trod the slippery pavement in her spike-heeled shoes as easily as on carpet while Jess Grunbaum, tottering now and again, quoted the famous actress who had vowed never to cross Nash's spoiled domain.

"What, *never*?" inquired Furnall. "Surely she'd break her vow on a night like this."

"Such a wonderful night," murmured Eunice.

"In such a night stood Dido . . ." chanted Bob foolishly, ". . . In such a night . . . did Jessica steal from the wealthy Jew . . ."

He was surprised to receive a slap on the arm from Miss Grunbaum.

"Steal my eyes!" she said, with a falsetto giggle. "Jessica took her rights. She marched *forward* – into the wide, wide world. And shouldn't we all do likewise? The beauty of Nash's crescent belonged to his own time – this belongs to ours. There *is* beauty here, even if Violas by the dozen won't see it." She steadied her heels in a pause to point with both hands at the high, flat walls.

"It moves – and yet it moves! "cried Bob, bowing to her.

"You mean it curves," said Furnall. "They haven't quite destroyed the curve—"

"No, by gum!" said Bob, grinning. "But that's not slick up-to-date, is it? I thought curves had quite gone out out!" He offered his arm in advance for a second slap.

Laughter pealed, but from Eunice came the faintest chime. She had fallen silent as the others chattered, and Bob's silly joke brought Dorry to her mind. The child must be home by now. Her long steps lagged rather than hastened. She wanted no sister-grained talk tonight, to break her new mood of warm indulgence. It was unlikely that Dorry, snug in bed, would care to hail her, however surprisingly late. Eunice dawdled with her companions at the lower circus, and endorsed their one-taxi plan. All to escort Miss Grunbaum to her Bloomsbury flat; then back, with the two men to Maida Vale. It would make her later still – but since the men agreed to "finish" together, she preferred being the last of the women to leave them. The extra measure of Furnall's company was worth the cost of Bob's increasing silliness.

The farewell grasp of the ungloved hand was close, prolonged: it enfolded her more cheerily than her veil of moles, as she made noiseless ascent of the gloomy stairs. Without touching a switch she reached her room and listened, sensing the blankness of an empty flat. Empty of other being; empty of Dorry. The surmise, or rather the certainty, was not pleasant to hold. She flooded the place with light, and searched – in vain. Dorry had not returned.

For a moment her heart reacted to alarm. But in the next it eased.

"I'd be a fool to worry," she assured herself aloud. "The kid's only done as I've done – but made it later. She'll be here before I'm in bed."

Passing to her desk, she unlocked it, ignoring the neatly-piled accounts to fumble in a drawer. Among the papers were photographs. Relics of the past, banished from wall and shelf and place of easy handling, to lose their barbs in dust of neglect. A sweet, not sharp, compulsion urged a peep at them now. But with her fingers on a card, a click startled her, and thinking it was Dorry entering, she closed the desk and waited. No sound followed. She moved into her room with the photograph in her hand, and sat down to gaze at it, entranced.

Herself. A girl of seventeen, in tennis kit. Pre-war kit. A sleeved muslin blouse, a full-pleated white serge skirt. The same long features, but more abundant hair, dressed high in front, a bow of ribbon behind. Droll, absurd – yet even in the faded print, electric with youth and vitality. The glow reached out, merged with the new radiation from the meeting with George Furnall.

"Vin" – she murmured – "Dear Vin – dearest—"

Tenderness, benign and profuse, streamed through her. Evocation of her husband, it seemed, was the source of this healing warmth, of which Furnall was the medium. She saw Vin in his flannels beside her young presentment. Ardent, smiling at her, alert with health and vigour, in the full spring of his big, fair, muscular body. (Bob was like him – the resemblance was superficial, physical only, but it was the reason of her kindness to Bob.) He had taken this photograph with a new camera, his birthday gift to her, immediately after the game – and immediately before she had refused, for the third time, to marry him. And the very next day she had run to him, and they had eloped.

"Dear Vin – dear boy – dearest—"

In all these latter years of remorse and repentance, she had never thought of him with such pure affection, untouched by bitterness or despair. It was like a release of long-pent impulse, gentler than tears. It was like bromidal tonic, soothing and regenerative. She sat with the photograph in the cold bedroom, not feeling cold, and undressed without lighting the gas fire. As she drew on her black pyjamas, she hesitated, kicked them off, and opened a cupboard near the stove. From a dainty case she took a nightdress, a lace-edged length of peachy ninon, with round neck and baby sleeves. Her slight body looked girlishly feminine in it. One like it had adorned her on her wedding night. The colour was Vin's favourite, and became her dark, clear skin. As she snuggled into bed, she stroked the soft clinging stuff with fingers as soft, as tender with vicarious caress. A drowsy languor beset her, and in a few minutes she was asleep.

She did not know it was two hours later when a creak and stealthy footfall in the corridor disturbed her. She half-woke, listened hazily, and thought – "Dorry's in"; and fell asleep again.

V

Business at Paris

IN the late dawn Dorry tossed on her bed of iron knobs. So the mattress seemed to her aching, wakeful flesh. The cocktails and champagne of her merry evening had the reverse of a soporific effect. And the events which were the intervals of drinking had exactly the same vinous air. She was electric with repercussions.

"Good old Rita – damn her! Interfering cat – luck's angel – I don't think! Curse her – bless her!"

The dual refrain convulsed her pillow. She hissed and sighed over the crucial moments of her night's escapade, stifling a fit of laughter to fall into a shuddering bout of relief – and regret. The scenes unrolled from the moment she joined Blake Pellew in the taxi. The kissing of hands (he'd learnt that abroad or from his foreign friend) and surreptitious pats on neck and arms while driving and dining slid into bolder caresses in the dark theatre during the acts. She'd known he was "hot stuff," and enjoyed the thrills of knowledge in the safety of public places. A man of the world, of experience and polish, literally trembling with passion for her! The cocksure little heart thrilled, not in response, but with subsensory gratification. Blake had "fallen for her" in deep earnest. Not his ardour, but his admiration, allured her most – the fact that she was "his style," not only in face but in figure. Her giggles of reminiscent delight began over a scrap of dialogue after the curtain fell.

In the foyer they had met, by tacit arrangement, a couple familiar from previous occasions. Dorry approved the man's choice of play. "It's lovely – I'm enjoying it ever so – going to be awfully exciting, I'm sure! And isn't Gladys *too* sweet!"

"She hasn't gone off – much," said the man.

"Oh, how *can* you? – she's divine! Is it true she used to be fat? Anyway, she's just perfect now, slim as a lath, and tremendously smart. Isn't she, Rita?" But Rita, as usual, was unenthusiastic. She shrugged the bare bones that were her shoulders, stared impassively at glancing men, and smoked in silence. Dorry appealed to Blake. "Isn't she, Blake?"

"Rather angular, I think," drawled Blake. He produced a fresh cigarette, and the other man offered him a light, saying in an undertone – "Ah, you like a plump little chicken, eh?"

Dorry pretended not to hear, but the giggles forced their way through the chatter she addressed to Rita. She was pleased and amused, though she did not like Serl – that was the only name she knew him by, and she had no idea whether it was a first or a last, an abbreviation, a nickname, or even a slurred pronunciation of Cyril. It was smart in Rita's circle to be casual about strangers, as about everything else. Often Dorry's curiosity got the better of her, and she asked crude questions which were seldom answered. Prudence, therefore, or the vanity which paraded as sophistication, compelled her to abide in ignorance of facts concerning the tall, thin-lipped, thin-waisted man who had lately appeared in Rita's trail. All she knew was that he had come from South America, and that everybody called him by the sound she mentally spelt S-e-r-l: to her it suggested the foreignness that was less in language than in intonation, less in act than in mannerism. That he was dark and combined feeble features with a bold gaze hardly justified her impression that he was sinister, and the coarseness she found in his speech was not due to the use of low words. For the matter of that, Rita, when she spoke at all, which was seldom, had a spade tongue, and swore badly. And strange to say, Dorry did not consider Rita coarse.

After the last act, they met again in the foyer. The play had impressed Dorry, beyond her interest in the slimming tactics of the leading actress – even beyond her observation of the audience, and of the new long evening gowns, sweeping the slimed flags as their wearers waited about for car or cab. "A pity," thought Dorry reluctantly, for though she liked the draggle tails of lace and chiffon, she liked better the display of her own shapely ankles and calves. Parallel with the thought coursed her chatter about the play. She appealed now for a decision on the ethics of the theme. Was it right for a woman to kill her crippled son, for the sake of an illicit child born to his brother by the cripple's wife? Bishops had denounced it, charming ladies had argued in defence. Blake jibbed at the murder. But there was no sin in the wife's liaison with the healthy brother. "Nature must have its way," said he, pinching Dorry's arm. They were walking along the Embankment, having drifted to the river in the fine, crisp, sparkling air of the night. Dorry tottered happily on her high, Spanish wooden props, glad they had come safely through swirling traffic to the dark stone walk. Lights flashed across the river, too far and spasmodic to affect Blake's amorous pressures under the spangled cloak. Serl, on the outer edge near the kerb, remarked that nature was equally justified in the removal of the unfit. He derided someone's notion that the immorality of the piece lay in the mother's plea of justification. "She's too sentimental about it, if anything. There's no immorality in putting such a chap out of his misery, and clearing the way for two normal people to live their sex life." He spoke in a reedy voice, bending from his waist to look aslant at Rita. She responded for the first time.

"Bloody rot," she said.

Dorry laughed heartily. She was fascinated by Rita, not the least of whose charms was unexpectedness. Dorry had never, in fact, met a person at once so natural and so opaque. Rita spoke, moved, grimaced, scratched her body, did as she liked without affectation or embarrassment, yet you could not gauge or see through her. But it was not the puzzle of her personality that attracted Dorry, so much as the marvel of her structure and gait. Bony rather than thin, she strode or jerked, or stood stock still, without grace, but with a subtle sophistication that drew much wider notice. Her head was small, and its shape had beauty, of a kind that secured her sittings to such sculptors as were anxious to model the "'30 type." She wore her hair lank and straight, with a lack of dressing that seemed like neglect. Against the startling red line of lip her complexion was muddish, and Dorry had an uncomfortable feeling sometimes that this perfect being was dirty. Often at close quarters her skin smelt rank; and one of Dorry's reasons for disliking Serl was, that he had an air of sniffing, doglike, round a careless mistress.

It was Rita who ruled out the Asulikit in favour of the Klatch. Dorry was a little chagrined; the Asulikit was bright and fashionable, while the Klatch proved dingy and dull. Blake's attentions, however, diverted her, and the wines were rare. She felt very gay and very hazy when Blake proposed they should all go to his flat in Jermyn Street for a final drink; and could hardly remember how long it was before she found herself sitting alone with him there. The others were about somewhere – in the kitchen, Blake said, making coffee. It wasn't a kitchen, she argued, vaguely but persistently: she remembered having passed through it to the other room. There was certainly a gas-ring in a corner, and a smell of coffee. Yet she had no recollection of tasting any. She hadn't wanted it, of course, there were so many other drinks. The dim light added to the haze in her mind. She felt sure it was brighter when she entered. Blake got more and more ardent as they sat together on the divan, and suddenly he asked her to go away with him. She did not explain that though she was only seventeen she had decided not to try that sort of thing, in fact preferred to get married – nor even that she had no objection to marrying him. But she pointed out that it would be highly inconvenient to her to be transported to Spain, where the sanitary arrangements were rotten; and anyway her sister was expecting her home at that very moment. He ignored the last remark, and made an alternative proposal. She could easily announce a week-end visit to friends, and join him in France. "It's just as filthy there—" she remarked. "The water" – (she did not know that she was saying 'wad'r')–"the water lets you down the sink Euny says—" Too much in earnest to laugh, Blake went on to emphasise that he must cross in the morning, and gave her details of his whereabouts if she had to follow alone. Business for his firm, who were arranging the Spanish contract, necessitated a preliminary stay in Paris. There they would spend the weekend together, and then, if she liked him well enough, she could accompany him further. If not, she could return home comfortably, and her sister need not be troubled in the matter.

The promised delights were anticipated by such caresses that Dorry found it difficult to be prudent. Prudent, that is, not only in behaviour, but in plan. Her hard-headed concentration on a matrimonial escape from her bondage to women was deflected. Even more than she longed for

embraces, she longed for a certain status and indepen-
dence, and now she was caught on a wheel of passion and
confused as to direction. If she swung with the wheel,
would it crush her, or speed her to her goal? If she resisted,
would she put a brake on her chance of arrival? She had
really no time to consider, bemused as she was, and with
Blake rushing her defences.

"Say you'll come, little Dorinda – sweet Dorinda—" he
urged, and she yielded her lips if not her voice in assent.
The next moment, finding herself sinking on the divan, she
screamed loudly.

"What the hell," said Rita, in her toneless pitch, standing
by the curtain she had drawn from the middle doorway. As
no one answered, she advanced and stared at nearer quarters.

Blake had risen and begun to tilt an almost empty bottle
over a glass. Dorry sat stiffly giggling on the divan.

"What's up?" said Rita.

"Nothing," said Blake. "Dorry's a bit hysterical, that's
all. Have this drink, girlie—"

"Quit," said Rita. She knocked the glass almost out of
his hand. "She's had too much. Come on, kid – get your
things."

She fetched her own wrap and the two handbags, thrust
Dorry's cloak over her, and drew her to the outer door.

"Serl's snoring it off," she said, as a faint hiss and snarl
became audible – "You can look after the pig. I'm taking
baby home."

She who seldom smiled, and had a brief, ugly staccato
laugh, now grinned widely as she made abrupt farewell.
There was an odd change, that might have been kindness
or perversity, in her manner to Dorry all the way to Maida
Vale. Cursing the taxi service, the post-midnight charges,
inadequate lighting of short-cut routes, and comparing

them with experiences at a similar hour in other cities, she was as unusually loquacious as Dorry was unusually silent. But not once did she refer to the incidents or escorts of the evening. When she drove off alone in the taxi, Dorry had no idea of her destination. Was she going back to the pig, or to some manless – pigless – nook of her own?

Neither very curious nor very grateful, Dorry crept to bed, congratulating herself only on unchallenged entry.

*   *   *

A not-too-chastened Dorry rose early, breakfasted on tea and rye biscuit, and was in Oxford Street before Eunice left her room. The shop kept everyone so busy all day that there was no opportunity for interrogation, which Dorry hoped more to postpone than to evade. Eunice, however, showed no concern about the night.

A diversion had arisen with an urgent order from a provincial customer, who dealt in abdominal belts and surgical corsets of peculiar construction. Previous supplies derived from France, mostly after troublesome delay and misunderstanding. The maker was an illiterate and conservative old man, whose home was his factory, and his family the only employees. Letters, telegrams, even telephone talks could not effect satisfactory delivery of a sudden order. The superiority of his goods, and their special nature, with which some of Madame Eve's reputation was involved, forced the firm to deal with Monsieur Faille against inclination. The profits, however, were considerable: and wholesale custom in other goods was often bound with these transactions. Madame Eve could not afford to dispense with Faille et Cie.

"But oh!" groaned Hava, "if only the little wretch understood business!" Exasperating, above all, was the fact that a personal call could wrest, in no more than a couple of days, articles (apparently always on hand and available to local trade) which would not, in response to the most pressing cables, reach London in as many weeks. Such orders seemed, from this side of the Channel, to necessitate special and prolonged manufacture: and leisurely Monsieur Faille could not be hurried. If you came, found, and took away – voilà! Last spring Mrs. Casson had descended on him and discovered the secret of expedition. In the autumn Eunice had gone over with Dorry. The success of these visits, not made specifically, continued to contrast with the failure of impersonal communication. And now, suddenly, imperatively, and most inconveniently, came a demand from their customer, an important corsetière in a country town, to supply within a week the needs of a client bound for India.

"He won't do it!" lamented Hava, laying down the pencil with which she was drafting a message. "It means going over and sitting on his doorstep. And that's impossible for us this week. With the stocktaking, and the new goods, and the special trade, and the rush, and—" she lowered her voice, so that the accountants busy in the outer office should not hear through the half-open door.

"Out of the question," agreed Eunice. She thought swiftly of Saturday.

"But I'm afraid it means losing Angeline. Her stock order isn't in yet – it looks like being conditional, she's begun to sniff at us lately. Since Freb's travellers have been all over her. Suspects we're rather small fry. And *she's* growing. Means five hundred a year to us."

"Gross or net?" said Eunice, trying to keep her wits on practical affairs.

"Net, of course," said Hava, with some surprise. "Haven't you just handled the account? Good payer, too. We can't afford to lose her, or even to share her with Freb's. They've a good imitation of this line. We must make a sacrifice."

"But how? We can't go. At least *I* can't. And I don't see how you—"

"Shall we wire Denise?" said Hava, mentioning a friendly agent.

"Made a mess of it last time," said Eunice. They stared gloomily at each other, then turned at the sound of a sharp, high voice.

"What about *me*?" it said. "Can't I go across and do the job?"

"You?" said Eunice. "What nonsense."

She frowned abstractedly and took some slips of paper from Dorry's hand. The girl, who had come in drooping from the outer office, turned with alertness to Mrs. Casson.

"It isn't nonsense. I've been there with Eunice and I know exactly what to do. You've got to have the goods here by Wednesday, haven't you? I'm free. You can spare me. My passport's all right. I'll cross tomorrow and be back by Tuesday night, or fly, if you like."

She was curbing her eagerness, standing still with her usual air of pert confidence. A flippant smile marked her last words. Hava Casson eyed her shrewdly and checked an impatient sound from Eunice.

"Sit down, Dorinda." Mrs. Casson's voice was kind, slow, but decisive, and she pointed to a chair. "I don't think we'll let you fly – yet. But tell us how much you know, exactly."

Eunice, listening uneasily, was called away. When she came back, Hava was giving Dorry instructions – not in regard to the order for Faille's, but for calls on other Paris firms.

"Denise will meet you," she concluded. "I'll wire her at once. She'll help you lots. But don't let her pry too much—"

"I won't," said Dorry emphatically. She burst into a laugh.

Eunice reassured herself with appreciation of Dorry's keenness – "She's taking a deeper interest in the business, at last." With Blake Pellew gone, Dorry was at a loose end, and this was at least a new excitement for her – far safer than men. Incontrovertibly she was equal to the trip, and would resolve an awkward situation. Surely she could not get into mischief with so much to do, in so short a time, and with Denise at her heels. . . . Eunice refused to recognise a sense of relief – that Dorry would not be at the flat on Saturday, to watch a delicate bud of friendship sprout from a past she judged, or misjudged, an abandoned dust-heap.

VI.

Journey's End Begins

MRS. JOHNS stayed on at the flat to clear. She looked drier and more abject than ever, but whether in contrast with the gaiety of the rooms, or through some addition to her woes, Eunice did not know – and it must be admitted, did not care. Outside rain fell between drives of blustering wind: indoors the firelight played on amber-curtained walls and groups of daffodils. The three guests came to tea, and the hours flew so swift with talk and content, that no move was made to disperse or dine elsewhere. They agreed that hot tinned soup and cold chicken, with fruit and wine, gave sufficiency and ease before play-going. Jess Grunbaum wore a sleeveless frock under her coatee that would carry her anywhere through the evening. Eunice changed, from a jumper and skirt in which she looked schoolgirlish, into a gown that matured and transformed her grace. She had bought it the day before; a simple but expensive sheath of apricot satin, shot with deeper flame at the long folding points. She had forgone her lunch to visit a barber, and her head was a sable crown of gleaming rhythmic waves. The outward harmony seemed composed from within. "Den was innen, das ist aussen," hummed Furnall. His eyes, approving her, were tributaries that fed her spirit. It moved her like a lake on which she floated, swelling, expanding with the wings of a swan. Bob more than once forgot Miss Grunbaum. And when he remembered, he urged extension of the party. He was willing to give up his two booked stalls, since no more were available at that theatre. But Eunice demurred. She said she wanted to see *Journey's End*, which Miss Grunbaum had already seen. Intent on division, she refused to go on to a night-club, either in pairs or in quadruples. She meant to be left with Furnall for the rest of the evening: and she was also resolved to retire early. That, of course, was pure business consideration. She must be up betimes to meet Hava at the office – their alternative arrangement to continuous Saturday work. A final check of certain matters had to be made before Monday.

Aware of Hava's surprise at her evasions, she had not cared to invite her to the flat, according to a first impulse. She wanted Hava to see Furnall: yet she did not want those quiet, shrewd eyes to rake his effect on her. She had also thought it would be "nice" for Miss Grunbaum to meet Hava. But now she wasn't sure. Jess Grunbaum differed from the Cassons almost as much as she resembled them. Possibly they had less in common than she supposed. In any case, another opportunity might come. Today, she decided, she must herself be free. Free to attend – to engage? – George Furnall's thoughts!

They went out together – last. She contrived it without, she knew, the notice of either man. If Jess Grunbaum saw, it was with less amusement than gratitude. Little as the younger woman was "catty," she could not but resent too much outshining. Her own interest in Bob might not be serious; still, one's chosen escort of an evening should be single in mind. There was no doubt that her conversation – or her attention to his – would hold Bob amply, if Eunice were not there to be looked at.

When Jess and Bob had gone, Eunice both hurried and dawdled. At her bedroom mirror she lingered with puff and stick, her reflected gaze startling her with light: in the kitchen she was quick, abrupt, flinging instruction on the turn of her heel.

"Please lock up carefully, Mrs. Johns. I've left the inside keys. Don't forget to put them in the usual place. And – er – Mrs. Johns – er – you can take the rest of the chicken and the cut fruit."

Eunice stammered from habit at the offering. It did not check her motion of haste towards the door. But she paused as Mrs. Johns caught her wheeling glance.

The woman was standing at the sink, her narrow back bent over steaming plates. She turned only her head, with its straying red wisps, and her eyes seemed drenched in greasy wet.

"Oh, mum," she said in her thin, plaintive tones – "Oh, mum—"

Eunice felt vexed. Furnall was waiting, her frock might catch a whiff from the culinary debris, and this dismal creature, instead of saying Thank you, began to whine.

"Well, what is it?" she asked, less sharply than she thought. For Mrs. Johns, either encouraged or driven by inward stress, burst into disjointed speech.

"Oh, mum, it's my baby – he's been that contrary this week – it's not his fault, the little love – it's his father – I knows it. He's turned the gells against me, and now he's turned the baby—"

"Nonsense," said Eunice. Her vexation increased. She looked from the drab woman to the drawing on the wall. The dainty lady still hung where Dorry had pinned her.

"It's true, mum," mourned Mrs. Johns. "He turned against me this morning. When I washed him he pushed me away hard, and said quite cross – 'Oh, mam, there's picky your hans are – I don' like 'em – I don' like you – I don' like picky hans—' It cut me to the heart, mum—" the poor fool stood with waggling chin, the released tears rolling down her face. She held out her hands. "They were purplish-red, swollen, cracked, blistered – a hideous sight. "Picky, they are – p'raps you remember, mum, what the children in Taviton calls rough skin. It's the cold weather, o' course, and chilblains, and the basement steps to clean in the raw mornings, and no time to dry 'em proper—"

"I'll give you some stuff. You can rub it in at nights, and each time after washing—"

"Picky," repeated the woman, staring at her hands. "They was smooth and white when he was born – no, I mean when the other one was born – just like *them*, mum—" She touched the drawing suddenly. It hung loose, and came off in her fingers.

"They'll be all right again with a little care," said Eunice impatiently. "Don't worry. Good night, Mrs. Johns."

She closed the door in relief.

"The woman seems dazed," her surprised mind recorded. "Perhaps she's taken to drinking, too—" The thought rolled lightly from the pleasant moment of rejoining Furnall. As they walked to the stairs he took the cloak from her arm.

"Don't you feel the cold?" he asked, holding it out. The landing air was raw and damp, but she smiled a negative into his serious face. "How that colour suits you—" he went on softly. "It makes you bloom like a peach—"

She gave a violent shiver. Hastily he pressed the wrap upon her shoulders.

"You see!" he said. "Of course you feel the cold!"

"Only gooseflesh," she protested, but she shivered again as they descended, clasping the fur around her. An obvious compliment perhaps; but the words had been Vin's – odd that he should use the very same! It was enough to make one feel the tread upon a grave. Yet surely – surely – Vin would not mind?

Still less, she assured herself, would he mind their sitting together to watch *Journey's End*. For there on the stage was shown the madness of his world – his, and Furnall's, and hers: shown for the new appraisement of those who lived on, and those who only followed. She knew at last what the verdict should be. Her brother's face came vividly before her – gay, careless, then drawn and haggard, with shifting eyes and irritable brow – Tom, Tom, *I do understand, I know now, I know*. The scenes of trench warfare, its filth and degradation, its pity and terror, drawn with quiet art and conveyed with realism in a single dug-out, beat on her sense with retributive force. She sat as if in spell, unable to smile, while the "comic relief" drew vociferous acclaim in the crowded theatre. "How can they laugh?" she murmured to Furnall. " It's easier to laugh," he whispered back. "And they really understand that best – that, and the sticky school-boy stuff—" He felt, glancing sideways at her grave, rapt face, as if he were uttering blasphemies: and ashamed of cynicism, he tried more closely to fit himself to her mood. Who should know better than he the motive of her sighs?

But he was uneasy at her earnestness until he succumbed to it.

"Left her sense of humour at home," he mused, in a last fling of detached reflection. "After all," he said aloud, "what is a sense of humour? I used to think it was a sense of proportion. But that isn't what makes these asses laugh. And – anyway – what's the good of a sense of proportion that makes you swallow muck?" He could not help grinning at his unintentioned pun, and then frowned severely to retrieve it. By the time the curtain fell, he had adapted himself wholly to his companion. She could – and did – express her feeling with impunity.

"How vile!" she said. "To think we could let all that go on for four years, and call it right! What monsters we were! – Stupid, unnatural—"

Her words suddenly rang echoes to her ears, thin, hollow, a long way off. She was embarrassed, disconcerted, until she caught the sympathy in his face. It seemed to spread over the girl she had been.

"No, no—" he said. "Only lack of imagination. Some people see things a thousand miles off. And some can't see what lies before their eyes. And the same power of vision doesn't always come to the same kind of people."

"But sense – pity—" she stammered.

"Not necessarily missing," he said. "Only not present in the right combination."

He soared very wise to her appealing look – very wise and kind, dispensing godlike balm. He could not help a slight giddiness at his height. . . . They sat in silence until the end, when she leaned unconsciously against him in the dark and said:

"It must never be again – *never*—"

"Let's hope so," he said, moved, but whether by the idea or by the pressure of her arm, he was not sure. As the lights came on, they stood together to the strains of "God Save the King."

"You're helping to make it impossible." Her murmur filled the pause. "That's what your work means, doesn't it?" He nodded. "I'm so glad. It's fine." Her dark eyes glowed, more richly than the flame leaping in her dress as she turned. It lit his nod into an act of dedication.

His public work? He had begun it on an impulse less ideal – though honest enough, he considered. The zeal of his youth had long been tamed. He belonged to a cause made safe by popular favour and ruling policy; if, like his fellows, he was stirred more by ambition than altruism, there was no reason why the two should not travel together. But now he felt a spirit touch him – a wandering spirit from the past – and it touched again to those fine issues that spring from sacrifice and pain. Let scorn come, out-casting – searing, maybe, in fresh fires of hell – yet must the one so marked crusade for humanity's redemption. In high mood he moved beside this gracious woman who believed in him; envisaging her faith, hearing his own noble phrases ring from crowd-hung platforms. What matter whether he uttered them himself, or wove them in obscurity for others to proclaim? The *righteousness of pacifism must ensue.* So his leader spoke, standing erect, one hand on lapel, the other raised – a Biblical strain in his eloquence even when blunted and vague. Bible truth. Politicians' truth. Furnall recoiled from parallelism so crude as to bring again the breath of blasphemy. With the arm of Eunice Fleet in his, he walked into Leicester Square, saying aloud in gay, excited tones – "Forward, St. George!" His smile of self-mockery was sweet as her own.

Ahead and above the great signs flashed, brilliant colours darted up and down and across, or zigzagged in endless crazy chase. A myriad lights dappled the shining river of the street, rain no longer fell, but the pavements were wet, trickles ran below the kerbs, and the procession of car-tyres sucked and slithered on a surface of marble slime. Well-dressed people sat in the cars or swirled from doorways, looking for vehicles or simply drifting about – a mass of males in black and white, sleek-polled and tall-hatted, a larger revolving mass of women, young and old, hair and faces as assorted in hue as the flimsy trails below their furs and brocades. Here and there a jewel gleamed from hand or throat, a bare bosom cleft the hug of wraps. But eyes as rich as Eunice Fleet's, skin as pure, motion as fine – where could they be matched, thought Furnall proudly, as he piloted his companion along.

"Shall we walk on?" he said. "It's cleared up and the air's delightful. You're not in a hurry?"

"Not a *great* hurry," she said. Her earnestness was eased with companionable flair. "I like the theatre crowds. Everybody looks so jolly, though there are some comic sights. One always sees a lot of dears who look as if they've walked out of a Victorian music-hall. The funny thing is, you never see *them* step into a hansom, like that smart couple there – Americans, probably. It's strange, isn't it? – how in spite of all the changes, some people remain just the same. And who could think that just a few years ago there were air raids over London, and almost everybody had someone in the horrors beyond?"

"Yes, the streets and the crowds were much the same – except that there was a lot of khaki about, no electric signs, and no miners or soldiers begging. There were people who looked jolly enough. They kept their spirits up, of course, by going to theatres as usual, and pretending there were no 'horrors beyond' – or that if there were, it was quite in order, and anyway, all the fault of the Huns."

"They know better now," said Eunice. She turned a face brilliant through its gravity on Furnall, and he did not answer. They were standing in a traffic block, waiting to cross the Haymarket. A double line of motors swung like curved chains round the corner from the circus, until a policeman spread his arms and split the links. As they moved between, Eunice felt a drift of moisture on her cheek.

"Oh, what a shame!" she exclaimed. "It's begun to drizzle again."

"Let's get a taxi," said Furnall, "and go somewhere for supper – unless you'll ask me to share your crusts again tonight?"

She shook her head.

"No, I won't – I mustn't be late. No taxi, please. I can't waste time with you in a swell place, either. But if you like – I'll spare ten minutes for a coffee and sandwich at the first handy bar. What about this?"

They looked into a window stacked with delicatessen, then smiled at each other in mutual consent. The little café was busy with custom. Men and women, mostly of foreign appearance, were consuming colourful viands at tables and counters. It was difficult to find an unoccupied seat. A corpulent waiter bustled up to help, and led them down a step to an added wing.

"They give you good coffee here," said Eunice, "and delicious smoked salmon. Hava Casson and I drop in some-times—"

She looked around with reckless assurance. It was pos-sible Hava was sitting there already, or might come in at any moment. She did not care. Why shouldn't she be discovered wasting time with an unknown young man? Primed and satiate with righteous pleasure, she would sleep sound and wake early, fit and alert for their morn-ing's work. And her private life was no longer a concern of Hava's – as Hava's must cease to be of hers. Strange things were happening to them both. Who could have thought that Hava Casson, the shrewd, practical business-loving woman, a realist if ever there was one, would yield her all to a fantasy? And who could have thought that the wreck of her own life should come to seem whole, rounded, reset in mellowed memory? Here in the midst of the London nocturne – outside, the garish shine of the circus, with its roar and flow of traffic and mundane seekers of fun; inside, the riot of appetites, smacking lips, cups, plates, spoons, coins, guttural calls – she was raised, balanced in rarefied air, gossamerlike, a fairy threading translucent beads on a filament of romance. It was a mood as remote from the ghastly trench as the frothing life around, yet somehow bound with it, a strand of rougher weave in the fairy's delicate plait, so that she felt its rasp on her skin as her companion talked.

"Do you know," he was saying, "that this place was shut up during the war? The German owners were kicked out. But now they're back, and flourishing. More popular, it seems, than ever."

"Good," said Eunice. "That's one of the signs of sanity, isn't it? Shows how the world can recover from madness. I'm glad we came in here. I'll come oftener now."

"With me, of course," said Furnall, so softly that Eunice was not sure she had heard; she looked beyond him at the next table, as if she had not.

"Vin knew it would be so," she said suddenly. Her balance had tottered for a moment, the filament had slipped her grasp. She caught it back with Vin's name. He could still, it seemed, sustain her. "He said it helped him most of all, next to his faith in the right – the certainty that people would return to their senses and reverse every war belief."

"You remember all he said?"

"Not all." She smiled deprecatingly. "You know I didn't listen, much – or understand. But I've got his letters." She paused; her smile trembled to the brink of the old sunk well of pain.

"Perhaps, some day, you'll show them to me?"

"I – might. They're – rather private—"

"Of course. I didn't mean—"

"No, no – it isn't that. But—" She could not voice her fear that she must come ill out of the perusal. Instead she went on – "You shall read them – I couldn't show them to anyone else – but you'd appreciate – everything."

The afternoon talk had skirmished the past, with Vin's history as open mark. But no intimate thing had been said. Bob and Miss Grunbaum knew the official facts. Furnall had reason to know more, and told what he knew. But not all that he guessed. How far she wished him to probe her relations with her husband, Eunice was not sure. But she would trust his judgment as much as his discretion. His wordless look was reassurance, – more—

She decided to hurry, after all, when the frugal meal was over. Must get her beauty sleep, she said. And knew already that she would be lying awake for hours, not unhappily.

On the way back she refused again his offer, broached casually in the general chat over tea, to reserve a seat for her on Tuesday night. His chief was to address the first of a series of public meetings, and the Prime Minister was expected to attend, with a Cecil in the chair. She sparkled at his urging before she remembered Dorry.

"I'm terribly sorry. But my little sister's due back from a weekend trip – I have to meet her on Tuesday evening at Victoria."

On Wednesday he was leaving with Sir John for the Midlands, thence to Wales and the North. There would probably be further meetings in London later on. On his return he would ring up and let her know.

"I'd like to come to one of yours," she said.

"Mine?"

"Well, you're coming out on your own, aren't you?"

"You're a witch, Mrs. Fleet. Or has Jess Grunbaum let you into a secret? Don't tell her I've improved on it, though! I don't think even *she* knows how definite it is. There's to be a by-election in the South soon, and I'm to stand."

"I'll come to your first meeting – and most of the others. I wish I could canvass for you—"

"You'll have to shut up shop and do it!"

They parted in heavy rain, but she scarcely noticed it. Running up the Seneschal stairs, she hummed a little tune and only knew it when a couple passed her at the top, staring unduly. They lived on the floor above, and had often crossed her entrances and exits – but never had they heard her sing. Quickly she slammed her door, conscious and embarrassed. Tom's youthful charge, amused and affectionate, came to her ears – "Of course you hum, Euny – no use denying it. Maybe you don't know you do. But that's how I can always tell when you're feeling pleased with yourself!"

She turned on the corridor lights and went to the kitchen, fumbling for the secret nook where the keys should be. It was a fad of hers, ridiculed by Dorry, that each room should be locked when the flat was unoccupied. Mrs. Johns observed the rite when left alone. The keys were there, but to the user's surprise, proved unnecessary. Each door that she tried was not locked. In some alarm she examined the rooms, but found everything orderly and intact. "Queer," she thought – "Mrs. Johns forgot she hadn't locked up when she put the keys away." Such a thing had never happened before. Without removing her cloak she went back to the kitchen and switched on the light. Spick and span, as usual – but on the scrubbed deal table, a neatly-tied brown paper parcel. She opened it. Inside, wrapped in grease-proof sheets, were the remains of the fowl and fruit she had told Mrs. Johns to take. So the food, too, had been forgotten.

"Must have had something badly on her mind!" Eunice put the parcel in the larder vaguely recalling the woman's distress. Back in the bedroom, the matter passed from her thoughts. She took off her clothes by the cheery sizzle of the small gas-fire – "It hums, like me," she said aloud, with a childish laugh – and put on a dressing wrap. "Perhaps it's Dorry not being here that makes me behave like a kid – I've lost the older-sister-cum-mother feeling." She laughed again, half blithely, half shamefacedly. One could not become younger. The load of experience was not removable, even when it changed into something precious – like a diamond tiara, that aged and burdened while it enriched. Certainly a tiara could be taken off. But years? She looked at the tennis-girl standing boldly on the chest. When she brought her here the other evening, it was to call up memories embodied in her form. Now she bent to inspection with more objective intent. But as she touched the photograph, the telephone called, and she ran to her desk. Perhaps – perhaps it was Furnall—?

A feminine voice spoke – a voice she knew but could not place. A metal-thin, timbreless voice. It asked for Dorry.

"Dorry is not home."

"Can you tell me where she is? I expected to see her tonight." As Eunice hesitated, the voice went on – "It's Rita speaking. I've been to your place, Mrs. Fleet—"

"Ah – yes – But Dorry is in Paris."

"Paris?"

The voice had not varied its inflection, but a faint whistle was suggested. Somehow it irritated the listener.

"Yes. She had to go off suddenly on business."

"I see." A pause. "Do you expect her back?"

A curious form. Not *"when"*— But Eunice did not consider it.

"On Tuesday," she said curtly.

"Oh – on Tuesday." The repetition had a hint of mockery. "Thanks. Good night."

The receiver grated, but not before Eunice heard a staccato laugh. A little indignation touched her. What was the creature amused at? She had an unpleasing recollection of a stick of a girl, with shapely ragged head and cool eyes – a minx whom Dorry worshipped, in her indeterminate flit from fashion to bohemian shrines. But Dorry and Dorry's friends and their vagaries could not hold her now. She

went back to sit at her dressing-table and study her
girlhood self – to study and compare, for she gazed with
close attention from photograph to mirror. Younger, fresher,
smoother, the cardboard face – in the glass were unexpected
lines, cavities, shadows. The older eyes had richness, and
meaning spread from them to firm contours of flesh and
bone: a chart for the wise to trace, in search of clues to
treasure. Only the fond, without prescience or discretion,
would dwell too long on the simpler script. Yet such
advantage did not comfort the woman, envious of her
maiden years. She drew what satisfaction she could from
lesser points, or what might seem lesser to legitimate, as
distinct from piratical, scrutiny. Such as the difference, for
instance, in coiffure.

The tennis-girl wore her locks in a high, piled front, with
anterior waves rising steeply. How much more exquisite
the grace – above all, how much more youthful the lines
– of the close-moulded head in the mirror. A sleek flow of
hair set low from a parting, to lie in coiled intimacy with
nape and ear. Eunice moved her chin in accord with the
swinging panels, and from each angle saw a faultless
response. She stood up and assumed the girl's careless
pose, grasping her handglass as a racquet. Indubitably the
effect was improved, nor was it due to a satin triumph over
serge. Style – charm – poise – these had increased in her
a thousand-fold. When she chose to exercise them, her
powers could transcend in similar measure the raw ghosts
of the tennis-court. And why should she not choose?

"You mustn't get slack," she addressed herself. "Even
beauties can't afford to. And though you're not a real
beauty, you can look it – sometimes. It's rather marvellous,
considering—"

She sat down again, and with unsparing gaze, checked
her defects. Mouth too straight, nose too narrow, chin too

long, cheeks uneven. A grave list of irregularities. Lines and hollows came into another category, with the grey hair disclosed at a parting. She snapped it off hastily. Oils, tonics, astringents, creams: she knew such remedies and could apply them. But she knew, too, the finest cosmetic of all, surer than the most cunning distribution of rouge and salve to enhance a pale complexion and sensitive mouth. A vital urge. A radiance from within that lit up eyes and skin, spreading, transforming, creating, to such effect that men stared and marked her out, and Hava would say, "You're very handsome tonight, Euny – you've come alive!" She it was, too, frank enough to say, though not quite as Dorry said it – "Oh, my dear, you're plain again – you're as near being ugly as possible – what's got you now?" Hava Casson understood. She knew that with Eunice it was not as with other women, who lost or regained their looks according to the hour. Even Dorry, whose features were lovely, "went off" in fatigue. But Eunice could be beautiful when physically spent, or plainest while at repose. She herself had no control over the agent: a scene, a presence, a word, thought, glance, might spark or quench the current of her spirit – might fill the lamp with glowing life, or drain a dull, cold shell. She did not speculate on reasons. For years the motion of her soul had been casual and slow; if, now, a giant force propelled her, she was as loth to plumb volition as resist. Safer, perhaps, and sweeter to let it carry her along, content to feel it beneficent.

She gave up toilet thoughts and went to bed, lying awake as she had foreseen. Her brain was restless, and she talked in her mind, as she had never talked in fact, with Vincent and the man who had resurrected him. A resurrection so concrete that it projected into dreams. But when she slept, she no longer ranged the past in terms of the present. Awareness of continuity was lost, and she lived each link of her life within its unit. The child in pigtails screamed as the youth jumped in the harbour: the tennis-girl flouted her swain: the spoilt daughter raged at a triumphant step-mother: the galled wife shunned her husband: the widow's heart turned from poison into stone. Each moved towards the other without knowing it. But long before the fairy came to thread her beads, a loud noise – louder than the ship's syren drowning her childish scream – pierced the sleeper's ears. She sat up bewildered in the morning light, hearing clang and chime – was the *Dorinda* leaving dock? – was it Armistice Day? – Confusion cleared to knowledge of her doorbell ringing, shrill, insistent, prolonged. Stumbling into slippers, snatching up a wrap, she rushed to the hall and unlocked her outer door. A policeman stood on the threshold, asking for Mrs. Fleet.

Part Two

PAST

1

IT WAS A bright day in spring when the pleasure-steamer *Dorinda*, favourite of the Granger-Forsett Line, made her first trip of the season along the Somerset coast. It seemed as if the whole population of Taviton had gathered to share in the event, so thickly they pressed the edges of their fine new dock – Father's dock, Eunice Granger called it to her schoolmates. They knew as well as she did that the dock was owned by the town. But the town itself would not have minded the term: since Father was Tom Granger, who had in every sense that mattered "made" the dock, and was the genial master of it.

The families of the Line were there in strength. Tom with his two sons and daughter, Mr. and Mrs. Forsett with their only child: all except Mrs. Granger, who was an invalid, and in any case too "genteel" a person, Taviton held, to hobnob with the crowd. The term, still lingering here into neo-Georgian days, conveyed the contrary of disrespect and no hint of snobbery. Tom, the son of a coal-trimmer, was thought – not least by himself – to have made an upward match when he married the delicate schoolmistress.

Mr. and Mrs. Forsett, like their partner, were of hearty strain, and so was their daughter Lallie, for all her pretty face and mincing ways. The boss's Eunice was not quite so "free," the dockers observed, and nodded appraisingly when she passed by. Her mother's daughter, she'd grow up tall and dark in looks, and a bit reserved. But only a bit. She was friendly enough, and full of spirits. Her pigtails tossed in the breeze as she ran to see the steamer leave the side. With syrens hooting, sailors shouting, a mass on deck singing and cheering, a duplicate mass with duplicate noises waving farewell, the scene was enough to excite the most ladylike child of fifteen. It excited another, not at all ladylike. She was a slum sprite, a gawky thing of tatters, with soiled skin showing through socks and sleeves, and wild eyes in a craving face. Somehow she had managed to slip through the barriers; and as the gangway was pulled, she leaped after it, rough hair flying with reckless legs in a mad attempt to board. Down she went, hair, legs, and tatters, into the widening channel. Before the horrified crowd could change the text of their clamour, another figure leaped from the vessel itself. It vanished for some moments into the mud where the girl had sunk, then emerged at a lower level of the dock; in the form of a limp clot of rags upon a pair of broad shoulders.

On the instant of that second leap, Eunice Granger was the first to shriek. Why, she never knew. The big, athletic youth, poised for expert dive, was as strange to her as the child he rescued. She was not one who screamed easily, and the sound she made, lost though it was in a concatenation of discords, seemed to her to pierce the heavens. She all but fainted in her father's arms as she dashed back to the office doors.

Her first meeting with Vincent Fleet. How heartily she joined in the laughter at his indignation on losing the boat.

"But I didn't lose it!" he protested. "It lost me!"

Tom Granger promised him free trips for the rest of the season, and invited him to The Laurels on Sunday.

The trippers' friends gone, the half-drowned child removed, the reporters busy at telephone, Vincent, dried and re-clothed in the private office, looked at Eunice. She coloured, thinking of her scream. But unable to say a word, she heard Lallie Forsett chime in.

"Oh, and you must come and have tea with us, too, Mr.

Fleet – mustn't he, mummie? I'm sure we'll all be delighted to see you again – such a brave, brave thing to do—" She went on cooing and chirruping, to her chum's intense disgust, and the hero's embarrassment. Only Eunice noticed that he did not accept the invitation.

It seemed that Vincent would never have come near either The Laurels or The Poplars, had not Mrs. Granger sent for him. She had made inquiries, and found he was an assistant at her old school. They got on so well together that Vincent became a frequent visitor.

Tom Granger joked about the attachment, and the boys grew "sarky" at their mother's interest in a "potty whipper-in." They could not, however, ridicule the intruder on any other ground than that of his profession. He beat them at their favourite sports, land and aquatic: rowing, swimming – and tennis, which they and their sister practised strenuously, on their own and town-club courts. Eunice was one of the few girls of that time who took the game seriously. She was impressed by Vincent's prowess, and willing to profit by his help. In other things, however, she found his earnestness a bore.

Her own careless life was infinitely charming to her then. She played, danced, sailed, flirted, with the gusto of a free, healthy girlhood: the spoilt daughter of the richest man in Taviton, a popular belle of the town. She was not as pretty as Lallie Forsett, but far more brilliant and attractive. Lallie grew jealous and cunning. Eunice saw through her manoeuvres with Vincent, and laughed at them; partly because of her own indifference to Vin's attentions, and partly because of his indifference to Lal's.

She was sixteen when her mother died. The friendship with Vincent deepened through his grief and sympathy. He had not forgotten his own mother, and the aunt who kept house for his father could not fill her place. His devotion to

Mrs. Granger was rare and sincere. In the year that followed, Tom Granger, junior, married, and his younger brother went to sea. The Laurels became a quieter and lonelier place. Yet Eunice hardly lost her spirits. With buoyant ease she recovered from the gloom of her mother's passing. There were hosts of friends to draw her back to gaiety, and her father encouraged the return. Most of his own leisure was spent at The Poplars, where the Forsetts cheered and fussed over him. Whenever Eunice went there, which was seldom, the men were deep in port and dominoes, or else planning trips to racecourses, in which she did not care to join. The Forsetts had a passion for racing – which was probably the reason why James Henry was junior partner, though ten years older, and the original founder of the Line. It was not a reason acknowledged by him or his wife, who shared his tastes, though very much younger and considerably more ambitious than himself.

There was no tennis-court at The Poplars, and Lallie was too lazy to play well. But she had the family craze for horses. One day she showed Eunice a new bracelet, which she said came from her winnings at a race. She was fond of jewellery, but her lavish adornments hitherto were of glass and paste. Eunice saw at once that these stones were good.

"Must have cost a pretty penny," she observed. "How much did you win, Lal?"

Lallie laughed; a shrill, insinuating laugh.

"More than you can guess, you ninny. But your dad had a bit on too, and as I'd given him the tip, we pooled. He's keener than ever now. We're all going to the Derby."

Eunice pouted. Her birthday fell on Derby Day, and her father had promised her a special treat. She did not regard a jaunt to Epsom as coming into such a category, and refused to go.

"All right, duckie," he said in his jovial way. "Please

yourself, and do whatever you like. We'll fix up a grand party when I come back, and I'll give you a lovely surprise."

But the surprise came earlier, and she did not attend the party. On the day she became seventeen, she woke with a headache, and saw rain creep down her windows. The big car had left the garage so quietly in the early hours that she had not heard the departure, but as she peered down she recognised fresh tyre tracks in the sodden path. They were like ruts made in her feelings, for grievance grew high around them, and she retired to bed, unsoftened by the paternal cheque among the presents on her tray. She told Mary to ring up the friends invited to a tennis-tea, and cancel all arrangements. But in the afternoon her mood, though still solitary, improved, and she went out in a rowing boat to a favourite cove, on the other side of the bluff protecting the harbour. Here the streaky red crags rose sheer to green downs, from a small pebbly beach unreachable by land. She moored her boat and lay under the rock, with a book which Vincent had lent her. She stared at the title and repeated it idly – *Trooper Peter Halket of Mashonaland.* Vincent admired Olive Schreiner and possessed all her works. Eunice had finished *The Story of An African Farm* moved by the fate of Lyndall, but the Trooper bored her, and she lost interest in him. In any case she could never read for long. She flung down the book, suddenly realising that her headache had gone. Rapidly undressing, she ran into the water and began to swim. The air was still moist with drizzle, but she loved bathing in soft summer rain. Lunging out in long, vigorous strokes, or floating rigid on her back, a delicious sense of unity pervaded her; body, air, and sea seemed a single element. As she always did when in the water alone, she slipped her shoulder-straps, and let the sea embrace her young, slight breasts. Rowing back in the boat, under clearing skies, she resumed not only her clothes but her highest note of good humour. A light wind played, the sun came palely through a ripple of blue, and flecks of light gilded the lead of the sea. She was hungry and called loudly to Mary for her tea, then rushed to the telephone. She meant to call up Vin, whom she had put off with the rest. He must be just in from school. "I'm down to tea, after all," she'd say – "and fit for play. I haven't asked the others. If you'd like a singles—" She smiled wickedly at the imagined light in his face. She knew how to bring it there, and what it meant. Such a nice face he had, especially then! He was a dear. Even when he kissed her – Eunice suffered kisses. She wanted them, even angled for them: yet at the moment of commission grew averse. Not so much, she admitted, when it was Vin. Somehow Vin was different. The difference, she felt without admitting, was that Vin loved her, and the other young men didn't. They admired her, they competed for her favour, but she did not sense in any of them that intense hunger for herself which devoured Vin. His kisses, as a matter-of-fact, were fewer and more awkward than any she permitted. She recoiled from them without repugnance, but with a vague alarm that made her more perverse.

Petulant at hearing that Vincent was not home, and his whereabouts unknown, she went alone to the garden to eat strawberries and cream. And just as she dropped into her canvas chair, he came dashing through the gate with a new camera; the present he had gone into the town to buy for her.

On the court they had a fierce singles, and then, standing under an old pear tree, he "snapped" her. She dropped her racquet and came across to learn the trick of a new gadget on the box. They were very close together, she was leaning to his chest, and suddenly he kissed her cheek.

"Sorry," he said humbly as she rebuked him. Then – "No, I'm not sorry – Eunice, darling, I want to kiss you again – always. Won't you marry me?"

"Of course not," she said laughing, though rather softly, touched by the vibrations in his voice. "Don't be a fool, Vin."

"I'd be a fool to love you and not want to marry you. Why can't we, Eunice? Don't you – like me well enough?"

"Perhaps. But anyway, we're too young to marry."

"You're too young to be left alone, darling. Your home – it isn't what it used to be when your mother – and besides – oh, Eunice, I want to take you away – to look after you—"

There was a queer solemnity in his words, a deliberation that did not strike her until she thought of them next day. It was the third time he had proposed since he got his mastership at the County School. Of course he wasn't well off, and she was practically an heiress. But he said coolly – there was always an air of commonsense about the wildest things he said – that he didn't care what her father meant to do about that. Her money could be tied up in any way she chose – he would have none of it. He could provide for her out of his salary, and the proceeds of his text-books (he had already written two that were in great demand) and they could live in the house which his mother had left to him. His father, just retired from civil service on a pension, was prepared to leave with Aunt Carry for Mold, where Miss Fleet had certain properties of her own. All these would come to him eventually. And he was working hard to gain further distinctions: everyone said that he had excellent prospects. All this she drew from him in teasing mood, amused by the mixture of assurance, worldly wisdom, and ingenuousness with which he revealed his plans. Yet – "too young" – she cruelly pronounced each time, in spite of his mature airs, his achievements, and his five years' seniority.

These days of courtship stood very clear in her mind. They came back more fully than later events, greater and of tragic import in her life, but too overwhelming in their force and rush of sequence to let memory limn each facet in the whole.

That birthday's end broke the outline first. She had agreed to join the Fleets at some entertainment in the town, which was over at an early hour. They left her at the front gates of The Laurels, and when she walked through, she was not surprised to see the windows blazing with lights. The big car stood in the drive before the door, and the chauffeur was busy removing bags. Her father's voice roared from the hall.

"All right, Hinkin – leave 'er be. You'll take us round to The Poplars after supper."

Eunice waited in the shadow until the door closed, and the chauffeur had gone round the side. She followed him cautiously. So the Forsetts were staying to supper. Her annoyance had gone, but somehow she did not want to see them tonight. She'd slip in unseen, get to bed, and tell Mary to discover her asleep! Her morning headache could be prolonged for the occasion.

But as she crept past the uncurtained kitchen window, she was astounded to see Mr. and Mrs. Forsett within, giving orders to the cook, and disposing the contents of packages they had brought. Such familiarity exceeded, it seemed to her, not only their range of intimacy, but the bounds of neighbourly manners. Where was her father? If in his room upstairs, she might meet him on the landing. The dining-room was lit, but not the lounge: its French doors were probably unlocked. She would get temporary cover from the garden terrace until they were all at table.

Turning the handle lightly, she walked in. Thick carpet deadened her step, but as she advanced, the moonlight showed her two figures in a chair. She stopped, clutching a small table that nearly overturned. In the chair sat her father, with Lallie Forsett on his knee.

She gasped and choked, her teeth bit sharp into her lips. Her only thought was that her father was very drunk. She had seen him in that state before. Yet this—

Lallie saw her, and got up with a skip. She giggled brazenly.

"Fancy, here's Eunice," she said, and Tom Granger's clutching hand relaxed. He did not hiccough, but his voice was thick. Eunice knew at once that it was not with drink.

A babble of sound in her ears.

"Oh, duckie – didn't know you were in – bit early on the scene, but never mind. Now you know – you see, Lallie and I have fixed things up – lovely surprise I promised you, eh? – I won't say a new mother, but a new sister – ha! ha! You're such good pals already, it's sure to be all right. We'll have a slap-up party on Saturday to celebrate – your birthday, duckie, and my engagement—"

She could not remember whether this was said at once, or pieces joined when the older Forsetts were there, and the lights switched on. They all kept saying things together then, half coaxing, half dictatorial; all except Lallie and herself. Lallie watched, smiling and giggling, while she stood staring and speechless – until her father advanced, with an uncomfortable propitiatory gesture that heralded a caress. She warded him off; and then her voice came in deadly release.

"You – you ought to be ashamed of yourself – I'll never speak to you again – never – and as for you" – she poured her furious glance on Lallie – "I always knew you were a slut—"

Hubbub arose from the parents, but she fled upstairs and remained there with locked door till late in the morning. Throughout the night she fought the sobs that nearly burst her heart. They should not hear her cry, they should not know of anything she did. Vile and foul the world – those who could act thus, and the rest, who would simply grin or jeer. Except Vincent. Thinking of him, she dressed hurriedly at last, and went out with her attaché case – just as she used to go to tournament practice at the club, when she lunched and changed there. Mary and cook might report as they chose. She lunched, however, with Vincent. His afternoon happened to be free; his father and aunt had gone for the day on a Channel trip. They were able to talk unhindered. She told her tale, and waited for his rage and sympathy.

"But, Vin – you don't seem much surprised!"

"No, dear."

"You knew?" She started up, aghast, accusing.

"No, no, I only guessed—"

"Why didn't you tell me?"

"How could I, Euny? – how could I speak of such a thing, not being certain – but – dear, I realised what it would mean to you—"

"Yes, I understand – I understand now what you meant yesterday. Vin—" She came close to him in the little room shadowed by a sycamore – "You wanted to marry me – to take me away – because—"

"Because I love you, dear."

She smiled, not taking time to savour the words, and spoke fast and urgently.

"Then let's go at once, Vin – now – today—"

"My darling!"

He took her in his arms, and she submitted, feeling the sweetness of protecting love. If difficulties there were, she neither knew nor cared; Vincent surmounted them. They went away, were married, and spent a happy month abroad

– Paris, Switzerland, the Valais Alps: Vincent happy in her, and she – happy in having blunted Lallie's triumph, in having robbed her father of content, in having escaped the yoke of filial misery. She had vowed never to enter The Laurels again, and never to countenance the Grangers. But Vincent wore her bitter fury down, less by argument than tenderness. The proud, spirited girl had found a master, so like a charming slave that he could soften her will. Actually, she attended the wedding: young Mrs. Fleet, who had filched priority of bridal, and now filched congratulations, from the "slut" walking the aisle with old Tom. Young Mrs. Fleet, with her brilliant young husband, the popular "sport" of Taviton, the "educationist of promise" acclaimed by the county press.

Eunice read the tributes with complacence. She accepted Vincent's mental superiority, like his athletic dominance, as an adornment of herself; and she accepted his devotion, the sacrifices he made to lavish gifts on her, his way of placing her pleasure foremost, as her natural right, the simplest matter-of-course. She saw in him neither an extreme unselfishness nor an unusual purity of love.

2

But the young wife had little normal time in which to make discoveries about her husband. They were married scarcely a couple of months before Europe was at war.

Eunice had, perhaps, less excuse than most women in not knowing what it was all about. From the first moment – or at least from the second, for primarily her husband, like other men, was merely shocked and incredulous – Vincent applied himself to study causes.

"There isn't any justification for war," he said. "Especially in times like these. Various arguments, of course, are always advanced in justification. Usually they are exactly the same on both sides. But it's obvious there must be certain differences in fact. So let's get at the facts—"

Nothing, however, was more difficult. Facts are not available for consideration during war. And even if they are, people strongly object to such consideration. Tom Granger, junior, did, for one. He said to Eunice, shaking with emotion (Eunice did not know whether it was patriotism, pugnacity, or simple anger), "Your husband's a damned fine talker. But this is the time for action. I'm off—"

And off he marched, to the nearest recruiting station.

Vincent, however, went on talking. It made Eunice uneasy, and finally she listened. An expression of horror worked her features.

"But, Vin—" she said. "The Belgians—?"

"Not such innocent victims as they make out," he said. "Of course I don't mean the mass – *they* never know in any country what their bosses are doing. But the Belgian diplomatists are responsible with the rest—"

She cut him short. An explanation of secret treaties and counterplots in the chancelleries of Europe could not compete in her mind with the picture of fierce Uhlans destroying women and children in their march to the English coast.

"We're all in it now, whether or no," she said.

"*I'm* not in it," he said. "I'm not in the mad stampede. I'm outside – with Burns – and Macdonald. I stand by them. Or rather, I don't stand by anyone particularly. I stand by my reason – by my conscience."

It was the first time she heard the fatal word in connection with the war, and she did not even notice it. She said indignantly:

"Are you a Socialist?"

"Why, darling, you know I am," he said, smiling. "Haven't I tried to convert you? Only you always were a bit of one, anyhow. Unconsciously, perhaps. I've only tried to make you conscious."

He put his arm round her shoulders, but she pushed it away, looking at him pensively, almost sullenly.

Yes, she knew. She had gone with him to lectures, tried to read his books and refute his arguments. The end was always kisses – less of agreement than of loving kindness. Their differences served merely to increase her good humour, because he found in her opposition proof of his beliefs, and somehow the proof flattered her. She claimed, for instance, that her disgust with the "lower classes" was a sign of her lack of sympathy with them. Hating "low common things," ugly habits, coarse talk, sordidness, she shrank from the vulgar boys, the sluttish girls, and rough adults, with whom Lallie hobnobbed in school and street. Lallie called her a snob. It was because she smarted from the epithet, applied in Vincent's presence, that she revealed how it was earned. There was a girl at school – one of a very large and very poor docker's family – an uncouth creature who was brainy and had won a scholarship. Without money to buy books, she had stolen some from Lallie's bag. Lallie didn't sneak to authority – she went on being friendly with the girl, exacting payment (by long instalments of infinitesimal sums) instead of return; but in a dozen ways she humiliated her before others, and extorted services from her.

Eunice, who loathed the culprit, enabled her at last to discharge her debt to Lallie, and to procure her whole outfit for the term.

"A loan, I said," explained Eunice, "until she'd qualified for teaching and got a post. I knew she couldn't pay for years. But I thought it only right to save her self-respect – if she had any after Lallie's treatment. Lallie said I was an idiot. She said I was worse – a hoity-toity. Snob, she calls it now. Because I wouldn't speak to the girl ever, if I could help it. It wasn't her being a thief. But she was so abominably common – and dirty. Lallie didn't mind that a bit. I did. The creature *smelt* – I don't suppose she ever bathed – and I couldn't breathe near her. You see – I can't bear those sort of people."

Beginning with the idea of justifying herself, she also meant to prove to Vincent how impossible it was for her to share his views. And he only laughed delightedly.

"Why, of course, you're absolutely right to hate filth and poverty – but don't you see – it isn't human beings you can't bear – it's the dirt they're cased in. That's Socialistic – that's my sound Eunice – sound in heart and brain—"

She was pleased by his commendations, even while bewildered by a sense of contradictoriness. Inarticulate, she stifled her demur – "Aren't there dirty humans – I mean humans who *like* dirt?"

But now resistance hardened, too deep for blandishment.

"I've never been the least bit of a Socialist. And I didn't think you were, either – not seriously. And anyway, it's all different from what I thought. One can't be a Socialist now."

"Now more than ever," he said. A little stubborn line came over his right eye. She had seen it before – in her favour. "The time to stick to principles is when they're being flouted. I've always believed in the co-operation of peoples, not in their mutual destruction. I see no reason not to believe in it now. And if I believe it, I can't join in with those who don't, or pretend they don't."

After that, he talked *at* her, rather than to her – since she showed reluctance to argue. But her ears were open and receptive, more to the hints and silences of others than to

Vincent's actual words. Her family's disapproval spread to friends, and finally to strangers. The hints became taunts and the silences vocal with threats. An able-bodied young teacher had no right to stay at home when weaklings were rushing abroad in defence of their country. And when it came to poisoning pupils' minds with pro-German treasons – well, something ought to be done about it! She tried not to transmit the sense of alarm and hostility until the day when Lallie met her in the street, and presented her with an envelope addressed to Vincent.

"We aren't sweethearts now, of course," she said with her most impudent, provocative air. (As if they had ever been!) "But I've written him a love-letter, and I don't mind your seeing it—"

She flaunted off before Eunice had sufficient wit to refuse the missive. When Vincent broke the seal, he found, wrapped in a blank sheet, a white hen's feather.

"The beastly cat" – cried Eunice, her face livid, her limbs jerking with rage. She tried to snatch the quill and fling it in the fire, but Vincent held it in cool examination, a little smile, grim, hard, upon his lips.

"I'm sorry you should mind so much, darling."

"Mind? – Don't *you* mind?"

He shook his head.

"Then you ought to – it's horrible – a frightful disgrace – being branded as a coward—" She stopped breathlessly to see how the term affected him. He shrugged his shoulders.

"Do you really think this a brand?" he asked, plucking the feather to shreds. "Silly action of a silly girl—"

She was not appeased by hearing Lallie dubbed silly – even by Vincent, so chary of labelling her enemy.

"It isn't only Lallie," she said sharply.

"I know. But – does my wife think me a coward?"

"Oh, what does it matter what *I* think."

"It matters, to me – far more than what others think. Tell me, Eunice."

"I've never known you afraid," she said, still angry. "But that isn't everything."

"Of course not – if you mean just physical courage. I'm not claiming credit for it. And I'm not sure that physical cowardice is a "frightful disgrace" – it's a disability, rather. But *moral* cowardice – that's another thing. I don't intend to sink to that, if I can help it – and if you'll help, too. Won't you, dearest?"

"I don't know what you're talking about."

"Yes, you do." His look pleaded with her, but she rejected it, staring away and pressing her lips mutely together. He took a stride round their pleasant little sitting-room with its new rugs and chintzes, and its wide window patterned by the sycamore. Afterwards she thought of him as like the tree – too big for the room. His limbs spread within, strong and energetic, almost pressing on walls and panes as did the branches without.

"You know I don't believe in war – in armies slaughtering each other as a way to peace and prosperity, not to mention justice. The whole thing's savagery. And stupidity. And waste. You've heard me say so a hundred times since this war started. I didn't expect you'd want me to behave as if I thought differently."

"Nobody thinks differently – except the Germans. But we've got to stop them doing as they like and coming here—"

"Most of them are not doing what they like – wretched conscripts! – only what they are forced or deceived into doing. We aren't likely to stop them by the same tactics. And even if we succeed, by turning ourselves into brutes and liars—"

She sprang round with such a flaming air that he stood still, abruptly.

"How can you abuse our men, who've left everything to go and fight in defence of our country? Tom isn't a brute and liar. He's as brave as you, if not as clever – and there are heaps even braver and cleverer, who've gone out willingly – heaps are going now, every day, before they're *shamed* into going—"

She broke off with an hysterical gurgle.

"My dearest girl," he said gently, but not moving to her. "I did not mean to abuse the soldiers – certainly not those who think it right to fight. But since it is not right for me—"

"Why? Why? Oh, I don't want to hear all that talk again – but why should you be different from other people? Dad says" – she squirmed visibly at remembrance of her father's jibe – "you're setting yourself up as a sort of Jesus Christ—"

He smiled a little, but replied in grave tones.

"Your father says Socialists are irreligious. He seems to want it both ways. If I admit I'm modelling myself on his Master, which of us is the greatest blasphemer? On the whole, his idea of me is more complimentary than Lallie's."

She did not speak. There was a pause before he added, suddenly:

"Eunice, do you want me to enlist?"

"I – I—" she stammered, and burst into tears. For the first time, he did not attempt to soothe her. She was so amazed, having expected caresses and capitulation, that she checked her sobs to peep at him. He was looking anxiously at her, but with such a remote and saddened gaze that she could not read it. Grievance welled up, hot and strong. Couldn't he see how dreadful he was making her position? Everybody sneering, insinuating, insulting – even her own offers of service ignored or evaded. Not that she yearned to make bandages in the Mayor's Parlour with Lallie, or come across the latter's ubiquitous friends in other centres of war-work. But to be treated as if she had a taint, because her husband hadn't rushed to the front, and was, moreover, suspected of pacifism and pro-Hunnishness – it was intolerable. Naturally she didn't want him to leave her and be killed. But everyone had to make sacrifices in these days. Perhaps by the time he had finished training, the war would be over – in spite of increasing complications "out there" and at home. And even supposing he had a little wound – Tom had been wounded twice already and gone back to the trenches none the worse – it would only make her prouder of him and more solicitous. He who had been the town's hero on many civil occasions, would shine with a brighter glory than any at Taviton; and she, basking in it, would reward him with her gracious delight.

No sense of inadequacy marred the presentation of her point of view. And so little did he combat it, that she was lulled into hoping he might yield before the Military Service Acts were passed.

His protests against conscription might be discounted in common with the genteel constitutional opposition raised by Members of Parliament, and the fiery but harmless speeches of Trade Union leaders. All these made a fairly loud noise *before* the passage into law. A louder noise proceeded from the patriots. What was tradition, what was the ideal of free service, what the dread of civil slavery, in face of the national peril, and the countless shirkers walking the streets? The measure established, all must conform: and though compulsory performance of duty was a detraction – still, that might easily be forgotten in the performance itself, with its potential scars of honour and glory of medals – perhaps, who knew? – the V.C.?

Contrary to the expectation of Eunice Fleet, thousands of young men refused to conform. And among them was her husband.

The legality of resistance could not, it seemed, be denied – in the first instance, at least. One had the right to claim exemption before a Tribunal on the ground of conscientious objection. But what was legality to her, who felt degradation in the claim? It was no less than a charter to Lallie and her friends to mock and flout – to her family to nag and rage – to strangers, to pile odium on abuse.

She moped indoors as the day of trial neared. Sometimes Vincent coaxed her into evening walks in the war-gloomed streets, barren of comfort to body or soul – yet less racking than the intimacy of their firelit hearth. Once she accompanied him to a dingy room in the Labour Institute. It was the only place in the town where she was welcomed with unequivocal regard. And she shrank from it more than from any other.

The members of an oddly assorted group, greeting her with anxious smiles, were almost all strangers – probably as much to each other as to her. It was not hard to see that these artisans, clerks, and professionals, came from various spheres, unlikely to have known contact hitherto. Intellect and occupation had divided them less, perhaps, than habit and temper. Yet here they were together, close as branches of a single tree, grown overnight like Jonah's gourd.

"Cranks," she thought, watching them silently under her sullen lids. These boys with excited eyes, men with mobile jowls, their womenfolk – mothers, sisters, friends (few wives, she noted, with odd satisfaction), all strung in a tension not so different from hers – they were thin, thick, robust, weak, pale, ruddy, a mixture of humans in no way distinguishable at sight from patriots. Only their talk—

"Comrades," the chairman was saying – "We have faced the situation frankly from the beginning, and must continue to do so. . . . We knew we were taking a course that would make us not only unpopular, but hated – what is worse, misjudged. We are accused of evading our duty, while in our view we are performing it – both to our country and to mankind. . . . Though coming to it in different ways, we reached the same conclusion – that we could not bear arms against our fellowmen. . . . Some of us think this particular war unjust and unnecessary. Most of us believe all war to be wrong. We hold that human life is sacred, and deny the right of Governments to compel us to inflict death. . . . It is not a paradox to say that the violation of our convictions has become the violation of the law. In this fellowship we pledged ourselves to resist conscription, no matter what the penalties might be. The penalties are now being imposed, not for breaking the law, but for acting in accordance with it. The conscientious objection clause in the Military Service Act gave us the right of exemption. But the Tribunals before which our claims are being presented, refuse us this right. . . . In this district, as in most parts of the country, there has not yet been a single case of total exemption. It does not seem likely from their attitude that there ever will be such a case. . . . The fact does not intimidate us. It is for the Government, and not for us, to fear the consequences of persecuting conscience, whether by legal or illegal means—"

"Cranks," Eunice told herself again, in wary unease: and her nerves remoulded them to fit her dislike.

The chairman's face was sanctimonious; his high voice vexed her drums. The boys wore their eager air falsely, since it aped that of youths who ran to the trenches. (As if these did not know they faced no real dangers – no risks – and – no glories?) She frowned at the secretary, a brisk, short-haired girl, for her resemblance to the secretary in the mayoral Parlour. The other women offended in the opposite style. Some were too dowdy to matter in their shabby coats and appalling hats: the younger had clothes in character

– misfits, wrong jumpers and skirts, absurd necklaces; a mixture of the jaunty, the frumpish, and the crazed. She warmed to none of them, not even to her shy little neighbour, who might have been any age from thirteen to thirty, being lost in a man's ulster, with only a mop of brown hair visible over a small face set with birdlike eyes. A shrivelled nut on the seat would have claimed as much attention. All the more startling, then, when the thing stood on its feet, and in a full, deep voice responded to the chairman's call – "Now, comrades, we'll take our watchers' reports. Perhaps Miss Fennick will begin."

Miss Fennick began. She undid her ulster, and revealed her child-like frame. Demure, fragile, shrinking, she told in her unexpected voice how she had attended three Tribunal sittings in three different courts of the county during the week. At one the public was ejected. She was finally allowed to remain on a plea of relationship.

"I said I was the C.O.'s sister," she confessed. "Was it wrong? I don't usually tell lies, and didn't expect to in this cause. But I'm not sure it was a lie. That C.O. was a stranger, he wasn't even an N.C.F.er – but I felt he was as much my brother as Harvey is—" She turned to her left, away from Eunice, and put her tiny hands on a youth sitting there. He smiled at her with the same bird-like eyes under a similar mop of hair – "As every boy here is – all of you – all, all, my brothers—"

Her voice rose on a sharper note, and she flung her arms wide in a passionate gesture. There was a hum of sympathy. Eunice shrank further into herself, averting her gaze. She hated that note in the girl's voice. She hated the gesture. She repudiated the idea of Vincent's brotherhood to the silly little snipe. . . . With reluctant ears she listened to the discussion that followed.

There were anxious inquiries as to the procedure of

Tribunals – but none, to her surprise, on ways of escape and evasion. She had been convinced this was the main concern of the group, and in fact had a secret, barely conscious, hope of gaining useful information thereby. It was almost as disconcerting to find that the experience of claimants, probed – before dismissed – by questions held gross and irrelevant, drew as much laughter as indignation. The amusement seemed to her affected, so strained was its mistimed ring. A certain "poser" was specially hailed, as the stock resource of investigators of conscience. "What" – it ran – "would you do if a German attacked your mother?" For all the fun it evoked, serious replies were retailed: but useless, deplored one, to say that individual assault was different from mass-machine war, that brains and moral suasion might foil attack, and even that force need not involve butchery. The investigator, like the German, was not there to reason with you; but to expose your effort to "save your skin" – "Dirty skin," added one of the judges, whose other occupation was selling baths. "How often do you wash it?" – commercial zeal was flanked by the military, whose representative hurled his comment – "You haven't the pluck of a mouse" – and the final charge of presiding authority – "what would happen if everyone did the same as you?" – "There would be no war," you assured him with fatal logic, and were thereupon consigned to the Army – the proper place for the practice of such beliefs.

But how it worked there was not so glibly reported. A sergeant was known to have boasted – "We can tame lions in the Army." Obviously he anticipated no difficulty with lambs – or mice. The methods of taming were screened by barrack bars, but peeping Toms spread rumours of flagellations, frogmarchings, live burials, and other tortures characteristic of medieval inquisitors – and modern Huns.

The group, no longer laughing, talked strangely about these things, as if sharing in martyrdoms, of which not Heaven but Parliament must be compelled to take note. Eunice could not grasp it clearly. The talk had an utterly unreal sound. She heard as if with the surface of her sense. It was like seeing the wrong side of an embroidered cloth, all the threads mixed and ragged in a confusion of design. Watching some of the faces, she saw the eyes of youth blinking more and more excitedly, the men's chins taking a grimmer set, the women's cheekbones showing taut beneath their skins: but her own emotions of discomfort were getting too much for her. The air of the room was close, stale tobacco reeked from walls and floor; the cold current from the open window gave her a crick in the neck, and did not stem a rising nausea. Suddenly she felt that she must get away. She looked appealingly across the room to Vincent, who was filling up forms for the secretary. He nodded in recognition of her signal. But as he began to move towards her, he was checked by the hand of the Chairman. A silence in which Eunice was bound but not absorbed ensued. The high voice dangled, a chafing rope.

"You have heard, comrades, how some of our friends, and several unknown to us, have met the full blast of prejudice which sways the Tribunals in dealing with C.O.'s. Those who are to meet it in the coming week know what to expect. We know, too, that they will bear their witness as steadfastly as the soldier in the trench bears his – as the rest of us mean to do when our turn comes. We were not deceived by the trick of separating married from single. Now, as we expected, the liability comes to all. We need not assure each other of support, in a trial which depends on the individual conviction of right. Not all of us have the power of speech or pen to help us in expression – even when expression is allowed. With little hope of establishing a case, we nevertheless look forward to the chance of making it . . . chiefly, we want those who are going first to know, that those who are left will do all that is possible to secure justice, and to arrange for the care of descendants. We are fortunate in Miss Fennick – in many of our women associates, who have undertaken the task . . ."

The rope tightened unbearably. She felt that if the voice continued another minute she must lose hold of her nerve, betray her vertigo and her disgust at once. Only pride in aloofness, and horror of contact, prevented a rush to the door. Somehow, she kept rein, eased only by complete lack of concentration on the speaker. Surely – surely he was ending—

"Comrade Fleet—" She could not shut these words out as mere fretting sound – "Comrade Fleet is among those who are due to go up. . . . He has not been amongst us long, but we know him too well to be surprised at the fact that he is not claiming to be exempted for doing work of national importance in his profession, as, of course, he is entitled to do. . . . He means to stand out solely as a conscientious objector—"

The tightness broke. A huge, soft darkness whirled. The sourness in her mouth staunched by a handkerchief, she stood as if by a giant stroke of will.

"I – must – air—" she said.

Tiny clinging hands merged into Vincent's grip, holding her at the blessed open door.

"I'm all right," she said, smiling. Her lips felt like snow, but the effort had really revived her. The thought sang in her mind that now Vincent wouldn't respond – he wouldn't stand up before them all to declare that the chairman was right – that he—

Instead, he was muttering a brief apology for withdrawal.

"Sorry – my wife isn't well – I must take her home—"

A murmur of sympathy. Of course they thought she was upset by their talk. So she was – but not in the way they imagined—

Vincent imagined it, too. He was solicitous and tender, whispering pet names as he half-carried her down the spiral stairs, through the alley court into the street, wide, dark, comfortingly cold. Khaki figures slouched by, whistling, and girls squeaked from shop doorways.

"I'll get a cab, darling," he said, peering about. "There ought to be one in the rank over there – come, my precious—"

He would not listen to her demur, and presently she was glad to snuggle into the rickety cab. In spite of her wish to walk in the air, her legs felt shaky, and her head ached. She breathed gratefully at the open window, leaning on Vincent's shoulder, his arm around her.

"Sweetheart," he said, "you mustn't take the reports you heard too seriously. There have been a few bad cases, of course – injustice and bullying, but that's bound to be stopped. I expect to get a decent hearing, and perhaps—" he hesitated, stroking her hair.

"It was the stuffy room—" she murmured. But it did not seem worth while confuting his assumption. Besides, – she pondered his last words, and began to think a little more coherently.

"Do you mean you may get off?" she asked. "I thought they said there were *no* exemptions granted now."

"Oh yes, some," he said. "Only from combatant service, though. Still, our Tribunal knows it *can* give total exemption – which is more than most Tribunals will admit, even yet. I may make them give it to me."

"How can you make them?"

"By convincing them I'm genuine."

"Well, of course, you are—" she said, with a sigh.

He laughed and kissed her forehead.

"Thanks, darling. It's almost a pity you aren't allowed to testify to my convictions – especially as you've tried your best to alter them!" His tone changed to wistful appeal. "You're coming to the court, aren't you?"

"Oh, yes," she said. A new confidence illumined her. It was obvious that he was being optimistic for her sake, and that those horrid "comrades" had ground for their reports. But he would at least be given non-combatant service, since he was "genuine." Then things must straighten out. He wouldn't have to kill Germans, like a real soldier, but still – in all else it was much the same – uniform, training, an officer abroad – the Red Cross was in the Army after all—

She knew better than to discuss it with him. But the idea stayed in her mind. She could have become cheerful again – if only her body hadn't begun to behave peculiarly. It was letting her down, not only in stuffy rooms, with uncongenial people, but at home, alone, in the garden, in the street. Quarrelling with her father, being haughty with Lallie and her clique, manoeuvring with Vincent – none of these things could acidulate her system for long, while her physical poise sprang back like truest steel. But it was failing to go back. A languor and lowness of spirit beset her. She wobbled with a sense of central strain, of sick inertia. It made her what she had never been before: gloomy, suspicious, and extremely irritable.

*   *   *

When the day arrived she set out bravely enough. At her freshest in the mornings, she put on a bright blue suit with a blue felt hat. It was a note of defiance as much as of taste. Lallie hated her in blue, which she claimed as her own natural colour. "It's for blondes," she would point out acridly. "You oughtn't to wear it ever – why, don't you know it makes you look *darker*?"

"That's exactly why I wear it," Eunice would retort: provokingly, inexplicably, to Lallie, who never understood that Eunice chose a special lilac blue – a dye with a pink instead of a steely tinge. Actually it warmed the olive of her skin, and made more striking the dusk of eye and hair.

But Lallie was not there to criticise that day. And it was just as well. For the clear frosty dawn slid to a dull meridian, with slush outside and stife indoors. Squeezed between Miss Fennick and a shabby old dame, on a narrow bench in a dark gallery, Eunice lost the spirit of her suit. The foul air above, the strange proceedings below, dazed and inhibited her.

She had not been in a court of justice before. It made no difference to her – as it did, apparently, to Miss Fennick – that this Tribunal was not meant to be ordered like a trial at law. She was disconcerted only at seeing, not Lallie, but Lallie's father. Among the half-dozen men on the bench, more or less familiar as tradesmen, lawyers, councillors of the town, sat Harry Forsett. She had known he was a magistrate, but never took the fact – or indeed, anything about him – seriously. He was a man of "better" education than her father, but to her, as to Tom Granger, Forsett was an insignificant and futile person. Often he was fussy enough, like a fly buzzing with the sound of a wasp: he could make a fuss without making an impression. She discounted him even as a factor in the family intrigue (as she regarded Lallie's marriage) to restore the Forsett dominance in the Forsett-Granger Line. It was Mrs. Forsett, much younger than her husband, who was ambitious and forceful. She had probably stirred him to his magistracy. But it was he, not she, who sat on the Bench: and Eunice asked herself uncertainly – would Forsett's presence help or hinder Vin?

It did not seem to count for much in other cases. As applicant after applicant appeared, Forsett's scant grey head dipped left and right, to listen to the consultations of colleagues. But he seldom contributed to them or asked a question.

Eunice knew little, at first, of what was going on. The drone of sound from the court well was mere sibilance, with an occasional bark from Bench and door. Phrases did not come clearly to the gallery unless one strained for them. But for Miss Fennick's whispers, she would not have understood what happened when a figure bobbed up, spun for some moments in a whirlpool of mumblings, hisses, staccato shouts, and was escorted away. Miss Fennick had to be discreet in her whispers, which were sternly "Sh-sh'd" by police.

"They ought not to be here," the odd little person kept repeating, giving the uniforms at either end glare for glare, if not sh' – for sh'. "They haven't any right to behave as if it was ordinary police court business – it's scandalous – they shouldn't be here at all—"

Eunice said nothing. She knew of no reason why the police should not be present, behaving as usual. The atmosphere, and the suspense of waiting for Vincent, had begun to set up ferment in her veins, or she might have been amused – contemptuously amused – at the mixture of rebellion and timidity beside her. The little creature was breathing in gasps, her eyes receded and obtruded in a tense cameo of a face. Why was she so worked up? – it was not her brother's turn today. But then – "they" were "all her brothers" – absurdity!

Frowning, Eunice leaned forward, concentrated, and began to follow the procedure below. It was not, however, her concentration, as much as an unusual stillness, that made it possible at last to hear clearly.

"That's a C.O.," came her companion's nervous, reckless whisper. "I don't know him. It's another of those isolated ones. Religious, I think—" She, too, bent her neck to listen intently.

The applicant was a youth with the round face of a schoolboy. He was pale, his hands fumbled, he looked confused. Trying to reply clearly to a question, he hesitated, was snapped at by another member, silenced. His statement was simple, his speech uncultured.

"I am a servant of Christ. I have always tried to follow His teaching – Love your enemies. I don't believe in fighting and shedding blood."

The chairman addressed him severely.

"But don't you know what a great preacher said in church the other day? – that to kill Germans is a divine service in the fullest sense of the term?"

"No, sir. I – I couldn't do it."

A member on the chairman's right pointed a finger at him.

"Come now, you know that Christ used whips to drive bad men from the Temple?"

The youth twisted his hands.

"But not to kill, sir."

"Oh indeed, He'd have killed them right enough if He'd had a gun—"

The boy shook his head, but made no reply. A member on the left said quickly:

"What would you do if a German attacked your mother?"

"I – I'd pray, sir, and trust her to God."

From a corner seat a military figure jumped up.

"Do you really mean to say you wouldn't kill anybody?"

"Yes, sir. That's what I mean."

"Good God! What an awful state of mind! You ought to be in a lunatic asylum!—" He waved his hands, snorted loudly, and sat down.

The chairman consulted with his colleagues on either side. Forsett's head nodded with the others. A minute later the presiding voice announced:

"We can't allow your claim. You're fit and able to serve your country. Next case."

The youth remained still, staring as if bewildered. A policeman stepped forward and placed a hand on his arm. Eunice glanced aside, hearing a soft thud next her. The shabby old woman was on her knees, praying.

"Lord Jesus, save my boy. You know, Lord, what a good-living boy he is. Regular in Sunday School. Always quiet and hardworking – only thinking of helping me since you took his father. Dear Lord, save him—"

"Sh' – sh' – silence there—"

Miss Fennick wrung her tiny hands, and suddenly stood up. She saw the lad below led off by a policeman. She saw another uniform stoop to the old woman on her knees.

"I protest!" she called out loudly. "I protest against the presence of police—"

Before she could bring out another word she was seized.

"Now, then, miss – stop that! Come along out—"

"Very well," she gasped, her little figure wriggling. "You need not hold me, if you please. I'll walk out at once, though you've no right to make me."

She was hustled, nevertheless, through a gaping gallery. The old lady stumbled after her.

Eunice sat still, her face cold, the nostrils lifting fastidiously. Two more cases were despatched below. The brother of four soldiers appealed in vain to be allowed to carry on his crippled father's business. The cripple, present in a bath chair, was told he could employ a girl. How should a conscience claim get preference over that? But the next appellant was a butcher, well known to the Forsetts and the Grangers as a patron of their Line. He was the largest importer of chilled meat at the docks: largest in the physical as well as the commercial sense. Hale and jovial, he sat exchanging pleasantries with the Tribunal, who granted him a second exemption of six months.

"Work of National Importance."

Eunice, angry for the first time, repeated the words to herself in disgust. A little bile came into her throat. She had eaten some of that man's beef a week ago, and it had made her very sick. "The worst bilious attack I've ever had," she declared, explaining her refusal to order more. It was hardly a reason for her anger now, as she knew too well. A revulsion that was neither rage nor reminiscence travelled through her frame. She drew back and closed her eyes, then opened them again. Who was this? A dark, spruce young man with a high forehead, and an intonation that reminded her of someone she liked. A friend – a school-fellow. A fine, handsome, good-natured girl, whose family had removed to London. They had taken strongly to each other – she and the monitor with the queer name – Hava. Vincent, who knew everything, said it was the Hebrew form of Eve. There had been a certain delicacy in discussing it with the girl, after whom small boys called in a mocking chant – Hava – Hava – nobody'll have 'er. Somebody had, though. Rumour came that Hava was married, long before she herself ran away with Vincent. She sighed, pressing her handkerchief to her mouth. Unheeding the drone below, she thought – what sort of business have I made of my marriage? Stupid to think of that now. The young man's voice was remarkably clear. Surprised, she heard him say:

"Yes, but it is my knowledge of the evils of conscription

that make me oppose it. My grandfather left Russia because *he* opposed it. It's a tradition in my family. I shall never be a conscript. I shall never be a soldier."

"But you are a foreigner?"

"No, I was born in this country, and my father, who was brought here as a child, became a naturalised British subject before my birth."

"Still, you don't feel quite like an Englishman?"

"I have always fulfilled every duty as an English citizen."

"Then why don't you now?"

"I am asking for exemption from military service in accordance with English law."

"Law!" said the Chairman peevishly. "I suppose it is. But I don't agree with it at all. It's a totally unnecessary clause!"

A solicitor on his left said hurriedly:

"But you're living in a country that has an army and navy, and I take it you accept their protection?"

"I didn't ask for it."

"Then you should leave the country."

"I can't."

"Why not?"

"The law prevents me."

The lawyer muttered inaudibly, while the chairman, who had found another opening, called out,

"Look here – aren't you – er – of the Jewish persuasion?"

"Yes."

"Well, then – the Old Testament is full of fighting."

"It is also full of the advocacy of peace. The ideal of universal peace was first proclaimed by the Hebrew prophets. 'Nation shall not lift up sword against nation, neither shall they learn war any more.' How can this come about if warfare is continued? One nation, or at least some members of it, must take the first step by refusing to arm. I believe

I am doing my duty, both as a Jew and as an Englishman, by refusing to engage in the slaughter of my fellow-men. I believe in the brotherhood of Israel and of all the peoples of the earth. I wish to work for peace and the realisation of Isaiah's vision."

"What would you do—"

"Mr. Chairman—"

The German-attack-your-mother questioner and the military representative both sprang out at the same time. The military man's voice was loudest, and won.

"Mr. Chairman, we've had enough of this rubbish. Are we to sit here all day listening to cowardly shirkers? Let me tell you, young Abraham or Isaac or Jacob or whatever your name is—"

"My name, as you are aware, is David Stone—"

"I don't care what it is. I say you'll have to join up and serve as a soldier, or else – you'll be" – he swallowed – "you'll be shot."

"That doesn't frighten me. I shan't be the first of my people, from the time of my great ancestors, whose names you have taken in vain, to meet death rather than give up principles."

There was a hum in part of the lower court and a corner of the gallery. While the ushers were suppressing it, the chairman said abruptly,

"Claim dismissed."

The young man bowed with an elaborate flourish – it was the only touch of excess in his manner – and walked smartly away.

Eunice shrugged her shoulders and crossed her feet. She heard a whispered exchange behind her.

"Who's 'e? 'As 'e got German blood in 'im?"

"Dunnow. 'E's a Jew."

"Jew? Dirty dog."

"Dunnow. I heard there's a lot o' Jews in the Army. One's gone from our street. And Fred wrote there was two in 'is camp."

"So they oughter. Fight the ones in the German army."

"Ay, the Huns got plenty too, I heard."

"Who's this big fellow? Not another conchy? 'E looks British."

"Ay, but yer can't never tell. Jus' listen. Somethin' 'bout internationalist on his sheet. One of them socialist conchies. 'Old on! Blowed if 'e isn't that champion, Fleet!"

"Sh' – silence there!"

Eunice, rigid now, stared below. It was Vincent. He looked up at the gallery, smiling, while his statement was being read. Though he could not distinguish her, even in the blue suit, she knew he smiled for her. She pouted, became more conscious of the foul air, the nausea at her throat. Her left hand pressed the seat, bracing her and keeping free a space.

There was an unusual stir on the Bench, a louder droning in the well. Ushers might bark in vain. Almost everyone had heard of Vincent Fleet. Several members of the Tribunal knew him. She noted Forsett's uneasy grin, his fingering of his collar, his sudden fit of coughing. Was he preparing to intervene? The chairman, who had no personal acquaintance with the applicant, showed familiarity with his name.

"We gather you have strong political views, Mr. Fleet," he said, in a more deliberate tone than he had used. He looked at a piece of paper on which he had jotted some notes. "But surely a political objection to the war does not come into the sphere of conscience?" He nodded his head sideways at his colleagues, as if to ask approval of a crushing phrase.

"It does, with me," said Vincent, in his pleasant way.

"My political and moral views are alike. I think the war is the result of a wrong political conception, which means to me a wrong outlook, morally and spiritually. I am concerned with the welfare of the masses in every country. I regard war in general as a stupid and inefficient method of settling international disputes – I regard it also as organised murder. And I cannot in any circumstances be a party to murder, or pledge myself to commit it."

Harry Forsett poked his scraggy head forward.

"Surely," he said, "you would defend your country if it were invaded?"

"Not by military means. I believe there would be no invasion if there were no preparations for military defence."

"What nonsense!" exclaimed another member. "D'you mean to say that if we had no army and no navy, the enemy wouldn't march in?"

"Yes. An unarmed population gives no provocation and excites no fear. If there were no provocation and no fear, there would be no enemy, and no invasion."

"That might be so, if everyone thought as you did – the Germans as well—"

"Exactly," said Vincent, smiling.

"You're talking of the millennium!" said the largest member of the Tribunal. He was an elderly man with a prominent paunch, on which his beringed hands rested. "That's all tommyrot. We have to get on with the war now we're in it, and our brave fellows fighting to keep the Huns out. Aren't you ashamed to be letting them down? Are you willing to let others lay their lives down for you?"

"No, I am not willing. Are you?"

"Mr. Chairman, I protest."

"Young man," said the chairman, "you're here to answer questions, not to ask them."

"I wish to know," said the stout man venomously, "whether you think it isn't good for a shirker to be put across someone's knees (he looked down, but obviously couldn't see his own) and *spanked* – as you spank your boys when they disobey you!"

"Pardon me," said Vincent, "but I never do that. I should feel myself a failure as an instructor of boys if I could not influence their minds without chastising their bodies. Like members of this Tribunal, I was appointed neither to spank nor to insult, but to consider, intelligently and judicially, the state of mind of any youth who opposed my views."

The man behind Eunice nudged his mate.

"Proper bloody teacher, 'e is," he whispered.

"'E can talk," grunted the other.

Forsett was saying hurriedly:

"Would you undertake work of national importance?"

"Well, sir, I am doing it now. If I remain at my post—"

"Oh, no," said the chairman. "We can't allow you to do what you like—"

He leaned back at a whisper from Forsett, and then continued—

"You have put your case quite well, Mr. Fleet, and we believe you to be genuine. I understand you are qualified in first-aid and ambulance work. Will you join the R.A.M.C.?"

"No, I cannot do that. All forms of military service are equally abhorrent to me. In the R.A.M.C. I should be as much a soldier as in the fighting ranks."

"But you would not be asked to fight. Surely you cannot object to saving life? You have quite a record, it seems, in this respect?"

"I cannot help to save men in order to send them back to the trenches. I cannot help others to do what I will not do myself. It is impossible for me to assist in the organisation of war."

The military representative, who had restrained himself with difficulty hitherto, now burst out—

"But you must do something, man! What *are* you prepared to do for your country?"

"Work for peace."

"You can do that at the front."

The chairman and his colleagues became busy in consultation. Forsett was unusually animated, dipping his head right and left, bending over to as many as he could reach. He sat up stiffly, with a sly, conscious air of rectitude, as the chairman cleared his throat.

"Mr. Fleet, we have carefully considered your case, and have decided to grant you exemption from combatant service."

"But—"

"Next case, please."

Eunice started from her seat, and got through a wedge of people towards the door. As she passed, one of the policemen gave her a sympathetic smile. There was recognition in it, and she hastened away, flushing deeply. Vexation turned and doubled on her. Was she, now, to be ashamed of being known as Mrs. Fleet – as the wife of a self-confessed "conchy"?

Vincent awaited her in the public lobby.

"Well, darling, I hope you're not too disappointed – after all, it's only what I expected."

"But you're free – you're finished with it!"

"Not at all—"

"But I heard! They said you were genuine – and they granted you exemption!"

"They said I was genuine – and did *not* grant me exemption."

She did not understand, pouted, looked sulky. There were people standing around. He took her arm and said softly:

"Never mind, darling – don't worry – it'll be all right. At least they've given me a technical ground for appeal. So there's still a chance of my getting the total exemption I'm entitled to."

"And you'll have to go through it all again?"

"Why not? It's another chance of putting the case. But you needn't come a second time, sweetheart – how pale you're looking – it's been too much of an ordeal for my poor little girl. Let's get away from this place—"

She accepted his concern without comment. Her query had been reproachful, prompted by her own reactions to the "ordeal," not by his. She looked for no sign of strain in him. Wasn't he fit and sanguine, sure of himself, confident of his case, cool and imperturbable in the presentation of it? Those lines around his mouth, the shadow in his eyes, were for her, of course, not for himself. And rightly so, since she was the victim of his stubbornness, his perverse disassociation from his fellows in the national stress.

Outside, they were surrounded by Miss Fennick and her brother, with others who had arrived to hear results. She stood mute in the midst of their distorting chatter, which lauded Vincent and rated the Tribunal. She had left the gallery in relief, satisfied with the verdict, uneasy only at the idea that old Forsett had contrived it. (Her father must have "got at" him, overpowering the influence of his women, and her bitter joy at thwarting their malice was dashed at the idea of such obligation.) But how puzzling, how exasperating – to find that what she thought success was deemed a failure. What of the Jew? What of the Christian? Were they haloed with triumph – or defeat? The chorus was discordant. Miss Fennick had a pocket-book full of notes. She had talked to each C.O. as he came out, made friends with relatives, arranged visits and an exchange of information. She flourished her notes with glee. Eunice stared at her in silent disgust. Was she making a hobby of collecting C.O.'s? She should not collect Vincent. He would disappear from the pages of that book into the records of the Army. Non-combatant. The Appeal Tribunal, these rebels said, was unlikely to go further in concession. And on this point they were probably right. Why, indeed, should total exemption be given, even though the law allowed? Vincent must accept the decision: she would see to that. The hand-kerchief at her lips became a weapon. She could strike with it. For over a week, the suspicion, then certainty, of the cause compelling its use, had been hidden in her mind. Now was the time to bring it out – to tell her husband, make him share the knowledge and the burden. His view of duty would collapse, a playhouse of cards. Instead, a solid structure should be raised, built to her design.

She smiled, waved her hand in farewell to the group. Almost sweet ran the acid dribble.

*   *   *

Miss Fennick's notebook was not quite negligible. Eunice Fleet was to be indebted to it for her detailed recollection and true appraisement of events set in the trials of that day. She learned from it how the Appeal Tribunal, moved by news of British disasters, the need for fresh men to throw into the furnace of war, an agitation against teachers who bred disloyalty in schools, and speeches in Parliament on pampered C.O.'s, made short work of the appellants before them.

Harry Forsett was not there to intervene for Vincent. And in any case his intervention would not have availed. Not only was Vincent's claim dismissed, but his non-combatant certificate was withdrawn. He was ordered to report for active service.

The result was in no sense a surprise to Vincent. But it came to Eunice as a shock.

She sat at home making toast in the cosy little room. Though the season was advanced, she liked an early indoor glow. The curtains hid the panes, the standard lamp was lit, the china service laid on a table near the fire. The prim young maid placed a kettle on the ring, and retired to her own tea in the kitchen.

Vincent was late, but Eunice did not fret. She knew how cases dragged, and that Vincent might be last. Anxiety could not touch her. Everything was peaceful and settled in her mind. Last night they had sat together for hours in the big chair – she for a long time on his knees, until he made her lie back in the deep, soft seat, while he squatted on the rug, his head against her. They had had a long lovely talk.

Her news astonished him, undoubtedly; he was more pleased, too, than she anticipated. At first she thought it was relief at the explanation of recent moods, her bodily alienation from him. More concern for her was exactly what she expected. Plans bubbled from him immediately, new provisions for her comfort and safety while he "must be away." No more definite term was used just then. She could live quietly at home, or go to Mold and stay with his aunt (his father had died in the previous year); or Aunt Carry might come to Taviton. Miss Fleet was a simple, homely soul, fond of Eunice, and Eunice liked her well enough. As for a doctor and nurse – he suggested names, proposed looking up credentials, getting further advice. Neither knew much about doctors. They were both strong, healthy from childhood, had never since needed medical care.

"Why," he said, – "there's Miss Fennick's sister – the married sister she lives with – I believe she's a maternity nurse. I'll inquire. If she's really good, you might see her."

Though she frowned, Eunice raised no demur. Why bother to object just now? Besides—

"I've heaps of time," she said lightly. "It's only just beginning, after all."

"Darling, are you really happy about it?"

"Oh, yes. Especially as *you* are, – I thought, perhaps, you mightn't be—"

"I know, dearest. This isn't the best time for children – in a way, it's a sad fate to be born into a war-ridden world. But let's hope it'll be all over by then – he'll know nothing about it."

"*He*?"

"Well" – he laughed a little consciously – "I feel it must be a boy – don't you, sweetheart?"

"Yes – I do."

"Of course it won't matter if it's a girl. But I'd like a son." He was silent, gazing into the fire. She saw their gorgeous boy in her arms. What was his vision? She could not separate it from her own – the vision or series of visions, that had already come to her. Not that she had particularly wanted a baby. Playing with dolls, incipient maternal emotion never wove a serious thread into her growth. Marriage did not develop the instinct. It seemed something for a future, something for which she was not ready yet. The birth of Dorry antagonised rather than hastened desire. Yet it was the spectacle of Lallie with her child that won her, in the first realisation of her state. The feeling was much the same, though not as urgent, as that which turned her marriage into victory. Revolt against Tom Granger as husband to Lallie, deepened against him as father to Lallie's child: deepest was the grudge against Lallie's new role, adding a strange jealousy to her wounds. She did not wish to see the babe, or acknowledge its sister-hood. But seeing it, she had to crush an attraction towards the dainty mite.

There came to her the lure of the group – madonna, infant, worshipping folk. But the shape it took was triumph over Lallie. She, the graceful mother; in her arms a gorgeous boy – wasn't he the fruit of true romance? – wasn't his father the young, handsome, athletic Vincent Fleet? How the girls they knew would come crowing over him – "Oh, isn't he too sweet? Look at his darling toes – diddums kissums then!" – The older women with their critical advice, the men respectfully admiring, strange passers-by halting at the pram – how this daily homage would supersede the rival shrine! Messengers would go to Lallie as now they came to her, with eager tales of growth, enthusiasm spiced with malice – "Have you seen the Fleet baby lately? He's marvellous! Walks about already, straight and tall, and not ten months! Mouthful of teeth and eats everything. Isn't Eunice *lucky*? She hasn't had an hour's trouble with him. Sleeps all night and never cries. Doctor says he'll pass the infantile diseases grinning. Never seen such a healthy kid. . . . Eunice says she's glad he walks on his own, without even holding his hand – she couldn't possibly lift him any more. Of course his father does. What can you expect? Vincent's crazy over that child. Begun to train him already for the junior races!"

She leaned down and stroked the brown head at her knees. A demonstration rare with her – she felt the quick thrill vibrate his muscles.

"Oh, my love – my precious wife—" He wound his arms about her, and rocked her gently. They did not speak until she said, "Vin, I'm drowsy – I'm nearly asleep."

He carried her upstairs, undressed her, tucked her into bed, set a jug of water on the table at her side. She drank thirstily during the nights.

"You're to rouse me, mind, if you want anything else – or if you're just feeling queer – anything—"

She had confessed to waking often lately. Her sick sensations came late in the day, not early as with many other women. But that night, light against his breast, she slept throughout without a break. She did not know that it was he who was wakeful, listening to her breathing in the dark, restraining his longing to press her closer in his arms.

As cheerfully as he set out, next day, he returned to tell her what had happened. His face did not alter before her blank, resentful stare.

"Impossible. It can't be. They couldn't mean that—"

"They meant it all right. But it makes no difference, dear. My position is the same as it was before."

"But you could have gone into the non-combatant corps!"

"No, I couldn't—"

"But you could – you would – Miss Fennick says numbers of C.O's have joined it, and they're quite genuine—"

"Of course, my dear – why not? – if they reconcile it with their consciences – if they think and feel that way. I don't, that's all. Conscience is an individual affair, and each must judge for himself."

"Yes – each must judge – according to circumstances. And our circumstances – *now*—"

"Darling." He put his tea-cup down, and took her hands into his. "According to conviction, not according to circumstances. And nothing is changed, now, except that you are more precious to me than ever—"

She resisted his caress.

"Then you ought to consider me more. Can't you see how much easier it would be if you joined – the Red Cross – or the—"

"Never." His smile thinned. She drew away, and huddled in her chair. "Besides – don't you see, Eunice? – today's decision has closed that way to me. You must accept it."

There was a pause before she said:

"Then what's to happen now?"

"I suppose I'll get a calling-up notice to report at some depot or other. Then – when they find I haven't turned up, they'll send for me."

"Send? You mean they'll fetch you? – A policeman?—"

"Now listen, dearest – you mustn't get upset or excited. You know it's bound to happen – you heard all about the procedure at the Institute. I'll be charged as an absentee and handed over to the military. And I'll refuse to serve, get court-martialled, and sent to prison. That's all. I'm strong and determined. Nothing can affect me. Probably the war'll be over by the time I've served my sentence. Anyway, I'll keep my end up all right – and you'll do the same. You must take good care of yourself. I saw your dad today. He thinks I'm stark, staring, etc. – washed his hands of me – but of course he'll keep an eye on you. I've written to Aunt Carry. And I got to the bank in time to arrange—"

She was not listening, though her large, strained gaze was fixed on him. Her mind stuck at the one word – Prison.

"But, I say – you've had no tea, sweetheart. Come, I'll make more toast – and Alice can bring a fresh pot—" he went to the bell, but she jumped up, her handkerchief to her mouth – useless handkerchief.

"No, I don't want it – couldn't touch a thing. I feel sick—" She ran out of the room. When she returned, white, languid, eyes dull in their sockets, he pulled up the big easy chair and settled her into it, with a new novel he had brought from her library.

"There, dear, try to read, and forget about me!" he said coaxingly. "I must get to work – I've tons to do. When Alice has cleared, I'll bring all my papers here." He wasn't going to work upstairs, away from her. She turned the pages, conscious of his glance, wandering to her from his manuscripts. When an hour passed, he came and sat on the long arm of her chair.

The tension within broke into a spasm of relief.

"Vin – Vin" – she said – "you can't leave me – not like that – you can't possibly – you mustn't—"

"Love," he said, "if I had a choice between leaving you and staying – of course I'd be tempted – to stay – but it's not – I haven't a choice. There isn't any sense in dragging me away – I'm no good to them – but that's the folly of things now. Leave you I must. And since I must – I won't leave to do that which would betray us both—"

She wanted suddenly to beat against him – to clamour, to rend. But her hand lay helpless, her tongue mute. She who had always felt strong was held in weakness. Vincent was a mighty bar before her – iron, not cold, but red-hot, against which her buttery ram melted to oil. She couldn't move him, she couldn't pass the limpness in herself. The melting oil soaked back into her flesh, blotting her fibres – nauseous, clogging. She couldn't fight: she was devitalised.

Not long ago she had seen, somewhere, a queer reference to a pregnant woman. The writer called her "dumb" – "a dumb creature, fettered, locked away, the door fast" – unable to call out, to release her thoughts. She was like that now. She – not he – was a prisoner. Caught, trapped, bolted in.

The simile recurred to her time after time. The days were bad, the nights grew worse. As they lay in bed together for the last time – how was she, or he, to know it was the last? – her restlessness roused him just before the dawn.

"What is it, darling? Can I get you anything?"

"No. It's just this awful feeling—"

"Sick?"

"No – nothing definite – just an awfulness."

"Poor little girl." He gathered her up, petted her, smoothed her hair.

"It'll go off, darling – it's sure to go off – can't last very long. Then you'll be well again – my bright girl – and happy – waiting for me – waiting for our son."

She sighed.

"Can't you see him, Eunice? A fine, upstanding, grand little chap. God grant he'll have a decent world to come into. Do you know, this has made me keener – I know I'm doing the right thing. I'm not only responsible to myself. I'm responsible to my child. We'll teach him to hate war, won't we? Anti-militarist from his birth. No toy soldiers and games of destruction. Gosh, I can see him—" he chuckled. "Running ahead, what? But I'd like you to know, darling – I'll be thinking of you both."

She writhed in his arms. He tried to lull her into peace.

"No more talking – you must sleep. Let's have this pillow down – there. Now you can rest your shoulders more and still get air. Not too flat, not too high. That's better, isn't it? Now snuggle in. Bye-bye, darling—"

She lay rigid, staring into the dark, her mind fumbling. So that was how he felt. Keener – this has made me keener. Oh, mockery. Must she travail to send him further awry? To spawn a son of shame? – Grim humour twisted her lips as she thought of the phrase – a *gaol delivery*.

It lit the secrets of her mind, which, fumbling, found a key. She clutched and held. Why not? – oh, why not? She could open her cell herself. An effort – a little will – perhaps a little suffering – not much, she could bear that better than months of this. . . . A greyness slit the parted curtains, trembling at an open casement. Dawn's first scout came spying in the room. It touched a jutting chin, the tip of a nose, the edge of a brow over staring eyes. Ghostly, imp-like, the wavering beam sprayed an odd malevolence on the face. As well that the blind husband was asleep; even his waking blindness might have seen.

*   *   *

Vincent was arrested at his school. At least his wife was spared the sight of his removal by police. She did not visit him at the station, nor was she present next day at the court, when he was charged, fined two pounds, and handed over to a military escort. But for the vigilance of Miss Fennick and her group, knowledge of these events might have been late in reaching her. It was not until he was at the barracks that she received a note from him, smuggled out by a soldier. It asked for more details than it gave, begging her not to grieve, and assuring her he was well and happy – "except for our separation. Oh, my darling, it torments me that I can no longer help and comfort you. But I console myself in the belief that you will endure with courage this time of trial for us both. I know that my Eunice is brave as she is lovely. . . . Come and see me, dearest, before I leave this place. Laura Fennick will tell you how it can be managed. I long to see you and learn from yourself that you are not too lonely and unwell. Aunt Carry must be with you, if you sent the telegram. . . . Let me know at once if there is anything else you need done. The Fennicks have a way of getting messages through. But try to come yourself, my own. I may be here a week – perhaps less – it's difficult to know. I can't add more – the man is waiting – it's my only chance of sending this. My deepest love to my precious wife. Your Vincent."

She read it and dropped it on the fire. Her eyes were dull, her movement listless. She could hardly grasp the inquiries of the gentle old lady, who had asked the messenger into the kitchen.

"Answer? No. Yes. I suppose I must. Let him wait a little longer."

"I told Alice to give him tea and sandwiches. He doesn't know whether he can take a message back, but he'll try. Do you want to speak to him?"

"I? No. Give him a shilling. I hope he doesn't talk about Vincent to Alice."

"Poor dear Vin! You say he doesn't tell you much about himself?"

"Only that he's in good spirits."

"Well, well, that's a blessing. Mind you give him my love, and say I'll stay a month. Perhaps he'll be home by then. Poor dear, why doesn't he give in? The man says he'll have to in the end, so he might as well now, and save them trouble."

Aunt Carry, the Forsett-Grangers said, was a fool. Gentle and kind, but a downright simpleton. Her words seemed wise enough to Eunice. Yet, she, too, apart from the standards of patriotism, believed Carry Fleet to be a fool. It was a good thing to believe. Only a fool – and a spinster fool at that – would be useful to her now.

Next day she set out for the barracks, nearly two miles outside the town. Miss Fennick joined her as she left the tram, pointed out the path to the gates, then retired to wait "round the corner."

"It's best they shouldn't see too much of me," she said, "I'm afraid I'll have to scheme my way in often enough. They're not too keen even on relatives. But you're a lawful visitor today. Please make the most of it."

"How do you mean?" said Eunice. She was far from pleased with Laura Fennick's company, but she almost wished, at this moment, to retain it.

"Why, get all the information you can. Find out how they treat Mr. Fleet, and what the next step is likely to be. If there's anything illegal, we'll report it."

"He hasn't complained."

Miss Fennick looked at her oddly.

"No, he wouldn't – to you." The last words were not said aloud. Miss Fennick had learned that Mrs. Fleet was not to be told of any "unpleasantness" that could be withheld.

The barrack walls loomed too soon for Eunice. She was challenged outside, but presently admitted. A guard took her across to the sergeant-major. There was activity and bustle in the square. Men were at drill, there were loud, sharp commands; officers walked smartly about, salutes were exchanged. An elegant young captain gave her a side-long look as he marched a company by.

Her face burned a moment, leaving her cheeks more sallow. What was she doing here? The sergeant-major acknowledged her claim with a scowl.

"Yes, you can see him," he said, and his thick grudging voice paused, while he scanned her a second time. He was a local man, and knew the Grangers by sight. Down in the mouth, as any lady would be. He called a corporal and entrusted her to him.

"Pity you didn't persuade him to behave more sensible," said the soldier, as they walked towards some huts in the field.

"I couldn't," she said.

"H'm. Pr'aps you'll 'ave another try." His tone was meant to be encouraging. "We've had some funny women come here to see C.O.'s. Seem to make 'em worse, that's a fact. Can't understand it. Don't they want their menfolk to protect 'em?"

She did not reply. It was not for her to echo Vincent's comment: "Far from protecting women and children, war endangers their safety, wrecks their homes, and turns them into widows and orphans."

One hut stood away from the rest in a swamp of mud-brown grass. She picked her way across without saving her shoes from slime. The soldier unbarred the door and roared—

"Private Fleet!"

There was no reply from the hole. It seemed black until

she peered more closely, saw the wooden sides, an open window high at the back, and a man on a seat bending over tins. He was rubbing them vigorously.

"Private Fleet!"

Still the man did not look up. But he spoke – Vincent's voice, pleasant and courteous.

"No sich person here, corporal. *Mr.* Fleet, if you please – or Vincent, if you like—"

The corporal's eyes bulged, his throat gurgled. He restrained the first result, and shouted—

"Here's your wife to see you."

A tinny clatter, and Vincent had bounded to the door. Her hands were seized; his eyes devoured her. Hers ranged dimly on his rough shirt and trousers, his hairy skin. She hardly heard his low stutter of greeting – ". . . But I knew you'd come today – I hoped – I knew – Eunice, how are you feeling?"

"Not so bad," she said mechanically.

"That's fine – that's jolly – come, dear, you must sit – but not inside – no, it's rather poor for a lady, corporal, isn't it? Can we use the bench outside?"

The corporal growled assent, and moved a few feet off. They sat together on the strip of wood, he still holding her hands, gazing into her face.

"How dreadful – this shed—" she said. "It looks all wet and slimy—"

"Oh, it could be worse – there's a tarpaulin on the ground – and plenty of air. Tons better than my cell—"

"Isn't this—?"

"No, I'm lucky to be here today – my proper home is off the guardroom – not nearly so comfy, I assure you. I've been chucked out because of the large number of drunks and other C.B. cases – well, you don't know what all that means, but never mind, darling. Tell me about yourself."

He asked her questions, and she answered, but her mind was held by his unkemptness, the wretched hut, and the presence of the soldier, gloomily kicking the mud a yard away. She kept her head down as Vincent talked. Her voice came stiff and reluctant in assurance about comfort, about Miss Fleet, about her ability to "carry on." She winced as he poured endearments on her, then called her his "true pal," standing by him in his need.

This was rather unlike Vincent: in fact, there was an unusual extravagance in his words. She was too flurried to notice it at the time. Once she interrupted him with a nervous glance around—

"Can that man hear? Is he listening? He looks an awful brute." Suddenly she remembered with distaste Laura Fennick's injunctions. "Is he – is he horrid to you?"

"That fellow? No, he's quite decent. Best of the lot, in fact."

"But he yells so—"

"My dear, that's the Army. They all yell here. I'll end by yelling myself. But no fear – I shan't follow their example – not in any way—"

"He thinks I've come to persuade you—"

Vincent laughed.

"Good idea. You must tell Miss Fennick that. They'll let you in oftener."

"How long are you to be here?"

"That's hard to find out. Nobody knows, and nobody tells the truth. But it looks as if they've stopped court-martialling—"

"What – altogether?"

"I mean *here*."

"Then you'll be sent away?"

He nodded.

"The rest have gone to Kinmel Park – there were eight

C.O.'s in the guardroom with me the first day – they went off next morning. I don't know whether I'm to follow. As soon as I find out, I'll try to let you know – or the Fennicks. Keep in touch with them, darling. There's a guard here – the one who slipped the letter – he's gone off for a while – they're a bit slack with me now. Know they can trust me not to run, I suppose." He grinned. "Not that I could get far if I did. But that guard – he'll take a message. Sympathetic, I believe, though he doesn't say so. Curses me as much as – that is, he doesn't show it. I think he's an objector who hadn't the guts to stand out – like lots of them – not that I blame 'em, God knows."

"Why are you dressed like this?"

"'Dressed' is good. It's the minimum I'll put on. Didn't expect to see me in khaki, did you? They took my clothes away, so what could I do? Had to cover my nakedness – Well, darling, I know I'm not as handsome as I used to be – I could do with a shave and trim. I suppose I'll get it later. Too much cropping, maybe!"

He rattled on, so that even if she could have forced her aversions into speech, she had no chance. His guard returned, the corporal stepped up close, and curtly told her she must leave. She rose, and Vincent stood mute beside her for a moment.

His sudden kiss fell scant upon her ear, as she jerked away in bitter embarrassment. Not once did she turn her head while crossing the field. As she reached the barrack square, the smart young officer she had met before came up alone from the staff quarters. He swung a cane and stared as he passed her to the gates. The sergeant-major saluted, the guards stood to attention. He acknowledged their homage with a supercilious flick. The same complacent ease was in his second look at her – deliberate, curious, quizzical. She flushed again with searing inner heat. How dare he think her game for insolence? Ah, but now – anyone might dare. Symbols, branding in her new estate. She, who ought to have been offered only the graces of military life, must now receive its snubs. Honours – gallantries – were not for one who trailed in the mire of that detention hut.

*   *   *

The rest of the week heaped obloquies upon her.

A bitter press campaign followed accounts of war-objectors' trials. Pacifists in general, and Vincent Fleet in particular, were denounced by scribes and correspondents in local papers. The best-known "shirker," whose fame turned into infamy, was shown to have a suspicious record, despite honours gained in sport and profession. He had been a socialist and a rebel against the Empire for years. His text-book on New Methods in Schools contained an ambiguous chapter on Patriotism. Such standard phrases as he used were unsound, since they omitted laudation of the Flag, discounted lessons celebrating its range, and urged "namby-pamby" substitutions for military drill. The teaching of a pernicious internationalism was advocated. "The author is a man who refuses to do his duty to his country," wrote the editor of the *Taviton Post*. . . . "This man, who wished to introduce into our Schools a system to pollute the minds of our children, to undermine their devotion to our glorious Empire, and weaken their sense of a noble heritage which it should be their pride and honour to carry on – this man, instead of fostering patriotism, as he was paid to do, sought to destroy it. His writings, which ought to be suppressed by the authorities, are full of rank sedition. He is revealed at last in his true colours as a traitor and enemy of his country." – "Perish the skunk!" wrote a correspondent. "He should be placed against the wall and shot at dawn, or else handed over to the Huns to taste a sample of the methods he admires." – "Let us rout out all such foulers of the nest," wrote another, "We have reason to believe that Vincent Fleet was not the only pro-German skulking behind the shelter of his profession. There are many who have not yet been forced to go before Tribunals and expose their views. These dastards – females as well as so-called men – are a menace and a scandal. Let us rout them out of their funk-holes!" – "What," clamoured others – "*what is the Council doing*?"

The Council discussed the matter at its next meeting, and called upon the Education Committee to act. A course of investigation into the opinions, conduct, and character of the teaching staffs of the town was forthwith adopted. Several peacemongering members lost their posts, and among them was Laura Fennick. Eunice was not much concerned at this development. She was sensitive only to the dishonouring of her own name in the public press, and its early consequences to herself.

First, there was a raid by detectives, who seized private letters and school papers in their search for seditious matter. It was a humiliating experience, followed the next day by the flight of her maid. Alice said tearfully that she had meant to give notice at the end of the month, as her parents objected to her being in the house of a conchy. But her young man, who was C3, and worked in munitions, refused to walk out with her if she remained another night.

Anonymous letters of abuse reached Mrs. Fleet by post and hand. Every day, it seemed, stirred some dregs to fermentation. Friends passed her in the street with averted eyes, or worse still, stopped to condole. The Grangers and the Forsetts who called, complained tauntingly of a common disgrace. She would not visit them, and wished they would not visit her. Her manner, if not her words, conveyed this to them – with evident effect, for in most cases the calls were not repeated. Only her father continued to come and she could not show him the door. The old man still doted on her, though he doted more on Lallie and the child. The filial bond tugged crosswise at his heart, in these days of stress and soaring dockyard profits. He missed his sons, and was burdened by their wives. Both claimed immunity from relationship with the "shirker" – most loudly when they began to shun Eunice as she shunned them. Their stinging comments reached her, and did not help to rouse concern for their husbands – which they and the old man expected her to show. Her affection for her brothers, like so much else, was warped by the patriotic storming at her doors. Such furies could not release her from her secret cell. They drove her in more wickedly upon herself, to twist the key within her palm, and devise unholy use.

In this dark mood she received an urgent message from the Fennicks, asking her to take a visitor to Vincent.

A young man from Cambridge, member of the Council of the Fellowship, and editor of its journal, had travelled down on Saturday to address the dwindling branch, and learn the fate of those in duress. He was specially anxious to see Vincent. They had met once, and exchanged some correspondence. "Our friend must leave tomorrow," said Laura Fennick, "but Sunday is a good day for the barracks – the slack time, in fact, when it's easiest to slip a stranger in" – She was unable to go herself, and it was inadvisable for a man to make the attempt without a woman. Naturally the right woman was the prisoner's wife.

Her impulse was to refuse outright. She was ill, she could not leave her bed. The excuse need not be wholly false. The mere thought of the barracks was paralysing. She had resolved not to go again, even if Vincent remained there for weeks. But the message came through Aunt Carry, who had met Laura Fennick in the town. Miss Fleet liked the Fennicks, though she could not understand them. She believed, however, that they meant well by Vincent, and was induced to add her own plea on behalf of the strange young man. "They say he may be able to help poor Vin, if he can get a talk with him now."

Aunt Carry could not be evaded, fool as she was. And at the moment Eunice did not wish to exhibit herself to the old lady in too ruthless a light.

She went to the barracks, accompanied by the Fennicks' guest, and hardly exchanged a dozen words with him. His presence, the forced visit, the air of conspiracy, it seemed to her, which the Fennicks imposed, were so obnoxious to her, that she scarcely looked at him, took no heed of his name, and had no idea that he was being considerate to her because, though she was obviously sullen, she was as obviously unwell and unhappy.

They found Vincent alone in the guardroom cell, a foul-smelling, ill-lit, unventilated dungeon: it had retained its character throughout centuries, in the old stone quarter of the castle barrack. Her loathing turned to self-commiseration as she clung to the iron door. Vincent seemed to her as cheerful as before. He did not mind the horror, she thought. He was even more unkempt, and perhaps paler – but the dim light on dirty whitewash might make the ruddiest look wan. He coughed a little, too. Who wouldn't in that atmosphere? How was she to endure five minutes of it without choking, or worse, being profusely sick? So powerfully did she concentrate on avoiding this catastrophe, in the presence of the vulgar guard and the polished youth, that she was almost oblivious of the talk in the cell.

A new sense of wistfulness in Vincent's smile – and what was that to her? – his eager hail of her companion, their mutual spur of confidence in themselves, their cause, their Fellowship – all swelling her resentment – summed the impression left at last, by the tide of her sick alarms. A curious relief marked the ebb of that tide – the fumigating smoke of cigarettes, avidly accepted by prisoner and guard. Perhaps that was why the fact remained in her mind, a sort of beacon to memory's future mariner. She must have noted, at any rate, as she crouched against the door, how the visitor struck a match and held it for ignition, once, twice, thrice, with his slim left hand.

As they came away, the youth subdued by farewell and her detachment, it was easy to leave him to the group waiting at the corner. She excused herself from some rites of hospitality at a member's house, and hurried off alone. Easy, too, it seemed, to forget him.

But not easy to forget her plight and determination. Two days later she heard that Vincent had left the barracks. The Fennicks were feverishly on the trail, and promised to send her news of the next location. A bitter smile stretched her lips as she passed the message to Miss Fleet.

"Oh dear me! Now you won't be able to see him at all – unless it's not too far away. Perhaps he's been taken to Oswestry – or Rhyl – didn't Miss Fennick say some of her friends were there? That's not too far from Mold. Hadn't you better pack at once, Eunice, and come back with me this week? We needn't stay here longer, dear, surely?"

They stayed, however, for another two months. Because Eunice slipped on a landing and had to be helped to bed. It was not like her to be clumsy or clamant. But she moaned so much and looked so queer that Miss Fleet proposed to send for the doctor. Eunice asked her to telephone instead to Mrs. Benton. Miss Fleet, who had known no Nurse Benton in her time, was inclined to argue, but yielded to insistence. The nurse came promptly and proved a capable sort of woman, who took charge with assurance. She stayed the night, and decreed that Eunice must remain in bed at least a week.

"Jolted her inside rather badly, poor dear – but its nothing serious. Rest will cure her. But she must rest *absolutely*, and see nobody except yourself, Miss Fleet. . . . Shock, too, you know. And all this trouble about her husband—"

"Yes, yes, of course. How poor Vin would fret if he knew! People have been rather unkind, I'm afraid – though it's natural with so many men killed and wounded, poor souls, and the war going on worse than ever, and the Germans doing such dreadful things – that awful *Lusitania*, and the raids, though of course we're too far away to get them, but one never knows on the coast, does one? – and all this rationing and standing in queues for a bit of meat and no butter – so of course people say shocking things about Vin, though I'm sure he didn't mean any harm. You may be sure, nurse, I wouldn't dream of letting anyone come and upset her, unless her father – I know she doesn't want to see him, though. But oughtn't the doctor—?"

"Oh no, not at all necessary. I'll come in every day. Just bathing and massage, you see – I'll manage nicely. And with your care as well, she'll soon be on her feet again, well and strong as ever. Of course, if you wish it, I can ask Doctor Fearns to come along – but I don't see why we should trouble him, I'm sure."

Eunice heard the conversation as she lay in bed, her eyes closed, her teeth jammed against betrayal of her body's rack, but with the same odd smile fluttering her lips. Miss Fleet saw neither its bitterness nor its malice. She thought poor dear Eunice was being sweet and brave, in the face of cruel disappointment. For Caroline Fleet, innocent spinster as she was, knew the meaning of the hemorrhage Nurse Benton attributed to the fall.

But she did not know as much as Eunice had learned in

the first month of married life. She was not familiar with young wives who met to parade their state, and whose homes were centres of an exclusive freemasonry, into which a bride was initiated with rites that marked off a pool of surmise from a sea of knowledge: a sea in which one might swim or sink, though not for lack of ropes, lifebelts, both ancient and modern paraphernalia of rescue. New matrons stripped to stark nudity. It seemed the only way to advice and skill. Even Eunice, shy of revelation, was not above prying on others. There was more than curiosity and abandon in these antics, inspired less by a wish to outrage Mother Nature than by the necessity to understand and harness her. Experiments were made in the interests of the race as well as in the possible extermination of it. Things went wrong sometimes, of course. The woman who jumped from a window (or, as one might say, dived from rock to rock) and broke both legs; her friend who slid on the garden path in frosty weather (skating on literal thin ice, to be drowned in ensuing flood) – and others who made maladroit play with hatpins and knitting-needles, not yet out of date or septically guarded: all provided lamentable warning of rashness and excess. Abortions were not really popular, in view of private as well as public penalties. The technique of control was simpler, less harrowing, less costly, and even more varied, though not as highly developed and as clinically available as it was to become. . . . At the same time, if one were unlucky enough to drift too far, with or without precaution, it was wise to know which boat to hail, which pilot to trust. Names were whispered: a particular name reached her ears too often for Eunice to forget it.

She lay smiling, aware that it was Miss Fleet's ignorance, rather than her knowledge, that made her obdurate. With little suspicion of accident, and none at all of Nurse Benton's ministrations, the good soul insisted on sending for Doctor

Fearns. He was not her "regular man," but she had heard
of him, and was no stickler for the person behind the
medical label. Doctor Fearns came and examined the patient.
He looked rather grave and pursed his mouth, staring
reflectively from bed to nurse. Mrs. Benton was too competent to withstand his gaze. The droop of hers, however,
was no gesture of deprecation, except in the formal and
complimentary sense. She had, as a matter of fact, recently
saved a baby for him (admirable nurse, who knew the law
of balance!) and with it a handsome fee – and some reputation. He was unlikely to be churlish with her. Why
should he wish to be – if the case was going well? As far as
he could see, it was. He smiled and said so, somewhat
drily, gave a few directions, and took abrupt farewell. Miss
Fleet trotted into the kitchen with light feet and lighter
heart. She was really in her element, fussing over milk and
barley foods, and instructing the charwoman who had
replaced Alice. But most of all she felt the importance and
the embarrassment of writing to Vin.

As soon as news came of his whereabouts, a letter was
sent, dictated carefully by Eunice. Either to save Aunt Carry's
susceptibilities, or for some other reason, few words were
used, and those none too bald. The fact, however, was
made clear to Vincent, that his wife no longer expected to
be a mother.

The frantic reply from his new place of detention did not
surprise the invalid: it was frantic, of course, with concern
for her. He made no reference of disappointment about the
child. But who should know better than herself his feeling
on the point? Smiles grew in distortion on her lips. Now
they should see! With one turn of her secret key she had
released herself and him. Pain – danger – some transitory
but hellish fear – had she not imposed them on herself in
greater measure than on him? But she was free!

And he, too, must rebel against his conscience into freedom. *"Keener"* – yes, to come home to her, to take up arms, be a soldier, a husband – and a father. Oh, of course, she would grant him his fatherhood; later, when he had made amends, when she was ready – "You precious little ass," said an older Eunice, looking back at the figure in the bed – "You crass, unutterable idiot!"

The apostrophe had no special relevance to Vincent's failure in response. He became neither a soldier, a husband, nor a father. Even if it were clear to him that the last two states depended on the first, he showed no signs of acting on the knowledge. Instead, he was court-martialled for disobedience to military orders, and sentenced to a hundred and twelve days' hard labour. On his way to Wormwood Scrubs he pressed into the hands of a Fellowship Scout who greeted him at the turn of Ducane Road, a note begging Eunice to write and come to London as soon as a visit was allowed. She did neither. He never heard from her and never saw her again.

*　　　*　　　*

At the end of two months, when the first visit and the first letter fell due to the prisoner, Eunice and Aunt Carry left for Mold. The long blue sheet covered in Vincent's minute scrawl (his normal writing reduced to half-size in the attempt to double allotted measure) lay folded in the elder lady's handbag, undisturbed by wifely claim.

Eunice was pale and languid, and if she grew increasingly fit, grew also increasingly sullen, in the rural seclusion of Miss Fleet's farmhouse home. The farm itself was run by an ageing Welshman, whose wife was a distant connection of Aunt Carry's, and looked after the long, low, whitewashed house. The couple had no children, and all their men, except for a cripple, had been taken into the Army. They "made shift" with one or two women until the arrival of a youth, strong and energetic, but entirely unskilled in the lore of cows and produce. How, indeed, should an urban accountancy clerk became a dairy expert, except in the course of resisting military demands? For Wallace Paige having unsuccessfully claimed exemption before a Tribunal and been court-martialled and imprisoned in what was now an established routine, had been released under the Home Office scheme of alternative service.

Miss Fleet was greatly interested in this product of conscience and politics, and invited him to tea in her parlour to explain his position. She had already approved the arrangements into which her bailiff had entered for the employ of the young man, on terms exceedingly favourable to employer and Government, if of doubtful benefit to the "shirker." But Eunice refused to share the interest or draw the moral which appealed to Aunt Carry. She ignored young Paige in house and fields, where he whistled in either real or affected blitheness as he drove cows or loaded hay on wagons; and was unmoved by Aunt Carry's hopes of a similiar development in Vincent's situation.

"Why shouldn't Vin come out to work here, too? I can apply for his services, Morgan says – we're still shorthanded, with all that corn rotting in the second field, and the milk wasting. Why shouldn't—"

"Why – why—?" said Eunice impatiently. "Because the Government won't let a conscientious objector work for relations. And anyway Vincent won't accept the scheme."

"But why?"

"What's the use of asking Vincent 'why'? He'll only repeat what he wrote, about not compromising his stand in any way, and all that stuff. He'd sooner rot in prison as the corn rots in the field."

"But, Euny, dear, we mustn't let him. We must try to persuade him—"

"*You* can try."

"Euny, dear, why shouldn't you write – in any way you think best, of course—"

"I've told you once for all – I won't. If he's stubborn, so am I. He'll be out soon. If he changes his mind, I'll meet him. He must understand by now what my silence means, though you try to cover it up."

"But dear, he's so fond of you – it must hurt him very much—"

"I hope it does. Let him suffer as he's made me suffer."

Though her vindictiveness shocked Aunt Carry, the old lady could not gainsay it. She feared Eunice was in the right. "Poor girl!" she thought, as she sat in her window, watching Eunice wander restlessly down the shrubbery path. "Poor girl! She feels her life is blighted, and no wonder. Such an unmentionable disgrace. We can't go anywhere – it's awful answering questions about Vin – and it's so bad for her to mope about. Oh, dear me, dear me! Why won't the dear boy be reasonable?"

She cried gently; then consoled herself with plans for bringing them together after the dreadful war was over. Meanwhile she would send a post card to Miss Fennick. She knew Eunice disliked the link with the Fennicks, who "encouraged" Vincent in his stubbornness. But since there was no other way of getting news of him, she risked the wife's displeasure – compromising on the card, for her fingers itched to write an indiscreet letter.

No reply came for many weeks. By that time Vincent's sentence expired, and he was sent to "rejoin his unit" at Kinmel Park. Another court-martial followed, and a second term of imprisonment. Such messages as came from him varied little. Generalities, still confidently expressed, of faith in his "principles" – and in the love of his wife. It seemed

all was well with him. The women's horror of prison was
to some extent modified by his own apparent lack of it. He
did not, it was certain, share their notion of "unmentionable disgrace," which loomed above the physical aspects of
incarceration. Locked cells might or might not be comfortable: according to the Press, they were not only safety
shelters, but health resorts. Laura Fennick's letter conveyed
a different impression.

It was a lengthy epistle. She began by apologising for
her delay.

"The fact is, my dear Miss Fleet, I've been running about
after my brother, and getting into all sorts of messes. But I
had to get him out of his mess, which was a much bigger
and more dangerous one. As you know, Harvey was
turned down by the Tribunal. After arrest he was not taken
to the local barracks, and I had great difficulty in tracing
him. . . . In the end I found him in a military prison, where
he had no business to be. But I had to fight hard with the
authorities to get him transferred. . . . In the first place I had
to *see* him. As visits were barred, this looked like being
impossible. However, I've decided, like Napoleon, not to
recognise that word, especially in war-time. . . . I let my
hair hang down in ribbons, and my size favoured the
illusion that I was a chit of thirteen, tearfully anxious to
persuade her erring brother to 'give in,' become a good
boy, and go forth to kill his fellow-men as ordered. Having
succeeded in impressing the Governor with this view of
my designs, I was led to a waiting-room. Suddenly I was
asked to step into the corridor, from the further end of
which my brother was being brought up. I can't describe
my sensations on seeing him. He seemed to be at death's
door, so limp and ghastly, and even at a distance of a few
yards the marks on his hands and face were plain – marks
of a whip and chains! I made a leap for him and at the
same moment he rushed to me. We had just got our arms

round each other when it seemed as if an earthquake took place and we were swallowed in the roar and crash. What happened was that the warder flung himself on us and tore us apart, bawling at the top of his voice. Harvey was pushed against the wall, where he stood or rather nearly fell, white and trembling, while I was shaking all over and thoroughly scared. I let the tears gush out in earnest, and the warder's shouts subsided into a growl.

He was a brute, of course, but we had really outraged him. To touch a prisoner is a frightful offence – like a transgression against the Holy Ghost! He told us of it in his resentful growl – '. . . Whatyer mean by it, huh? Got a good mind to march yer back to the cell, 507, an' not let yer have the visit at all!' – 'Oh, please,' I said humbly, 'it's my fault, I'm sorry, I didn't know it was wrong, I won't do it again—' 'Yer'd better not try – well, yer can thank y' lucky stars it's *me*. Git inside. Prisoner fust and behind the table – see?'

Still stunned by the cataclysm, we took our places opposite each other, the length of the table between us, and the brute standing scowling and listening to every word we stammered out. You can imagine how difficult it was to speak at all. And I had to pretend to plead with him to 'give in.' My heart was boiling, as if the earthquake had really taken place inside me, and hot lava streaming through my veins. I saw his eyes bulge and his lips quiver at me. 'What, Laura – *you* – *you* tell me—' Somehow I managed to make him realise the trick, but it did not help him to explain what they had been doing to him. It was enough for me, however, to read his face – his looks – and the marks – 'You're ill,' I said, 'Have you hurt yourself? Have you been falling about like you used to when you had epileptic fits?' I winked as if I were blinking my tears. (And I needn't tell you I'd got over my sensitiveness about lies!) 'Yes,' he said, 'I've hurt myself against rods and iron things—' The warder shuffled his feet and coughed and I said quickly, 'Then you ought to be moved to hospital. Why don't you give in and let the doctor attend you properly?' 'Never,' said he, – 'But you'll die if you go on like this,' I said – 'You know you've only got one lung, anyway. Don't they know it here?' 'I've refused medical examination every time,' he said, 'and always shall. But of course they forcibly—' 'Time's up,' said the warder, and before I knew where I was I'd been hustled out and Harvey marched from my sight. Hollow echoes of their feet going down the corridor – then clank – bang! Doors were slammed, bolts shot, chains rattled, harsh abrupt shouts startled the walls. I wonder if you think, as I used to, that the horror of a prison is its solitude and deadly silence? I know now that there is more horror in its noise. Sudden yells, clankings, bangings. There is nothing human about these noises, like the noises of a street – or a school. And Harvey never could bear sudden sounds.

I didn't go home. I went straight to London and worried every sympathetic M.P. I could get hold of. There aren't too many and they were not all in town – and they're overworked with these cases – Snowden, King, Ponsonby, Anderson, Edmund Harvey – (my brother's proud to be his namesake) and the rest. The result is that Harvey is now in hospital at Walton, and likely to be released altogether soon. I shan't rest until this happens. Of course my talk about epilepsy was eyewash – Harvey has never had a fit of that kind. But it's true that he has only one sound lung – that's not too sound, either – and is in a serious state. He was ill-used brutally at the military prison, but it's denied or excused on account of his 'obduracy' – refusal to obey orders, to carry kit, to salute, march, etc. If my brother dies, I shall never forgive not only the militarists, but the civilian jingoes who have hounded to his end a sick boy, quite useless to them in any case. The local doctors knew that he was physically unfit, and though he refused medical examination from the start, when he could have got off as a C3 type, they certified him as A1. But he won't die if I can help it. By hook or crook – I don't care how literally – I'll get him home, where my sister and I can nurse him.

You will understand how my time and attention has been taken up. My own case gave me some trouble, too, but I don't care what happens to myself, except in so far as I must find a job and earn money somehow, for my brother's sake as well as my own. I'm only sorry that I can't do as much as I should like for other C.O.'s. But I advise relatives and friends to keep on the alert and foil every act of cruelty and injustice. Many tragedies have happened already where there has been nobody to care or to investigate in time. Do you remember the case of a religious C.O. who appealed at Taviton on the same day as Mr. Fleet? The Tribunal trampled on the poor lad – a simple, sincere Christian – and allowed the military representative to say he should be in a lunatic asylum. I don't know whether this played on his mind. He was sane enough, but completely bewildered by his treatment. His poor old mother was unable to keep in touch with him, and though I arranged for a visit, he felt himself lost and abandoned. They said he developed melancholia. I know his spirit was broken. He was released from prison last week, only to be sent to a mental asylum. God knows whether he will ever recover.

It is as well to realise that the depression which attacks our men in prison is much more dangerous than physical disease. I am so glad to hear from you that Vincent Fleet is cheerful. He has an exceptionally strong mind, of course, and sound nerves. But even the strongest must feel the strain of such experiences. I am sorry Mrs. Fleet has not been well enough to visit him, and hope with all my heart that she will be able to manage the next visit due. It isn't only that a personal visit from dear ones helps to comfort a man, but as you will gather from all I have told you, it is the only means of discovering hardship and injustice. Prison letters are censored and no description of routine is allowed, much less of abuses. I don't wish to alarm you. Mr. Fleet may not have been ill-treated, and his health may not have suffered, though I know that he was affected by wet conditions in the barracks here, sleeping on marshy ground for several nights without means of drying and changing. He had a nasty cough at his first court-martial. Later on he was in hospital with influenza. Probably you know more than I do about all this, and I shall be glad to hear of his complete recovery. I'm not surprised to know that he won't come out on the scheme. It's a dirty trick to split the movement . . ."

The letter ended unintelligibly. A second one, almost as long, came next day.

"If for any reason Mrs. Fleet finds she cannot pay the next visit, I will try to do so, if you let me know in time. That is, presuming I am not in gaol myself. Not only have I lost my job through the persecution of irate patriots, but they are trying to stop all my peace work. I've just returned from canvassing some streets in our suburb with a petition, asking the Government to negotiate for peace at the earliest favourable moment. It is a perfectly innocuous document – too much so for my taste. But I did not get many signatures. One man threatened to report me to the police; and I daresay he has done so, or will. Another drove me from his door, more in sorrow than in anger, but his polite insults were no less venomous. It's a scandalous shame, he said, for a female to go about preaching peace *now*, when we are just ready to fight the unspeakable Huns on something like equal terms. A premature peace, he said, would be the greatest calamity that could befall us, and those that preach peace now are enemies of the human race. – As if every hour that we continue this bestiality, we are not doing irreparable injury to the human race, destroying and muti-lating the best of our kind, and giving licence to the worst. Who are the real enemies of mankind – we who want to stop at once this senseless waste and havoc, or those who want it to go on, in order to satisfy their hatreds, their blood-lust, and sense of revenge, which they call their sense of honour? – When I said as much to the man who had begun to argue with me, he also looked round for a policeman.

The women, I regret to say, proved just as disappointing. Some were timid and cautious, afraid to do anything without the sanction of their men. If *they* think it's right to go on fighting, said one, I suppose they must. Others were bellicose themselves. They abused me at the top of their voices and nearly scratched my face – though being what are called ladies. How dare you go behind the backs of our men, said they, while they are fighting and dying for you? But surely, said I, it's because they are fighting and dying that we must work for peace quickly, to save as many as we can. And anyway, I said, I never wanted them to fight and die for me. If a man thinks a woman is worth fighting for, in the sense of killing and being killed for her, perhaps he has a right to act on his opinion. But what right has a woman to place such a value on herself, as to expect a man to give his life for her? I don't believe that any woman, and especially any stupid, ignorant, bloodthirsty woman, is worth the sacrifice of a brave man's life. A woman who believes that war is necessary, ought to be prepared to fight herself, or at least take the risks of engaging in war as Nurse Cavell did. Women who allow men to kill and be killed for them are the worst cowards, shirkers, and hum-bugs, unfit to live themselves or carry on the race . . ."

"Good gracious!" said Miss Fleet, taking off her spectacles and putting them on again. Her fingers shook with agitation as she held the schoolbook sheets.

"The girl's raving," said Eunice. The expression on her face as she listened had turned from sullenness to rage. But they did not discuss "the girl's" opinions. Miss Fleet was more concerned with the idea that Vincent might be ill or maltreated. Eunice would not credit either possibility.

"He's in a civil prison," she pointed out. "And even Laura Fennick doesn't suggest they maltreat prisoners there. You know that she exaggerates everything. And she's a self-confessed liar, who won't scruple to use any means to get her own way."

"Oh dear me," said Miss Fleet, scandalised by the stark terms "nice" women were now employing. "She seemed such a sweet, truthful girl, and so quiet, one can hardly believe – But Euny dear, you *will* go and see poor Vin, won't you, next time? You're so much stronger now, and of course I'll come with you—"

"You!" said Eunice. The scorn in her voice was modified by a patronising warmth. "You mustn't think of going near a prison – it would upset you for weeks. And I'm sure I couldn't stand it, either. Miss Fennick can do as she likes. But I see no reason for her interference. I'd rather you didn't write to her again."

The sullen look came down like a shutter on the long, pale face. Miss Fleet gazed wistfully, and was silent. She was fond of Eunice, and grateful for the signs of affection that flickered in return. But the proud, wilful girl intimidated her. The urgings of a deeper collateral love and pity shrank back confused, and the plaintive "Whys?", "Can't we's?", "Shall we's?" lessened daily.

*   *   *

Tom Granger came home on leave, and Eunice returned to Taviton to see him. In any case the letting of Sycamore Cottage to new tenants required her presence. She was not quite satisfied with her agent's report of affairs. The elderly couple who had taken the house for a term wished to renew their agreement; but the agent stated he had received an offer of nearly twice the amount from a young pair, who were anxious to settle in immediately. There seemed no reason to doubt the fairness or the profitable nature of the transaction: but Eunice had an uneasy feeling about the old people. She knew them personally, and had made an amicable arrangement with them for retaining a room, which in fact meant the facility of using her home if she returned for a brief visit during their occupation.

On arrival, however, she found them packing up in happy mood. The man – a branch-manager of a multiple firm – had been promoted unexpectedly to another town, where a married daughter lived, and they were eager for the change.

Her mind relieved, Eunice telephoned to the agent, making an appointment to see the prospective tenants at his office in the morning. Then she settled down to await Tom's call. It was understood that she would not meet him under their stepmother's roof, nor under his own, which was also his wife's.

The brother and sister seemed, however, uncomfortable in each other's company, though no hostile third was present. Eunice was troubled at the change in smart, vigorous, hearty Tom. He was slack and listless in his shabby uniform; his haggard face had lost geniality. Always the garrulous one of the family, he was strangely laconic. After the first greetings, his assurance that he was "all right," a desultory interchange about Albert, who was with the Fleet, he had little to say. His silences and abruptness disconcerted her, and stiffened her own reluctance to talk.

"I've heard all about Vin," he said suddenly. "Where's he now?"

"In prison," she faltered.

"I know that. Which?"

She told him. He drummed with his fingers on the table.

"Been to see him there?"

"No."

"How's that?"

His stare confused her. She flushed.

"I – I couldn't."

He continued to stare, then dropped his lids.

"Oh, your illness, of course. But Gladys says you've been better a long while." There was a pause. "Sorry, Eunice, you've had such rotten luck—"

A longer pause. Then he said:

"When's the next visit due?"

"In a few days, I think."

"Don't you know for certain?"

"Yes. The tenth."

"That's the day after tomorrow. You're going, of course."

"No."

"No?"

She did not speak or look at him.

"Why the hell not?"

"Tom!"

"I said – why—why not?"

"I don't know why you should ask – in that way. You don't expect me to run to prisons, do you? – to see a man who refuses to do his duty?"

He got up and stood near her, glaring. She noticed the red streaks in his eyeballs, and the twitch of his wrists.

"Christ! So you're like the rest of the swine, are you? And I thought *you* had a heart!"

"I don't understand your language, Tom."

"Don't you? I don't understand yours. Thought you had pluck, too. Always knew how to get your own way. And now – you haven't the guts to stand by the only man in the family with sense."

Her head dropped. Instead of the haughty uplift she intended, her whole body sagged pitiably. He blinked, and scratched his chin.

"I thought you'd be different. Have all the women gone rotten? – listening to the preachers, I suppose. There's a fine lot here. Seen this?" He pulled out a local newspaper, and pointed to a headline – Clergy on Reprisals. He began to read in the hesitant, squeaky voice he had always used for unwonted recital.

"'Every effective stroke must be utilised,' said the Bishop to one of our representatives, who was received at the Palace. 'The object of our reprisals must be to do material damage to the enemy, and not to punish them for killing our women and children, though in carrying out our object it may unfortunately happen that non-combatants and women and children may be killed—' Bloody hypocrite. Here's another one, our Wesleyan minister, love 'is 'art – 'As we are at war with the Germans, we ought to go with our aeroplanes there, and do as much damage as we can.' – Why don't the swine come over and do it then, instead of spouting in pulpits and palaces? Ought to be shoved into the first aeroplane and dropped out with the bombs. Christ!" He flung the paper down and began to walk about. "Gladys says it's grand stuff, putting heart into the troops" – He spat and used an epithet which made his sister jerk her hands to her ears. "I couldn't talk to her – but I thought you – and now you tell me you've turned your back on your husband, because he don't believe in this rotten mess, and they've chucked him into clink. Haven't you got any decency? I'm ashamed of you." His tones were muffled, but when he stopped before her again, they rose into the squeak. "What a crew to come back to! I'll get to blazes out of this pretty quick. But Vincent – stuck in that cell, waiting one chance in months to see you – and you're not going! Euny—" he stuttered a little now – "you don't mean it, eh?"

"I do," she said stubbornly.

He burst into a loud laugh.

"Then *I'll* go! He'd sooner see me than nobody. And I'd sooner see him than anybody. Hell! That's a good one!" He laughed again, and seized his cap. "The tenth, is it? Last day of my leave. I'll sprint tomorrow and do it. So long."

He was out of the house before Eunice could move. She was bewildered rather than angry, and more hurt than either. Hurt, for the first time, with a rankling of guilt.

"It's Gladys," she assured herself. Her blatant sister-in-law – Gladys of the protuberant eyes, the flat cliff-like upper lip, and nagging, insensitive tongue – had got on Tom's nerves. "And he's working it off on me."

A changed Tom, indeed. The old or rather the young Tom had never been nervy, could never have worked off spleen in such nakedly circular terms, on the sister he had humoured, spoilt, admired as a superior being throughout their youthful lives. The early family pattern was smashed: the pattern of two sons with their father, simple, common-place, united in worship of the only girl, more refined, more fastidious, more cultured than themselves – a lady in her mother's image.

She was late next morning at the agent's office. The young couple were there, awaiting her. She greeted them pleasantly, and nodded in acquiescent manner to their proposals. The agent joked and laughed, an easy atmosphere prevailed, and the close of the interview hung on formalities. The husband, a portly youth very conscious of his uniform (he was doing clerical work at a recruiting depot), produced his pen and began to screw and unscrew the cap. The wife told Eunice for the twentieth time that she adored the cottage, thought it was furnished with charming taste, and considered it an ideal home. She was a vivacious girl in a smart hat and a rather long, full, summer coat, which she suddenly opened and slid back on her shoulders.

Almost as suddenly Eunice stopped listening. Her look set hard, and in a few curt words she excused herself and retired to an inner room with the agent. There she delivered her fiat.

"I won't have them. Not if they paid *four* times as much. It's useless arguing. My mind's made up."

"But, my dear Mrs. Fleet – *why*—?"

"She's going to have a child. I can't have children in the house."

Nothing would move her. The house could remain unlet – but she would not alter her decision. To the agent she was cold, unblushing, a senselessly obdurate client. In her bed that night she let her stubbornness run fluid, and wept bitterly for her lost motherhood. Not with remorse or regret for what she had done. Her heart renewed its rage against her husband, rage still fed by righteous self-pity. The blood in her veins had seethed with gall the moment she saw that another woman's child might be born in her home. In that moment she had known that she could not endure it.

Her house – hers and Vincent's – furnished as much with their thwarted dreams as with the toys of her "charming taste" – to become the "ideal home" for a stranger's firstborn! An intolerable vision. One that her instincts leaped at once to blot. Bad instincts, perhaps – cruel, spiteful, jealous: but none the less true and powerful.

Who was responsible for her plight, her ignoble reactions, her violation of the hopes of the innocent? – who but Vincent himself? Their life together had failed. She charged

him with the flagrance of the failure, absolving herself in
the flood of her tears.

*   *   *

She walked about the streets of Taviton on the tenth,
vaguely aware of commotion in the town. People were
hurrying hither and thither, there was a block of vehicular
traffic at an unexpected point, brazen music sounded, and
something like the tail of a procession wound ahead. Troops
marching through, perhaps. She did not look at passers-by
or listen to their talk. She was afraid of recognising, of being
recognised. Her visit home was hedged with aversions,
and she meant not to prolong it. One more interview with
her agent, and perhaps another with her father. Then off
again to Mold. At least there was a respite there from
familiar sights and sounds.

She walked about, careless of the fact that her husband
and her brother were facing each other with bars between.
It did not strike her as ironic: a soldier giving up his last
hours of leave to comfort an imprisoned C.O., whose wife
not only stayed away, but prevented the visit of a friend.
Eunice would not have liked such a version of her silence.
But she knew that silence was construed by Miss Fennick
as an intention to make the journey herself.

It happened that the girl could not have gone, though
she would have had no difficulty in finding a deputy.
Aware that Mrs. Fleet was not "in sympathy," Laura
Fennick did not guess the extent of the wife's feeling: she
could not imagine a deliberate will to let the visit go by
default. When, therefore, she met Eunice in the High Street,
her surprise was mitigated by the information that business
having called Mrs. Fleet to Taviton, Mrs. Fleet's brother had
gone to Vincent in her stead.

Fortunately for Eunice, who was not a good liar, and too conscious of having described Laura by that name, her brief announcement was not examined. Laura Fennick had no time for talk. She had been rushing by when they met, her midget figure in disorder, her hat awry, and a ribbon of material streaming from a rent in her sleeve. She clutched a bundle of pamphlets, a number of which slipped loose and strewed the pavement. Her head swung from left to right, as if in search of someone or something. It was obvious she was distracted and in haste.

"Come back with me to the hall, Mrs. Fleet," she urged. "Have you been there or were you just coming along?" But without waiting for a reply she took a step forward, jerked her head about, and added – "I'm looking for MacDonald and Mrs. Swanwick."

Eunice was startled. The bare statement had in it the elements of shock, even to one aloof from "peacemongering" campaigns. She had seen posters in the town, advertising a public meeting to be addressed by notorious pacifist leaders: she had seen, too, alongside these sheets, others in larger and tri-coloured type – red, blue and white – calling on loyal citizens to oppose the meeting and attend a prior demonstration in a church hall. These bills were signed by the minister of the church and a local Member of Parliament. They had achieved success, according to Laura Fennick.

"A hooligan's success," she said bitterly and a little breathlessly. Her short steps danced to outpace the other's reluctant stride. "You must have seen the procession – a lovely sight, wasn't it? Drunks and loafers, headed by our Bloated Parliamentary Patriot" (she emphasised each initial letter, so that they stood out in capitals), "waving the biggest Union Jack. Brass band playing 'Tipperary,' and 'See the Conquering Hero.' The other conquering hero was at the tail end, shepherding his flock. They smashed the doors in

and stormed the platform. Police couldn't or wouldn't stop
them. Our speakers had no chance – even Jimmy failed to
get a hearing. The police made him leave with the others
from the back. I think the men are all right – but I'm
anxious about Mrs. S. – couldn't find her anywhere. We got
separated at once. I was pushed all ways by the mob – the
audience and the hooligans were a frightful mix, and I was
lucky to get to an exit at all – intact. Except for this—" She
held her sleeve up ruefully, and tried to tuck the streamer
into the rent.

The hall which was the scene of conflict stood away in a
turning from the curved main street. As the corner came
into view, the crowd seething beyond spewed out clots,
each of which, dispersed by police, broke into straggling
pedestrians. Eunice had no intention of joining them: but
even as she stopped, Laura drew her into a side street and
thence into a lane, from which they emerged upon the back
doors of the hall. The space around was clear. Suddenly a
man dashed from the further end, waving an umbrella at a
taxi which followed. As the girls came up, a figure stepped
from one of the arched doorways.

"Why, it's Mac!" said Laura. "Thank Heaven *he's* all right.
But how funny Mog looks with the gamp—"

She giggled. The man gesticulating at the taxi had suddenly opened his umbrella wide in the sunshine, and screen-
ing the advancing figure, hustled it to the kerb. Laura dashed
forward, but the men jumped in and were driven off. She
ran after the taxi and disappeared round the bend.

Eunice stood still for a few seconds, then went back
through the lane. Her heart, to her own surprise, was thump-
ing a little. She was relieved to have escaped her companion: but her paramount emotion was a queer sense of having
had a big moment.

The smashing of a peace meeting scarcely touched her.

The Bloated Patriot with his gang, the hunted pacifists, Laura Fennick's fuss – the whole thing was repellent, and she oughtn't to have let herself be drawn into the ragged sequel. Ridiculous as well as disgusting. No wonder that even Laura laughed (hysterically, no doubt) at the little stout man opening his gamp in the sun to hide the long-limbed fugitive. A Charlie Chaplin-like scene. Yet she could not as much as smile, because in that preliminary instant, meeting the eyes of the man who stepped from the arch, she was aware of greatness.

There before her, in a brief space which sufficed for vivid impression, was the man who centred in himself the vituperation of British loyalists. The most hated and reviled man in his country: the hero of a small outcast group. She did not know the extent of that faint span of honour. She knew, however, that Vincent worshipped him, as a strong young mind worships a master.

A vivid impression, but contradictory. Tall, spare, a figure at once humped and erect – sagging and firm – shabby, almost trampish, with a gold chain sparkling under the loose coat – wild dark locks rumpling a powerful brow, a sensitive nose over a coarse moustache, a chin sunk yet proud; a deject, scarified, fleeing man with a kingly, indomitable air. The glance of those deep, fiery, indrawn eyes struck like a lightning shaft.

Confused, Eunice hurried through the lane, took a wrong turning, and found herself on the frizzling edge of the mob. The main entrance to the hall was barred, but people still swarmed around; a loud-voiced man in a clerical collar harangued them from a stand, and shouts, bursts of laughter, and shrill whistling answered him. A drum was beating a little way off, and suddenly there was a rush, men and women pushed and screamed, and above their heads and upraised arms a figure was hoisted. It was the leader of the patriots. Eunice saw his huge red puffy face, his rolling venous neck and tremendous paunch. Waving his hands, and letting them drop in strangely feeble flaps, he emitted hoarse, indistinct sounds. His supporters yelled back and hoisted him still higher, so that his feet in thick, unlaced boots could be seen slipping feebly, like his hands, over jerking shoulders beneath. He opened his mouth again, but instead of words, a yellow froth dribbled out.

Eunice skirted the High Street and turned into a café. It was still early in the afternoon, but a number of persons were sitting at the little tables. She chose a curtained recess, from which she had a side view of a similar niche in the opposite wall. A lady occupied it, quietly drinking tea, looking so calm, so peaceful, so remote from stress and turmoil, that Eunice felt as if a soothing hand had been laid on her own harassed soul.

Without curiosity, she stared across. The lady's large hat did not conceal her face. It was large, too, but clearcut, and rather fine in its composure. She was fair, and seemed to have a mass of straw-coloured hair. Her blue eyes gazed unblinking at her cup.

Eunice sighed. Calm – quietude. As well to rest here for a little while, until the street was clear of rowdies. The agent's office was only a short way up: but she debated now whether it was worth while seeing him. Her business could be done by letter. Suppose she went home, packed her few things, and left at once? She would send a wire to Mold. Why stay another night, to be racked and pestered at every turn?

She moved out of her niche to find a waitress, and came face to face with Laura Fennick. The small creature clutched at her.

"Oh, you're here! I thought I'd try this as a last resort – I suppose you haven't seen Mrs. Swanwick?"

"I don't know her—" began Eunice stiffly. The other, peering around, gave a little cry:

"Why, there she is – at last" – and bounded across to the opposite recess. The calm lady received her with a smile.

*　　　*　　　*

Eunice was not surprised to hear, when she was back in Mold, of Laura Fennick's arrest under the Defence of the Realm Act, for distributing seditious literature in the streets. The fact that the literature in question was defended as innocuous, being passages from the Sermon on the Mount, a speech by Snowden recorded in Hansard, and a newspaper report of the trial of a C.O., strung together by a plea for the just administration of the Military Service Acts, did not modify her crime. The law was outraged, and so was the sentiment of the war-blown public. Laura received a sentence of three months' imprisonment, reduced on appeal to six weeks or a fine. She was, as a matter-of-fact, extremely fortunate. More important persons than herself were sent to prison for six months on a similar charge, without alteration of judgment on appeal. The visiting Recorder who revised her case was possibly less enamoured of "Dora" than the local justice; and possibly, too, he did not think the little girl before him was a great danger to the State. Her sister paid the fine, to Laura's disgust. But since their brother needed her at a critical stage of his own incarceration, she could not insist on going to prison. And she agreed that two nights in a cell made sufficient martyrdom.

Eunice read of the case in the *Taviton Post*, which was sent to her at Mold. No communication passed between her and Laura, nor did Aunt Carry dare to write as much as a post card to the "dangerous little crank with distorted views." Aunt Carry was sorry for the foolish young woman,

who was quite nice in other respects: but it was wiser, as
Eunice said, not to invite correspondence that might be
subject to proceedings in a court of law.

Aunt Carry had no idea that Eunice herself was weaken-
ing in the matter of letters to prison. But then the old lady
had not been shown the message which arrived from Tom.

"For God's sake, Euny," the brother wrote, "go and see
your husband. Pale as a sheet and thin as a rake, with a
cough that shakes him to pieces. He hadn't much to say.
Think of that! His being mum upset me most, and I told
him a lot of lies, though I hope they aren't, not all. Said you
were pining for him and so on, but wasn't equal to the
jaunt. You'll go next time, though, won't you? You're a
sport, old girl, I know. Knocked out a bit, but it's not like
you to sulk because you've had a blow. Sorry I left in a rush
without seeing you again. Make it up some time. This
lovely war'll be over in ten years or so. I'll come home
every birthday – I don't think. Well, cheerio!"

A week before "next time," Laura Fennick was on her
way to Liverpool, wrestling with the task of her brother's
release. She managed, in the midst of her distractions, to
send a brief reminder of the date to Mold. It was so brief
that it was curt, and like a command. But Laura had no
dictatorial intention. She did not credit Eunice with avoid-
ance of the visit. She wrote in a hurry, and on a pre-
cautionary impulse, which familiarity with C.O.'s helpless
relatives had made recurrent. The message, however, had
an effect contrary to her wish. Eunice, almost ready for the
journey, abandoned the idea. She would not be driven into
going. Tom was bad enough. But how dare that wretched
little crank presume to order her? She tightened her lips
perversely, and decided not to go. A letter, perhaps . . . that
was different. She might write to Vincent at last – as uncom-
plainingly, as solicitously, as she could. Her magnanimity,

she thought, impressed Aunt Carry, whose additions were cut down ruthlessly to an expression of fondest love. She agreed, however, to mention Wallace Paige and commend that blundering youth's meed of national service.

The letter was not easy to write. She dallied with it for days, excised and altered (she was particularly careful not to be too affectionate – that would be "encouragement," exceeding the purpose of a considerate, though irrevocably aggrieved, wife). Several copies were made before it was despatched. What an affront, therefore, to receive it back! But the covering sheet from the Governor contained an astounding piece of news.

"Private Fleet" – it ran – "has rejoined his regiment, which was ordered abroad on active service. He is now somewhere in France. No doubt a letter addressed to the War Office will be duly forwarded."

Eunice showed it to Aunt Carry with a hand that did not shake.

"Good gracious!" said Aunt Carry. She fumbled with her spectacles and read the letter twice. Then she looked at Eunice in consternation.

"Oh, my dear, what does it mean?"

"It means," said Eunice smiling – "it means that Vin has given in at last."

*   *   *

The information conveyed in the Governor's letter was technically correct. Vincent had earned a slight remission of his second term of imprisonment – whether on grounds of health or conduct was not clear: at any rate he found himself, much sooner than he expected, back at a military camp. Here he prepared for a third court-martial; and here, also, he found a friendly soldier willing to smuggle letters.

But though neither the friendliness nor the willingness of the soldier was at fault, the letters – pencilled jottings on odd scraps of paper, margins, flaps of envelopes, cigarette packets, lavatory slips – took a long time to reach their destination. The soldier had his own preoccupations, got drunk several times too often, was "C.B.'d" without, he contended, due cause, brooded on his wrongs, and then, being a humorist, over-celebrated his rights. Finally he forgot everything in the excitement of being ordered to France, with two days' special leave. Somehow the scraps of letters were kept intact throughout his adventures, and in the end were held up only for lack of stamps. The money Vincent had given him had been used for more urgent needs. Fortunately it occurred to him at the last moment that stamps didn't matter, one of the two "gals" (it worried him a trifle that he couldn't remember which of the two – "fancy" or wife – should be the recipient) would doubtless be glad enough to pay up double. So he wrapped up the bits of cardboard and paper with a contribution of his own, tied the brown bundle with string, scribbled over it one of the two addresses, and squeezed it into a pillar-box.

In this way Laura Fennick received the first intimation of what had happened to Vincent Fleet. She did not stop to read the bundle through. The freshest of the writings, and the soldier's note, were enough to send her flying from home.

"Dear Madam" – wrote the soldier – "Please excuse my posting without stamps I got none and don't like to wait till I do. Your friend was treated very bad because he won't do nothing. He's a sticker no mistake I wish I had his guts if you'll excuse me Madam. But he's no match for the army and if he don't give in on board ship or when they fix him in irons at Bouloin like they did the other conchies he'll be up against it no error. So look out. Excuse me madam not signing my trew name but I don't fancy clink myself. I adsum.

Yours respectfully,

T. ATKINS."

Laura flashed like a meteor from Taviton to London, trailing a shower of telegrams like angry sparks. She had achieved one miracle and was ready for another. Her brother, discharged from prison, was at home, safe in the skilled care of their nursing sister. She was free to cope with the "newest outrage" – the Army's defiance of civil authority by continued despatch of C.O.'s to the front. The practice had not been as successful as patriots hoped. One or two victims of physical torture had "given in," and added some doubtful soldiers to the fighting ranks: but the rest, though paraded before troops and solemnly condemned to death, remained inflexible. Yet they were not shot forthwith. Parliamentary friends having acted in time, they were reprieved at the sixtieth second, and their sentences commuted – to ten years' penal servitude. It was not believed that the army in France, having more desperate work in hand, would be troubled with more of this recalcitrant and demoralising material. But the army at home thought differently. Relays of objectors crossed the Channel, to be "lamed" by crucifixion and the ordeal by paper. Being "read out" to death was a pretty grim farce, as effective as the real thing. To Laura Fennick it was incredible that the actual shot never followed. She had no faith in the military machine and none in official assurance. Accordingly Whitehall and the Fellowship – which had its own Records and Departmental offices, with the difference that its short-haired, tea-drinking staffs proved prompt and efficient – were riven with her alarms. It may have been due to her, as much as to the inevitable course of events, that Vincent Fleet came back again to an English gaol.

But he did not serve his third term. The war, despite Tom Granger's prophecy, did not last as long. Release came to Vincent from a different cause. A week after his return he was in hospital with pneumonia. One day Eunice received a message from the Governor, asking her to come immediately to her husband, who was seriously ill. She was in Taviton, having been urged home by Laura Fennick. As they were leaving together, a telegram came to say that Vincent Fleet was dead.

*   *   *

Young Tom Granger had perceived, to his sister's propitiation, that she suffered from a blow: but that blow, vast to her senses hitherto, shrank to a pin scratch before the hammer of widowhood. It struck, and all her past seemed blotted out. Her future had no existence.

Vincent gone! Vincent, who had always been there. Infantile years did not count. Life – memory – began with Vincent teasing, admiring, desiring, holding. The central point in the pattern of her days, whether bright or dull. The background on which to lavish all her moods, kind or cruel. A responsive background, but responsive always with the colour and note of love. And it had vanished. Completely, irrevocably. There was nothing to see, to hear, to tread on, to lean against – nothing but dark, empty space.

Thus the ego, reeling under the blow. If she had cared for him at all, was not this but selfish caring, the grief of the deprived? Laura Fennick thought so, observing her tears. She wept gracefully, since the tears were only for herself.

But it was obvious she was dazed, in fact stunned. She took no steps of any kind, allowed everyone to come and go as they pleased, submitted to be directed and fussed over by her father, Aunt Carry, even her sisters-in-law, hardly able to conceal their satisfaction in a righteous doom. There was not much to do for poor Vincent, but Laura Fennick did it all, or arranged for it to be done, decently and expeditiously.

Too decently and expeditiously for the little creature herself, whose grief spilled over into protest. Her services were offered and accepted without bias. She was useful in emergency, as full of resources as the sea of fish. Promptly to hand, aware of the right course to adopt, the right person to see, the right message to send, the right train to catch. Ready for any journey, for any obnoxious errand. But she soon exceeded her welcome and the duties of a mourner. The Grangers heard with horror that she proposed to raise a clamour – for inquiry, investigation; a public poking into the treatment of Vincent Fleet that might blow clouds of scandal – over the Government, the Home Office, the War Office, the prisons and military camps, said Laura; over the family, said old Granger, and put his foot down sternly. Since Eunice, stricken mute, made dumb assent to the stamping foot, the stranger could do nothing. She may have had reasons for refraining. The "family" received her consideration, but not her sympathy. Her bright brown eyes were hard with scorn, even while she proffered help. How were they to know that she would have avoided the Cottage, and ceased all contact with its owner, but for the dead man's injunction – "Do all you can for her?"

On the day before Miss Fleet's departure, the three women were together. Aunt Carry renewed her plea to Eunice to accompany her back to Mold – "for good." On this point the widow was resistant. She would not give up the Cottage. Aunt Carry might stay as long as she liked: but if Aunt Carry was obliged to live in Mold, Eunice meant to continue alone. She could not explain her feeling. But it was simply that the farm, once a refuge from Vincent, now seemed a desert from which she could not reach him. They had never been together there; it held for her no symbol of his being. Here, in their home, she might regain at least the illusion of their partnership. It was a scarcely conscious clinging to his spirit.

"Don't you think mine's the best plan, dear Miss Fennick?" persisted the old lady.

"I suppose so," said Laura abruptly. She addressed herself to Eunice, lying on the settee. "Get right away from it all. Forget you ever had a husband."

Eunice took no notice of the crudely bitter words. She wished to say, "I don't want to forget," but instead she murmured languidly, "Vin would not like my giving up the Cottage."

And at that Laura burst out in anguish – "Oh my God, isn't it rather late to think of what he would like? Why didn't you think of it before? Why did you keep away from him? Why didn't you write a single word? Why did you let him die of a broken heart?"

"My dear Miss Fennick!" Aunt Carry was aghast. She had never seen the little person in such a state. Laura seemed beside herself. She had sprung from her chair, where she had been sitting in quietude, with legs dangling childishly above the floor, to a strident posture near the settee. Her lifted arm shook alarmingly.

"You killed him, and you know it!"

Eunice turned her head and looked at her, but did not speak.

"Dear me, dear me, Miss Fennick, what a dreadful thing to say! Poor Vin's sudden illness in prison—"

"Sudden, indeed! Not so sudden. And as to prison – yes, that and the barracks, hardships, persecution, the war and the whole beastly business – enough to break the strongest man, body and spirit. I know that too well. But Vincent wasn't broken by *them*. He could have got over his illness, serious as it was. Wasn't my brother worse? They believed he was dying when I brought him home. But he wanted to live, because he knew *we* wanted him – my sister and I – desperately. And weak as he was, he lives. Vincent was strong – healthy enough for a dozen – he need never have got into a hopeless state. He had rough times, God knows – but he could have recovered if he'd wanted to. But he didn't – because his wife, whom he loved so dearly, turned her back on him, refused to have anything to do with him, ignored his appeals—" She choked, struggled, recovered her voice on a hysterical note – "I say she is his murderess!"

Eunice had withdrawn her gaze, but lay without moving, silent and pale. Miss Fleet watched her in alarm. How strange that she did not rise in haughty rage and banish the offender from her sight. Protest came tremulous from the old lady's lips.

"You have no right to say such shocking things, Miss Fennick. Of course you've been very good, and we know you feel it. But naturally we all loved poor Vin – even if we didn't agree with his ideas—"

"Then why didn't she visit him – why did she never write – oh, it was cruel, heartless, to treat him in that way. He longed so much for just a word – each time the disappointment was awful – he could have stood the blanks between – but the deliberate silence – the deliberate staying away – when he realised that – it was too much. He couldn't stand the thought that his wife had abandoned him. He couldn't stand that, so he just gave up—"

Eunice did not lift her face or her eyes, but she spoke now, almost in a whisper:

"How do you know?"

Miss Fennick snatched up her attache case and opened it. She drew out a packet and flung it on the settee.

"Read those," she said harshly. "Some are for you and some for me. They were mixed up when I got them, so I read them all. I couldn't bring myself to show them to you. Because he— But why shouldn't you read them? Not that you don't know what you've done. He was the finest man I ever knew. And you let him die like a dog."

Eunice did not touch the packet near her hand.

"I didn't," she said, in the same low tone. "I didn't know he would die. You oughtn't to say that. Besides, I *did* write – in the end—"

"The end – oh, yes! What was the good of that? When it was too late!"

Eunice spoke up a little strangely.

"Why didn't *you* try harder? I suppose *you* wanted him to live – didn't he know you wanted it?"

The fire died out of the little creature's bearing. She seemed to droop.

"*My* wanting didn't matter to him. It was you – only you – he thought of. But it's true I didn't try hard enough. I didn't write or inquire enough – I – I had my hands full – but – I could have tried more, I admit—" She threw her head back stiffly – "Oh, what was the use? It was only *you* he cared for – and it was *your* failing him that mattered."

There was defiance in the admission as well as in the charge. For a moment they stared deeply into each other's eyes. Eunice seemed to be seeing Laura for the first time. She had never been more than half-aware of the small person, the nondescript creature moved by a certain amount of unpleasing but occasionally useful energy. Now she saw – the same slight exterior. But it had grown, expanded with some inner significance. The face was bolder and more vivid. It had definite features, set in warm russet skin; two glowing eyes, a piquant nose, a pair of rich mobile lips, a dimple-cleft chin. Above was a finely-moulded brow with soft hair drawn across. Signals from within gave fuller meaning to a face already set to receive them: a face to interest – attract – a man, in tune with the spirit behind.

Disturbance followed the impression. Eunice frowned and made her first impatient gesture: warding off Miss Fleet's anxiety, relieving and intimidating the old lady at once by reacting in her normal manner.

But Laura Fennick was not abashed by it. She stood there looking an embodied accusation. Some hidden conflict, and not the widow's repudiatory air, made her rush away, crying as she turned – "I can't forgive myself – I can't forgive *you*!"

*   *   *

Miss Fleet went back alone to Mold, her relief double-edged. Reassuring as it was to see dear Eunice moved out of her mourning daze, stiffen rather than collapse under a wicked charge – that charge itself revived Aunt Carry's doubts. Of course Laura Fennick was a crank: of course dear Eunice had been the victim of poor Vin's wrong-headedness. She had never sent him a harsh word, she could not have prevented his succumbing to pneumonia. Nevertheless, dear Eunice – sweet enough to Aunt Carry herself – had been hard as a wife, perhaps fatally unkind.

The old lady pondered in agitation all the way to Mold, and came to judgment with weeping eyes. A rare spot of gall embittered the gentle tears. Poor Vin was in his grave. No Fleet remained to cheer an old aunt's age. The Grangers' claim to Eunice, stronger than her own, must be riveted by sorrow and propinquity: she found she could relinquish it, not unwillingly. A spot of gall can be a powerful dissolvent. It eats into affection, it spreads from human tissue to legal document. It was to affect a clause in Caroline Fleet's last testament, when she had pondered still longer in the remoteness of Mold.

But of this, even if she had known, Eunice would not have complained. She was careless about money as about love. Enough had always flowed around her to make it seem inevitable and constant. Apart from her home, and Vincent's nest-egg in the bank, the inheritance from his parents which passed to her, there was her father's generous allowance. Her bond with old Miss Fleet was slight enough. But no mercenary link had held it.

Eunice brooded for a time over Laura Fennick's packet, without any attempt to examine it. She had no curiosity about the contents. Letters, documents – information of trials, sentences, whereabouts, prison regulations: in and around these there could be only familiar fact and opinion. Familiar and exacerbating in reminder. She thought she had forgiven Vincent everything, even the deception he had not practised on her. Wasn't it natural that her anger should revive, that even the shock of his passing did not quite dissolve it? For even his death spread the taint of his living shame. Gladys Granger proclaimed it in the hour of mourning – "Fancy one's husband dying in prison!" The insult, thrown like a missile from the cliff-like mouth, scarcely penetrated the widow's mind. Only the thinnest glaze of her anger remained. But such a glaze may keep another's rage from soaking through. When anger, however, is gone – when the last thin glaze melts away, then insult and accusation sink deeply within. Roaming about house and garden after Miss Fleet had left, trying to help her maid in household tasks, Eunice brooded on the packet and the scene with Laura, remembered the censure in her fierce words, in Aunt Carry's remorseful bearing, in Gladys

Granger's malice, in Lallie's patronising condolences. But none of these things stung. It was not that she could forgive in every case as she forgave dead Vincent. It was simply that she was weary of rancour, and that there was a great gap in her heart that felt like a bottomless pit, into which everything might fall – good words and ill – without filling a fraction of space.

Once as she stood in the middle of the room, staring through the window at the broad-leaved sycamore, she recalled how she had rushed to Vincent here and asked him to marry her. The warmth of his hug enfolded her an instant, then faded away. How cold, how empty, the room – how much colder, more empty, the space in her heart. There was no Vincent in the world to calefy her. If she might strike a ray from his written words—? She moved to a drawer and fetched the packet, sat down at a table, and pulled out the file of papers.

A medley of bits, soiled and crumpled. Laura had fastened them together with some attempt at order. But they were not easy to follow. One could only try to read them as they came – here and there a blue or white form, prison and army sheets, their margins filled irrelevantly; but mostly odd scraps torn and stained, webbed with faint pencil scrawl, some almost illegible through criss-crossing. Full paragraphs alternated with disjointed phrases, quotations, accounts of punishment in task and diet, dates, names, reports. A few of the jottings could not have been messages. They seemed like diary notes. How they were concealed was a mystery. One or two must have reached Laura in earlier days, for she had added them with dated comment. Others had been folded into a cover of envelope shape on which Vincent had written "Keep for me." But the soldier must have unfolded and mixed them with the rest, as Laura surmised and noted. The same thing had happened with the letter to Eunice, which was separated from the inscription of her name and address. Though more familiar with his writing than Laura could be, Eunice found classification more difficult. But that, after all, did not matter much. She read each scrap that her finger turned. The reports to Laura had the fraternal intimacy that the wife might once have resented, with disdain if not with suspicion; if she winced now it was for other reasons. Two sentences recurred throughout – "Keep in touch with my wife" – "Don't tell my wife." They received a ghastly illumination from the rest of the text.

*   *   *

. . . Found an inch of pencil today, no matter how. Priceless jewel. Wonder if I shall ever catch the post. Most likely catch P.D.

. . . Worse than Mil. detention. Frightful combination – being cut off, shut in, caged, put away in a box 11 by 7 – with the constant surveillance of spyhole. Knowing one can't move, sit, stand, breathe, without an eye looking on – perhaps a sudden shout, an order *not* to do what you are doing, or to do what you are not. . . . Oh God, what a worm, what an insect one feels.

. . . It was funny at exercise that first day. The savage-looking hulk in front with a fierce beard I took to be a murderer at least. He was the gentle Quaker H. But the meek little man behind was an old hand. He whispered to me – "I'm here for trying to do a man in. What'r you here for?" – "For *not* trying to do a man in" – Pause, then whisper again – "Gawdstrewth!"

. . . If I only knew about E. otherwise calm, confident,

never clearer in my mind, never more certain. My soul is free. All the free souls who have been in prison before me . . . great task given us to do. Not only now. After it's over – the slaughter, hate, chaos, wreckage – new world to come. Work for reason, justice, brotherhood. Ideals must come to earth. Practical schemes. Wish I could communicate with F. and A. Can F. visit me? Three allowed. But only want one first. Six weeks yet. E. will come. I'll see, I'll hear her. God bless my d. God keep me to the mark . . .

. . . Conquer it. Strength. My mind's my own. Another month – 672 hrs. – 40,320 min. before I can write home – before I can get letter. Eternity, where is thy sting? . . .

. . . I wish I knew about my wife. Please keep in touch with her – if away, write as often as you can. She must be making a very slow convalescence at Mold. I'm eagerly awaiting news . . .

. . . So they sacked you for refusing to Trafalgar. Good girl. I heard just *before* I got out. How? Things travel round the exercise yard. B – you remember him? was behind me (He's still there). In front was a C.O. from Cardiff. When I passed the news, he said (ventriloquially, of course) Traf-fic-vulgar. Laura, forgive him – it was the best he could do. . . . Cheerio. Keep out of gaol if you can. If you can't – well – bring in your "lustre and perfume." Remember Cowper? *You'll* never be "a weed." . . .

. . . No, I don't want to go back. At least there's the human touch in camps. Harv. was unlucky. You've done marvels for him – good thing you got hold of Furnall. – The men here are decent. Some of them listen, which isn't good for the army, but mighty good for the world. Of course they say the conchies are mugs. But one said, "We're bigger ones, if you arsks me!" Expect to be read out today. Here are the names . . .

. . . She didn't come. Why? Why doesn't she write? Aunt C. says all's well. My d. can't mean to be cruel. How can I go on if she – no, I won't think it. If L. could talk to her – no, I can't let L. on to this. Not fair to my d. She'll come next time. She'll come. She'll come. I'll will her. No, she'll will herself. . . .

Sorry my last letter home was two weeks late. Hope my wife wasn't too anxious. Naturally I couldn't explain! No letters, no visits – it was pretty hellish. Punishment, of course. For passing bread to another chap. He's always hungry, poor devil. I'm not. At least not now. Once I found an insect in my dinner, and it put me right off. Anyway, the stuff gives one indigestion. . . . It's a rotten system. No wonder criminals are made in prison. Some of us must look deep into this when we come out for good. . . . This time my window is of opaque glass, so even when I reached it by stretching my bones, I couldn't see out. Beastly disappointing. Silly, but it "got" me. P.D. again for sulks. A likely cure. Don't tell my wife. . . .

E. can't be forgetting me. She can't, already. Already? It's a year – ten million years. I forget a lot myself. Why I'm here. War, peace, work to be done. Not really, though. One frets about little things. Nonsense. It all comes back. As to forgetting E. – what a joke. As much as if *she* could . . .

Hospital again. A relief to know flu' is cause of depression. Awful nights, sleepless. Worrying about E. Why doesn't she write, is she well? Feeling all is lost. Haunted by facts of war learned in camp. World seems full of irredeemable horror. Will the ghastly business ever end? My effort – efforts of comrades – puny – futile. Who cares? Why am I shut away from the world – from my love – Eunice, Eunice, I want you, I want to shout your name. Am I getting dotty?

. . . Thank God for physical ills. I could bless the pain in my chest. Doctor's been. Blunt, but fairly decent. Says there's nothing wrong but a cold, touch of flu'. Says I'm sound – of course I am. Cough's nothing. Mustn't tell E. Think out cheerful letter. Perhaps she'll come.

Refused the scheme. It's a trap. Must be. Poor Aunt C. She can't know. But if E. – if it made her change. . . . Five have gone. Good chaps, straight, never give in. Why not? I'd have E. back. I could go home. See her, no bars. Have her to myself. Oh God, I must, I will. I wrote God. Who is He? Where? Still small voice. Conscience. Am I a C.O.? Aren't the five who went? Nothing to do with me. Don't go by others. Is it right for *me*? If it's only for E. – only – only my life, my love—

> But there is yet a liberty, unsung
> By poets, and by senators unpraised,
> Which monarchs cannot grant, nor all the powers
> Of earth and hell confederate take away:
> A liberty, which persecution, fraud,
> Oppression, prisons, have no power to bind;
> Which whoso tastes, can be enslaved no more.

Good thing I memorised Cowper. Never thought *The Task* would help me to sleep.

Notes for next Court-martial.

I still believe war to be wrong, a savage and utterly futile method of settling disputes. I still believe it my duty to humanity to refuse participation in the present war. All I know of the conditions prove the soundness of my belief. There seems to me no sort of justification for the continuance of slaughter and destruction, when the negotiations for peace which must eventually take place might as well begin today, and save millions of men from injury and death. . . .

I have been asked to accept "alternative service," whatever that may mean. Some C.O.'s have accepted it. They
have never had any objection to doing national work under
a civil authority. They believe they have successfully resisted militarism, and see no difference between civil work
outside and *inside* a prison. Everyone must judge for himself. To me "alternative service" seems a kind of industrial
conscription. And as I am opposed to every form of conscription, as to every form of war, I cannot agree to undertake it. . . .

I believe in the freedom of personality. Military discipline crushes this freedom, paralyses the will and judgment
of the individual, and enslaves him to a cruel and con-
temptible system. . . .

. . . So here I am, waiting for the usual farce. But there
are all sorts of rumours. Last week seven C.O.'s went out
from here to France. It isn't supposed to be done now, is it?
Thought the Fellowship had got it stopped. That lot were
frog-marched to the station, while the band played the
Dead March. I haven't got all the names, but I'll write
down as many as I know on the back of this. . . .

I hear that King and Snowden have kicked up ructions
in the House about B— and H—. Good work. All the same,
I don't think too much fuss ought to be made about hardships. There's the inevitable comparison with the sufferings
in the trenches. It's the spirit of persecution that's so revolt-
ing. . . . Loss of liberty, loss of human dignity. . . . Not
always the big things, but the little things, bring degradation, paralysis of the higher faculties. The stage when
one can't think – when one's mind gets numb. . . .

Physical ill-treatment can be serious, of course, for the
weaker chaps. This is the roughest place I've been at. They
think nothing of using handcuffs and ropes, kicking the
bound, chaining one to walls with hands upraised. Yester-

day I refused to do pack drill. They stripped me and turned on the hose – with sewage water. Worst of it was standing for an hour, drenched, in a bitter wind. It's pretty bleak up here. I can't get rid of my cold. Don't tell my wife of this. I wonder if you have seen her lately. . . .

If only they'd get on with the C.M. But they say they mean to break me first. What fools. . . . Two more C.O.'s came in today. Their names are—

Things are easier now. The officers have stopped roughing us. The men won't do it. Not bad fellows. They don't get much better treatment themselves. There's a particular brute here. . . .

I hear we are to be sent to France. The idea is that we shall be given the chance of disobeying orders at the front, where of course we are liable to be shot. I'm not sure that wouldn't be the best thing. But I don't really pine to be a martyr. And strange as it may seem, I'm not sure that I'm quite sick of my life. So I think something ought to be done to checkmate these military fellows. Or do the Big Civilians want it as well? Has Asquith gone blotto? Parliament doesn't seem to mean much nowadays. I've heard of Ponsonby's magnificent speech. Do you ever meet Furnall? He ought to know about things. . . .

My guard's just told me – marching orders any minute. I'll write again when I can. I've some scraps I want you to take care of. I hope to see you yet. But if not you'll know I've served my turn. You'll keep in touch with my wife, won't you? Do all you can for her. Yours in the hope of a saner world,

V. F.

The last? There was nothing more on the clip. "Yours in the hope" – and the end – Eunice clutched the papers tight, let them drop, and her hands fell limply over them. Her face was rigid, staring. The muscles round her heart seemed

to be contracting: in the great empty space a core of pain
grew fast.

"Vin – my Vin – my poor darling—"

She sobbed tearlessly. The tale of his suffering, unrolled
before her, was frightful, unbearable. What had she done?
What had they all done? Why hadn't she known of these
things before? Why hadn't she *thought* of them?

Laura Fennick knew, and wanted to show them up. She
was right. They ought to be exposed – they were illegal,
unjust, un-English. She forgot her own acquiescence in the
punishment of shirkers. But she had not imagined brutali-
ties like these. She would never have approved even in the
heat of her anger, of such treatment of any C.O. And especially of a C.O. like Vin – brave, sincere, fastidious – oh
God, her own husband, whose body was dear to her—

She pushed the papers away, covered her eyes with her
hands, and bowed her head on the table.

He was dead. It was too late. Nothing could be done.
And nobody cared. Her family, condoling with her, rebuked
and made light. "It's a pity, but it can't be helped. Perhaps
it's for the best." Lallie made it clearer. She said, "Buck up,
no need to mope. There are thousands of young widows
who deserve more sympathy – widows of men killed in
fighting for their country – and *they* are quite bright and
cheerful."

Yes, that was it – those widows were covered with glory
– widows of heroes greatly praised. Perhaps they felt the
sorrow of bereavement just the same. When a dear one was
lost, could one stop to consider *how*? But one did – one
ought, at any rate, to find the sorrow eased by the balm of
homage. "He died for his country – *you* gave him to the
country – be proud of the sacrifice – smile, rejoice!" Mothers
rejoiced in the sacrifices to Moloch. She shuddered, hearing
Vincent's voice. He had said it long ago. He was spat on for

saying it – cursed – hounded. So he died in shame. And she, the widow of a shirker, an outcast, a felon, must not presume to bewail her loss, must hide her double load of disgrace and pain. But it was pain alone she felt. More on more pain. The anguish of bereavement and something over. She had lost her husband, her gay companion, her lover – "the finest man I ever knew." Must it matter *how* she had lost him? Oh, Heaven, it mattered horribly – but not in the way the others thought. Only in Laura Fennick's way. Laura knew – understood – accused. Whom did she accuse? Everybody. Herself. Most of all, the wife.

Eunice felt the spasms round her heart leap sharp and stringent. She gasped and lifted her head for air.

"Vincent, I didn't mean – I didn't mean to add to your suffering—"

But she did. She knew she had meant it. She had told Aunt Carry so.

"I thought – I thought it would help to change you – to make things come right again—"

Yes, but she had meant to punish him, too. She could not deny her vindictiveness. It loomed black before her, blotting out the light of her justifications. For all the while, he had been crying out to her, beseeching her, even between the lines of his official letters, the few brave half-defiant, half-formal protestations that sensitive Vin knew his jailers must read. Who but his wife knew how sensitive Vin was, how shy beneath the ready flow of talk? And if he had not always been so patient, so blindly loving – if he had grown angry with her, excused her less, wanted her less tenderly – if she had not loved him, too, in her spoilt, stubborn soul – could she have read so clearly in those scraps his misery, his desperate need, his despair at her abandonment of him?

Eunice groaned and seized the papers. She wanted to put them from her sight. The file would not go smoothly back into its case. A twisted slip blocked a corner and she pulled it out mechanically. It was something she had not seen before – a close-folded sheet, fastened with a pin. She opened it and read.

"My beloved wife, why have you never written? If you couldn't come to see me, surely you could write a message? I don't mean to reproach you, dearest. I know my poor girl has been very ill and very miserable. But if you could only realise the torture – to count the days and nights, every hour and every minute, for a sight of my love – to hunger in vain for a word. Nothing else hurts as much. I said I could stand it all, and I have and will. Every fresh punishment is only a further test, after all – But if only I could have seen you once – oh, my darling, that day when Tom came instead of you – when he said you had sent your love and cried because you hadn't the strength to come – I felt distraught and overjoyed at the same moment. To have the assurance of your love was heaven. Don't let me fall to hell again by doubting that I ever heard Tom say it – by doubting Tom himself. I want it from yourself – in your own dear hand, at least. My darling, you must be better now. Don't let the past grieve and weaken you. Nurse yourself for me, my precious wife. One day this terrible separation will end. The dark cloud of war and suffering must pass, men will come to their senses. That day cannot be far off. Again I am in the hands of the military, ready for my next court-martial, and any other chance to witness to the truth. But it is hard to be merely passive, hard to be able to do nothing but resist. And so hard, darling, to have no word from you – except the blessed word through Tom. Good old Tom. He wished me luck and told me to stick it. Wasn't it great – Tom saying that on his way back to the trenches? When you write to him tell him how grateful I am. I couldn't say much at the time, I felt all choked up. My paper's running out. I hope you can read this. Are you at home or in Mold? How is Aunt Carry? Are you together? Does your father help you? Do you see Laura Fennick? Write at once and tell me everything, dearest – or at least send me a few words to tell me you are better and stronger, and still love

Your always loving husband.—

Burning tears were in her eyes. Tears that seemed to come from a lake of fire and scorch her lids. She pressed the dirty paper to her mouth.

"Forgive me, darling – forgive me! I didn't know—" She shivered with self-horror – "It's true what she said. It's true. *I* killed you. *I* am your murderess."

The pain surged up, brimmed over the edge, fell into the great pool of Vincent's agony. She gave a choking cry and tumbled from her chair. The little maid ran in and found her, unconscious on the floor.

*   *   *

Another summer came, another winter. Armistice Day in November, 1918, silenced the guns of Europe. The capitals rioted in joy or terror, according to the degree of chaos and rebellion with which the war of exhaustion had invested them. Victory and defeat might have been interchangeable terms. In the lobby of the House of Commons members shook hands without speaking, Mr. Baldwin wept openly, and outside in the streets people sang and capered. Neither tears nor laughter could touch the millions in each country who had died by foul means, the millions more hideously injured, the yet uncounted millions condemned to mental ills, broken homes, broken careers, broken lives.

The hospitals were full of cripples. And the gaols were

full of C.O.'s. Fifteen hundred "absolutists" remained in strict confinement. Thousands of "schemers" awaited in vain their remission from penal routine. Men continued to hunger-strike, to be forcibly fed, to be released, re-arrested, and sent to "rejoin units," with the prospect of a fourth court-martial. In the spring of 1919, while Members of Parliament were still asking questions about dying prisoners, and one honourable colleague approved discharge "on condition of employment in the cleansing of army latrines," a new Conscription Bill was introduced. The Secretary of State who moved the second reading declared – It is perfectly clear that the War is not yet over.

At least it was over for the dead, and for the widows of the dead.

Eunice Fleet took less rather than more note of events. She drifted through the days with her burden of pain: days bleak with deprivation, gnawed by unceasing self-reproach. She shrank deliberately from family and friends, her aversion changed in quality from the old. To share their interests was treachery to Vincent. She looked for occupation that drove her furthest from their scope. Her pride and hardness seemed to them greater and more inexplicable than ever. But in reality her mood was neither proud nor hard. She was soft to helplessness, bare, exposed, and vulnerable. She had no will for rages or rebuffs. Too easy laceration came from every contact.

The family, however, soon lost concern in her. News came one week of Albert Granger's death by submarine. A fortnight later his brother was reported missing – "wounded and believed a prisoner." No confirmation arrived of this report, no proof of wounds or capture. Tom Granger joined the ranks of unknown warriors, whose bodies never found a recognisable grave, whose scattered limbs went hurtling compass-wide, in company with bits of wailing shell.

The loss of his sons hit old Granger very hard. Their immunity till the last stage of the War had made him complacent. Things had gone well with him in every way, except for discomfiture through Eunice. In spite of her "contrariness" he loved her, and counted on her rehabilitation in the Granger-Forsett world. He could not rid himself of the feeling of having wronged her, nor did the feeling lessen with the raptures of his second marriage. It was a pity about Vincent: but with his passing, the family situation must improve. Euny would "come round," Lallie relent. Women-folk had their spites and jealousies. He did not mind so long as they fluttered about him, reciprocating fond attentions.

But Tom and Bert – he had missed them sorely, his deepest hopes were stored against their return. Sons of his flesh, they were sons, too, of his spirit, their dad's joy from early days of easy accord, of pride in their fitment to his steps. Boys – men – they were part of his life, his business, his ambitions, his struggles and success. Their places waited, they were to help and carry on, to be the father's props and more – his sturdy, wide-branching trees. And now . . . what cruel strokes had cut them down, uprooted, flung away, disparted each strong fibre to wasteful, sapless end. No happy family reunion. No office conferences. No schemes of joint new enterprise. No passing on of Granger to Granger in a greatened prospering Line.

It was the patriot's lot, this "giving" of sons – how often he had heard and used the phrase. A drear lack of comfort he found in it, in the closing weeks of war. Old Tom became noticeably old. He wilted, he lapsed. There were days when he did not reach his office, but wandered far from the docks. Things fell slack under Forsett's guidance, and his partner did not seem to mind. At home he was humble and pathetic. Lallie had "no patience" with him, she sneered and nagged, or went away and left him to himself. Her absences were of earlier origin. War-work had taken her beyond domestic life, her friendships and pleasures excluded him. Little Dorry, his little idol, his little pet, whom her mother had tired of sooner than of her dolls, and long ago left to the care of nursegirls – sweet little Dorinda, hailed with joy, and named after the finest steamer of the Line – she was too young, the darling, to understand; too young to share an old man's sorrow. His daughters-in-law were no solace: Gladys, the elder, raved and extorted, complained of her position and the rights of her children, a couple of snivelling girl-babies too much like herself: Bert's wife, Susie, was a flippant thing, earnest only in her study of fashions, and rather too pleased with the fit of her new black frock. It set off her blonde hair and skin to such effect, that in six months she exchanged it for a second wedding gown. And none too soon, the gossips said.

What the gossips said of Lallie, only her husband and Eunice did not know. Eunice might, perhaps, have caught stray comments, if her ears had not been dulled to all but echoes of her pain. In any case she had lost interest in officers, and could not have distinguished between the American and Australian types that brightened the streets of Taviton. Lallie, however, was skilled in Army lore. She weighed distinctions with a nicety of discrimination that for some time puzzled the officers themselves. Each left convinced that he stood high in her favour: but as to which stood highest – one, at least must have been surer than the rest. For he came back two years later and carried her off.

The gossips, it may be guessed, were not surprised. Nor, by that time, were Tom Granger and his daughter.

An ill tide had set in with the passing of Tom's sons; his family disrupted, his health failing, his affairs rushing to disaster. The great shipping slump that followed the war completed the ruin of the Forsett-Granger Line. Harry Forsett threw himself from the harbour bridge one night, and his wife died a few months later. Old Tom Granger lived feebly on. He had his darling "baby," and just enough means to keep her and himself. "The Laurels" was sold. So was "The Poplars." So was Sycamore Cottage. Eunice had left Taviton long before, and was fortunately not dependent on an allowance that ceased, with other amenities of the Granger home.

*   *   *

If much of the incident of the early post-war years came back to her blurred and incomplete, the blur was through the mist of tears that formed, unseasonably, uncontrollably, as she sat at home or went about the town. Her mind obsessed by Vincent, by pictures of his prison solitude, the torment of his pale, pleading face, strained in anguish to catch her withheld word, would seize upon her suddenly. Walking past the shops, riding on a tram, in the midst of hustle-bustle and moving crowds, the vision would descend as clear as when she lay sleepless in her room or in silent intervals of work. Those were not graceful tears that she shed; no drops of silver dew, no crystal gems, cool on a lucent bed: brine from red rims, they stumbled clumsily, in blobs on her nose, in streaks upon her chin. She hardly thought of wiping them off. She hardly cared that a woman weeping in the streets, openly, unobtrusively, must be a focus of attention. Her pain absorbed her, remorse freed her from shame. Once only she returned a glance of recognition. It came from Laura Fennick, brushing by her in a busy square. She stopped, and Laura stopped, their glances interlocked. Laura said hurriedly, brusquely – "Why are you making such a spectacle of yourself?"

Eunice whispered, "Have you forgiven me?"

"No," said Laura loudly, and walked away.

But the next day she walked into the Cottage. Eunice was on the settee near the window, staring vacantly at the sycamore. She was not crying though the stain of tears riddled her cheeks. Her eyes turned to Laura as she entered, but she did not rise.

"I say," said the visitor, flinging off her hat and sitting down on a small, stiff chair. "I thought I'd better come and see you before I go away again. You know I'm at Bournemouth? Governess in a family there. My brother's in a hydro, and I can be with him quite a lot." She waited a moment, as if in expectancy. But Eunice said nothing. "Well, if you *want* to know, Harvey's much better – but not well enough, even yet. The doctor says he needs mountain air. Abroad."

There was a considerable pause. Then Eunice said,

"Do you forgive me now?"

"I forgive you," mumbled Laura. Her small face opened, expectant again. But to her surprise, Eunice did not change expression. A low wail of anguish came from her instead.

"But *he* wouldn't – Vincent wouldn't forgive me ever—"

Laura jumped up.

"You make me sick," she said. "I don't understand you. I never did. But I understood Vincent. And I know perfectly well that he'd forgive you – he always did and would. Why, if he knew you felt like this about him now, he'd – he'd—"

She moved nearer, gave herself up to outstretched arms. They fell on each other's necks and wept together. Soft rain of tears, that washed and did not scald. Eunice dried hers quickly, and smiled at her guest, fumbling for her handkerchief.

"You'll have tea with me," she said, and rang the bell.

"I've got a friend outside," said Laura. "A girl who – she's a cousin of the Jewish C.O. who went before the Tribunal with Vincent. Do you remember him? He's been ill, too, and is in a clinic in Switzerland. Hannah's going to ask him to let me have particulars – I might get Harvey there, you see—"

"Bring her in," said Eunice.

The girl was lithe and dark-eyed, with a round face and talkative manner that set them all at ease. Still in her teens, she must have been at school when the spruce young man declared his inherited aversion from conscription. She did not speak of him at once; but dismissed the rigours of the war in an animated account of the rigours of the peace.

"It's awful to see the wounded soldiers limping about – would you believe it, six legless men came into my tram this morning! And it gives one the horrors to pass the hospital. But the unemployed round the docks are an ugly sight too. Only one boat for loading this week – and you should have seen the hundreds of men. But you must know well enough how it is, Mrs. Fleet."

Hannah Jay's mother had a shop near the docks, and they were feeling the pinch of lessened trade.

"It's lucky I've a sideline of my own," she said with her brilliant smile – the flash of large white even teeth between full-rosed lips. She was so obviously ready to be questioned that Eunice, warmed by reaction to Laura and the cordiality and freshness of the stranger, asked graciously,

"And what is your sideline?"

"Corsets," said Hannah Jay.

Corsets. A prosaic, alluring word, that was to bring change, adventure, enterprise, complete diversion of the currents of her life, to the pale, languid woman on the settee. Hannah Jay suggested it herself, remarking on that pallor.

"Do you know, I was just like you – white as a ghost. Anaemia, nearly pernicious," she said, her round cheeks glowing. "The shop didn't agree with me, and our doctor

said I needed to get out all day into the air. So when my
mother's friend, Mrs. Wise – she used to live in Taviton,
perhaps you remember her daughter Hava at the Inter-
mediate? – Mrs. Wise is Madame Eve, a smart *corsetière*
with a good business in London – when she came down on
a visit to mother, and to see if she couldn't set up an agency
here, it seemed like a godsend. I agreed to call on ladies,
and got a lot of orders very soon at a good commission.
Then I began to go out of town, too, with recommendations
to ladies living on the coast – it's pleasant walking or
driving round by the sea and some of the villages inland.
My health's improved enormously – and so's my pocket! I
admit I didn't like the idea at first. But it isn't the usual sort
of commercial travelling. Besides, girls have to earn their
living these days, and business offers better openings than
professions – though my little sisters are studying, and I
shall help them."

"You don't mean to confine yourself to travelling, then?"
said Eunice.

Miss Jay gave her a brisk, admiring glance.

"You're sharp, too, Mrs. Fleet," she said, laughing. "You're
right. I'm getting to understand the trade pretty well –
measurements aren't the whole of it, by any means! One of
these days mother and I will fix up a machine or two, get
machinists, and open a branch on our own. It requires a
little capital, of course. In the meantime I'm establishing a
connection."

She was only shy of discussing her cousin.

"Miss Fennick here thinks he's a hero – but nobody else
does. Of course we admire him in the family, but we don't
like to spread the news, even now. Jews have enough to
put up with in the way of prejudice. Plenty were killed in
all the armies. Several I knew in Taviton fell in France.
Hava's husband was killed in Palestine – on the English

side, of course. But all that's forgotten if you mention C.O.'s. People talk as if a Christian C.O. was an unnatural coward and traitor, but a Jewish one a *natural* kind!"

"I don't agree with you," said Laura – "You're hyper-sensitive, that's all – the prejudice against the C.O. is the same every time, no matter who he is—"

"But you've told me yourself there's been discrimination between religious and political objectors," said Miss Jay, shrewdly. "Anyway, *I'm* not setting out to make distinc-tions. Not even between the C.O. and the soldier. They all did their duty, I expect. I'm thankful I didn't have a brother, though I always used to long for one. I'm the eldest of three girls – the others are twins and still in school – my father died when I was five. Poor Mum's had a hard struggle to bring us all up."

"Yes," said Eunice sympathetically. "It's bad enough to be left a widow – but with children—"

"Oh, but my mother says that was her great consolation – having us – even the twins, who were only six months when father died – she wouldn't be without *one* of us!"

Eunice got up from the settee, and arranged the used cups together on the tray.

"It gave her occupation, I suppose," she said.

"Occupation – and love," said Hannah Jay, smiling. "You see—" she stopped suddenly, dismayed. Mrs. Fleet had turned abruptly and walked to the window, where she stood looking out, a tall, thin figure in a black dress. She seemed to have forgotten her guests.

"Have I put my foot in it?" whispered Miss Jay to Laura, who shook her head and shrugged her shoulders non-committally.

"When I need a corset, I'll let you know," said Eunice, wheeling round and holding out her hand to Hannah. Her face was kind and composed.

"I'll get you a lovely one," said the girl, in eager relief. "And then you'll be able to recommend Madame Eve to your friends."

"Of course," said Eunice, smiling. If there was an ironical glint at the thought of those friends, whose intimacies she had so long forsaken, Hannah did not see it. The maid came in to remove the tray. And the three made cordial farewells.

*   *   *

How much later was it that the idea came to her? She could not remember. A certain relaxation set in that day, which led to greater self-possession. The sharp core of agony dissolved. Pain did not leave her, but was diffused more bearably through her quick, resilient system. The effect was that of hardening and control. No longer abandoned to despair, she neither wept nor catechised her grief. Film cleared doubly from her eyes. The horror of loneliness yawned like a pit, but looking about her with dispassion she saw the feasibility of stepping out of bounds, of finding a new entrance to life. The two girls concerned in the change could have helped her. But Laura disappeared and did not even write, except for a card from Bournemouth, and another, much later, from Switzerland. She was either too rapt in the fresh experiment with her brother, or doubtful of her generous impulse to free the guilty. Hannah Jay might have been forgotten, but for the accident of a laundry returning a favourite belt in tatters.

Eunice had never worn a regulation corset. She was too straight and too flat – an unideal figure in days when curved hips and bosoms were admired. As a young girl she was urged to use padded stays, and mocked for keeping her athletic bones untrammelled. Already a change of taste was setting in, and *brassières* instead of pads ruled the bust under waistless jumpers. Eunice was still without need of artificial aids; her body had developed from its bony stage, but the slight swell of breast and diaphragm kept firm and unobtrusive. Her fragile satin belt, dishevelled by the laundry, had been more ornamental than useful except for the suspension of stockings. She decided, however, to replace it. And then she remembered her promise to Hannah Jay.

It was instructive to be measured by that young lady. The intimate process gave full rein to her tongue, though she could temper candour with discretion. She did not mention names when she told stories, of fifteen-stone clients who wanted sylph-like effects, and gentlemen devotees of waists – their own.

"Gentlemen?" said Eunice, lifting her brows.

"Oh, yes," said laughing Hannah. "Our best customer is the heir to a titled family – they have a country house here. He was wounded in the war, poor fellow, and isn't much of a figure – but he was never much before. When he got his commission he went to Madame Eve, who made officers' belts a speciality. But it was a real corset he wanted, plenty of whalebone, and waist. When he found our branch he was delighted. We've repaired his old stays and made him new ones."

"And do you measure him?" asked Eunice idly. She was more interested in the girl's play of feature than in her story.

"Oh, no, I really couldn't. Mum attends to him, of course. But it seems he's rather shy and very *refined* about it. We had a much funnier case last week – one of our neighbours, a shipping man you probably know, but I mustn't tell who. He'd worn belts of a special kind for years, and gave Mum most precise directions. *He* wasn't the least bit shy – a cool customer, I can tell you!" Hannah's black eyes squeezed into long-cornered lines. "It sounds hardly decent – but as soon as he began to give the order, he unbuttoned his trousers and let them slip right off! Mum was scared stiff, and I – well, I might as well confess, I was peeping through the glass panel between the fitting-room and the shop. But it was all right – he wore a long shirt to his ankles – and he was terribly serious and particular! Of course it made him look even more comic. Mum daren't even smile, and she guessed I was behind the lace curtain, trying not to explode. We were both nearly in hysterics when he left."

Her chuckles were infectious, and the pictured scene absurd. Eunice joined in. It was a long time since such a sound had been heard in the Cottage.

"It paid us, though, to attend to that order. The belt turned out perfect – better than any he'd ever had elsewhere. The old chap was pleased as Punch, and seemed delighted to pay Madame Eve's stiff bill. So we had a big commission as well as lots of fun!"

"It seems to be a profitable business," said Eunice.

"Ra-a-ther!" sang Hannah. "Not so much with the ordinary stock as with the specialities – and of course there are the luxury lines. One must know how to handle it – the *whole* of the business, I mean. There's the artistic side, too, not always profitable in money but it gives tone and reputation. That side appeals to me because it's so delightful and interesting. Style and materials have changed so much from the old stiff variety – or rather lack of variety. Lovely pliable brocades cut to individual design. Corsets can be beautiful things when you *make* them—"

"For beautiful figures?"

"Well – not necessarily. A beautiful corset, cleverly designed and fitted, can make *any* figure beautiful – almost!"

"One must know how to handle it!" mocked Eunice.

"Exactly. It's marvellous what you can do with a stomach,

for instance – push it up or down out of the way. In the old days you just lifted it and got an extra fashionable bosom. Now it has to go round this way." She illustrated her words with lively gestures. "Busts and ridges in between get lost in *brassière* tops – but you don't have to trouble about all that sort of thing, Mrs. Fleet. You've got the perfect basis for Madame Eve's daintiest creation. I know you hardly need to wear more than a suspender strap. But if you let us make you one of the new silk girdles, you'll love it – and it'll be a glorious advert for the firm. Naturally, any orders we get as a result from your friends will earn the usual commission – for *you!*"

There was a pleasant excess of banter in everything she said, but beneath it, her eye looked out on Eunice in a shrewd, tentative way. The strange thing was that Eunice looked back at her with an almost similar expression.

"I wonder," said Mrs. Fleet – "I wonder if that would improve my health."

"I'm sure it would," said Hannah Jay. "More than Doctor Billiams' Brown Bills for Bilious Bankers."

They left it at that with unspoken understanding. The position of the Forsett-Grangers was not unknown in the town, and the affairs of Mrs. Fleet not difficult to guess. They were of special interest to Mrs. and Miss Jay, anxious for a coadjutor in their corset agency.

Eunice turned the idea over without resentment, rather with indulgent speculation. She was aware that she must decide on a course of activity, and of necessity one that added to her income. Sycamore Cottage must go, and with it the routine of the past. For some time she had performed secretarial duties at her old tennis-club, but the post was to be filled by an ex-service man. She did not feel inclined for further clerical work. No professional opening was possible. In any case she liked the prospect of business. She wanted above all to find a niche for herself that did not depend on her relatives, and would not interfere too much with personal liberty. She was prepared, therefore, for the development that followed a telephone call from Miss Jay.

"Your order is being despatched from London tonight," said the official monotone. Then the personal chant crept in, "Shall I bring it round tomorrow, Mrs. Fleet? And, by the way, Madame Eve's junior partner, Hava Casson, is coming down for the week-end. She's bringing her girl for a holiday by the sea. Ruth's being fixed up with friends for a couple of weeks, but Hava can't stay away from business just now. I wonder if you'd like to meet her?"

"Yes, I would. Please bring her with you to tea."

*   *   *

Hava Casson's visit stirred Eunice to premonition. She felt it a turning-point. The two women met with curiosity. Profoundly different, they resembled each other in more than common experience. Strength, pride, reserve, sensitiveness they had in equal measure, but in unlike quality and kind. The springs of being moved in Hava Casson more slowly, to more tenacious purpose, with deeper certitudes. At first sight she looked a large, complacent woman, her reddish hair, blue eyes, and milky skin composing an illusion of easy content. But as her sturdy, well-built frame had no fatty surplus, so her character had no sloth or vapidity. This, however, was for the future to reveal. At their present contact, only their pleasant schoolgirl memories came to fusion, with the aid of eye and ear in signs of change, maturity, emergence from parallel griefs.

In their young days they had liked each other, in passing, casual fashion: the liking was confirmed, a seal set upon it, and augury given of increase. A contract, indeed, was actually signed. Eunice Fleet undertook to promote the Jay agency for Madame Eve's wares, over a social as well as geographical area, at a wage and commission no lady need disdain. She was to go to London every month at Madame Eve's expense, to report and receive initiation into other aspects of the trade. Such a liaison office between headquarters and Taviton, where the Jays were bound to the soil, might become an asset not only to both places, but to herself. – At least it was potent with value to her future.

Eunice entered into her job with energy, if not quite with enthusiasm. There were phases she disliked, days that were blank with failure and dull with distaste, but she plodded on for sheer horror of the pit escaped. The distraction that she needed grew gradually into an interest, and with wider prospects, into an ambition. She was an intermediary for a year. Her visits to London were pleasant spells of hospitality at the Maida Vale flat, where Hava Casson lived with her mother and her child, and equally pleasant but more strenuous spells at the shop near Oxford Circus. Mrs. Wise was the presiding genius at both places; a little round-chinned grey-haired woman, with a foreign lilting voice and a benign manner, who had stitched Madame Eve's products on her hired Singer machine, years before she trained apprentices and set up a workroom away from home. Now Madame Eve was jointly her daughter and herself. They directed, and others stitched. Hava had a head for figures of the mathematical kind, and for executive business organisation. Mrs. Wise still did a considerable amount of cutting, as skilfully and indispensably as she cooked in her kitchen. Eunice enjoyed her food, and the little old lady enjoyed her guest's enjoyment. It was she who encouraged her daughter to persuade "zat poor lonely gayl" to come and live with them. Not that she had not a shrewd eye to the "lonely gayl's" interest in the business. Her own physical powers were failing. She concealed from her daughter the warnings of doctors, and her secret, increasing pains. As long as she could, she meant to work in shop and home; but knowing her time was limited, it seemed to her a good thing to ensure a partner for Hava as sympathetic and capable as "zat lonely gayl from ze contree where we used to live."

The plan was carried out. Eunice sold up her home and assembled her assets, including the little that dribbled in from Aunt Carry's estate. Poor Aunt Carry was dead. She had passed away peacefully in her sleep some months before, and Eunice bore no malice for the disgruntled will. The farm lands, house, and stock went to the Welshman and his wife. Other property that should have come to Vincent and his heirs was consigned to remoter links in the family chain. Only a small part of Vincent's inheritance through his father came to his widow. She put all she could realise into Madame Eve's, and became a shareholder, an important member of the staff, and an addition to the household at Maida Vale.

The severence with Taviton seemed complete. She left it with relief, sick of its load of misery and inertia. The happy days of youth weighed nothing in the balance. They had been due in large measure to her father, from whom she was still in alienation. His patience with his wife added to offence, his worship of Dorinda was a senile slur. She took no notice of the pert, pretty child. Instinctive advance was followed always by deliberate recoil. She wasn't to be lured by artful pussy tricks, nor by the fatuous pleas of the darling's old man. The darling's brat was no sister of hers, she declared – an insult that was more a rashness of the tongue than a calculation of mind.

But when she left Taviton, the worst had not happened. News of Lallie's flight gave her no satisfaction. Yet she had

little sympathy with the discarded old man. His downfall
in business and domestic affairs seemed a logical result of
treachery and decay. Hard judgment here was not eased
by penance, since she could feel no liability. Her own prospering fortunes brought neither ruth nor stiffening. Work
increased, rewards accrued, new friendships widened life.
The spectacle of London filled any gap, with distraction if
not with pleasure. Her natural poise developed. She grew
more competent, more gracious, less myopic. But though
her brain matured and her body richened in sensory power,
her heart stayed numb and dry.

Then suddenly the filial string was pulled. Old Tom was
dying, and she hurried to his bedside. Opposite knelt a
little sobbing figure, flaxen curls pressed over a limp, horny
hand. "Take care of my baby," begged the father's feeble
voice. "Promise me, Euny – I'll die easy if you promise."

She promised. And a week later two black-clad sisters
arrived in a taxi at the Maida Vale flat, with bags contain-
ing all the younger's possessions.

*   *   *

Dorry was just fifteen, and in her infantile pathos looked
about twelve. The short black frock made her seem frail,
though she was plump and solid enough. Her small, pretty
features were too subdued to be pert, in the wistful droop
of strangeness and mourning. She clung to the big, bold
sister with touching trust as they went about the unfamiliar
streets, sat in roaring underground trains, jumped on and
off buses and moving staircases, and, later on, queued for
palatial cinemas.

But Dorry was neither as helpless nor as young as she
appeared. London suited her to a T as she wrote when
trying out a new fountain pen. Very soon the fledgling

began to preen its wings, to make its own audacious hops, choose its own tit-bits and perch where it pleased.

She came to Maida Vale at an opportune time. Mrs. Wise had died some fifteen months before, after an operation in a nursing-home. Hava Casson missed her mother, and her own daughter, now a student of King's College, missed even more the domestic care of her devoted grandparent. They decided on a change that had been broached much earlier. When the lease of the flat expired, they would buy a little villa in Golders Green, and install a housekeeper to carry on Grandma's traditions. Such a home would re-create the family atmosphere in a fresher and more modern way. A garden and other amenities would add private and social charm. Mrs. Fleet was invited to move with them. But she showed no liking for the scheme, which seemed to her inconvenient and troublesome. The flat in Seneschal Mansions satisfied her needs. When events dovetailed, it offered a ready solution to the problem of Dorry. Eunice renewed the lease for herself – an arrangement that suited everyone. The only hitch in its working was domestic. A succession of honest slatterns and efficient rogues made the discovery of Mrs. Johns seem heaven-sent. She did not sleep in nor remain all day, but her few hours morning and evening were enough to keep the flat in exquisite order, and to provide adequate service when the mistress was at home. Mrs. Johns was in fact the old-fashioned "treasure," so seldom a feature of the modern menage. Dorry might criticise her lugubrious face, but she did not need to see it often. Off to her commercial school after breakfast, Dorry met Eunice for lunch in the West, and for tea in the office. Sometimes they dined out together, or spent the evening with the Cassons at Golders Green. Eunice and Hava always had business to discuss in extra-office hours. Dorry had her own work to continue. She was assiduous at her

studies during the first year, and grateful to her elders for
any simple pleasure. But her industry and her spirit of
acceptance both wore out as she became an easy Londoner.
She made friends in and out of classes – fleeting, quick-
changing friends – and began to resent supervision. Long
before she was seventeen, her position was established by
the drive of her own personality. Her clerical contributions
to Madame Eve proved less useful than direct service to
clients. In this sphere she showed eagerness and efficiency,
though both these qualities fluctuated with her whims.
Either through natural flair, or because she was keen to
emulate Eunice, whose poise and success in salesmanship
she began to envy, Dorry became a favourite in the "Salon,"
with ladies who liked youthful smartness and flattering
attentions. She grasped their "points" with a zeal that was
really the measure of her interest. Actresses and society
folk were models she delighted to study at first hand. She
pried upon and copied their beauty secrets with a *naïveté*
that amused them. Sometimes they took her out to tea (not
without an eye to reciprocal business favours) or introduced her to friends.

Eunice might discourage these marks of patronage, and
"nip" their results, both in and out of the office: but fresh
buds would sprout and even blossom, beyond the range of
sisterly sunlessness. Intimacy with Blake Pellew was, perhaps, the only solid fruit to ripen in this way. How solid
and how ripe Eunice could not know, however shrewd her
suspicions. The more threatening and strict the elder's
temper, the more dexterous the younger in evasion. And
when at last Eunice grew slack, through a new preoccupa-
tion of her own, sap and greed reached an appointed end.
The fruit was plucked, the juice extracted, the pips and skin
cast away. A wiser but not much sadder Dorry trod the
routine of Madame Eve's, and stepped recklessly on her

sister's skirts. That sister, meanwhile, walked with head in the clouds, sensing a solar effulgence. Why should she heed the drag at her hems? – she, who had come so far in sodden garments, dried in the furnace of remorse? Her long travail seemed over. The sun above, illusory or not, stirred life in her bones, and shed a gracious warmth on all within her sphere.

Part Three

PRESENT

VII.

A Drive. And a Recipe for Happiness

THE policeman has been standing at the door for a very long time. He does not know that Mrs. Fleet's dreams have been unduly prolonged, her memories springing detail as her subconscious mind renewed its strain. But he is aware that it is an early call to make upon a lady, and apologises, though not too meekly. After all, he has his duty to perform.

"Sorry to disturb you, miss – madam. But there's been a – bit of an accident-like—" The policeman, a young fellow not long from the country, stammers a little at the panic in the lady's face, at the way in which her hands, clutching her wrap, fall and reveal a lovely nightdress. He has seen pyjamas before, even in his village. But only his old mother at home wears a gown, a long calico cover-all, frilled at neck and wrists. This revelation of scant gauze and lace is distractingly different.

"Dorry!"

The name could not pass her lips, which parted, trembling. The policeman spoke more quickly.

"It's Mrs. Johns, ma'am – I believe she worked for you?"

"Oh, yes – yes – come inside, constable – what's happened to Mrs. Johns?"

"Put her head in a gas oven." The policeman's eyes turned reluctantly to his note-book. "All over when they found her. She had a husband and four children, but she didn't leave any message for them, only a letter to you. It says she's sorry she can't come no more, but she couldn't stand the picky hands. Nobody seems to know what it means. Husband says she's been queer for months. You'll have to attend the inquest, Mrs. Fleet."

"Oh – must I, constable?"

"Afraid you must, ma'am."

Relief had given place to dismay and sorrow – not so shattering as might have been, but keen enough in an employer concerned for her staff. And Mrs. Johns was no ordinary servant.

The policeman lingered, repeating details. But she dismissed him abruptly. What a ghastly business! She moved to the window, and threw it wide to the air. Grey dawn was already blue morning, the sun glinted on roof and pane, the trees in the square spread bright green arms. A young welcoming note sang in the sounds of the street. Lightness raced in the atmosphere, in the currents of her blood, thwarting the heavy shade of the policeman's tale. Yet she could not but let her thoughts droop to its weight. Poor Mrs. Johns! Poor broken drudge!

A sordid tragedy, the newspapers would say. In a slum kitchen was found the body of the basement tenant, who helped to clean, cook, and wash in part payment of rent; and one morning took advantage of the early hours to use her landlady's stove for other purposes than the lodgers' breakfast. A mean, dirty trick upon the landlady! Her gas and good nature depleted in one stroke – or in one turn of a tap. A mean, dirty trick upon the husband! Four whining orphans to rob the drink from his throat. A mean dirty trick upon Eunice Fleet – not that it wasn't a grace *her* stove had not been used! None the less, an indefensible act, to leave that message to her about the "picky hands." Must she add a suicide to her burden of guilt?

Half real, half assumed, the spirit of mockery played with the depressing event. It was unfair to load a gloom on her, upon a morning so sweet, so potent with pleasant moods. Exasperating, unlucky, reedless Mrs. Johns. Poor wretched soul.

Another ring – the telephone bell. She stared at the instrument. Who could be calling at this hour of Sunday? All her friends and acquaintances must be abed. Perhaps Hava, urgent in reminder— She took the receiver in a languid grip, which tightened suddenly. The response to her bald Hallo was overwhelming.

"Hel-*lo*! Is it Eunice? Good morning. This is George speaking – George Furnall."

"Oh – good morning. Aren't you early!"

"Early? But I've been up hours. Mean to tell me you're still in bed?"

"No – the phone's in my sitting-room."

"Don't say I got you up?"

"I won't, because you didn't. But as a matter of fact, I'm still in my nightie."

"I say! Why haven't I got television! Is it very charming?"

"The policeman thought so – he couldn't take his eyes off!"

"What? What's that? Did you say policeman?"

"I did. But I didn't mean to – it doesn't matter—"

"Great Scott, doesn't it? What's a policeman been doing in your flat? I won't ask for the moment why he had the damned cheek to admire your – negligee – but – what the devil did he come for—?"

"Really, there's no need to swear—"

"Shan't apologise. Please tell the tale. It can't be too bad, eh? You sound all right?"

"It's a sad one, though. I'm very upset about it."

"Tell on."

With an effort she brought a solemn note to her voice. It stayed and deepened as she recited her news.

"What a shame. I mean for you. Shocking thing, of course. But too bad you should be dragged into it."

"It's my own fault – I'm partly responsible."

"But how? Because of your kindness to the woman?"

"My *lack* of kindness. I ought to have realised – I ought to have sympathised more, made the poor creature feel she had a friend who cared. A little fellow-feeling at the right moment – a little scrap of insight, a word in season – just at that last moment – it might have made the difference between life and death—"

"My dear Eunice – absurd!"

"You think I'm foolish?"

"No – too divinely wise! But you're talking of a scrubby little char—"

"Ah, I haven't made it clear. It's hard to tell her story on the phone. But didn't I describe her? She wasn't that at all – but quite delicate-minded and sensitive—"

"Now you're talking of yourself."

"But – George – listen—"

"I'm listening – you bet I'm listening."

"You must believe me – it's serious – I'm most un-happy—"

"Poor girl! You'd soon get rid of that if I could see you. Think I'd let you harp on such morbid stuff? On your own showing, the woman was sick of existence. The drunken brute probably beat her blue that last night – and between him and the howling kids in that cockroach basement, no wonder the gas oven tempted her – and would have done no matter what you said or didn't say. Don't worry about the inquest – I'll tell you what to do about that. . . . No brooding, please. I've a good mind to come right away and stop you—"

"Oh no, you mustn't—"

"I will – I'll start at once—"

"But by the time you get here I'll be in my office. I told you of my appointment with my partner today."

"Well – I suppose I must let you get on to it – so that I can take you off early. You know you're coming out with me this afternoon."

"I didn't know it."

"You know it now. There's a Kreisler concert at the Queen's Hall. I've got two tickets, and you're coming with me."

"Really?"

"Really."

"You're much too positive, young man."

"You're much too – conscientious, young woman. Sundays aren't meant for labour, anyway. How's an idle fellow to get through without you?"

"I thought you—"

"Please don't think. Just leave it all to me. Where shall we meet for lunch?"

She laughed frivolously. She did not recognise herself. Neither the situation, the form of banter, nor the feeling of nonsensical joy seemed to belong to her. They were all too Dorrylike. Yet she must be Eunice – Eunice Fleet, junior partner of Madame Eve's.

"But, George—"

"Yes, Eunice?" His drawling of her name was soft, beguiling. Strange how his voice affected her. It was not deep or strong – rather thin, in fact, but pleasant and sometimes muscial. There was a little break in it now and again, like an echo of boyish breaking, that touched her nerve centres, sent fine vibrations behind her shoulders, up the back of her throat, the crown of her scalp. She could hardly go on speaking for a moment. Then summoned her common sense.

"I've got to finish my job today. Just *got* to. Understand? I'd love to come with you – Kreisler's my dream – but truly, I can't. I'm lunching at Golder's Green, probably late. Too late for the concert. Impossible to get free in time."

"You're an obstinate wretch. But I can't help adoring – obstinacy. It's something I haven't got much of myself. That's why I'm letting you off. But only partly. Will you be ready by three? – three-thirty? – three forty-five?"

She laughed again. He took it for assent.

"Then I'll call for you – what's the address?"

"But Kreisler? – Your tickets?"

"I'll pass them on. We'll go for a drive instead. I've got a new two-seater I want to try out. At least it isn't quite new and I haven't quite got it – I'm thinking of buying it from a friend. He's only had it six months, and he's had to go abroad. Last night I found a letter from him asking me to use it or sell it for him. I'm just off to the garage for it. A little gem, you'll see!"

"But you haven't driven it before?"

"Just once in town, through Regent's Park. We'll let her rip through Surrey, eh? Great West Road, Staines, Guild-ford, Hog's Back or the Punch Bowl – anywhere you like—"

"Oh – I—"

"You're not afraid?"

"Terribly!"

He chuckled and jeered.

"Sounds like it! I can't imagine you afraid of anything. Except a bogey. And you can be sure *that* won't survive my driving!"

It scarcely survived the conversation. While preparing breakfast in the kitchen, she certainly was aware of Mrs. Johns, stark with ginger head in oven. The grim vision alternated with a bent figure at the sink, turning to blink piteous eyes – or fumbling at the door before she left, in vain self-expression – "He says, I don't like your picky hans' – the little love – it cut me to the 'eart—" But in the sitting-room, drinking hot tea at her dainty tray, the pangs of pity and regret were intermittent as her mouthfuls of food, though in no way connected. A stimulant beyond hunger diverted appetite, and drove it from the power of gloom. She told Mrs. Casson of the policeman's visit without a hint of self-reproach, accepting commiseration on the loss of service, and the waste of business hours at a coroner's court. Both women agreed the case was pitiable, in the sub-personal tones of humane employers. Furnall would have found nothing morbid in their talk. Nor did he find it in his companion of the delightful country drive.

When they met, he scanned her a little apprehensively beneath the bluffness of greeting. He disliked the strain of melancholy he suspected in her. But her smile, her easy bearing, though slightly subdued, had a sparkle that reassured him. Her quietness was light, not heavy: it was a foil to his own dash and masterful approach, as he sensed with a growing triumph. He was used to competent women who were not attractive to him, and to attractive women who found no competence in him. Eunice Fleet was different in charm and response. That such a rare creature should be shy with him, was a tribute to his power over her. It astonished her even more than himself. Shy! She had never been shy of an admirer before, and had not known the capacity to be in her. It was evoked suddenly and overpoweringly at Hava's door. How freely she had chattered over the telephone! Her very glibness then tied her tongue now. She felt it incredible she had been so bold. As she sat beside him in the little open car, his slight dapper form towered dominant, his closeness enveloped her, his elbow on her sleeve abashed her sense. Her glance adventured in meeting his, as he beamed magnificently upon her.

Yet all the morning she had dallied with the idea of his subjugation – to her. The early phone call was significant. "Up for hours" – unable to sleep – why? because he was thinking of her? – desiring her? – Pulses beat faster while she mocked herself. Absurd to let her fancy run too far. Men today didn't fall in love so easily and wholly. They didn't lose rest and sink concerns in pursuit of sudden passion. Even Bob, who really loved her, who preferred her company to that of any other – even Bob could stay away for weeks at a time, and amuse himself with different women. True, she discouraged him, had never exerted herself to keep him. With Furnall she knew herself otherwise. Her powers of fascination had come into play. Not deliberately, perhaps – not fully or with conscious intent. Instinctively, without purpose or reflection, she had put forth her lure, had called her idle faculties into use. There was no effort and no sense of strain, as happened on the infrequent occasions when she tried to secure the attentions of a man. Only too naturally did she exercise a charm that was instant magnet to Furnall's steel.

But evidence of response must not delude her. Love or passing attraction – she need not ponder deeply on a bond so mutual. She forgot, in fact, to ponder at all. She forgot, as they raced over Wembley in the exuberant air, that Vincent was concerned in the bond, and that she had believed its sweetness due to him. She felt a great release of new, fresh being, tremblingly new with untried strength. A delicious spirit in her matched the soft, quick breeze, that caught in her face – and in his. It was like sharing breath together.

"Why so silent?" he rallied her suddenly.

"I'm observing a rule of the road – 'never speak to the driver,' isn't it?"

"'Never speak to a bad driver,'" he amended. "So you really haven't confidence in me?"

"Oh, lots – when you don't take your eyes off the road."

He turned his face deliberately to her.

"If my passenger doesn't talk, I'll keep on looking at her," he said. " And even if she does, I'm afraid I'll have to – occasionally."

"The scenery's nice," she observed, gazing ahead.

"But not as nice – to look at—"

They swerved rather sharply round the bend to a bridge, with two cars and a cycle whizzing by. But Furnall's control was full and precise, and he took the near curve rather well.

Their eyes met again, and she smiled with ease.

"He's cool," she thought, and he nodded amusedly, as if he read the words in her face.

"Flattery's good for me, you know," he urged. "Don't be stingy – you might give me a little now and again."

"Don't you see you're putting me in a dilemma?" she said. "If I talk to flatter your vanity and make you keep your eyes on the road, am I showing more confidence than if I *don't* talk – knowing you'll take your eyes off all the more?"

"Subtle, by Jove!" He laughed above the engine, louder as they climbed. "You can split hairs like a politician."

"Or a politician's friend."

"Lucky politician!"

"Where are we now?" she asked. "It's beautifully open up here. But I see the fields are breaking up, and building's begun."

"Yes, its changing fast. Now we drop again – we're running down Hanger Hill. Can you see old Doctor Clifford ambling up, munching an apple? Ever since I heard the story of his favourite walk, I see his ghost coming towards me here. I'm afraid he'll give it up pretty soon, now that the lane looks like becoming a street."

They crossed Ealing Common and ran into the Great West Road. The broad motor way was full of traffic, four-fold streams of old and new cars, carrying couples or families. Each driver with a mate went flashing away, the open coaches danced with bobbing heads, back panes of saloons showed peeping little faces, hands upraised in childish glee. A friendly common purpose strung the urban procession, though some were leaving and others seeking country space: chariots of the Sunday exodus, fleeing as if pursued, smart and dowdy, humble and ornate, strange and nondescript – limousine, sports model, "baby," "bike," steered by various humans linked in outdoor joy. Eunice felt herself integral in the line, rare sense in a solitary unit. She, with the rest, composed this moving world, partner and maker of it. A rare and a satisfying sense.

Past the waste stretches, the mushroom houses, the neo-Tudor "pubs" and garages, the factories with many a jazz device. Furnall bent to his wheel in sudden concentration. He tried to score off an overtaking midget, which "cut in" twice, escaping retribution.

"Fellow's in a deuce of a hurry," he complained, jamming on his brakes to drop behind. Oncoming traffic was heading very near.

"Why worry?" she said lazily. "We're keeping up a good rate, anyway. And there's a long trail behind."

"Yes," he agreed, peering into his mirror. "We don't seem the only ones to start late for an outing."

She sat back stilly and smiled to herself. It was a pose he had observed and called "mysterious" – a Monna Lisa-like mystery, he teased. But to her it was the simple expression of content. She did not know that her mouth, even then, had a close-pressed wistfulness that added secrecy to charm.

It stimulated Furnall to greater animation, and an almost reckless desire for speed. Such a woman beside him, incalculable, grand, cool yet electric in her shell, conferred powers beyond self-knowledge. He was lord of his machine, sovereign of the road. Metal leaped and slackened as he chose, a live steed harnessed to his touch.

The flat, bald beginning of the track to Staines grew thicker with hedge and tree-strewn gap, broke into village over bridge and hill: the lines of vehicles split and scattered, a bunch came together and dissolved, a thin tail vanished and left them royally alone. Furnall diverged into secondary routes, avoiding main traffic streams to find peace and beauty in narrow winding lanes. Eunice approved, though she criticised, too.

"There isn't room for another car to pass us here," she pointed out. "Suppose we meet one coming down?"

"So much the worse for the coo," he said. "One of us will have to back, no doubt."

The contingency did not arise. They wound to safety and glimpses of the river. More than once Furnall was lost, and Eunice refrained from comment. It did not matter to her where they went. She would have liked to know that Furnall felt the same, but he had come to a decision; and having announced their objective as tea at Dorking, he was bent on finding Esher. He found it, and they ran through woody Oxshott to Leatherhead and the foot of Boxhill. Eunice was not too much enchanted to be above longing for tea, as she readily owned. But she showed no disappointment at the refusal of her suggestion that they should stop at some quiet cottage in the fields.

"My dear girl," said Furnall emphatically, "you'd simply hate it. I've brought you out to enjoy yourself, not to drink slops out of a smelly mug, with chickens pecking at you, and no decent sanitation. These new road cafes aren't bad, but not too comfy, either, at mob-time—"

"Democrat!" she said, in gentle mockery.

"Not today," he admitted, with a smiling bow. "I'm taking you to tea with the Duchess. She won't be at home, of course – but we'll use her rooms and pleasure-grounds, and be served by a waiter who might be her grace's butler—"

She was not loth to acknowledge the charm of driving up to a stately mansion, discreetly blind to the trade signs above; of the carpeted hall where dainty tables were disposed, with porcelain cups and "artistic" paper squares; of the soft, unjazzlike music under the gallery, the service of stiff-shirted, languid youths, and the freedom to roam through ex-ducal privacies. She said nothing of the insipid tea and stale sandwiches, nor indeed did they trouble her. When Furnall took her out into the gardens, and made her climb the rhododendron hill, she was happy without reservations. Here at last they were alone in the domain of Nature: other couples wandered on the slope, but at the crest, the two who paused beneath the great trees to view a vast expanse of country, seemed left in a solitude of their own. And it was at this moment, while they stood together, breathing a little heavily from exertion – for they had climbed the steepest way, up a narrow flight of steps cut into the rocky mount – gazing in delight at the panorama below, then turning to each other as if in instinctive search – at this moment, Eunice was struck with a thought which made her clasp her hands and look at Furnall's, with eyes dilated, and a slight half-amazed, half-smiling parting of the lips.

"Oh!" she exclaimed. "Oh, George! I've only just remembered!"

"What?" said he. "Something pleasant, I hope? You have a genius for remembering, haven't you? What is it this time?

"Your hand," she said.

He looked down perplexedly, raising his right arm and letting it drop again.

"What about it?" he said. His tone was a little abrupt. "You know, of course, that it's artificial. Anyone could see that with half an eye. And I'm afraid I was a little clumsy at tea."

"You're never clumsy with it," she said. "And certainly I know – I knew all the time. But isn't it strange? I quite forgot while you were driving!"

He smiled suddenly – how delightfully, she thought, his face lit up, softening the rather hard line of cheek.

"By Jove, did you really? Now that's a first-class compliment!"

"Yes, it is, isn't it? And it's perfectly true! I didn't think of it once, from the moment you asked me to come, until just now! But how on earth – how did you manage it – well, of course, I know how you managed it quite – marvellously! – but how did you get permission— "

She was a little incoherent, an unusual ingenuousness eager in her face.

"I didn't. Fortunately it isn't compulsory – yet. Very soon there'll be new regulations, medical inspection, certificates of fitness, bar on defects, etc. That's why I made sure of my licence and took driving lessons early. The authorities know nothing about my hand, and don't need to."

He spoke in a modest voice, with a slight reserve, as if aware that his disability remained, in spite of skill. She was touched and moved. Impulsively she reached for the artificial limb, stiff in its glove, and gently lifted it. He looked at her, his eyes kindling. His left hand closed on hers, bare flesh on flesh, warm, quivering. She did not resist. They were standing together, their heads on a level. As he leaned forward, his mouth was near hers. She felt herself dissolving, yet stringent for his kiss. But on that transilient pause crude voices broke, two girls and a boy came bounding from the wood. Furnall released her fingers; they stepped from the path.

The noisy party passed, their shouts receding, and the solitude seemed as before. But the moment had gone, and Eunice struggled with a cold fit of embarrassment. She had turned away and was gazing at the view without seeing it, wondering what Furnall would say. His words came tentatively.

"Shall we sit down? There's a seat under that tree further back – unless you'd like the grass patch on this side—"

"Yes, it's gloomy under the tree, I prefer the open."

He spread his newspaper for her on the hollowed slope, and she carefully adjusted her dress. There was an akwardness between them that she dimly felt her fault – why had she become so stiff and icy-set? – Furiously she battered it down and recovered her poise.

"Do tell me how you lost your hand. I've never known that, you see. I thought at first – I mean when we met in the Asulikit – that it was the war. But of course you weren't in it at all."

"No – it was really the hand that let me off. I lost it years before – in fact, while quite a kid." His voice, too, was light again. Though she would not meet his eyes, she had drawn him back, near, but not too close. He lay stretched below her feet, plucking the grass and throwing handfuls away. Sunshine dappled the air, though barred by the trees behind. Warmth returned between them, an intimacy purely friendly, but comforting to her soul. She basked in it, and plied her questions. He answered easily, unfolding a past that was strange and dear to her.

As a boy of eight, George Furnall lived at his grandfather's house in Knightsbridge, in the charge of a youthful nurse. His parents were in India, where his father died. Before his mother's return, he was sent with his nurse to the country, for a holiday on her uncle's farm. He was a favourite there, and allowed to do as he pleased. The nurse relaxed her care in dalliance with her cousin, the farmer's eldest son. On a busy afternoon in the hay-machine shed, the boy prowled about unobserved, watching the chaff-cutting. Suddenly he put a hand to the grinding-knives, and screams of agony filled the hut. Two fingers were cut off before he was released, and the hand later amputated. It was a sad time for the boy, and a bitter one for his guardians. The nurse never abated her remorse. She married her cousin, and subsequently owned the farm, which provided the grown-up cripple with a refuge during the war.

"Of course I wasn't expected to be a fighting man, but the Army wanted me as clerk or recruiting officer or anything a left-handed chap could be. The Tribunals temporarily exempted me and ignored my C.O. claim. I was still at Cambridge, and intended for India. But all that went smash. C.O.'s were barred anyhow for the Indian Service. Not that I cared about that – as Russell said, no C.O. ought to have wanted it! In those days we were great sticklers for what we ought, and oughtn't, to want to do – the prisons and the camps were rent with debates, and as for the committees and the papers some of us ran – by Jove, we fought with hairs like swords!" – He grinned, and she smiled whimsically. Vincent came back now, hovering in his ghost-dim shade. The live man at her feet, bright with magnetism and success, went on chuckling loudly as he described his work of national importance, obtained through the Pelham Committee when the Tribunals became troublesome. "My activity in the Fellowship was too much for them. One member wanted to lock me up. Since I'd got to visiting gaols and kicking up a fuss about conditions in

them, I'd be safer inside. Well, I didn't quite agree with
him. There were times, of course, when I felt a bit too much
'outside'—" He hesitated for the first time, his voice dropped – "It seemed mean not to be sharing the conditions,
instead of setting questions about them – most of our Committee were arrested at one time or another – it was all a
mess, anyhow, stupid, and farcical – I didn't really escape
my bit of martyrdom—" He was silent in a pause that grew
hollow for her, in a cavern into which a word flung might
resound like a pebble. But when he resumed, the light,
even flow made music of the echoes. "They got me fixed in
the end. And that's where Nannie's farm came in."

She could not smile as readily at his picture of himself
driving cows through a country town.

"I had yellow corduroys and a straw hat, with a beard –
well, not the Café Royal kind – and I mostly fell over the
beasts as they lurched about. I had to tap them with a stick
to get them back into the road, and each time I tapped I
called them by name – that is, the name of each member of
the Tribunal – from Salisbury down – and every time a
passer-by stopped to watch my antics, I waved my stick
and shouted *'Work of National Importance'* – but though they
laughed, they didn't really see the joke!"

It was amusing, but she could not smile. Her whirl of
memories confused her. Was the reproach in them only for
herself? That poor Wallace Paige – his stay at Mold was not
the holiday that Furnall enjoyed with his Nannie. Aunt
Carry's gloomy bailiff complained that he was not "genuine,"
because he was not "religious" in Morgan's sense. There
had been arguments, quarrels, rebellion against petty task-
mastership – the boy had run away, had been re-arrested –
she had not been sufficiently concerned to know all that
happened, and Aunt Carry, of course, knew only what
Morgan told her. Furnall's experience was different. The

public charge of cows might have been a joke – or a humil-
iation – but mostly his work was play, as he boasted.
Playing while his comrades toiled and suffered, like Paige.
Or died, like Vincent, in absolute refusal. Refusal to – what?
To serve his country, said the patriots. To compromise, said
the ghost. Poor ghost! Poor? No – proud. Proud ghost.
Proud Absolutist. Against him, and his "class," had gone
forth the decree, pronounced by the chief Patriot in the
Cabinet – *I shall only consider the best means of making the
path of that class a very hard one.*

She winced as she listened to Furnall's drolleries. Then
rounded on herself for stupidity. How could she know
what his feelings had been? It was unfair to judge by his
present easy mirth. Perhaps a sense of humour had saved
him even then. No victim that she could remember had
shown much humour in the predicaments of war.

She looked down at the outstretched form; slim, dapper
even in relaxation; the dark hair neat on a skull masculine
yet fine; a jaw delicately cut yet hard and strong. A wave of
tenderness poured through her, an outreach of yearning
and solicitude. Poor boy – dear man! He, too, had known
his "bit of martyrdom," had suffered, endured pain and
deprivation; had fought for freedom, by pen and speech,
when such weapons earned more odium than the sword;
and had survived to fight again.

Wasn't it a privilege to have survived with him, to link
her strength with his in marching on? The past had no
reproach, but stimulus. She would be the new Andromeda,
arming the new Hector. Strange, inverted image! Its odd-
ness made her laugh. Easy enough to be gay at last. She let
her own music ring to enchant his ear, without too close
interpretation. There was risk in clarifying meaning – risk
of eye on eye unveiled, of hands abandoned to caress.
Somehow she was not ready yet. She must not yield so

rawly to temptation. Let present sober moments wait on what might come; they were sweet enough and sufficing to her mood.

So just before the sun had set, she made him leave the crest, and ran before him on the wooded paths. Other ramblers hastened with them in the fading light. It was fun to hurry amid echoing calls and mould-soft stumbling steps. In the park below the ranged cars began to hoot, and their movements made a changing pattern of space and crawling dot.

Furnall drove homeward over Reigate Hill and the Epsom Downs towards the Sutton by-pass route. He drove more slowly and less showily, not because of any subduing of his spirit, or check of darkness; unaware that his companions's animation both absorbed and curbed his own. Evening spread in opalescent tints, decking a faint new moon, and the velvet riches of earth and sky owed as much to the sun's lingering veils as to the sables of night.

The same mellow glow lit the communion of man and woman. By it they had found each other, it seemed, after years of trackless wandering. A sense of trust, steadier than the flicker of inspiration, gave their hearts repose, though both might leap again to adventure. They talked engrossedly of their separate affairs, important and trivial. Furnall sketched his chief's campaign, his own immediate and future course. He asked Eunice to decide on his subjects of debate, his choice of colours in notepaper, his mode of address to constituents in the pending election, and his purchase of the car. He advised her, in turn, on business and domestic matters of which he knew as little or as much, and approved her plans for developing Madame Eve. It interested him to hear that she was to rule in Hava's place, with a sister to raise in status.

"You must meet Dorry," she said, in generous warmth. "She's a real cute kid, as the Americans say. This trip to

Paris is a credit to her. But of course she's very young and needs direction. I have to look ahead for her. Now she's provided for, as far as the business is concerned. But whether she'll stick to it, I don't know. She's a pretty child, and rather giddy, I'm afraid."

"So a pretty little sister is another of your responsibilities. Aren't you inclined to take them all too seriously? You'll be worrying about *me* next!"

"Naturally. I'll worry until you're an M.P. And then I'll worry until you're a P.M."

His laugh had a queer gurgle in it.

"By Jove, Eunice, you're enough to make a chap conceited! You don't throw many bouquets, but when you *do* – By the way, I wonder if there's a hornet in that one? What would you expect me to do if I were P.M.?"

"Abolish the Army and Navy – and of course the Air Force," she said gravely.

"Oh, of course!" he mocked. "What a poisonous little sting!"

The return to Golder's Green took an hour longer than the journey out. But to Eunice it seemed shorter. She was not sorry that Furnall excused himself from Hava's supper. He had work to do that night in preparation for his chief: but he, too, perhaps shared her fear that the family in the villa would not maintain the atmosphere of the drive. For some reason he was not at ease with the Cassons. Hava was kind to him, yet a little critical in gaze: her daughter was aloof, not from intention – indeed, she seemed hardly aware of him. The small, darkbrowed girl with the luminous black eyes had none of the jollity of Miss Grunbaum, whom she resembled in other ways.

Eunice found her neither cold nor remote. Lying on large pillows in the pretty, pink-walled room, with curtains undrawn over leaded panes above the garden, she saw the door open and Ruth appear, hesitant and smiling.

"Come in, dear," she said, though not too cordially.

The girl glided to the bed and sat down, polishing her tinted nails.

"You look awfully well this evening, Eunice. The drive did you good. And I must say letting your hair grow was right for you. Girls with long slender necks ought to welcome the change in fashion."

"Am I a girl?"

"Of course. You look like one now, anyway."

"Thanks, Ruth. But your neck is slender, too – why don't you let *your* hair grow?"

"I'm too small. Proportion, you know. But keeping my hair short is a practical necessity. More sensible for a hot climate – and work on an orange plantation."

"And are manicured hands sensible?"

Ruth laughed.

"Gloves can be worn, perhaps; my hands are my weakness, I admit. But even that vanity may have to go, with the rest of my glad rags."

She held up her fingers to the light, rosed from a low silk shade. They were exquisitely shaped, fine and tapering, with white arcs curving on points of scarlet glaze.

"I don't understand you, Ruth – quite."

"No, old thing? My sort of stuff isn't in your line."

"But – anyone can – can be in love—"

"Why, certainly."

"And I see how love can make a girl give up a profession, comfort – luxury, even – to go and rough it in a strange country – digging—"

"Oh, I mayn't have to dig – not much, anyhow! Now that Mother's come in and bought land and labour, it's all so much easier. I daresay there'll be a certain amount of roughing it. But Palestine isn't a strange country – to me."

"I know. You've been there twice in the last two years. So being in love—"

Ruth got up from the bed and walked to the casement window. The young moon was showing through the trees.

"The same moon's shining over David." She pronounced the name with the broad "a," the only lingering intonation in her curt, quick speech. "And I suppose he's looking at it and thinking of me. And we're both thinking how much nicer it would be to be looking at it together. There! That's being in love. But you're wrong if you fancy it's the only reason I'm chucking things here so completely. Love isn't everything."

"Isn't it? Why are you so sure?"

"Do you mean you aren't? Heavens, Eunice!" She returned, laughing, to perch again on the bed. From the pocket of her mauve silk pyjama coat she drew a cigarette, lit it, and puffed away. "You're in a romantic mood tonight, I see."

Eunice grew warm before those luminous black eyes. She said in haste,

"That's where I don't understand you, Ruth. You're not a bit romantic – in fact, you're a real tough modern little chit – and yet – well, you can't deny you're sacrificing a lot to go and marry your – what do you call him?"

"My *chalutz* – my *pioneer* – a common labouring man. No, bless him, he isn't common – not even in Palestine, where there are thousands like him. Incidentally, he's a University graduate – or would have been, if he hadn't been squeezed out by the *numerus clausus*."

"Is he very handsome?"

"Not particularly." She blew a fume of smoke through pouting lips. "Not like your friend, Mr. Furnall—"

"Oh ! But – *he*'s not particularly handsome, either."

"There, you see! Love need not be blind."

Eunice turned her cheek on the pillow. She felt a sting of resentment at the flippant tone of the girl. But it passed in a moment.

"I beg your pardon, Eunice. I'm only rotting—" There was a pause before Ruth added, her voice changed – "Of course I love the boy I'm going to marry. He suits me perfectly. I think that's the great thing, don't you? Being suited?"

Eunice looked round at her kindly.

"Yes, I agree." A little tune sang in her brain – He suits me – George suits me – and – I – suit – him.

"But the point is – I'm sorry to disillusion you, Victorian maiden – I was suited before I met David. And that was when I decided to go back to Palestine."

"You don't mean—?"

"No, not another man. The country. Everything. Everything *except* love!"

Eunice stared, intrigued. The luminosity of the eyes seemed to spread over the face. No colour came into the olive cheeks, but a warmth, a suffusion as of light, made brilliant the delicate flesh.

"Your mother told me you didn't want to go, at first. Isn't it true?"

"Oh, yes, it's true – I didn't want to, at first. I'd planned a trip to Italy. But the girl I arranged to go with let me down. She joined a party of students for Egypt and Palestine. I couldn't find another companion at the last moment, so I joined them too." She reached out to the table beside the bed, and stubbed her cigarette on the plate-glass top. "What really made me go was the chance of visiting my father's grave."

"And that was why your mother went with you, last year."

"Yes, I persuaded her – I told her it was shamefully neglected. We had a new stone placed and lots of things done." She was silent, gazing at the table. Eunice watched her with pleasure. There was something vivid even in the quietude of the dark little thing. She was hard, like Dorry, wilful and self-absorbed, yet at the core of her something moved, unflintlike – un-Dorrylike? That she could not penetrate to it made awareness no less pleasurable – at moments almost exciting. When Ruth was not there, she forgot her: so alien from her own life were the girl's interests. But Ruth, being there, could not be forgotten, she aroused expectation and surmise. Odd words came from her next. "That was all Mother really cared about. But I went back to Palestine for the living, not the dead."

"So you had already met David?"

"Oh, no. Not until the middle of the second visit." Her glance came back to Eunice, arch, provoking, withholding.

"Tell me – how – where did you meet?"

"On the sands at Tel-Aviv. Mother and I were walking there one evening. It was delicious, cool and refreshing, after the heat of the day. There were crowds, but we didn't know a soul. We walked arm-in-arm, talking together – in English, of course. Then someone pushed against me and said – "Hebrew – speak Hebrew—" We were astounded. I stopped and glared at the fellow. 'Impudence,' I said. But he only grinned and said *'chutzpah,'* and walked away." She began to laugh very softly.

"Was it David? And what is cha-chut-chuzpah—?"

"It was David. And the word he used to me was the same as I used to him. Only the tone was different. And the intention, according to him. My first lesson, he told me. Not only in translation."

"So you went on talking?"

"No, not then – he disappeared. But we met again next day, quite conventionally. At least, as conventionally as can happen in Palestine, which isn't very. That is, outside the snobby official circles." She jumped up suddenly. "I'm keeping you awake. Do you hear Mother, making 'noises off'? But it's the first time you've stayed the night – it seems like old times, in the flat – and I thought you'd like a little chat before turning off the light."

"I've loved it. You never talked to me like this in the flat – you've never told me as much about yourself before, Ruth – I hope you'll tell me the rest some time."

"The rest's in Palestine. Come out and see us next year – or as soon as you can take a holiday from business."

"I'd like to be at your wedding in the spring."

"That would be the cat's cream."

She hovered at the door like a dusky moth. Then fluttered back to offer a swift kiss.

"Ni-night, Eunice. I wish you could be happy – as happy as I am—"

Eunice put her fingers on the wide mauve sleeve.

"What's your recipe? You mix something with love – but what is it?"

"Oh, I don't know! Well – perhaps it's belief in something – something big – not just in a man. Righto, Mother – coming. Now I'll catch it for keeping you up."

Eunice smiled her secret Monna smile. She lay back on the pillows, stretching her hand to the electric switch. Darkness blurred the room, her eyes closed, but she saw Furnall's teasing face, and her arms, still outstretched, softly enclosed the sleek bent head. Why hunt for recipes, with happiness at her board? Odd little Ruth must travel far for her dish. Eunice drew in the savour of her own, with delicate breathings of dreamless sleep.

She left the villa in the morning with Mrs. Casson. When she returned to her flat, it was homelike with the service of a temporary maid, provided through Madame Eve. The spirit of Mrs. Johns was exorcised: partly by the offices of George and Hava; partly by her own resolve to help the orphans, and make special provision for the infant who objected to picky hands. She faced the inquest with philosophy.

VIII.

Nice Little Sister

DORRY came back on Tuesday more "cocky" than ever. It was Rita's word, uttered like a sneer. A curious malice struck from the clipped, staccato tones. But to Eunice, Dorry's swagger was endearing. She reflected on it with humorous patience, even when it became a bore. "She's brought it off, and nobody's to forget it!" Mrs. Casson, too, was encouraging, since she appreciated the business exploit. Dorry could boast shamelessly, and did.

"You ought to see old Faille on his knees to me. Positively crept! I gave him a mouthful of my best French over his doddering delays, and he was humble as pie, all over me." Dorry smirked. She knew it was not her French that captured old Faille, who understood much better the language of her eyes. As for Denise – "That plump pussy! All she thinks of is hot chocolate with cream. Laps it up day and night. I fed her at cafés till she was sick, but she was always ready for more. They knew us at that place opposite the Madeleine. Glass of lemon for me and hot choc. for her. No wonder she can't keep her figure. *She's* no advertisement for *La Svelte Ceinture – sous ventriere* I called it, when she showed me how she fixed it on her skin, and she went into fits! But I wormed plenty of tips out of her. Saved her commission at Jeune's and Pierre's, and didn't let any cats out of *my* bag!"

She winked at Hava, who looked suitably impressed; then laughed so excitably that tears flushed her eyes. The way Dorry strutted and peacocked, Eunice began to feel, was out of all proportion. Almost as if other experiences had come her way in Paris, that gave her this air of cynical wisdom, of exaggerated slyness and maturity. Was Denise to be trusted? But questions could elicit no divergence from plan, carefully if hurriedly arranged. Rita, much less sisterly in challenge, may have understood better Dorry's fits of reaction. One day full of bounce and superciliousness, the next she was pensive and depressed. There was a violent quarrel with Rita of which Eunice knew nothing. But Dorry changed friends so often that such an incident would not have been disturbing. Nor did her sulks and snappishness trouble Eunice much. The little flirt probably missed Blake Pellew. A riddance that might well be spared comment! Eunice smiled and humoured Dorry, who resented rather than enjoyed the elder's indulgence.

"Thinks she can do anything she likes with me, now that Blake's off the map. Damn it! Treats me more like a kid than ever—"

This was Dorry's complaint to Rita when they met again. Rita was cold and indifferent, but not more than usual: and Dorry could not do without her. It wasn't only that she admired Rita intensely. It was the relief afforded by imparting confidences to her. Dangerous confidences. But one could say anything to Rita.

"I wish you'd let me share your flat with you." She made the proposition coaxingly, not for the first time since Rita had revealed that a girl she "digged with" had gone abroad. "I'll have to chuck Eunice in the end— Just as you chucked your aunt. It'll be worse than ever when Hava Casson goes. Can't call my soul my own—"

"Body, you mean."

"Same thing, Rita. Anyway, it's mine, and I mean to do as I like with it."

"Bloody little sop."

"Not so bloody as you think." Dorry imitated the other's ironic tonelessness. "I shan't throw it away. I'm more set than ever now – no ring, no anything."

"Got it, didn't you?"

"I will, though. Be a brick, Rita. Help me out of Seneschal. It'll be easier if I can say I'm fixing up with you. You might as well – honest, I won't interfere—"

"Oh, shut it, and go home."

On Sunday night Dorry was lying moodily in bed. She was alone in the flat. Eunice had gone to a cinema with Bob. She hadn't wanted to go. Bob came uninvited to tea, and stayed on, urging her – urging them both, since Eunice agreed on condition that Dorry went, too. But Dorry, who had a headache, and had been out of sorts all day – a flu' cold seemed threatening – offered convincing excuse. She didn't like the pictures at the theatre they were going to. A potty highbrow-place where Russian films were shown. She didn't want to see flickering fields of corn with peasants quarrelling over ploughs and tractors. Hideous faces they had, even the girls – rough pocked skin in the close-ups, with the sweat standing out like callosities, unpleasant and disconcerting. If it was a Greta Garbo or Constance Bennett or Ronald Colman picture, she would have been tempted to go, in spite of her headache. But it wasn't only the cinema that Dorry didn't like. She didn't like Bob. More accurately, perhaps, Bob didn't like her. She knew it, having set out deliberately to dislike him, if not to induce dislike. She did it because she could not bear a man to admire Eunice more than herself – or rather, to be "all eyes" for Eunice while hardly noticing "the kid." She suspected, now, that to return indifference with contempt was a mistake. But having achieved the mutual activity, she let it go on. Eunice was welcome to the swain. He was fat and dull, anyway.

Dorry yawned, and kicked her legs in the air. She liked looking at her legs. They tapered up prettily from the rumpled quilt. The ankles were daintily slender from any angle, as she twisted and pointed her toes. It was good exercise, too, and she had rather neglected her exercises since she came back. If her head didn't ache slightly still, in spite of the aspirins, she would have got out and performed on the rug. But there was one she could do in bed, a simple new trick – new to her, at least – for flattening the tummy. She had heard of it only yesterday from a chorus-girl, a big-built dancer with a marvellous tummy, flat as a pancake. "Used to be more like a drum," said the girl.

Dorry stretched herself rigid, elongated her knees, breathed in and out from the diaphragm, timing intake and projection with rhythm. The rush of air in her ears was disconcerting.

"Oh, blow!" she gasped disgustedly. "I'm in rotten condition. Get like Denise if I'm not careful. All very well for her – Frenchmen like 'em that way. And Blake's half-French, of course."

Thoughts of Paris were tantalising. She turned to the wireless box on the table near the wall, and plugged in vain. There was nothing on the ether – nothing, at any rate, that could be trapped. Or perhaps something was wrong. The new portable set had not behaved too well even in the sitting-room. Since she had brought it in here, she couldn't work it at all. The local Sunday programme was frightfully boring. Church stuff – sermons, oratorios, appeals for charities. . . . Even Gracie Fields was pressed into incongruous service. . . . Nothing worth listening to, except for the sense of company the voices gave. Weather and shipping news – not much better. One of the announcers had an attractive drawl – the slight clipping, the slight sibilance, the exquisitely balanced mince and coo of articulation, tickled her ears; she'd like to meet that chap. He wasn't meetable, though, even as a voice. She had switched on and off capriciously, trying in vain to get the Continent. Once she thought she caught the tones of the Italian lady – "Al-lo . . . Ro-ina . . ." Deep, full, vibrant tones, too much like those of Eunice to please her. But they didn't come through tonight. And now it was too late. Must be nearly eleven. Her watch had stopped, and she couldn't bother to consult the clock in the other room. Eunice would be in soon. Hope she won't bring that fat bear in. Dorry yawned again, and closed her eyes. She was getting sleepy. As she snuggled into the pillow, the telephone rang. She lay still a moment, listening. Then got up quickly and answered it. A man's voice against her ear – an unknown voice.

"Hello, Eunice. Glad to catch you in. I've just got back – straight from Euston this moment. How are you? Did you get my card?"

"Who is speaking?"

"Why – George. Didn't you – I can't quite get your voice – the line's buzzy this end – it's Eunice, isn't it?"

"No. She's out. I'm Dorry."

"Oh." A slight pause. "Then you're the pretty little sister—"

"Thank *you*, George, I don't know you, but you sound quite nice."

"Thank you – Dorry. You sound even nicer. I hope to make your acquaintance soon."

"When are you coming round?"

"Unfortunately, not just yet. Every minute's booked this week. All the same, I hope to see your sister – and you, per-haps? – at the Albert Hall on Saturday. I'm sending her a ticket for the meeting – reserved place. Shall I send another for you?"

"What sort of meeting?"

"Political. Speeches on Disarmament. Perhaps you aren't interested?"

"Not much. I couldn't come Saturday, anyway. Got a date."

"A what – oh, I see!" He laughed. "Well, we'll have to arrange something else. In the meantime, please tell your sister I rang up. George Furnall. Er – do you think she'll be in during the next ten minutes?"

"Don't know. She's gone to the pictures. With a friend."

"Oh, with a friend?"

She made a face at the instrument.

"Yes. I expect he'll keep her out fairly late. I may be asleep when she comes in. But I'll tell her in the morning."

"Thanks. Er – I wonder if I know him?"

"It's Bob."

"Oh – Bob!"

The tone, in spite of its sympathy with her own, caused another resentful grimace.

"Well, if you'll excuse me now, I'll pop back to bed."

"Awfully sorry. Do get back at once. But – I say! – if Eunice *should* come in during the next few minutes, will you ask her to ring me here?" He rattled off a number. "Thanks so much, Dorry. Good night."

Dorry's ears had already caught sounds at the outer door. She muttered "Good night" – clicked the receiver, and was in bed with the light off and covers over her chin, before the Yale key had been withdrawn. There were soft steps, a tiny tap, a whisper – unanswered.

Dorry opened her eyes to the darkness, half peevish, half amused. "George" had a nice voice – it sounded remarkably like that new announcer's – but he was probably dull. A political blighter. Where had Eunice got hold of him? Through Bob, most likely. He was much more "coming-on" than Bob. Pretty free with names in a brief space of time.

Well, Eunice could jolly well wait until she heard from him. Two men dancing on my lady! No wonder she gave herself such airs.

Dorry yawned once more and squeezed down her lids. But she did not feel as drowsy as she had done before.

IX

Politicians – On Platforms and Off

EUNICE was a little vexed with Bob. He ought to have been sitting at the Press table, but having made his arrangements with a colleague, he took her off to a couple of seats which gave a good view of the platform, yet could not easily be seen from it. Unwilling to fuss, she was obliged to abandon her reserved stall, towards which Furnall might look in vain.

Good humour, however, prevailed. She was interested in the occasion, for which she had prepared herself by reading current journals: and Bob had his uses in pointing out distinguished figures, both on the platform and in the audience. Everything about the demonstration proved pleasantly exciting. It was popular with all parties, and the leaders of each were to give addresses, supported by representatives of Church and Army. Pacifist organisations showed a natural zeal. In the procession that marched from Hyde Park women preponderated, many of them scarred from war-time campaign: now their banners proclaiming international goodwill flew in the sun without challenge, were greeted, indeed, by sympathetic murmurs, both outside and inside the hall. Eunice watched their entry with close attention. She thought it possible Laura Fennick might be among them. It would be amusing, almost thrilling, to meet Laura again, in an atmosphere at last congenial to both. In all the years since they had left Taviton,

Laura had made two brief appearances on Eunice Fleet's horizon. Once, when they met at a celebration of the forming of the first Labour Government. Bob had induced Eunice to accompany him there in his journalistic capacity; and it turned out that a fellow-journalist, newly appointed to edit a Labour weekly, was none other than Harvey Fennick. Brother and sister were together. Harvey, though deeply tanned, looked none too robust. He was braving his first winter of fog and sleet in the interests of his political cause. "You must be overjoyed," Eunice had said to him politely – "now that your old leaders are in office." He seemed far from overjoyed, however. "Now all our troubles will really begin," he said. "I'm afraid there are dark times ahead." Laura laughed at him. She was even more of a foreign visitant, and when in England, preferred being in the country with a group of associates to "working" – whatever it was she worked at – in London. The second time they met was when she sent Eunice an invitation to a gathering of the Association of Friends of Soviet Russia. Eunice, unimpressed by Laura's new enthusiasm, asked with an ironical smile whether it was shared by Harvey. "He's not as keen on Russia as I am," confessed Laura. In appearance she was curiously unaltered. Her short hair fell as brown and soft across her nut-like head, her little wiry figure could be as still or suddenly alert. But a subtle change transfused her manner. With all her optimism and zeal, no trace of sentiment recalled the younger Laura. "I'm afraid Harvey's in a backwater. Got in now with a set who might be called the neo-Fabians. Expect to permeate the jingo world with Socialist ideas, by colouring them Jingo! I've no use for that sort of chameleon. Of course, I'm in the opposite camp. With the Bolsheviks." She cut the other's smile with a challenging grin of her own. "Tomorrow I'm off on a long visit, to study the Soviet system at first hand. I may be away six months or a year. The A.F.S.R. want me to lecture when I'm back. Will you come and hear me?"

Eunice promised, obviously cool to the prospect. The year had passed without news of the odd little creature. She might well be in London now, participating in events in which the Women's International took a leading share.

There was no sign of Laura, however, in the near mass; and it was impossible to recognise any face in the further ranks that filled the great hall. For a moment Eunice imagined she saw her sitting at the Press table. But her view was obstructed and her attention diverted, by the uprising of the audience as the speakers walked onto the platform. Bob spoke loudly amid the roar of cheers

"That's the Prime Minister – there's Baldwin with the Field-Marshal – here comes Lloyd George, and – hallo! – what's going on?—"

Eunice was aware of commotion below. Bob leaped a row of standing people. He got back with difficulty as they began to sit down, and grinned delightedly.

"Woman threw a stink-bomb," he said. "She had a nerve! – sneaked into my place, I believe – but they soon got her out."

"Nothing's happened?"

"Only a smell." He sniffed. "She managed to shoot off a glass bulb from her paper bag – didn't you hear it break? Wonder who the little devil can be—"

"Was she very – little?" Surely it could not have been Laura?

"Don't know – couldn't see. They hustled her out in a jiffy."

"I suppose they arrested her."

"Oh, no – just chucked her out."

"But what did she *want*?"

"God knows – either more punch, or less!" He laughed. "Always some fanatic on the job at these shows. No harm, anyway – only fun. But I bet they had a scare down there. And the stuff has a vile smell. Look at Mac sawing the air to keep it off his nose!"

They had whispered through the chairman's speech. Now they sat silent, staring at the platform. Eunice glimpsed Furnall behind his chief, but it was unlikely that he would see her unless he turned his head – and even then only if she leaned forward. Somehow she felt stiff as a poker. Couldn't budge. But her vexation was lost in the thrill of recognising in the stately figure facing a rapt audience – rapt after thunderous greeting – the outcast avoiding his fellow-countrymen in a back street of Taviton. Times had changed. That figure, too, had changed. She remembered a shaggy, beaten man, impressive in the moment of humiliation, conquering in the act of retreat. His pride and dignity had wrested homage from a mind full of hostile scorn.

Age – eminence – acclaim of the fickle mob – did these things add to dignity or lessen it? The shabby refugee had shone a king to her rebellious eyes: and now those eyes, ready with reverence, grew hesitant, seeing no majesty. Not only virile prime had gone with the dark locks reckless on the brow. The grey crown curbed and groomed, the body trim with polish to the toes, were somehow dulled and drained. Weariness grooved the skin, sank below it, clotted the racing blood, the easy tongue. She listened, staring. Fire enough in gesture and voice, for those who stirred to rhetoric: but where was the molten steel, the quality of fineness that ran fluid from a muted man? A hot spirit that perhaps had waxed too high, spilled over in the furnaced years, then dried – in a blistered vessel, covered too late with glaze.

The sonorous phrases rang reverberations to her ears echoes of far-off speech, set to a new rhythm of the times. As if Vincent were speaking – and, incredibly, eating his words.

"People seeking safety by arms are like people seeking shelter under trees during a thunderstorm. . . . The sentiment of peace is universal, but the practice of peace is circumscribed. . . . We are going to Geneva to get the nations of the world to reduce this enormous, disgraceful burden of armaments. . . . The way is difficult. When you settle down to tonnages, to man power, to questions as to the kind of material to be taken into account, it is difficult. We must have no illusions about disarmament . . ."

She listened, and looked away. Her discontent returned. Why didn't Furnall find her out? Why didn't he meet her seeking eyes, and give her reassurance? He was young enough to have zest and confidence; to despise the barriers raised by tired old men.

The ex-Premier who followed was gentlemanly in another way. He showed neither strain nor fatigue, and talked with a genial air, as who should say – "A naughty world, my masters. But one might as well be pleasant, don't you know." He shook a finger in regret at Russia, whose bad manners might exhaust forbearance: and at least set Eunice wondering again, how Laura's study of that "armed and powerful neighbour" had ended. In a bomb of protest? Was it really Laura who had thrown it? And if so – if she or another – protest against what? Could it be – against willy-nilly, shilly-shally . . .?

The next ex-Premier was much less gentlemanly. His reputation for metaphors was not maintained. Nobody climbed peaks into arcadian valleys, or watched the dawn break roseate. He was glib but sardonic, a teller of unpleasant truths. "Let us be frank," he cried. And he was at least more explicit than the others. "Sixty countries signed the pact to renounce war. All had great armies. And since they signed, their armies have become greater and more powerful! They all renounced war, but they forgot to renounce preparations for war. . . . They kept Germany to her promise, but broke their own. . . . A Disarmament Commission had been sitting for years – and so far had hatched nothing. . . . The nations of the world were now spending over £800,000,000 to prepare for war."

She sighed, and looked around, bewildered, at the dense-packed hall. Bob put his hand on hers. She took no notice of it. Presently there was a burst of applause, and she muttered:

"Isn't it rather depressing?"

"What?"

"Oh – this sort of thing—"

"People cheering their leaders? – or all demonstrations for peace and plenty?"

"But I mean – what the leaders say about militarism everywhere – the way delegates agree on principles at Geneva, then go home to raise new armies and taxes for instruments of war—"

"Well, we must face facts—"

"Yes. It's honest of the leaders to admit the facts. But don't you find it depressing?"

"Not at all. You're young at this game, aren't you?" He smiled in tender drollery, but seeing she was grave, unlined his smile. "Don't you see, girlie, it means a harder push for peace campaigns – to get people to see sense, and act up to it."

"Act up to it – of course." As Vincent had done? She couldn't ask Bob that. He had been a soldier, cheerful in the acceptance of his duty. "Silly mess," he recognised. But if another war broke out – because men were too weak or too obsessed to stop it – he would probably "serve" again. Or consent that others should "serve." But George Furnall – George couldn't. She leaned forward, supple and eager, and again Bob pressed her hand.

"Let's go," he whispered. "Had enough of it, haven't you? Let's clear before the crowd, and find some tea—"

She shook her head, and at another outbreak of clapping, withdrew her fingers, pretending to join in. Poor Bob! Why did he bother about her, when she couldn't possibly – bother about him? She had asked him once. He had laughed with forced airiness, and quoted something – from or about Goethe, she wasn't sure which. It sounded like – "She was lovable, and he loved her: he was not lovable, and she loved him not." It wasn't true. She was not lovable – yet he loved her: *he* was lovable – yet she loved him not. Her half-impatient pity spread to sweeter thought, sweeter and more poignant. Surely, now there was lovableness in her? – but only for the man who had less. Was Furnall lovable? Not as Bob was. Not as Vincent had been. Warm, spontaneous natures. George was not like either: cooler, more calculating, more – cynical. Yes, she admitted it, with a little shock. Cynical, despite ideals, spurts of enthusiasm, devotion to a cause. Not in the flippant change of speech, such as Bob used, without diminishing the hoard of inner faith: but in waste of real stock – of deeper values. Yet – if he loved her? She leaned still further, careless of Bob, intent to concentrate her gaze on George, compel him to look at her. A lady was on her feet, proposing a vote of thanks. She had a fluent platform manner – fluent, but dull. The energy of her phrases was oiled with platitude. Furnall was listening, not too attentively. Now and again he glanced away, exchanging signs with Jess Grunbaum, who sat at the other end of his row. Eunice bored her will into the back of his head, ordering it to turn. And in a moment it turned. Her smile caught him full. He beamed in response, half rising and waving his hand. She drew back, still and quiet, but in her veins the blood ran gaily, acknowledging the sun.

*   *   *

George, like Bob, parried her criticisms, but with more authority in humouring her seriousness.

"My dear girl, you're in a hurry. Didn't you grasp what the P.M. said about patience, and step by step? Statesmen can't commit their countries to drastic courses, which the people mayn't really want – and which in any case might make worse international complications. And aren't you inclined to pick on the dark side? Of course there are forces against. But just think what's been achieved in spite of them." He described England's reduction of arms, the progressive "baby-walk," of the infant League, the pacific spirit spreading throughout the peoples of the world. It was important, while nursing this spirit, to take no risk of danger, no chance of countercheck.

She smiled, with more pleasure in his familiarity than in his arguments. She could not, indeed, think too clearly while he addressed her. It was otherwise when she was alone, reading newspaper accounts of belligerency in the East, faction in the West, mock air-raids over London – "If young Londoners adequately realised the fascination of work with the searchlights" – rhapsodied a journalist – "I can imagine them flocking to enlist in a battalion like the —th!" Wireless talks on international problems moved her more than lyric verse.

She discussed these problems with Hava Casson, who was so sensible in comment – marginal comment of busy partners, alive to the economics of their time. Pros and cons of tariffs, trade walls and barriers between nations – the higher the walls, the fiercer the hate? – profits, taxes, bank-rates, employment costs. Hava was not losing interest in commerce because of relinquishing sound business for adventure. Her combination of shrewdness with idealism brought, in fact, a stronger note into pronouncements on humanity. She was sure of the triumph of pacifism – "it's the only thing that'll pay in the end." And perhaps this

very optimism, too bland for the other's secret doubt,
blurred frankness between them. How could Eunice, conscious of her doubt, let Hava see that faith in world-peace
was bound with personal passion?

To herself there was no confusion in the fact. World-
peace was Furnall's career – and therefore the development
of her own. If he wavered, it must detract, not from a
standard, but from the perfection of the triangle which she
and Vincent had begun. She wanted George to see the
design as she herself saw it: a thing complete, yet shaping
still out of the ideal that drew the parts together. An ideal
that was a power, if not a reality, since having once disrupted and impoverished her life, it was now annealing,
making it stable and rich. Deprecation seemed a double
treachery. She strove to avoid it in herself, mere novice or
late disciple; and dreaded it in others, those who had
served from early time and seen the cycle round. In George,
particularly, who must believe – and reassure.

She brought him tales, therefore, to confute and pooh-
pooh, as if she were a child in his presence, which, in a
way, she was. Why, she asked, if the world was more
pacific, were Archbishops still preaching the war-guilt of
Germany? Why did a woman leaving a Peace conclave,
clutch her husband's arm and hail a hawker in the street
offering toy cannon for sale – "Oh, Jack, there's the very
thing for our Freddie's birthday!" Why did the French
announce a new plane, armed with five machine-guns and
eleven bomb projectiles, able to carry a ton of explosives, in
addition to crew, with a range of 1427 miles and a speed of
150 miles an hour? Why should the B.B.C. devise novel
measures to conduct war-propaganda, as was suggested in
an evening journal of repute? Why did shareholders of
armament firms include clergymen, Cabinet Ministers, and
members of the League of Nations?— Why – why – why—?

George, of course, could either scratch his head and deplore these things, or show the balance against them. So long as he maintained the front, and boasted his own and his chief's generalship in the conduct of the peace campaign (strange how pacifists used military terms!) she was content. But if she brought more than tales – if she posed problems and suggested solutions, his response did not always satisfy.

She pondered, it seemed, the proposals of national representatives at Geneva. Some wanted to reduce all armaments to what was called a general "safety" level; others, to abolish specific weapons, such as bombing planes, or tanks, or submarines; yet others, to ban chemical warfare and the use of poison gas. But nobody offered to refrain from every kind of armament in any circumstances. The "abolition of war" was a fancy phrase, an aim confessedly remote. How could it be otherwise, with Asiatics learning late but efficiently the tricks of the Western world? Or with the Westerns themselves still embroiled in petty spites, discarding old tricks for new, perfecting rather than rejecting the machinery of hate? Lofty persons spoke of salvation, not by riddance of arms, but by the invisible process of "a change of heart," a "new spirit" in mankind. Hava said this spirit was as old as Isaiah. It was familiar to generations as the "will to peace." Every nation had it until stampeded into war. Even the rulers had it, or at least proclaimed it, to justify usage of material to hand – the inanimate material, and the animate who wielded it, to destroy the opposite animates – whenever some crisis occurred, some muddle which their wits or their wills could not solve otherwise.

There was only one thing essential to a state of no-war, which the animates could effect while the inanimates lay piled. The Hebrew Prophets advised it, the Early Christians had practised it. Vincent and ten thousand of his fellows had confirmed their wisdom. But thousands more – millions – must be urged to make the "will" concrete in the same way. Refusal. Refusal to kill, to be "deemed" a soldier, to handle any instrument of carnage, to engage in any process of military craft. If men would not fight, if men were not *compelled* to fight, even in a single country, there could not be a war.

Having arrived at this ingenuous conclusion, so simple, so obvious, so effective, that it put all the complicated weavings of politicians to shame, Eunice was aghast to find that the politician to whom she submitted it laughed at her. At first she thought it must be in derision – not of her idea, but of her belatedness. Of course she had not made the discovery when Vincent did. She had not even seen it when he showed it to her. And her blindness had stricken them both. She deserved to be mocked. But not by George. Why should he laugh at her now, when she acknowledged the truth, and proposed that he should make his platform on it?

He stopped laughing when he saw that she was hurt, took her hand in his, and explained. It was not that he disbelieved – how could he? And there was a lot in her notion of getting the Powers to agree on – well, even a *modification* of compulsory service. But he could not take an extreme stand at the outset of his public life. The political course was full of dangers. One had to appeal to the electorate on the main – perhaps the "safe" – issues of the hour. The peace question was important, but in view of other aspects of the appalling world economic position, not yet foremost, in spite of the campaign, the war-cloud in the East, the tangles at Geneva and Lausanne. His chief said—

She didn't gather what his chief said, confused by his eloquent eyes and the way he stroked her hand. She knew, however, that his objections were of expediency; and she countered them by saying that if he was right, and the matter not timely, then the outlook must be hopeless. According to the signs, there was bound to be a "next war," which might really prove to be "*the* last war." The horrors would be greater than ever. And perhaps it wouldn't matter if objectors weren't listened to then – for everyone, militarists, pacifists, soldiers, civilians – *everyone* – would be swept away in holocaust—

At which he laughed again, but so tenderly, so obviously charmed by the spirited sarcasm of her speech, that she forgave him. And then Dorry came in and the atmosphere changed. And she realised a long time afterwards that it was their last talk together on the great subject.

But not, of course, the last time it was discussed in general terms, when she listened and said very little. The talk of men – of Bob and other friends – had more interest for her now than her silence made them guess. She drew impressions which might have caused surprise, or more probably, she thought, amusement. George had taught her at least to smile ironically at herself.

Vincent's ghost walked no less effectively these days. He had become for her a standard of comparison, from which not even George was exempt. There had been about Vincent something fiery as well as gentle: something stern as well as sweet. She could not imagine these things combined in George – or indeed in any "modern" man she knew. They were apt to be petulant rather than angry, and much too pliable to be fixed. Austerity and fire were not in them, except as sparks that drifted in the wind. Perhaps they could not be sufficiently in earnest: perhaps the crucible of war had left them waste. The conviction did not sadden her, since with George she felt assurance – that as her own ash stirred to flame, she could enkindle his. In him a brand of altruism smouldered still. As for inflexibility – she might blow cool as well as hot upon the mould. Vain, perhaps, of her power over him, and rash in estimate. But happy. Happy in the growing sense of love and hope.

She criticised, therefore, with kindness. Furnall's friendship with Dorry increased her patience with both. They had taken to each other from the first, though there seemed a little mystery about that "first." When Furnall came to the flat one evening, with Bob and Jess Grunbaum, Dorry was just going out. He acknowledged introduction with a grin – "Oh, but we know each other – your pretty little sister and I – had a jolly chat on the phone when you were out—"

"Oh, really? "said Eunice, and Jess chimed in, "And did you know she was pretty on the phone?"

"Of course!" But George Furnall was no fool. "I admit it helped that Eunice had told me so before. What I discovered on my own was that Miss Granger was *nice*!"

"Cat!" thought Dorry, who disliked Jess Grunbaum, and attributed motive to a careless phrase. Either in despite, or because Furnall's words mollified, she made a point at once of earning his praise. They got on well enough to make her inclusion in other evenings, both at the flat and elsewhere, an easy if not inevitable result. As Dorry generally avoided her sister's friends, this was a new departure, not without inconveniences. But any sign of amiability on Dorry's part was welcome to Eunice. The girl's ill-humours had become a problem that only pleasanter preoccupations made tolerable.

X.

The Marrying Sort

DURING August the sisters spent a holiday in Frinton. It rained most of the time, or was cool and windy. Dorry thought the people in the hotel were putrid; the celebrities who sometimes took villas on the coast had gone, very sensibly but inconsiderately, to the Riviera; there was never anybody decent on the front when Dorry and Eunice blew along the grass above or kicked the sand below. Dorry could not swim like Eunice, who enjoyed the buffets of the North Sea waves, foaming at their lead-green mouths; so, without sun-bathing, she hated the sea. She hated golf, too: and the nights were dead as mutton. One had to run over to Clacton to see any life, and the services – bus and train – were the last word. "Why don't we get a car?" (The putrid men in the hotel took other girls for rides.) She snapped and complained until they returned to town. If Eunice had not held herself in – if she had not been happy enough to make the holding easy – the two would have quarrelled every day. At home and in business, the friction increased. Dorry seemed to be getting out of control. Her head, thought Eunice, was turned by admiration, the flattery of customers and friends. A series of successful sales raised her to giddy heights. She wanted to fly before she could walk. She demanded impossible terms, a partnership for which she had not qualified, a status which Eunice was dangling in reserve: alternatively, a lump sum with which to "clear out" and establish herself otherwise. "What can you do, silly child?" – "I'm not a child. I'm older than you were when you married. There are lots of things I could go in for, and plenty of people to back me up. Rita designs gowns, and I could sell them, I suppose. I'm sick of corsets, anyway!"

Eunice was perplexed, unable to yield, unwilling to take drastic measures. Then suddenly the welcome change. Dorry stopped threatening and demanding. Partly Mrs. Casson was responsible. She suggested an arrangement which gave Dorry a larger share, without too much control or excessive drain on funds. Eunice, as Madame Eve, was undertaking extra burdens for the year, and Dorry's acquiescence was a relief to all. Eunice had other things to attend to. An accumulation of matters to settle with Hava Casson, who was leaving in October; details of buying and selling for the end of one season and the beginning of another; a visit to Paris; a dispute in the workroom between cutters and fitters; and building changes, a new shop front-age, an extension of premises and lease. In addition, her voluntary charge of Mrs. Johns' orphans. . . .

All this kept her busy till the autumn. She did not feel it mattered that weeks of interruption lessened rather than increased her personal contact with George. He, too, was occupied with his chief's work, and his own candidature for Parliament. As the election week coincided with the Cassons' departure, she was unable to help him as she wished. Instead, she released Dorry, who was lured by the novelty of canvassing into fresh enthusiasms. For one thing, she learnt to use Furnall's car. He seemed to humour her as Eunice did, to treat her in the same way, but with masculine impunity, as "a nice little kid." He took her out in the car while Eunice was away, and was amused by her desire to drive it. The lessons proved a practical benefit to him. Dorry was expert enough to take charge on polling day, and carried relays of electors to their booths. It was she who made most fuss when he failed to top the poll – by a "mere" few hundred votes. She wanted a recount, and suspected a plot against him when no grounds were announced.

"Never mind, Dorry," he said, patting her shoulder – "we'll do it next time—"

Eunice smiled half-heartedly at them. She, too, was disappointed, and in more than the election. George was more friendly than ever, yet they had got no nearer to each other. She had thought it enough for a time: but her heart, dreamy-content beneath the routine of life, woke up in hunger. She began to crave for something less tacit, for more definite tokens of their bond. Was he more disheartened than he showed, and by apparent indifference in her? Had she neglected him too much? Had she let her business absorb her to the exclusion of his, which was even more deeply her own?

She had expected him to win his seat, to plunge forthwith into the Parliamentary arena. That would have served as a new starting-point for both. Already she had decided on certain changes, to fit in with his. Even the date was allotted in her mind: the day of his maiden speech. (It must follow his induction very quickly, she thought.) She would be in the House. Thenceforth she would be often in the House, lunching with him, devising ways of making herself companionable – necessary – indispensable. She had absorbed knowledge from Jess Grunbaum, and spent hours at St. Stephens with her before Parliament had adjourned. Several afternoons and evenings she had wasted in the galleries. Wasted? She ought not to have used the word. She ought not to have ridiculed the pompous legislators, stretched on their benches or prosing on their feet. Particularly she ought not to have sneered at the "clubroom throng," and "the holiday seekers," while empty leather heard the speeches on reduction of Air Force grants or warships. Where, she asked, was A.? and B.? and C.? – not to mention X. and Y. and Z. They might never have been thrust into gaols or chased from platforms, for denouncing war and slavery. Now that they were acclaimed as leaders, lifted into office on a tide of favour, they were silent, or absent – or, worse still, made specious opposition – when voice and vote were needed to turn crusade into law. "Is there no sincerity in politics?" she fumed, indignant. "Are pacifists in power willing to take the risk of war, and not the risk of peace?" Jess Grunbaum shrugged her sturdy shoulders. "Proselytes are always over-zealous," she observed, "and it's hardly like you to be crude, my dear. Office isn't power. And people may change without being insincere. Above all, one must be loyal."

"To what?" asked Eunice.

"You mean to *whom*?" Jess pointed to a picture of the Premier on her desk, and smiled – her cool, discreet, black-eyed smile, with a twist at the corners of her mouth. It soothed Eunice as little as the strong Parliamentary tea, served to them both in a private room.

"Loyalty's in your blood," she said, and thought of Hava. How strange that those two disapproved of each other. And then she thought of Ruth, and her half-light, half-thrilling tones. *Belief in something big – not just in a man.* But only men could bring about the something big.

After all, she was young to the game, as Bob had pointed out. She must not be hasty in judgment. And there was no question of her judging George. Encouragement – that was what he needed. And though he had lost the seat – until "next time" – her scheme need not wait. She repented her laxity with Dorry. The chit must work harder, get less time off. At least they could arrange alternate hours "on." The manageress she had been training was turning out well, competent and keen, acceptable to the staff, already able to relieve her upstairs.

She must be free to spend more time with George. And – she must become more desirable to him. Walking out of her office with this thought, she smiled at herself in the *salon* mirror, to the surprise of an assistant near by. The girl peered slyly backwards, and caught her employer's frown. But the change of expression was not meant for the spy. Eunice had noted a sallowness of skin, too deep a laugh-line, unlustred hair. She must pay an early visit to a beauty-parlour.

It was Friday, a very tiring day. Orders were being completed, extra work rushed through, special clients interviewed. Dorry slipped off, evading Eunice, who had a late appointment with a country buyer. "Shan't get away till eight, I suppose," she had grumbled at lunch. But after Dorry had gone, a telegram came to postpone the call. Eunice locked up in relief and hurried home.

There was a possibility of George coming in. Though he had provincial engagements for the week-end, he might not leave town till Saturday, in which case he would look them up on Friday night. He had said he would phone, but she received no message, either directly or through Dorry. He must be coming. She had not asked anyone else, hoping that Dorry would go out, as she generally did on Fridays. It was a long time since she had been alone with George. Her heart lifted at the prospect, and the bus seemed unnaturally slow. Why hadn't she got on the "pirate," which had stopped at the same time, and now dashed along in disregard of the general's ten-m.p.h. crawl, cutting in and out with glorious recklessness? There it was in front of her, vexatiously ahead. But even the pirate was obliged to honour the signals in Oxford Street.

The long row of hooded lamps fascinated her. The automatic halt they produced in streaming traffic was a new feature of London. No policeman to stem the course with extended arms, a human bar that frowned or smiled, or even if impassive must breathe visibly. Nothing to heed but colours that flashed in change. Red-yellow-green. The checked stream flowed again in prompt release. She saw the portent of the signals. Mechanisation. Soulless mould of discipline. The machine without a god, or a god removed and reduced to slavery. Progress? Advance? A world of switches and obedience to a flash. Suppose the flash led only to destruction? Against that lurid glow, glimpsed in mock-prophecy, how pale the wick of human freedom. Of individual right. Of liberty of conscience. And yet— *How far that little candle throws his beams.* Shine on, dear Vin. You lit the way before. And now, with George, I'll throw a wider ray.

The brilliance of that ray was on the Edgware Road. Its shops and crowded barrows showed friendly life, swarming and varied in joys. The mothers dragging children home, the fathers pushing prams, the hawkers' gusty voices and loud-speakers' blare, made common human highway to fair goal. The bus jogged on to Maida Vale. Before it stopped at Clifton Gardens she jumped from the step, and ran along to Seneschal. She leaped up the curving flights with long, lithe tread, and turned the little Yale key in her lock. Sounds fell welcoming into the narrow hall. The wireless was on, strains of zigeuner music, a soft yearny background for Dorry's laugh and a light-toned masculine burr. Eunice smiled involuntarily. George had come. She would slip through the corridor to her room and titivate herself. But the sitting-room door was open. She paused in her glide and peeped in. The radio set was on the writing-table, and Dorry stood beside it, lovely in her new dinner-frock. No wonder she had rushed to try it on. The colour was her favourite china-blue, a cold and garish shade that almost stridently announced her fairness. It emphasised the youth and littleness of her. The style was simple, too; a slight frilliness below, and two tiny infantile sleeves. She sprouted out of it, a Botticelli imp – a cherub with a sweet, wilful pout. George was half-sitting, half-leaning on the table, his arms folded, a benign and amused expression on his face. Eunice felt a queer pull at her heart. She had the sudden sense of him that often overcame her – the feeling of a dear yet aloof personality: the forbidding and sacred sense of a stranger who was yet most preciously familiar. How could Dorry take such liberties with him? He was looking down at her, and must be thinking what a pretty chit she was. And she, of course, knew he was thinking it. And no doubt she had just said something saucy and pert. It was nice of him to humour Dorry, to indulge and spoil her, as if she were – already – his "little sister." Eunice almost sprang into the room, so strongly did her impulse to him move – with something else, some instinct of alarm. In that very second Dorry put her hand on his knee, and said, with a quivering lip, quite seriously—

"But I *do* mean it, George – I really do. Rita says I'm the marrying sort."

"A lot she knows about it! And a lot you know what *she* knows – luckily!" His hand caressed hers, and she snuggled close. Her eyes seemed to stray a moment to the door, then returned to stare, very wide, at him.

"Listen, now, Dorry – I don't like all I hear about this Rita. You must give her up, once for all. She – ain't – no – good – to – you." He chanted the last words in time with the new rhythm wailing from the wireless band.

"Very well, George – if you want me to." Dorry was climbing the knee, he bent to haul her up, and she joined her arms round his neck, digging her chin into his cheek.

"You know, George dear, I'll do anything you want."

He held her to him, and began to kiss her – playfully at first, then quickly, passionately. She was giggling; smothered, breathless giggles of delight.

"Little darling – sweet little darling – my little love!"

The wireless dance-music broke into louder jazz, drowning any sound from the door. But in the ears of Eunice there was neither noise nor silence. Petrified one moment, the next swift-moving to her room, she stood staring vacantly into the cheval mirror that checked her stride.

XI.

A Sweet Predicament

DORRY had "fallen for" George at sight. So she informed Rita, to whom she hastened with the news. He was the most charming man she had ever met. A high-brow who didn't talk over her head like Bob, and a gentleman, whose eyes answered hers without the lewdness of Blake's. Rita's allusions to the engineer no longer goaded.

"That bounder! He'll crawl back to his old hag yet," she said, and dismissed him finally with contempt. "I say, Rita – I'm going to drive his car."

"Whose?"

"The boyfriend's."

"I thought he was Mrs. Fleet's."

"He likes me best."

"Come off it. He likes the 'nice little sister.'" She almost achieved a simper of mimicry.

"Sister be blowed. He likes me for myself."

"Nice 'ickle self."

"He thinks it is. Honest. Don't grin, you pig. He's taking me to Brighton on Sunday—"

"H'm, the cat's away."

"—and what'll you bet, Rita? – What'll you bet *I* drive all the way back?"

She made further bets with Rita concerning Furnall, and meant to win them all. The fun of the wagers spurred her on, and even Rita did not believe for a time that the pursuit was serious. She knew the kid was mad on cars and meant to own one, even if it was only a second-hand Austin Seven: and of course she had no scruples about "booked" men. A sudden change in Dorry's appearance amused her.

"Pawned your ear-rings, kid?"

"'M—got sick of them." Dorry almost flushed, fingering her bare little ears. Not so long before she had made it a grievance that Eunice advised her not to wear the long, dangling stones. ("Said they weren't my style – made me look too old and sophisticated. Cheek! When she says sophisticated she means smart. She knows I'm smarter than she is – even if I haven't got her figure.")

There was no doubt that with the modification of her "smartness," Dorry was more childishly attractive. Under less heavy make-up, her fair skin bloomed more shyly, her mouth, freed of magenta tints, became a wistful bud. Grey eyes peeped innocent from unshadowed lids, the lashes lost their pincered, waxen stare, the silken curls fell soft behind the ears, no longer scrolled in serried waves upon each cheek. Rita's comment on the simpler coiffure brought frank acknowledgment.

"Big Boy saw me by accident one day, after I'd shampooed in a hurry and hadn't time to get a set. I thought my hair was a sight, flying anyhow over my head – but he just loved it! Said it looked adorable in its natural state, and why did I ever twist it into shapes?"

"Well, why *do* you? It isn't quite as natural as all that, even now—"

"Trust me! A man likes to believe he admires what's natural – but if things are too natural he doesn't admire 'em half as much!"

"There's a lot you don't know, kid – but not much you can't guess!"

In the artless effects, therefore, no less art was used. And

Dorry, sitting demure at home at her elder's feet, or clinging, a limpet third, to their company outdoors, sensed the
triumph of her tactic in Furnall's flickering looks. But
she felt no triumph when she spied the counter tactic of
her sister. Not that Eunice had any notion of rivalry. Her
instinct of adornment was simple and frank, as single as
her silence or her speech. She was absorbed in attention
to Furnall's talk without note of Dorry's imitative pose –
though a little vexed, perhaps, at her presence.

It is possible that Dorry had no deeper intent than Rita
suspected at first. She was always jealous of Eunice; always
ready, not only to flirt with any man, but to regard each
new admirer of her sister as a potential admirer of her own.
At what stage she became more serious, she might not
have been able to tell. But one day a conscious rage flared
up in her.

She had dressed rather blatantly for a Chelsea studio,
where a friend of Rita's often "threw a party." Though
eager to go, it vexed her strangely that Eunice seemed
equally pleased. As a rule the elder disparaged such affairs,
and was severe upon a laxity of costume. Tonight she took
scant notice of the backless, and almost frontless, sailor-
trousered pyjama suit with which Dorry skipped into her
room.

Eunice was, in fact, engrossed in her toilet. Dorry watched
her for some moments in silence. The process of creaming,
patting in lotion, applying a delicate-hued and finely sifted
powder, was neither novel nor complicated: but it was
being carried out with a peculiarly tender care. It was clear
that Eunice, absent to her companion, was alive to the
charm of her own pearly face. She was dipping into some
special preparations brought from Paris, and thinking
Dorry hankered after them, she offered their use, pushing
the jars to the edge of her table. Still looking in her mirror,

she raised a perfume spray, and lightly daubed the lobes of her ears. Then she picked up a pad and scrutinised her nails.

Dorry could have used her own to scratch her. Getting herself up for George, of course! Where was she going to see him tonight? For once too proud to ask, Dorry did not learn, could not even guess whether it was to be a *tête-à-tête*, a party – or only a public meeting. Eunice was damned secretive, often about nothing at all. Very well, she'd show her what a secret could be!

Running out abruptly, Dorry slammed the door, stood for a while outside it, clenching her hands. Her cold grey eyes were sullen with resentment. A voice rasped madly in her brain – "She shan't have him – she shan't! What *right* has she got?"

Repeating the words in brooded spite to Rita, she added, "I'll bring George the next time, see if I don't! He'd as soon take me about as Eunice – and sooner! I've only got to say the word. You should see the way he gives me the once-over. Why should I worry about *her*? She married once. If she made a mess of that, it's her own fault. War widows haven't any right to snoop up husbands a second time, while so many girls can't get away with *one*. I'm hanged if I let her spoil my chance!"

Rita laughed her startling staccato laugh, with no risibility in her face. The kid was really funny sometimes, especially on the marrying stunt. The oddest mixture of crudity and old-fashioned views, with up-to-date – sluttishness.

"A likely thing," she jeered nonchalantly. "If your sister's got her hand in, she won't let herself be cut out. What's your plan, anyway, kid?"

Her unusual curiosity was flattering, but Dorry wouldn't tell. She, too, could be guarded if she chose. Her secret should be her own until – until – she smiled provokingly, and pranced off in her trousers with a youth in a blouse and skirt. He was a pale-faced youth with very moist hands, which Dorry kept jerking off her bare waist. She wasn't impressed by boys under thirty: and she really loathed that pawing.

The drive to Brighton, and further motoring lessons, during the week that Eunice was away, had been the sole occasions when George and Dorry went about together. Afterwards the chance of being alone with him seemed remote. But Dorry meant to contrive it. She might ring him up, make some pretext, get him to take her out, pledge him to silence – it would seem just fun at first, then he'd be committed, then – well, then – he'd get to like it—

The course proved easy. It was easy because of the election, when she could go to him openly "to help," because Eunice became more and more involved at Madame Eve's, because George, as she foresaw, grew fonder and fonder—

Life relaxed very agreeably for George. His election prospects had never been too good, and results were far above his party hopes. The experience was useful, at the least, and he knew through Jess Grunbaum that his chance of solid favour had increased. He had proved himself discreet, though enthusiastic. "Sound" men, not wild ones, were in request in high quarters. The country was in a mess, and though extreme measures might be taken, they were unlikely to overbalance to the left. The leaders of the left had their ears cocked to the right. Meanwhile excitement subsided, his touring jaunts were curtailed: Sir John, without abandoning, moderated his campaign, and for health reasons took another rest abroad. Jess went with him to ward off imprudent mail. George had ample leisure, Eunice almost none. The nice little sister was always at hand. He drove her about London and the country lanes – or rather she drove him – shirked invitations to lecture in dingy halls, and even in drawing-rooms lent by titled

Labour ladies, and laughed more than he had ever done in his life at a girl's bold, innocent chatter.

It was not long before George found himself in a sweet predicament. For some weeks of Dorry's siege, he could not have told which of the sisters affected him most. Their physical attractions made exciting contrast. The younger was undoubtedly the brightest and prettiest. She lured the eye like a fascinating toy, as she sat in decorative dumbness or played with the wireless. Her glances made droll mischief with adorable impunity. In motion it was Eunice who conquered with her grace, the turn of her long, slender neck, the flush and ebb of animation as she talked. In absence, too, it was Eunice who came to mind. He knew her splendid and fine, a woman enriched by experience, brimming with gifts which it seemed – he was not sure – she might yield to him. Her voice filled his ears with its deep, musical note. What Dorry said in her thin, pert tones mattered little, held nothing for remembrance. Rosemary and pansies: such were the words of Eunice, compact of thoughts and memories, troubling even more than they pleased. They held him to high duty, they enlarged his sense of responsibility. Her voice was like a summons; a bell, solemn and thrilling, ringing in the future. The light, agreeable, drifting joy of the moment – that was Dorry. A bewitchment, a soft, enticing pillow, a feather-weight of charm. Had not a man need of ease in the world, even while he strove for right and justice? . . . Not that Eunice could not please the senses, in her slow, languorous way – she was no intellectual or ascetic. But fate had made of her a sieve, shaken by winds to separate gold from grit: a sieve that was good, no doubt, for a man with ambitions, with ideals, with pledges to fulfil. The winds that shook it were stimulus of the mind, impetus of the soul. It was a rare composition that Eunice Fleet offered. If, indeed, she offered it – to him. Her moods were variable, she had strange reserves and hesitancies. Criticism on her tongue chilled less, sometimes, than the exactions of her praise. She had, too, an odd humour of self-retribution. Her treatment of Fleet was hard on the victim, yet natural enough, in the ignorance and heat of those early war days. He saw nothing in the letters she had shown him to justify undue remorse. He said so emphatically, almost angrily. She took the impatience for herself, an exuberance of concern on her behalf: she could not guess how the voice from the grave annoyed him. Ignorance – heat – crudity. Everyone had a share. The C.O.'s not least. "Stubborn prigs – comically self-righteous" – was the modern verdict on them. His present sense of proportion made no demur. It recalled him to a smile in place of the excessive frown. So he smiled, and reassured Eunice. She was comforted, but not convinced. She said – "You don't know all – Laura Fennick said—" But Laura Fennick was a fanatic – had always been, and still was. Her own brother couldn't stand the extremity of her views. Eunice, he thought, had never loved her husband. Though even where she loved, she might take fierce toll. . . .

It was after he had first kissed Dorry that he began to analyse her sister. To allay, perhaps, his own slight sense of guilt. He tried to summon impressions from before, that must unconsciously have checked abandon. Lure remained, but not enough for passion: the bell still rang, but its echoes grew faint, for when he tried to listen, Dorry's tinkle drowned the clarion note. The charming little face dimmed a goddess radiance, too awful, perhaps, and remote. . . . In the end, there seemed no predicament. Only the sweet dimpling of Dorry in his arms, her roguish chatter in his ear.

"Well, of course, I've got a crush on you – and don't you know it! . . . Oh, boy, I'm so glad Eunice acts the big sister to you. I know all about it – she likes you because you remind her of Vincent. I can't remember him, but it seems you've got his kind of politics. I don't suppose you're a bit like him really, though, are you? Because Euny and I never cared about the same sort of—" "Men" she meant to say, but substituted "things." "I'm not saying anything against her, but she's frightfully old-fashioned in some ways. That's because she can't forget Vincent, poor dear. After all, the world's a bit different now, isn't it, and you have to act differently, don't you? Besides, Big Boy, you've got to be an M.P., and you can't if you're a crank, can you? I'm afraid that's why you lost those potty votes – because that beast who got 'em went about saying you were a C.O. and would let down our Army and Air Force. I did what I could with the mugs in the car – told 'em all he was a liar, and couldn't they see you'd lost your hand in the War? Didn't you? – oh, well, it doesn't matter! *I* don't care a toss what your old politics are! Now *do* behave, George, and listen to me – I was talking about cranks, wasn't I? Well, I'm afraid – honest, I am – that Eunice has become one her-self. The way she lectures you makes me wild. And she's the same with me. Always ramming sloppy stuff down my throat. Positively pre-War." (Dorry was proud of this phrase, which she had culled from the pale-faced youth with the moist hands. He did not use the popular slang of the talkies, but every time she repelled those clammy paws, he protested with – "I say, you're positively pre-War!") "I can't tell you how miserable she makes me sometimes – still, I know what's what, and as I often tell her, I'm older than she was when she married. . . . It's my belief Eunice doesn't care for anything as much as her business – she's wrapped up in it, and thinks I ought to be, too. It's partly mine, of course – I mean, I've got a share in it – but a girl doesn't want to be wrapped in corsets, does she? – oh ducks! Now I've said it, haven't I!"

XII.

Turning Tide

SHE had not closed her door. All the doors in the flat, indeed, seemed to be open. She heard George fumble with the speaking-tube.

"Taxi? Right. Down in two minutes."

Then Dorry's call—

"Run down, darling, and hold the man. I'll just get my wrap and follow in a jiff!"

A mumble of protest, but George went down; she heard the bang of the outer door.

Dorry moved about her bedroom, singing the refrain of the jazz melody—

> "Sweet and lovely – sweeter than the roses in May
> And – she – loves – me
> There is nothing more I can say—"

She sang at a high pitch of her piping voice, as if to assure the world – and herself – that she was in a blissful mood, the mood of a lover beloved.

Unable to bear it, Eunice came into the corridor, meeting the singer as she left her door.

"Oh – you're in!" There was falsetto surprise in Dorry's high tone. "George is downstairs – he's taking me out to dinner – we didn't know you'd come in—"

"Liar. *He* didn't – but you – you saw me. Left the door open on purpose, no doubt."

Dorry drew her breath in a gasp, then flung back her head.

"All right. You can think that if you like. What about it? You had to know sometime, the sooner the better. George – George is a friend of yours, of course. But he's in love with me."

There was both bravado and hesitation in her air as she stood, playing with the clasp of her short white coat.

"Yes, you've managed it very well – behind my back. I might have known you'd be up to your tricks. Off with the old, on with the new. And you're not satisfied with your own sort – you want – you want everything that belongs to me."

"George is my sort as much as yours. And I can't help it if he prefers me."

The insolence of triumph was too much.

"Shameless. Like your mother. Selfish, greedy wanton—"

"Leave her out of it. I know you hate me – you always hated *her* – and now you hate me the same. But she didn't care a snap about your hate and your jealousy, and I don't, either. I don't see why I should consider you. I stuck to Father and you didn't. You were beastly to him. He gave you everything – good times, plenty of money and dresses, everything you wanted. But he was too poor to give me anything. He said you owed me my share. But you haven't given it to me. Oh, I know you think you've been a marvel – generous as pie, I don't think! Stinting – *mean*, I call it. I've had to fight like hell for what I've got – and if it wasn't for Hava Casson, you wouldn't have done as much. Not that *she'd* have advised you to if it wasn't in her own interest – so that you can carry on easier and pay her off. Clever, all of you. I'm as clever, any day. I've had to look out for myself." She paused, panting. Her voice was still high, and very shrill.

Eunice stood silent, eyeing her with contempt. Then turned deliberately and entered her room. Dorry put a hand on the closing door.

"I – I—" she stammered. "We needn't quarrel, Euny. It would be awful for George. And it couldn't alter things. Honest. Don't you see? He wants me, and I want him." She withdrew her hand. There was a whirl of frills. She was gone.

Eunice walked about the room. She had thrown her hat upon the bed, but her long, dark coat was still buttoned tight. With hands pressed to thighs, her posture erect, her gaze upon the floor, she strode backwards and forwards, rapidly at first, then in a slackening pace that was stayed, as before, by the tall panel of silvered glass. She stared at herself as at a stranger, noting the heave of the slight breast beneath the close-fitting coat, the long slope of face blank and stiff, as though a shutter had lowered over it. But when the lids rose, two dark-glowing pits smoked below.

Anger had risen powerfully within her. She had felt it swell her veins till her body towered. Like a great tide it came in tumbling waves, lashing the walls of her being. When the tide was full, it was slower in surge, but more immense in pressure. . . . That little babbling brook that dared to cross her way – how easy to swamp it with the flood! Pitifully easy. . . . The stranger had a noble lift of head, eyes that emitted vital rays, a frame electric with power. The shutter rolled up, the lit flesh gleamed, a grandeur radiated, magical with charm. Poured over Furnall in its ample measure, it must draw him back, hold him – retain . . .

"I don't see why I should consider you."

Then, little trickster, why should *I* consider you?

Why, indeed, should she consider Dorry?

The stranger merged identity in herself, complete, self-confident, self-mastering. She flung her arms out, circling them back to enclose the fineness of her bosom. Her strong white fingers met on its crest. She seemed to be gathering up the magnificence of her person. Eyes spoke to eyes in brilliant passion. She must have Furnall. She *would* have him. He was hers by every right – of womanhood, of equal status, of shared experience, of common purposes. She needed him, as he needed her, to redeem their separate yet united past – to fulfil their future. Above all, to live the ripe joy of their present. Why should this grand ordained cycle be broken at the trivial touch of Dorry's fancy? Trivial – casual – a capricious child's lust for a brighter toy than any she possessed. Intolerable. Incredible. The gods could not permit it. And if the gods were mute and stirless, then she, herself, must usurp their state, and fend divinely for her own—

Facing herself in the mirror, drawn to the height of stature in flesh and spirit, she was intensely aware of the sea of wrath within. It was mighty, relentless, incalculable. Once before it had swept her in its tide – to destruction. She had let it burst the walls of her immaturity, to overwhelm the city of her life and its king. It had surged over Vincent and destroyed him. No less surely could it surge over Dorry and destroy her.

And then? She had moved away and resumed her parade, to return more than once and halt at her image, before the question brought her pride into pause. And then? Once more remorse? – regret – repentance? If not as deep and frantic – if not as agonising and vain – enough, perhaps, to vex and sting for ever: even – who knew? – to blight the last, most precious, gift of happiness.

Wrath, so dangerous in release and deadly in recoil. Wrath, the agent of evil, since the havoc it wrought was endless in effect. Must wrath be master of those who wished to avert the curse of mankind – the hate that severed kin from kin, tore apart communities, breached the neighbourliness of the world?

A stiff, ghastly smile distorted her lips, smudged the fine blaze of her uptilted face. She had lived too much with altruisms lately. Was this the moment – *this*? – she sneered. As well run after a thief with a jewel, dropped from the haul just snatched.

Thief – trifler – impudent chit. Dorry was all these and more. And yet – was simply Dorry. Her wraith danced beside the reflection of the mirror. It mocked and flouted, but held a wistful grace, an air unconsciously appealing. The face was the face of a child, for all its hardened eyes, its painted messages. The face of a little sister leaning for an instant against the comforting cheek of an elder. Dim behind peered the outlines of their father, old Tom with his rosed cheeks grey and sagging, his limp mouth open to plead – "Euny dear, take care of the baby – I'll die easy if you promise!"

The tide was on its turn, the swell subsiding. A shudder shook the long, taut, rock-like frame. Her hands dropped loose. She staggered to the bed and fell upon it. She could not – she could not wreck young Dorry's hope. And if Furnall wanted her – if he chose her in preference – if those wild kisses meant more than sudden lure—

The figure on the bed was limp and twisted, quivering with tearless sobs.

"But I love you, George. I love you. And I thought you loved me—"

In her ears the childish stammer, urgent with certainty,

"He wants me and I want him."

She groaned and crushed her face more deeply in the pillow.

*   *   *

When at last she was still, only the faint ticking of a clock broke the silence of the flat. The maid was out, there was no likelihood of callers, and if any came, she would not answer or admit. She had no wish to move, to dress or undress, to eat or drink – only to lie, unheeded and unheeding, sharp-closed with her grief. But presently the silence crept upon her sense, malign, intrusive. The vacant rooms mocked her solitariness. The tick of the clock changed from monotony to malice, jibing at a woman, abandoned. She sat up suddenly with ruffled hair and hot, dry cheeks, and flung off her crumpled coat.

She could not stay here alone the whole evening. She must go out – get some one, anyone, to accompany her into the streets, into a place of noise and glitter. She sprang to the telephone. Bob? No, a stranger would be better. There were male clients always wanting to take her out. One had tried to persuade her today. He was a decent sort – an ex-officer of high family. He had given her a club number – "in case she changed her mind." She had changed it with a vengeance. But when she rang through, the man could not be found. He had been called away, and though some message followed, giving another number, she would not pursue him further. A fickle humour disordered her will. A second name occurred to her. As she turned the page of the directory, the telephone bell shrilled out. She took off the receiver and heard Bob's voice.

Immediately a mood of resignation lulled her. Let Bob decide.

He was tentative and eager by turns. Might he call, might he join her party, might they meet somewhere? He was hardly coherent when she said – "Yes, come round at once – take me somewhere jolly – where's the hottest jazz?"

"The Asulikit," said Bob, and stammered joyously about a new band and the peppiest conductor in London.

"What – the Asulikit?" – Eunice laughed unusually loudly. "How funny! Yes, I said funny. Don't you? – oh, it doesn't matter. The Asulikit will do. – Yes, come right away—"

She rushed to her wardrobe and pulled out dresses. There, on the last hanger, was the ruby velvet she had worn that first magic evening. It was new then, yet she had not worn it since – through some idea of alteration, which afterwards seemed unnecessary. Meanwhile, it had hung neglected through the summer. It suited her still; its long, suave lines would look "undated" under the Parisian coatee.

She made a hasty toilet and put on the frock. Except for redder lips, a different twist to the hair, this was the same woman who had awaited Bob in the spring. With a derisive smile, she greeted herself in the glass.

"Where have I seen you before?" she asked. The phrase and the scene it evoked gave her a bitter delight. So she would sting and torture her pride, until it rose above humiliation. Back to the place where the whole thing had begun. She had not wanted to go there, or planned to contrive it. But since it fell out this way – this way she would go. Perhaps there was sanity as well as irony in the law of repetition. That which had been seen before and must be faced again – it was life's alternate course of good and ill. Perhaps the dish was always the same, and the different flavour only in the eater's mouth. At least one could absorb from it the courage of disdain. She felt strong and reckless as she braced herself, gave her lips another smear of wine-red salve, and drew on her little silver jacket. The door-bell rang with vigour.

"I say, girlie – you *do* look ripping!"

Again her laughter was too loud. But Bob, who did not know himself an echo, was charmed with her gaiety. He had not hoped for the luck of finding her alone, willing to be entertained, though he had a shrewd suspicion of

Dorry's capture of George. If Eunice guessed it, too, and was indifferent, so much the better all round. Her interest in George, he always tried to believe, was neither deep nor emotional.

"We'll have an early supper," he announced. "I bet you haven't had much dinner on your own—"

"Not much," she said, and led him to the door.

He put a hand on her arm in helpless fascination.

"Eunice, you're walking like a queen. I've never seen you grander. Ripping? – Why – you're absolutely *it*!"

She smiled at him over her shoulder, her eyes, lately so soft in their depths, bright with a concrete gleam. Her head was very near his forward-bending face, and for a second he thought she would let him kiss her. But the thought alone unnerved him, and the next moment she moved and opened the door.

"You're a silly boy, Bob, but a priceless friend. I don't know what I should do without you."

He tried to recover sober content, and follow her gratefully. She was kinder to him than she had ever been, gayer, if more fitful. It seemed she wanted to enjoy herself, and to make him happy. Tonight these two things were not separate. She tasted everything at supper and asked for other dishes, eating with a gusto that might or might not have been relish, and drinking all her wine. She danced with a vivacity that could not impair her grace, but she declined to tango. There was one long number and she said that the band, which crashed and wailed jazz as if demon-possessed, could not get the rhythm right.

"Just listen!" she said contemptuously, tapping her shoe on the floor to catch them out. She poked fun at the players, lost in grimaces; she poked fun at the leader, trying to subdue his jerks to the longer swing; she poked fun at the dancers, swaying and mincing in a diversity of steps;

then suddenly, almost in the last phrases of the music, she jumped up, and exclaimed—

"Come on, Bob. Let's try it," – and bewildered but pleased, he took her round. He had not seen, as she had, George and Dorry enter.

There she had sat waiting – waiting for Dorry and Blake. And instead it was George who had come and transfigured her life. Shouldn't be surprised if the Prince walks in, Bob had said. Her Prince. Dorry's. Hadn't she been waiting tonight for those two to appear? Why, when they came, did she forget her part? To disconcert with calm, to carry on a gracious flirtation with Bob, to pose with nonchalance, in superb and impressive self-possession. . . . Easy enough in theory. But to imagine her own behaviour without fore-seeing theirs, was a flaw in vision that tripped her up. The sight of them had startled her painfully, drawn the blood from the heart in a gush. To watch their attitude to each other – Dorry perking and fluttering, almost nestling publicly, George tender and playful, hanging over her as they chose a table, squeezing her hands, drinking from her glass, acting child to a child, hugging her as they danced – perhaps the fevered eyes saw more than happened, but enough was obvious – was unbearable.

She knew quite soon that she could not bear it. When Dorry caught her glance and shrank from it, to whisper to George and then bridle, toss her head, play her amorous tricks more openly (it did not occur to Eunice that the chit might be bold from nervousness) – when George looked up embarrassed and answered her stiff, imponderable smile, she turned to Bob, and said, still smiling,

"I'm tired, Bob – and I've a headache coming on. I'm afraid I must go home."

Bob rose in silence. He, too, had seen by this time – more than he wished to see. Not the couple, but their effect on

Eunice, fretted him. Poor Eunice! She walked out gracefully enough, but hardly like a queen. Her crown had
fallen, and she left it in the dust, even for him to stumble
on. She cared about that ass, after all. He was sorry for
himself, sorrier for her. But he knew better than to show it,
in words at least. She was quiet in the homeward cab, but
gave him cheery farewell. She wouldn't let him take her
up, spoke decisively, drew her hand almost roughly from
his clasp. She passed it over her head as she vanished.
Quite likely she *did* have a headache – poor girl – poor
lovely queen. Why did the asses get all the luck, only to
pass it by? He tried to console himself, going off *solitaire*,
that being a bit of an ass himself, some of that luck might
yet come his way. The part that wasn't an ass would know
how to treat it. Bob stopped at the corner of the street,
looked up the block of flats, until he saw a light flash at an
upper window. He sighed and waved a hand. But being a
modern lover, slunk away abashed because some women,
passing, giggled. "Ain't he soppy!" said one, in audible
comment. He was so abashed that he jumped again into the
cab, which, since he had dismissed it, was "cruising"
round. As he sat back, he eased his collar, and ruminated
until confidence returned. He decided to ring up Jess
Grunbaum – useful, companionable Jess. Eunice had not
promised to see him over the week-end, and he would not
press her again – just yet. Better let her alone for a week or
so. Perhaps she'd miss him more – and have got over the
dumps.

"Cabby," he said, as he got out, "do you think I'm soppy?"

"Not by the size o' this," growled the cabby, looking at
the tip in his hand.

Bob laughed, and doubled it.

XIII.

Jay-walking

THE card from Laura, inviting her to the lecture on "My Tour of the Soviets," had lain on her desk for a week. She had forgotten it, and seeing it now as she turned over household bills, picked it up and stared at Laura's name, printed in neat, fine type. Had Laura suffered in seeing Vincent caress her? There had been little opportunity for that. But she had known how Vincent loved his wife, who was unworthy of him. No wonder she had found it hard to forgive. But she had forgiven. And time had won her to new friendliness. Eunice flung the card down. She did not want friends. She did not want to hear lectures. She did not want to see Laura, now or any other night.

But the evening spread before her like a threatening cloud. Sullen and stifling if alone with her thoughts; thunderous if Dorry came and lit a quarrel. They had avoided each other over the week-end. George was away, and Dorry – she neither knew nor cared what Dorry did. Her own time was spent in Golders Green, at the villa the Cassons charged her with. They had practically sold it before they left, but owing to some misfortune in the purchaser's family, the deal had lapsed, and it was still on the agents' lists. Eunice had the keys of the house, which was partly furnished, and was to be let for a period if the reserve price – a fairly high one – was not reached.

Though empty of tenants, the place retained its fresh

and welcoming air. Pretty chintzes fluttered on leaded panes
as Eunice and her maid opened windows. The garden
threw up its charming face of paved lawn and border
shrub. Goldfish glinted in a miniature pool, a trellis arch
showed late roses, and the sun lay delicately over a dialled
stone. The advance of autumn here seemed part of summer's spell. The yellowing foliage of young tree and bush
was spilled luxuriance, and not decay. Baring branches
gave a view of further gardens, varied plots of grass and
rocky banks, mossed and sprawling with green life. No
high walls of private glooms, no towering hedge or fence
to ward off curious looks. Hava Casson had liked it so.
When others ridiculed suburban airs, and twitted her with
pettiness, she smiled her large, complacent smile and said –
"But it's nice to leave the town with its nobody-knows and
nobody-cares and live where your neighbour borrows pans.
It makes you feel you're human and a part of common
life." She had renounced it, nevertheless: but only for a
warmer – was it really a narrower? – sense of humanity, a
closer link with the common life to which she belonged.
The little house was meagre without that generous presence; yet something of her lingered and made it bright. In
the garden was peace without isolation. Nature trimmed to
pattern without too much artifice; birds rustling the leaves
and pecking on the grass; voices of children, people sauntering, others at simple tasks, not too near, not too far. A sweet,
kindly atmosphere. If she could find content anywhere,
surely it might be here. Hava had said at parting – "Why
not take the house yourself, Eunice – for a year, at least? It
would do you good. The flat's too stuffy, and shut up, especially in the summer." But the plan had not appealed to her
then any more than before; and now – now it was a mere
brushing thought, brushing against an unhappiness too
stiff to hold it. Except that when she got back, her rooms

seemed darker and more pent, no effect of her brief visit remained.

A full, heavy day at Madame Eve's, a reluctant return, a solitary meal – and this brooding dread of the later hours. Suddenly she took up Laura's card again, and read the details of time and place. 8.30 p.m. She glanced at the clock. A quarter past. Without decision, but as if moved by fate, she put on outdoor things and went to the meeting-hall.

It was somewhere off the Strand, a club-room half filled with faces she did not know. Laura was not famous enough to attract a crowd, and no mutual acquaintances had come. Slipping into a rear seat, Eunice was in time to see the chairman sit down, and Laura rise beside him. A Laura small as ever, but on her feet, fronting the public gaze, quiet and confident, enlarged with the significance Eunice had once found in her face, flashing out in personal encounter. That moment's penetration recurred less clearly than the timid, nerve-strung girl whom she had heard, in astonishment, making her first speech to her "C.O. brothers." How many of them, as strong and full of zest as Vincent, had survived into the frail speaker's world? How many of the survivors could still be acknowledged kin? Even the blood-brother had thinned the spiritual quality of that fraternal bond.

Eunice looked in vain to see if he were present. Her slow, circular gaze at the faces around expressed the sole curiosity she felt. Interest in the occasion she had none. She asked herself dully why she had come. To listen to Laura's steady voice was not so much a strain as a burden. But only as everything was a burden. She might as well sit among strangers here as anywhere. Even Laura, with her steady voice full of familiar echoes, talking of the benefits of co-operative farming, was a stranger to her now. The past was dead, it had lost its pain. The future held no shape. The present was simply something she had to drag – to drag. Her head nodded with heaviness. She was very tired. She had not slept much for several nights. But it would be silly to fall asleep here. If only she could keep this drowsiness for her bed. . . . Sitting very straight, her eyes wide open, she tried to follow Laura's speech. It was clear, concise – easy enough to follow. And it did not last very long. There were questions at the end, which she answered crisply. She knew her Russia, her Soviets, her Five-Year Plan, her methods of transport, production, distribution, tractor machines, peasant education, the path from illiteracy to the sum of culture – otherwise, a system of economics that solved the human problem. Her knowledge was precise, her faith profound, her admiration of this new-hewn world supreme. When Eunice came reluctantly to greet her, she said as if continuing her speech – "Go and see it all for yourself, as I did. It will wake you up."

"How do you know I'm asleep?" said Eunice. She talked automatically with a faint, false smile. It tried to match the real smile on Laura's unpainted lips.

"Everyone's asleep in this country. One day there'll be—"

"A rude awakening," said Eunice. "I'm sorry, but you're rather obvious, aren't you? I didn't expect a platitude from you."

"This isn't one. I might have said an earthquake. At the end of the *second* Five-Year Plan, Europe will find its workers in arms—"

She was annoyed by Eunice, and spoke more bluntly than she intended.

"In arms?" Eunice was a little stirred. She looked with more intentness into Laura's face, and moved closer.

"Did you throw the bomb?" she asked suddenly in a low tone.

"Bomb?" said Laura. Her voice was vague, for she was half listening to an urgent murmur from behind. Most of the audience were leaving. Groups stood about, and some men and girls hovered near, waiting for a word with her. "Might be as well to throw a bomb at some old fossils I know, doing all they can to stop the regeneration of the world—"

"Perhaps it wasn't you," said Eunice, vaguely also. "But you're not approving violence, are you? I notice you don't mind conscription any more – in Russia, at least."

"I said the Army was getting more educational advantages than civilians—"

"It's an army, all the same. What's it for? And what's the difference between a Red Army and a Blue?—"

"Why, lots," said Laura, smiling. "Don't you see—"

"I see prospects of another war – perhaps a world war. Surely you think that would be horrible?"

"Horrible, of course. But it might make regeneration come all the sooner—" She turned at a touch on her shoulder, and nodded quickly. "Excuse me a moment, Eunice. Will you wait for me? I'd like to walk some way with you—"

Eunice drifted to the door and passed out, forgetting Laura's request. "Where have I seen you before?" she thought. The phrase haunted her with a strange malevolence. Laura was different, yet the same. The world was different, yet the same. Modern youth, fresh-fashioned in speech and dress, and habits born of new facilities, was like its forbears, in chase of current toys and acceptance of doom. The few who rebelled would expiate their rebellion – or live on to conforming age. Wars – revolutions – violent reforms – murder and havoc in the name of re-generation. . . . Did the cycle have appointed end, or must it whirl in eternal repetition? Was there no advance except the mechanical? Did the human spirit progress? Was nothing gained, and all to learn afresh, by every new generation from the cradle

to the tomb? The same contents and discontents, the same
stupidities and greeds, the same crude pains and spoiled
delights? What then was the use of heroisms, sacrifices,
martyrdoms? Futile questions, that any fool might ask. Perhaps it was a fool's belief, that if a single growth reached
the light, it should not thrust itself back into the dark – to
fossilise. Perhaps even Vincent, if he had lived— The
thought was like a blasphemy. But inured as she had now
become to shock, she faced and probed it. Nothing seemed
immutable – except mutability. Nothing was sacred, inviolate,
immune. She laughed aloud – an abrupt sound that ended
like a groan. The policeman at the corner where she halted
looked at her.

She had taken the downward and not the upward
turning from the club, and had emerged upon the river
street. High new arc-lamps shone steadily bright, electric
signs flashed in and out of the misty blankness opposite.
The clanging trams were sailing halls of light. She crossed
the road and leaned upon the stone, hearing the water
swish heavily below. It had a cold and dreary sound,
unquiet as her heart. Dark shadows rose from the darker
depths. The air was raw, and her flesh crept suddenly,
though the nutria coat she wore was downy warm. For-
lorn, abandoned, she leaned there in her furs, as lost as any
ragged wretch upon the seats. She had eyed one as she
passed, hesitating, askance. The silver in her purse could
buy him comfort and relief, perhaps disperse his woe. The
world's stock of silver could not palliate her own.

Men going by glanced curiously at her. She moved, and
seeing children dart about a plinth, walked to their hiding-
place. It was late for such games, but the urchins who
made playground here had no routine of nurse and meal
and bed – perhaps not even a drunken parent to chastise
them. They bounced and glided round columns and steps,

with only a hiss or cackle to announce approach. Perhaps they were intent upon their play, perhaps they were avoiding official notice. But the policeman sauntering by took little heed of them. He had his eyes upon the lady in the smart fur coat.

She was aware that he had crossed the street to watch her. Aimless movements such as hers must rouse curiosity. She sighed and peered down the steps, where the black waters gleamed as they lapped. The urchins had run up and down with naked feet, splashing drops on her shoes as she stood. But as she felt nothing of the spray, so she thought nothing as the dull notes of the water reached her ear. Its rhythm remained with her, however; as the damp spots sank into the yielding *suède*. She lifted vague eyes to the train rumbling over the bridge. More lights. More bustle. More humans scurrying to their homes. One might have walls, chairs, carpets, and yet no home to scurry to. Or one might have only a bench to huddle on, and no policeman to watch – a scurry into homeless rest.

With the river's mutter on her sense, she turned and stepped lightly to the pavement.

"Good evening, officer," she said. The gurgle in her voice might have been amusement. Standing still, the burly figure stared at her, expressionless. "I wonder if you will help me?"

"What is it, ma'am?"

A slight, irrelevant resentment curled in her. No strange policeman had ever called her anything but "miss." She must have aged quite suddenly.

"Well, the fact is – one hears so much of these destitute creatures on the Embankment – I thought I'd just see for myself and – and try to assist one or two, perhaps." She laughed as if apologetically. "But when I went past that bundle of rags over there, I simply hadn't the nerve to speak to it."

"Just as well not, ma'am."

"Oh, but I should really be ashamed to go away and feel I'd done nothing. I mean – I don't want to know about them – but just – well, I wonder if you'd help me?" She opened her brown *suède* bag with the amber clasp. In rapid movement her fingers emptied a purse of silver into an envelope, and thrust it – a thick, bulging packet – into the policeman's hand.

"Please, officer – give this for me to the nearest bundle – or bundles – just as you think best. Good-night – thank you so much."

Before the slow eyes could read the inscription, on the business envelope addressed to Madame Eve – device to engage and disarm – she crossed the tramlines to the other side of the street. The policeman, staring in good-natured contempt, saw her next, standing at the corner where he had first noticed her. Her arms were crooked, the brown bag pressed closely to her breast. Not having looked in time to observe her flight, he did not know that in two seconds of it she had twice escaped death. As she crossed the lines a tram crashed at her heels; and then a charabanc, racing from the other direction, missed her by the proverbial hair. Unheard shrieks from a passenger in the coach, a driver's curse on "bloomin' jays," were the only comments on the incident.

As she stood for a moment at the corner, pressing her bag to her breast, Eunice breathed high in exultation. Her danger heightened her triumph over the policeman. How easy, with her lady's voice of patronage, of amused embarrassment, to deceive him! And if the tram or coach had caught her – how much more complete the deception! Plunging into the river was so obvious, that even a stupid constable could imagine it. But an accident in the street was different.

Sobering a little, but still in a state of mixed maze and clarity, she climbed the narrow hill into the Strand. Traffic was collecting for the close of theatres. Soon each empty bus would fill, the taxis circle busily about, the private cars congest all turnings. She ought to get ahead without delay. But there was no urge in her to reach the flat. Her steps lagged more and more as she moved along the street. Her spurt of exultation dropped to its anterior mood. "And I, of ladies most deject . . ."

The line of sombre music crept through her brain. A thousand engines throbbing, wheels rotating, gears' and hooters' clamour, could not still the voiceless dirge. She hardly knew from what store of memory it came. Bits from school. Bits from spoutings of Vincent. One year he had given his class *Hamlet*. "To be or not to be" – she could not even remember whether it was Hamlet or Ophelia who began that speech. Ophelia drowned herself, anyway, plucking flowers. If she had met a policeman, seen suspicion in his eye, would she have turned away, given her flowers to a tramp, dashed under a tram instead? How mad! But then – Ophelia was . . .

She stood on an island, waiting for the buses, to stop or start – she wasn't sure which. She advanced, then hesitated, then walked on. At once a shouting rose between the noise of engines and wheels, a screech of brakes, a din of abuse and cries. She was pushed, seized, held by rough hands, a crowd was breathing on her.

"Damn silly way to walk! – Can't yer see? – what the hell d'yer think yer doin'— Are you all right? – Are you hurt?—"

"I'm all right, thanks. No, I'm not hurt. Please let me—"

She struggled free. Though the voices shrilled, she moved fast and got away. But her arm was touched again, and a slight figure pressed on her.

"Sure you're all right, Mrs. Fleet?"

"Yes, thanks – I—"

She looked into the girl's face, and they walked on together.

"You remember me – I'm Rita—"

"Yes, You're a friend of Dorry's."

She said it coldly, but did not withdraw her arm. All at once she was trembling, a frightful weakness relaxed her legs.

"A close shave, that. Lucky the bus hadn't got up speed. I was sitting on top—" Rita stopped. She felt her companion sway. "I say – I'm glad you're not hurt – but you must have had a nasty shock. Come in here for a coffee – or a nip of—"

"Oh, no – I'm—"

The other drew her firmly into a glittering glass hall. The glare of lights and reflections made her still more dizzy and she was glad to drop into a chair. She was glad, too, that the thin, abrupt girl went on talking coolly, not about the accident or her shakiness; though a glance came now and again, sharp, raking.

"Been busy lately, haven't you? Dorry says everyone at Madame Eve's overworking. It's good to know there's a spot of business somewhere."

"We're lucky, I suppose. For the moment. It must be a bad time for art—" She racked her mind to recall Rita's "line." Model – actress – milliner – designer—

"Putrid. Nobody wants it. My stuff's commercial – it goes in patches." She sipped, smoked, and twisted her head about. The men sitting around stared hard.

Eunice began to recover herself. She drank great gulps of rich, soft coffee, and lit a cigarette. Remembering, suddenly, all about Rita, she sat up in her graceful, composed, rather aloof manner, which at once increased the girl's resentment – and approval.

"You do fashion-drawing, I think?"

"When I can get paid for it." Rita crossed her legs and raised the tip of a narrow shoe, offering it to the contemplation of a man at the table near. But as he bent slightly forward, she jerked her arm, with the cigarette extended in her fingers, almost jabbing his nose. Though she caught his glance, her face was expressionless as she continued to talk. "The best job I ever did was a cover for *Style*. Never had a model like it."

"No?" said Eunice politely. She observed the byplay with distaste.

"Modern lines, Victorian face— Just right for the debutante number. Gave you a surprise, though, didn't it?"

"Oh – that— you mean—"

"Your lovely char."

"Poor Mrs. Johns."

"Was that her name? Dorry called her Ginger. Gorgeous hair. Henna and a perm. would have done the trick – better than any drawing. What happened to her? Didn't she fall ill – die or something?"

Eunice did not answer at once. She drank the last drop of coffee in her cup, then said,

"She wasn't ill. She committed suicide."

Rita flicked her lids.

"Damn shame. What she do it for?" Her tone was flatly casual, but to her own surprise, Eunice told the whole story. She even added details of the orphans, again at Rita's request. It might or might not have been a sign of interest. As a matter of fact, Rita was considerably interested: not so much in Mrs. Johns and family, as in the employer's attitude. This proud, "superior" woman was not only the charwoman's, but the rebellious little sister's much-berated "boss." And Rita, though she mocked at Dorry, and affected unwrung withers, was a jade who had once been badly galled by an aunt, equally her "boss" and the arbiter of her youth. Her feeling for Eunice was mixed. Antagonism, partly vicarious, partly direct; admiration, obscure in the mind tonight in piquant solution. Rita, looking from her bus, had seen a curious sight. A woman deliberately court- ing public death. The angle of vision shifted with recognition in the street. But again and again it recurred. During the narration of the "char's" tragedy, tone and air more than words brought back an odd impression. "She was sick of her life. Naturally. . . . She *couldn't go* on. . . . I can't blame her" . . . The speaker pours out fresh coffee, leans back, puffs a cigarette: she is elegant, cool, almost nonchalant. But walking in front of the bus, a load of woe had hunched her back. Why had she walked so recklessly? "The little snipe's knocked her out. Clean out." Clever little snipe! To floor the arrogant, virtuous, insufferable "boss"! Yet the victim might be grandest of the two. When she straightens her back, displays a line of beauty, rare, aesthetically satis- fying – and what's odder, a human sympathy for sluts and drabs – well, the mixture grows too strong, the components fight, some headiness from one must overcome the other.

"Dorry never told me anything of that. But I don't see much of Dorry these days."

"No?"

Every time Dorry is mentioned, Eunice is brief, non- committal, stiff.

"She has another boy-friend, of course. Takes up all her time. Dorry always goes whole hog for things. But they don't last. Off with the old, on with the new."

Eunice was silent. Her own words, but with some hidden twist. The toneless voice had almost a lilt.

"Not that I blame Dorry for chucking Blake. You never liked him, it seems. He wasn't a bad sort. But he and Dorry never really hit it off. She found it out when they stayed together in Paris."

Eunice put down her cigarette.

"What did you say?" she asked. "When they stayed together? – Do you mean—?"

"Of course. That week-end she went off – on a business trip." Her short, sudden laugh ripped out. "I suppose you guessed. Blake fixed it up beforehand. But he wanted her altogether – I mean, to chuck you, everything, and live with him. Anyway, they stayed the week-end at an hotel, and then she came home – fed-up. Made me send all his letters back. He used to write to me, but he's stopped now. So I expect it's off for good. Well – that's nothing to cry about. She just had her little fling – a try-out. Girls do, nowadays, you know – or don't you," she added *sotto voce*.

XIV.

To Tell or Not to Tell

DORRY was in bed, and as usual, pretending to be asleep. But even pretence could hardly survive the noise Eunice made. The heaviest slumber must have been broken by her impetuous entry into the flat, the flinging down of objects, the bursting open of doors. Dorry's lock had never been attended to – how she cursed it now!

No soft tread, no whisper – "Dorry, are you awake?" – no bated retirement. Just the loud fling of a door, a rude click and flashing on of light, and an imperious call—

"Get up. I must speak to you."

"What's all the row?" grumbled Dorry, tossing her curls with a start. "Can't you let me sleep? I'm tired. I don't want to talk now—"

"Of course. You think you can sleep when you want to – talk when you want to – play when you want to – everything just as you want it, *when* you want it – at other people's expense. Even to the point of living with a man, and then trying to get off with another—"

Dorry had sat up quickly, appalled at the violent bitterness of the first few words. At the last, she gave a little shriek.

"You're mad. What are you talking about?"

"You know well enough. The nights you spent in Paris with Blake Pellew. Perhaps not the first time you slept with him – you little slut—"

"Slut yourself! How dare you talk to me like that?"

"Dare – *talk*? Is there anything you dare not *do* – cheat, deceive, abandon yourself—"

The strong, powerful tones quivered in their intensity – low-pitched on a string that seemed about to break. She stood at the foot of the bed, quite still, her hands clenched, only her face mobile with its working mouth and blazing eyes. The sea of wrath had rolled unchecked, and was pouring wildly over the bit of flotsam on the bed. Spluttering, jerking her arms, Dorry tried to stem and dodge the furious waves. She screamed denials, countercharged, bluffed, heaving her puny might in vain.

"You're mad with jealousy – that's what's the matter with you – you believe any filthy yarn you hear about me – Rita's pulled your leg, I know – she's always at it. Fine lady *you* are, to have such dirty thoughts and use such language to me! You'll be ashamed of yourself tomorrow, see if you won't! I tell you I never saw Blake in Paris—"

Eunice strode to her side, leaned menacingly towards her.

"Save your breath, you wretched little liar. You can tell your tales to George, and see if he believes you – after I've told him the truth."

"You wouldn't!"

Dorry leaped from the bed.

"Why not? Why shouldn't I save him from you? He's a decent man. And he's more to me than you are – even if I were never to meet him again."

"Oh, God, Eunice, *no* – don't – you mustn't tell him—"

She fell on the rug in her pyjamas, grovelling, seizing her sister's hands, pressing, tearing at them.

"Don't tell him, Euny – say you won't – please, please! I couldn't bear it! I'll tell you everything – honest, cross my heart, – I *did* stay with Blake in Paris – but it was the first time, I swear – and I didn't really mean to. I'd refused to go – and then that chance came – I thought I'd just meet him, and – and – you see, *I did* like him, and he was awfully in love with me, and I was willing to marry him. Then when he met me and persuaded me to stay with him – I wasn't bad, Euny, truly – I only thought it would make him marry me – he promised – do you understand? he *really* promised – but afterwards it turned out he couldn't, anyway. Because his wife's a Catholic and won't divorce him. He wanted me to live with him until – he said perhaps she'd die – she's much older than he is, and has some disease – it's all true, I know, he showed me papers and things – but I was wild about it. I said I'd been had – and I chucked him – I wouldn't have anything more to do with him – not even letters. And it was all finished before I'd even *seen* George. Oh, Euny, dear, you won't tell him – promise you won't – don't ruin me and make George give me up – it won't make any difference if he doesn't know – honest, I'd be ever so good with him – I love him, Euny, I do – I do – oh, promise you won't tell him – please – please—"

She was weeping frantically, her little rosy face swollen and streaming. Her body in the thin silk squirmed and shivered against the rocklike limbs of the elder. Hot tears fell on the icy hands she clutched, but her own fingers were as cold. Eunice held them fast in a sudden fierce grip, and swung her to her feet.

"All right – that's enough. Get into bed, quick."

She pushed the little convulsive figure into the blankets, rolled them over her, tucked them beneath. Her eyes were stormy still, but her voice had lost its bitter urge.

"Be quiet now," she said in a sunken drawl.

Dorry's sobs grew fainter. Her lids closed tight as she whimpered.

"You've promised, Euny. You – won't tell?"

"No, I won't tell. Go to sleep."

"G'night – dear – Euny—"

The lights clicked off, a dim figure glided through the door, head bent so that the mutter of "Good night" was lost to straining ears. A suspended whimper followed it to silence.

XV.

Postman's Knock

DAY after day to trudge these dingy stairs. It was a ghastly thought – a ghastlier necessity. Why had they never seemed so endless, the three curved flights over the dark, smelly landings? The smell came partly from the cleaning stuff – turpentine, beeswax, some unknown ingredient, blent with mustiness from the walls. Never had the odour so disgusted her, never had the passage from hall to upper floor been so oppressive. Because, even at worst, the rooms above had welcomed her with brightness and clean air. Gay curtains, flowers, open windows. But this evening found chill frowsiness within. Fog lingered from the day, the hangings were grimed, wood and walls sticky and sour, dead blooms drooping on slimy stalks. The maid was away with influenza, the daily char had not turned up. Fireless, dank, neglected, the flat was a murky cave.

Eunice felt like lead as she moved about. But she had felt like lead all the week. To the dull weight was added a thready sensation, not so much a pain as a vertiginous ache. It ran through heart and stomach, spinning cobwebs to the brain. If it stirred languor at all, it was only to repulsions. She filled a kettle, placed it on the stove, but did not light the gas. She was neither hungry nor thirsty, and without volition to simulate. A coal fire was laid in the sitting-room; though sprayed with soot and dust, it might have crackled at the touch of a match. Instead, she switched on a small electric heater, and watched its disc begin to redden. The pale measured blush, flameless and still, hardly tinged her fingers as she spread them close. She was cold: but a furnace would have made her no warmer.

Listlessly she drew the slimy flowers from each vase, wrapped them in paper, and put them out of sight. Then she sank down on the divan, opened a journal she had brought in with her, and stared at a page without reading it.

She saw life stretching before her – day after day of routine, spanning long, empty hours. The prospect terrified her. It was the first time she had felt terrified; the first time she had seen – futility. To be alone, stricken, thwarted, had never before spelled negation, an endless, purposeless blank. Even her lowest mood had held activity, some promise, however dim in apprehension, of change. She had been stunned with grief, had wandered in despair; but neither in stupor nor in pain had her spirit fainted utterly.

For years rage and hate had kept her strong, vibrating outwards to passing things, catching threads of their colour on the spikes of her nerves. Below, remorse might be gnawing at her, as the eagle at Prometheus; but still her soul was strong, indomitable, forcing her eyes from the gulf to the way of salvation. In such a mood she had swung herself free, worked and forged her business success, won friendship and material amenity. Her suffering had been a flame, that licked close to harden the vital core, not to consume it. She had grown tough, perhaps; indifferent and cool; but not insensitive – not dead. How easily she had stirred to new and vigorous growth. . . . But now – this blight had come upon her. A black and fatal frost. Misery without pain. Dull, depressing misery, making her footsteps lag, her veins sluggish, her brain fitful and vague.

She knew, without caring, that Madame Eve was affected.

Clerks in the office, assistants in the *salon*, machinists in the workroom – all were slackening in their turn as she slackened, all were touched by an instinct of something amiss in her. Errors went unchecked and unreproved. Clients were dissatisfied and not conciliated. Vigilance and tact no longer outran the standard of rivals, and therefore fell behind. There was no partner to correct and replace deficiencies. She and Hava Casson had been equals and mates. The others, even Dorry, were subordinates – without initiative, without the larger grasp and ceaseless concern essential to the conduct of business.

She knew and did not care. The only thing that moved her was terror of the long, blank hours – idle or busy, all long and all blank. And longest, most terrifying, the hours of the night. Sleepless, the minutes crawled decades. She tired herself with mental and physical tasks, she walked the streets from and to her office, but fatigue brought no more slumber than could be spilled in dreams.

Lying now, on the cushioned divan, she could not rest. The light hurt her eyes. She dare not turn it out, since the dark meant sharper consciousness. She got up slowly and went to the window, drew back the curtains as far as they would go, pushed up the sash, and leaned out in the raw damp air. The fog was thin. The square below, with its railed enclosure, showed almost clear. Branches of trees emerged with the beams of street lamps on them.

Trees. They called to her with friendly gestures, even in the still, mist-black atmosphere. And always she had answered. She cared for trees more than for flowers, though knowing less about them. As she had gone through most of life, accepting things or rejecting them without inquiry into their nature, so she was incurious about the kind or variety of trees. In early days Vincent had instructed her, discriminating between ash, beech, poplar, pine. The sycamore in their garden was individual and known, the unfolding of its red-stalked leaf marked each spring. As Pharaoh's Fig it spoke of shade in Egypt, kin with the Crusader's elm, while native oaks shed history with their acorns. Tufts of fairy lace meant larch, dark elegance was labelled fir . . . but names belonged to catalogues, lore to the student mind. For casual joy there were simply trees. Their outlines on a hill against the sky, their density in groves, their bowed or upright patterning of field and street, could fill an empty glance with trove. To gaze on them at leisure was to build a mood of grace, inhabited by secret harmonies. In rugged winter shape, as in bud-burst green or lush autumnal garb, the sense of beauty constantly abided. Now, for the first time, it failed to satisfy. She looked at the giant branches in the square and found no solace in their pride. Bleak and grimed, they towered dominant, disdainful of the mottled light as of the wreathing fog, sure of their roots, of arrested sap, of green bright foliage in potential hoard. Their gaunt and naked bark was strong with promise, and rich with fertility. They greeted her, but in their friendliness was irony. They mocked rather than comforted the barren thing she was. . . .

She closed the window, and with lax head, moved towards the kitchen. Supposing her child had been born? The thought was strange and curiously unreal. For years she had been free of it; had forgotten that the seed of life once lay in her body. Supposing she had now a son, or a daughter – almost of Dorry's age? A soft face to caress, a sturdy frame to prop, a voice to cry – "Mother, you have *me*"?

She stared round the cold kitchen in distrust. What had she come for? To light the gas under the kettle? She took a box of matches from a shelf, and fumbled it in her hand.

Of Dorry's age? Then she herself would be old – the

mother of a grown-up girl or boy would be old – her woman-hood finished.

"But I'm old, anyway," she said, addressing the stove. "I'm old – and finished." She stooped mechanically and opened the oven door. The black benches danced before her eyes, mocking her. And strange echoes mocked her ears.

I have been young and now am old. Yet have I not seen the righteous forsaken. . . . But I was not righteous, I drove Vincent to his death. I would have driven him, unrepentingly, to a shameful end in blood. And though I repented of his bloodless martyrdom, it has not been accounted me for righteousness. Therefore, O Lord, am I forsaken, and justly am I cursed. But deliver me, O Lord, deliver me from the body of this life, for I can endure it no more. Not a day – not an instant – not the breathing of a breath—"

Blindly she fingered the tap and turned it on. The released gas rushed to her nostrils, and she drew it in. Her brain was clear – at least a part of it, the front or surface part, which seemed extraordinarily light, beside the thick, heavy pressure behind. With this light, clear part she was thinking calmly. Kneel down, put your head well in, inhale as fast and as deeply as you can. All will be over soon, completely, quietly, without fuss, unlike the noisy and difficult process of an accident in the street. She had known for days that this must be the way – or rather for nights, since it was in those dreary nocturnes that Mrs. Johns appeared, advising her humbly but convincingly. Only one detail she refused. The cushion for her head. That would give the key of deliberation. And, even now, she preferred to baffle surmise. A pie on the upper shelf – matches in her hand to light the oven – a faintness as she turned the tap – a fall, her head striking inwards – at least there might be doubt, an appearance of misfortune. . . .

Nausea, dizziness, constriction, singing in the drums – was she imagining sensations before they came? The thready vertigo increased enormously at the first whiff – she took another and another, quickly. The quicker the better. But perhaps – not deep enough. She opened her mouth as well as her nostrils, expanded her lungs to the full. At the same moment a loud double knock split the silence of the flat.

Eunice sprang involuntarily to her feet. She gasped and spluttered, leaning against the scullery wall. Her temples throbbed, her heart beat in great furious thumps. Again the shattering knock. She shuddered violently. Who wanted her? Who would knock and wait until – until – she staggered into the hall and flung open the door. A postman faced her, grinning and chuckling. He seemed to her like an ape gesticulating in a swaying cage. What she seemed like to him in the dim light could have been nothing grotesque or fantastic. For he made a polite jocular remark as he handed her a packet and two letters.

She remained there after he had gone, standing and staring vacantly. Then she closed the door and stumbled into the sitting-room. The letters in her hand fell to the floor. With a sudden hysterical laugh she gathered them up. The large packet was for Dorry, the other two for her. Christmas was coming – "A merry Christmas and a Happy New Year." The postman had not said these words, but they were in his mind, in his grin and chuckle, in the loud knocks she ought to have recognised as his. He was rehearsing for the day when he would say them to her, and making her share in the rehearsal. Last year she had given him an unusually handsome tip. He was looking forward to another, he wanted to see her as often as possible in the preceding weeks, to greet her pleasantly, to remind her—

She laughed again, a sobbing, foolish laugh, sat down on a chair, and tore the flaps of each small envelope. The first was from Palestine. It contained an amateur photograph, with a message from Ruth Casson. The words were clearly written, but they were not clear to her eyes. She gazed at the picture. From the blur emerged a group in strong sunshine. Ruth in the foreground in a cotton smock, a large sun hat almost obliterating her head. She was helping to plant a slip of a tree – helping a young man whose heel was on a spade. He was a muscular fellow with bare arms and open neck, rising out of a collarless shirt. Beneath his own large straw he was looking, not at the ridge of earth at his feet, but at Ruth's face. Like her he was smiling widely, showing the gums above thick, irregular teeth. Near them were labourers similarly garbed, but a little way behind sat Hava Casson, at ease in a wicker chair, wearing an elaborate Ascot frock. The contrast was amusing, but not the cause of the faint smile that touched the beholder's lips. The smile was drawn by the merry, laughing aspect of the scene of sun and soil. An immense exuberance poured from the scrap of tinted paste. She turned it over and read, in Ruth's schoolgirl hand—

"Here we are, old thing – busy planting oranges – the last of 500, mostly put in at night. But as it's Friday, we're finishing early. We shan't get any of them to eat for seven years! – but David says that's nothing, as he hasn't to wait so long for *me*. He's got six up on Jacob! We're awfully happy. Expect you in the spring. *You must come.* Mother sends her love. She's too lazy to write, and I'm too busy."

The faint smile lingered on the unwilling lips. "Dear little Ruth." An odd, unsuitable phrase. Not even her own mother could have called the girl that. She was "little," and might be "dear," but the term meant something that was not either word, and was incongruous with – with what? The subtle sprite that Ruth had always seemed? The smart, immaculate, ambitious young Ruth, steeped in Cockney sophistications – or this careless child of nature?

Eunice put a hand to her head. She was still dizzy, and her fingers trembled. Again she read – "Expect you in the spring." Spring? The postman expected to see her at Christmas. The Cassons expected to see her in the spring. A few moments, and she would have passed beyond even the knowledge of their expectations. Why had they drawn her back – they, who knew nothing— She got up with an effort, feeling deadly sick. The flat reeked with fumes. Handkerchief to face, she reached the stove, turned off the tap, opened windows. At the sink she vomited freely. The cold air above was fresh on her clammy skin.

She tottered back to lie on the divan, shivering and perspiring. But sickness had gone, and she felt light all through, no longer dragged by chains from hair to heel. Relief and chagrin struggled dimly in her mind. I couldn't do it after all, she thought. Am I a coward – for not taking a coward's way? Coward. Who was a coward – what was cowardice? They said Vincent was a coward. Her hand sought the glass of water she had brought in and set on the table beside her. It displaced the letters, which fell again on the floor. She stretched uncertainly for them. Lying on her lap, she forgot them – until minutes, hours later, she looked down and saw the second envelope, opened but unread. She knew from the address that it came from Mrs. Baines, the foster-mother she had found for the Johns' family. Mrs. Baines sent regular weekly reports. Her present account of the older children was satisfactory, but of the youngest she wrote—

"I'm sorry to say, madam, that the baby don't come on as well as expected. He's lost another pound. As you know, he don't take his milk very well, and the rickets can't improve till he does. The doctor says he ought to be in the country, or somewhere in a garden with plenty of fresh air. Dear Madam, you know I does my best with food and care, but conveniences I haven't got for keeping a child in the air all day, especially in the winter, and I haven't got time to take him in the park for long enough. There are the others to consider. I shall be glad, madam, if you will come and see the little dear as soon as you can, and talk things over."

With the letter in her hand, she lay still until Dorry came in. A rather quiet and circumspect Dorry. She seldom allowed George to accompany her into the flat, though he did not know the full implications of her fear of "upsetting Eunice." She was careful, these days, not to upset Eunice – except when she was irritated, or over-confident, and forgot. Tonight she remembered so well that she almost tiptoed into the room. But Eunice greeted her amiably enough.

"You're early, Dorry. But I'm tired, and I was just going to bed. I wonder if you'd do something for me."

"Of course – what is it?"

"Make a hot drink – milk, or anything. I rather think I'm in for a cold – perhaps a touch of flu'. I'm seedy and awfully done."

"Yes, you look it. Been working too long as usual. And the weather's beastly; you'd better get straight to bed. Shall I turn on your fire? It's cold in here. And fusty. Gets worse every day. I'm ashamed to bring – anyone in. Hope Ellen turns up tomorrow and clears the mess. I'll make your drink and bring it to your room."

"Thanks."

"I say, Euny – don't you think you'd better ease off? Go somewhere after the Christmas rush. South of France wouldn't do you any harm—"

"Perhaps not. Perhaps I'll take a longer trip – a little later. Paris – Marseilles – Trieste—" She spoke languidly, then with more decision – "In any case I'll leave the flat pretty soon."

"Leave the flat?"

Eunice stood up, still shivering a little. She flickered Mrs. Baines' letter across the table.

"Read that."

Dorry read and shrugged her shoulders.

"You've taken a job on there. I don't see—" She checked herself. "But about leaving the flat – do you mean moving somewhere else?"

"Yes. To Hava's villa. It's a nice little place, and the garden's O.K. It'll be a treat to get back to from town in the spring, and jollier still in summer. Do me good – and give that kid a chance. I'll get a nurse in, of course."

Dorry suppressed a strong phrase with difficulty. But she could not altogether restrain herself. Watching Eunice move slowly to the door, she inquired with mincing sarcasm—

"You haven't decided to adopt it, have you?"

"No – I haven't decided. But it's an idea– –"

"Good Lord!" said Dorry. She was genuinely shocked. "You're potty. A charwoman's brat!"

Eunice stopped at the door and turned round, leaning wearily against the post.

"The child's dying," she said. "But if it pulls through, it'll be as good as any other. Mrs. Johns—"

"Oh, I know Ginger wasn't a low sort – like the father. But a *suicide*!"

"It might have happened here," said Eunice. Her voice had the mournfulness that Dorry loathed.

"Greek tragedy, I don't think," she sneered. She had no patience with the fuss over the Johns, and this development was – the crimson limit. Was *she* expected to live with a squalling sick child? In any case she detested Golders

Green. She was about to flash out in protest when Eunice, looking at her with a subtle change of expression, said dryly—

"You can stay here, if you prefer. I shan't give up the flat entirely. Of course, if you get married, I'll sublet it to you."

Dorry went on staring at the door after Eunice had passed through. The joy of liberation given by her sister's words was curiously dashed. One never quite knew what Eunice was getting at when she used that dry, emotionless tone. It wasn't exactly "sarky," but it had that effect, the wounding touch of a probe. Dorry lifted her shoulders again, put out her tongue, and ran into the kitchen. She filled a saucepan with milk and set it on the stove.

She was cold, even with a coat on, and she closed the wide-open window. But immediately afterwards she began to sniff, wrinkling her skin in disgust. "Beastly smell," she muttered, but forgot it in the reflection of her face in a small shaving-mirror – relic of a male Casson – that stood on the sill. How lovely her head looked tonight! That new hairdresser was a find. Expensive, but worth it. He knew exactly the right preparation for a platinum blonde – the "latest thing," which she happened delightfully to be. Instead of the yellowish tint she had been accustomed to hunt, the new shade was silver-pale. Her hair "came up" marvellously in it. Drawn flat across her forehead, to nest in close-packed curls below, each strand had a life of shining transparency, as if young moonbeams strayed beneath. One ear showed an oval-pink lobe, the other was completely hidden. The forehead itself, the little nose, the dimple of chin, the delicate-tinted skin, made a picture so cunningly devised that only nature seemed to triumph. And indeed the lovely curves of flesh owed nothing to art, but all to youth and natal gift. Never had Dorry been prettier. She smiled and simpered at herself, turning her profile from one side to the other. No wonder George had been so ardent tonight. Of course he was going to Geneva, and coming absence made fonder farewell. He was rather "peeved" that she wouldn't let him in to speak to Eunice – he said that Eunice, though she wasn't so interested in the League of Nations lately, would appreciate his mission – "*You're* too pretty to think, and too pretty to let *me* think," he said. She need not have been afraid to bring him in. Eunice had quite got over her tantrums. And it was absurd to be jealous of a woman twice one's age. In spite of her figure, and her ability, at times, to seem young without much "getting up," Eunice was old. And tonight she looked it. A regular hag. Dorry blew a kiss at her own enchanting reflection.

George was ardent, and she was likely to keep him so. But there was nothing settled about marriage. Men were funny nowadays. They did not seem to think that girls might want to marry as well as have good times, even if they were very young. At eighteen or so one needn't be in a hurry. But Dorry had heard that if one didn't marry early, one seldom married at all. Besides, she loved George and wanted to be his wife – much more than she had ever wanted to be Blake's. She hadn't been afraid of Blake. But she was afraid of George. The more afraid, the more determined – marriage with George was not simply an escape, or even a triumph; it was bliss. She shivered with delight at the idea of it. But she wouldn't stand for the other thing. Look at Rita. Ran away from her bully of an aunt with a man, and messed herself up ever since. *She* didn't care, of course. Thought that marriage was bunk, anyway. But refusing to live up to an aunt was not the same thing as refusing to live down to a mother. . . . That was Dorry's secret, unshared by a soul – her terror of the end report ascribed to Lallie Granger. A brothel-house end. . . . Rita went too far. She was clever, and though not beautiful, extraordinarily attractive – there was *something* about her – she could fascinate any man. And what's more, several wanted to marry her. But she didn't want that. She went too far. She said she must be free to change her men. And sometimes she must be free to have no man at all. Really, Rita was the limit – she'd say anything – that was why she was difficult to keep away from. But Dorry was keeping away from her now. Not only because she'd promised George. But because they'd had a frightful row over her telling tales to Eunice. Strangely enough, it was Rita who picked the quarrel, not Dorry – Rita who told Dorry to go to blazes and never come back to pester her with trashy yarns. "You took Blake away from me," she said astoundingly, "and you took George from your sister – aren't you satisfied, you greedy little worm? Stick to your George or chuck him – I don't care what the hell you do. But keep away from me."

Dorry kept away, disconcerted, but at the same time filled with complacence. She had never realised that she had taken Blake from Rita. It was a tribute that added so much to her conceit that she almost turned George Furnall's head that evening. Almost, but not quite. George took a lot of turning – into a husband, at least.

A pensiveness came into the shallow eyes. She did not so much frown as tighten brow and lip. The elongated arches stayed "put"; but the lashes flickered, and she noted their scant measure, to the point of thinking – "I wonder how the new kind would look, fastened on—" while the deeper mind employed itself with courtship *sans* proposal. But suddenly she smiled, radiant again, and forgot her deficiency of lash. Why, the "pottiness" of Eunice would pave the way! To have the flat to herself – to be free – and at the same time make her invidious position clear to George—

"Damn," said Dorry cheerfully. A hiss and sizzle behind her, warned too late; she turned to see the milk rise in a foam and flow over the stove. She dashed at it and lifted the saucepan. It was empty, except for a blackened layer of skin. And there was no more milk in the jug.

Luckily there was a lemon in the larder. She boiled some water and prepared the drink, disregarding the liquid dribbling down the stove, and collecting in pools on the floor. The oven door annoyed her. It stood wide open and was splashed inside and out. She pushed it with her foot and banged it fast.

When she carried the tray into her sister's room, the light was on, but Eunice made no sound. She was lying in bed, her arms flung out, her right cheek pressed into the pillow. On the left her dark hair flowed in a long, concealing wave.

Dorry set the tray down uncertainly. If Eunice was asleep, it might be as well not to disturb her. She tiptoed to the door, and stood there for a moment, watching the figure in the bed. It was still and silent. "Dead to the world," thought Dorry, and shrugged her shoulders. With one hand on the door-knob, she stretched the other to a switch. Darkness fell, and the door closed quietly.

September, 1932.

THE END

Iron and Gold

By Hilda Vaughan
With an Introduction by Jane Aaron

'I baked the bread made you mortal. For mortal you
had to be. Same as myself, fach. No different, see?...
When I'm gone, you'll be taking my place quite
natural... A chain o' women. All alike. Every link.
That life may hold unbroken.'

So a dying woman addresses her supernatural daughter-in-
law. For this is the old folk tale of the Lady of Llyn y Fan
Fach, the fairy bride lured from her underwater home to
become a farmer's wife on the Brecon Beacons. Iron and
Gold's retelling of the myth makes of it a psychological
study in the nature of marriage and the social construction
of gender roles. As the bride struggles to adapt herself, and
sees her gold worn away under the iron pressure of
conformity, both her difference and her acquired familiarity
eventually breed marital breakdown and tragedy. But the
human yearning for strange beauty, disruptive though it
may be, remains poignantly alive throughout the novel.

Breconshire-born Hilda Vaughan (1892-1985), in this her
eighth novel, first published in Britain in 1948, fleshed out
the bones of the old Welsh myth in ways which make clear
its continuing relevance for modern readers. This new
edition includes an introduction by Jane Aaron, Professor
of English at the University of Glamorgan.

This is the fifth in the Honno Classics series, an imprint
which brings books in English by women writers from
Wales, long since out of print, to a new generation of
readers.

£8.99

ISBN: 1 870206 50 9

Strike for a Kingdom

By Menna Gallie
With an Introduction by Angela V. John

First published in 1959, this novel is set in the fictional valleys town of Cilhendre at the time of the miners' strike. The murder of a hated mine manager exposes the tensions and secrets of this close knit South Wales community. It was described by critics at the time as an 'outstanding detective story that is genuinely different' and as a 'poet's novel' despite being a 'whodunnit'.

Menna Gallie (1920-90) was born and reared in Ystradgynlais, in the Swansea valley. She was six at the time of the miners' strike, though deeply affected by its impact on her community. Strike for a Kingdom was her first novel, hidden away for two years before she was persuaded to send it to a publisher. It was immediately accepted, and was highly praised, particularly in America. This edition has an introduction from the historian Professor Angela V. John, author of the biography of Lady Charlotte Guest and of a forthcoming biography of Henry W. Nevinson.

This novel is reprinted as part of the Honno Classics series, an imprint which brings books by women writers from Wales in English, long since out of print, to a new generation of readers.

£6.99   ISBN: 1 870206 58 4

ABOUT HONNO

Honno Welsh Women's Press was set up in 1986 by a group of women who felt strongly that women in Wales needed wider opportunities to see their writing in print and to become involved in the publishing process. Our aim is to publish books by, and for, women of Wales, and our brief encompasses fiction, poetry, children's books, autobiographical writing and reprints of classic titles in English and Welsh.

Honno is registered as a community co-operative and so far we have raised capital by selling shares at £5 a time to over 350 interested women all over the world. Any profit we make goes towards the cost of future publications. We hope that many more women will be able to help us in this way. Share-holders' liability is limited to the amount invested, and each shareholder, regardless of the number of shares held, will have her say in the company and a vote at the AGM. To buy shares or to receive further information about forthcoming publications, please write to Honno:

'Ailsa Craig',
Heol y Cawl,
Dinas Powys,
Bro Morgannwg
CF64 4AH.